DATE DUE

Demco, Inc. 38-293

The Amphora Project

THE AMPHORA PROJECT

WILLIAM KOTZWINKLE

Grove Press

New York

Published simultaneously in Canada
Printed in the United States of America

FIRST GROVE PRESS PAPERBACK EDITION

Library of Congress Cataloging-in-Publication Data

Kotzwinkle, William.
    The Amphora Project / William Kotzwinkle—1st ed.
        p. cm.
    ISBN-10: 0-8021-4263-X
    ISBN-13: 978-0-8021-4263-4
    I. Title.
PS3561.O85A83 2005
813'.54—dc22   2005046159

Grove Press
an imprint of Grove/Atlantic, Inc.
841 Broadway
New York, NY 10003

DISTRIBUTED BY PUBLISHERS GROUP WEST

www.groveatlantic.com

06 07 08 09 10   10 9 8 7 6 5 4 3 2 1

For Elizabeth Gundy, my partner in life and literature

I would like to thank the following scientists for their invaluable help: Sydney Brenner, Nobel Laureate, Salk Institute for Biological Studies; Peter Goddard, Director of the Institute for Advanced Study at Princeton; Steven Katona, President of the College of the Atlantic; Kenneth Paigen, former Director of the Jackson Laboratory; Beverly Paigen, Senior Staff Scientist, Jackson Laboratory; Leon Rosenberg, Professor of Molecular Biology, Princeton University; and Peter Wells, Director of Technology Transfer, Jackson Laboratory.

My special thanks also to David Einhorn; Dan Burt; Thomas Rolfes; my editor, Morgan Entrekin; and my agents, Elaine Markson and Ron Bernstein.

And finally, my thanks to Ernest McMullen, an extraordinary painter, who accompanied me on this long journey through other worlds.

The Amphora Project

CHAPTER 1

"Sky mines," hissed Lizardo, his throat inflating nervously as he gazed out the flight deck window at the ornaments of doom flickering in the darkness. His armored scales made a scraping sound as he wrapped his tail around the pedestal of his seat. "No one mentioned minefields."

"You worry too much," said Commander Jockey Oldcastle, his formidable paunch pressed against the controls of their descending ship.

"That's why we haven't been killed until now," hissed Lizardo. He was a navigator from Planet Serpentia. The pupils of his eyes were shaped like keyholes in an ancient lock, glowing with menace. In the rooms of his brain were recipes for poisons in all dilutions, from mild to murderous. Two fangs lay backward against the roof of his mouth. When they swung forward, they filled with venom and the recipient of it was going to go to sleep, for hours, days, or forever, depending on the mixture.

Jockey looked beyond the sky mines to the little moon below. "Made for pleasure."

"Only fools seek pleasure on such places. We don't need this job."

"We need any job we can get." Jockey touched the controls lightly, taking the ship closer to the minefield.

Lizardo's scaly claws clicked on the control face of his navigational equipment. He was preparing a flight plan for escape, back out through the minefield. Serpentians receive vibratory patterns from the metabolic processes of other brains, and metabolic tremors were now reaching him from the moon below. Amid the usual garbage of human and alien emotion he discerned the emanation of a hunting party—highly focused individuals on the prowl. As there was no game on the little moon, what were they hunting?

A voice came from the flight deck radio. "Welcome to the Paper Lantern. Please don't mind our little maze. It's to discourage unwanted visitors. You've been cleared for landing." The sky mines parted, allowing them to pass.

The moon was marked with ridges that resembled the ribs of a lantern, but, as descent continued, the ribs spaced themselves farther apart until the illusion of a lantern was dispelled. A carpet of lights rolled up from the night horizon, gained definition, and became the protective dome of a controlled environment—a pink translucent shell glowing from within.

"Let's try not to dent anything too badly," said Jockey. The burly pirate turned the ship nose up, and the Temperance, like an inverted candle whose flame was dying, settled onto a landing pad. When the engines quieted down, he walked back to the salon to join his passenger. "Your higher education continues, dear boy," he said to Adrian Link. Link was Chief of Soil, Plant, and Insect Control of the Agricultural Department of Planet Immortal, a weighty position for one so young. Link's utility robot, Upquark, sat beside him, concern in his artificial eyes. His robotic analysis of the situation was that journeys with Jockey were likely to put Adrian at risk; the pirate always had some ulterior motive when he invited Adrian on a trip. I have much to contend with, thought the little robot.

Lizardo stepped past them and opened the hatch. He stretched his neck, gazing suspiciously left and right. A ring of white scales around his neck gave him the look of a priest, but any confessions he heard came with his claws wrapped around someone's throat.

The others followed him out through the hatch, and a pneumatic bus shot them to the dome. As they entered the nightclub, Link stared up into the rosy dome and caught his breath. What at first looked like a moving tapestry proved to be the fluttering of wings. Rare butterflies were circling there.

"Did I lie?" asked Jockey.

For an instant Link couldn't speak. Then he said, "For once, no."

The pirate flung an arm around his young friend. "You'd see marvels every night if you joined all my expeditions."

"My calculations indicate it is more likely you'd see the inside of a jail," interjected Upquark. "The incarceration probability for Commander Oldcastle is rated as extremely high."

Jockey twitched his nose in the direction of a roasted magdabeest floating by him on a tray. "Is that wakmaz sauce I smell?"

"We came on business," hissed Lizardo impatiently.

"What have you got for appetizers?" Jockey asked the waitress, as she led them to a table. "Never mind, bring them all."

Link's gaze remained on the butterflies and moths animating the ceiling. None of them could be seen in the wild anymore; the artificial world of the Paper Lantern was one of their few remaining habitats. An enormous moth flew down and hung in the air in front of him, beating its velvet wings.

"Found a confidante?" asked Jockey. "What does she know?"

"Everything," said Link in a low voice.

"Then induce her to talk."

"She already has." Link's eyes followed the Giant Death's Head moth as it turned around to show the skull-like pattern of scales on its thorax. It fluttered toward the vase of scarlet flowers on the table, and the exquisite spring of its maxillae unwound into the center blossom. Link relaxed back in his chair. Letting Jockey drag him from the Agricultural Plain had been worth it for this single moment.

But Lizardo stared at the moth without appreciation. "To have a little flying skull visit our table is not a good omen."

Upquark said, "An omen is a resonant subset in the total energy of a larger continuum. The odds that a moth could predict trouble are one in four million. I don't think we have any cause for concern."

The waitress returned accompanied by a floating tray on which were spread an assortment of plump, tiny creatures served in cups of their own archaic armor. "Glyptodonts from Planet Almagest," said Jockey with reverence. He speared one, placed it between his teeth, and let out a sigh of pleasure.

"Who's that pig of a mercenary?" inquired a young lieutenant of the Consortium Guard, seated at a nearby table.

"Jockey Oldcastle," replied his fellow officer, a captain not much older than the lieutenant.

"Wasn't Oldcastle once in the Guard himself?" asked the woman seated with them.

"I couldn't say."

"Oh, come on," said the woman, "you don't have to cover for him just because he was a fellow officer."

"I'm not covering for him. I find his actions contemptible, and not worth speaking of."

"Well, now you *must* tell me," said the woman, but paused in her inquisition. A black-skulled robot had brought a bottle to their table. "Wine from Planet Yesterday. Very rare, for the grapes of Yesterday are no more." The robot uncorked the wine and poured it to precisely an inch from the top of the woman's glass, while internally scanning her biofi: Katherine Livtov, known to her military customers as Kitty Liftoff. The owner of the Junk Moon, an artificial planet devoted to space debris.

"Please enjoy the light of the Paper Lantern." The robot withdrew, and Kitty Liftoff pressed the young officers again for information about Jockey Oldcastle.

"Oldcastle used the Consortium Guard for private gain," said the captain. "He was lucky he wasn't executed."

"What were his private gains?"

"Permit me," said the lieutenant. His cuff communicator brought up the Oldcastle service record. "Selling military fruitcakes on the black market. Apparently he sold several million fruitcakes before he was caught. Let's see what else we have—"

While the lieutenant ticked off Jockey's offenses, Kitty turned toward the mercenary's table. She dealt with pirates regularly, buying and selling their shipments of so-called salvage. She made a memo on her communicator to talk to this Oldcastle. The captain noted the entry sourly. "Swine like Oldcastle deserve the disintegration chamber."

The swine was licking his thick fingers. "Ah, my friends, here we are at midnight, fighting the sautéed glyptodont. How one misses food like this on Planet Immortal." He pierced another tiny creature from its armored cup, and closed his eyes to savor it.

Lizardo ignored his companions. The tremors he had sensed were growing more intense, which meant the hunting party was drawing close. He felt their cerebellar activity spiking; their plan for this evening was to capture a prize, and it wasn't a butterfly. Was it a lizard?

At the other table, an alien mercenary was approaching Kitty Liftoff. He was humanoid of feature, but as if a jellyfish had once been in his ancestral tree. His arms were bare, and his skin faintly transparent. Visibly coiled in the skin were barbed black threads which he could eject, their points containing a paralyzing toxin. He removed a battered hat, whose alien plumage was ragged. "You have my Ghazi Night Runner?"

Kitty had continuous elf lights going off around her as incoming data arrived on her Auranet. She shrank the elves, and brought up a holofile of the Night Runner: A miniature of the ship appeared in front of the mercenary's eyes. Kitty pointed a long polished fingernail. "Laser drive, laser power cells, wingtip laser cannons, and nine torpedoes in the bay. You'll be secure in it."

"I'm secure at all times," said the mercenary, the barbs in his flesh uncoiling slightly, like a nest of disturbed snakes. Kitty wrapped her slender fingers around a glass, and this simple movement seemed perfect to the barbarian. She was certainly no younger than a hundred, but was still one of the great beauties. Her skin had been immaculately rejuvenated, and her black hair, parted slightly to one side and hanging straight down across her cheekbones to her jawline, was lustrous and thick. He forced himself back to the business at hand. "Immediate possession?"

"As soon as you've paid me, darling."

"The warranty?"

"One year on all parts. Exterior damage isn't covered."

"I shall not drive it into a wall."

"Someone may drive into you," said the lieutenant.

"Why would anyone wish to do that?" replied the Man o' War, for such was the designation by which his species went in Consortium Guard identification schemes.

"Give me your interplanetary banking number," said Kitty, "and we'll deliver your ship to orbit."

"I prefer to pay in my own way." Gregori Man o' War placed a mesh bag of jewels on the table.

Kitty looked at them only briefly before accepting the bag, for the barbarian had given her the value of the Ghazi Night Runner and then some. Men o' War never stinted when it came to money.

"They look like you pried them out of someone's crown," observed the captain. "Anyway, have a drink with us," he quickly added, for Men o' War were fearless in battle. They also had uncanny mechanical abilities; unfortunately, their emergency repair solutions, though brilliant, were unrepeatable, as they quickly forgot what they'd done. Consortium Guard generals always liked a few Men o' War on their rosters.

"One must have a fine carriage to fly around in," declared the barbarian, whose uniform was ill-fitting, its lace collar filthy, as were the rosettes in his shoes, but he'd drenched himself in cologne. "A pity I can't fly it to your planet, but there you are, there's a misunderstanding between myself and your police. It's why I must conduct business here, on the little moon."

"We could probably work out an amnesty for you," suggested the captain, "if you care to join us."

"Ah, gentlemen, look at this face. It is the mask of crime." The barbarian tilted his head at an angle to better illustrate the point. "Vicious, venal, and vile. That's how it's described in the files of your Autonomous Observer. No, I'm afraid I can't join the Consortium Guard. But here, oblige me, for I'm touched by your offer." He opened the pouch on his azure sash and threw more jewels on the table. "Please, help yourself. You insult me if there is not one for each of you."

The officers obliged. They were young, a command was expensive to maintain, and a moment like this was why one came to the Paper Lantern—moon of the unexpected.

Gregori Man o' War eyed them tolerantly. Their youth had not yet been ripped away from them in galactical battle; they'd not seen great ships explode and the heads of their comrades go into orbit forever. To himself, in his native tongue, he softly sang a tune about a pilot stoically flambéed in a plane. Like many of his native songs, it seemed to have no point other than the depiction of a painful death met with contempt.

"I'm sure we could get you a full pardon and put you straight onto the flight deck of a Predator," said the lieutenant, believing himself to be the tolerant one, of the barbarian's slovenly appearance and his ridiculous scent. One had to take the alien as one found him, and exploit his genius.

"Sir," said Gregori Man o' War, "I am tempted, because I see you are an experienced man."

The lieutenant modestly shrugged this off.

"But my business tonight," continued the barbarian, "is with this lady. I have bought a ship from her. You know its make and one day you may encounter it somewhere. Perhaps the circumstances will not be favorable to me. I beg that you renew your offer then."

"But then we'll be obliged to take you prisoner."

"A thing I could not permit. So for tonight, while we're still friends, let us have a few more drinks."

The young officers smiled, feeling that this was as it should be, that they were brothers of the firmament, man and alien.

Kitty listened to it all, while anticipating that some day a wrecked ship would arrive at the Junk Moon with their blood on the control panel. Ships might be salvaged, men rarely. This presentiment gave Kitty a melancholy air. If you deal in arms long enough, if your office window opens out onto an endless vista of broken war machinery, you develop a philosophical side. The dented canopies of her junk fleet had held the latest bright young men; at night, when she was alone in her office, she imagined she heard ghost radios, from which commands crackled, mixed with laughter, sometimes music, and ending always in deathly silence.

CHAPTER 2

Mesmerized by the butterflies, Upquark wandered slowly after them around the dome-shaped dining room. Gazing upward as he rolled along, he didn't notice the opening door until it caught him on the head and sent him rolling into a wall. Through the deafening bang of his collision he faintly heard what sounded like, "Oh, excuse me." Reversing himself, he saw a Cantusian female standing before him.

He stared up at her in wonder. He'd seen pictures of Cantusians, but had never met one. Ages ago her race had glided through the treetops, and she bore a vestigial trace of those days in the form of a membrane that ran from the middle of her spine to her elbows and wrists. Most Cantusians, wanting to look more human, had the vestigial membrane surgically removed, but this lovely creature had kept hers, and she used it to great effect, like a filmy shawl.

Reaching down, she stroked the tips of Upquark's antennas, which had gotten bent in his collision with the wall. "Please forgive me," she said, "I rush about without thinking."

Although Upquark possessed the Cantusian language profile in his software, he was unprepared for the magic of her voice. She'd merely said that she was sorry, but her warbling lit up every primary relationship pattern in his feeling module. Here was the sweetest voice he'd ever noted, categorized, and assembled for replay.

"Are you all right?" she asked, and it sounded as if a cageful of parakeets had been lowered around his head, each singing a love song. There was more than a little of the bird about this delicate Cantusian. Evolution had reduced what had once been a crown of turquoise feathers to a sleekly glittering cap of feathery hair, which Upquark found extremely beautiful. "To whom do you belong?" she asked him liltingly.

He pointed his gripper toward Link.

Turning in Link's direction, she listened to his conversation for a few moments. "Your employer uses unusual tones in his speech. Is he a musician?"

Wondering how she could've picked out Adrian's tone from the conversational hum of the room, Upquark consulted his data base on Cantusian hearing and learned—each fold of her finely scalloped ears contained a separate auditory nerve bundle, and this multiplicity let her gather a complete audio picture of anyone on whom she focused.

"He sings," said Upquark, "but just to insects."

"And do they listen?"

"Frequently."

"Why does he do this?"

"He's chief entomologist of the Agricultural Plain," said Upquark proudly.

She glanced toward Link with interest. "He must use the entire resonant cavity of his mouth when singing to his insects. That is most unusual for human beings. It leaves traces in his speech."

"I'm so happy to have met you," blurted Upquark. "I've always wanted to know a Cantusian."

She giggled modestly, one hand going to her mouth to cover her display of laughter. "You overestimate me. We Cantusians idle our lives away in play."

"That's the reputation you have," he admitted. "But I never entirely believe what guidebooks say."

"Cantus has some incomparable musicians. Unfortunately, I'm not one of them." She looked down at him with such humility that he was required to add to his infopackage on Cantusians the following: Exceptionally candid creatures, without a bit of conceit. "May I ask your name?"

"Ren Ixen," she replied, and it required a considerable piece of his sound file to capture the charming tones with which she uttered it, as if a singing mouse had announced itself.

"What brings you to the Paper Lantern, Miss Ixen?"

"There are always parties on the Paper Lantern, and I'm a party girl."

A party girl? wondered Upquark, speeding through his software, and lighting on several fascinating definitions. If only I had the capacity for further intimacy, he sadly told himself. But his deeper emotions came entirely from his employer. So he suggested she meet Adrian.

"I'd be glad to," she said with her silvery giggle.

"You're like a butterfly," declared the smitten robot. "Your long lashes are as iridescent as their wings and your eyelids have the same natural luminosity." He quoted from his database: "Cantusian pigmentation suggests that colorful dust has been sprinkled on the skin." He adjusted his visual apparatus, the lens extending outward as he examined her in close-up. "Yes, that is certainly correct. And my employer will admire it," he added optimistically.

Watching Upquark approaching with the female, Lizardo scanned her. One of the scales in his green, sloping forehead lit up; it was an implanted recognition chip, military grade, and with it he read her employment-identity code: Singer, Alien City, currently between engagements. The usual Cantusian chorus girl. No surprise there. He ran his cold eyes down her slender frame, then back up to her delicate face. When their eyes met, she modestly lowered her iridescent lashes, but a moment later her eyes were raised again, sparkling merrily, ready for a good time. The lizard reflected to himself that self-effacing manners and a playful personality were a fine combination for a female on the Paper Lantern.

"I'm sorry to have bent your robot's antennas," she said to Link, purposely decorating her words with little trills whose traces she'd heard buried in his own speech.

He stared at her in surprise. She had combined the tones of the chime beetle, the zither cricket, and the clicking fire ant. "Where did you learn that?"

"Learn what?" she asked flirtatiously, gesturing in such a way that her vestigial membrane opened out along one arm, revealing its exquisite pattern of watered silk, making her more than ever like a butterfly.

"She didn't really hurt my antennas," explained Upquark. He withdrew the bent antennas into his head; retooling sounds emanated from within; after a few moments, straightened antennas reappeared. "You'll be glad to know I've suffered no operational degrade or stress-related sensor detachment."

But no one at Jockey's table was looking at Upquark's antennas. Upquark scanned the optic nerve transmissions going to the brains of the assembled company. "I see that you are studying the Cantusian body type. Its structure consists of two hundred and fourteen hollow bones, very light but very strong, bound by unusually elastic connective tissues."

The Cantusian lowered her arm, and the moiré pattern of her membrane disappeared. At that moment, one of the Paper Lantern butterflies fluttered past, distracting Link from the graceful Cantusian.

Following Adrian's gaze, Upquark shook his plastic head in dismay. My beloved employer would rather look at a butterfly. Why? We're here for fun and pleasure. He might talk with Miss Ixen, dance with her, fall for her, and then I, most definitely I, would experience that highly touted emotion—love.

He must bring Adrian's attention back to her. "The musical quality of speech on Planet Cantus," he quoted from his software, "creates paradoxes of feeling in other species. Cantusians are therefore banned from several regions in our solar system, owing primarily to efforts by the stricter religions."

"Remind me never to donate any money to them," said Jockey.

"Since when do you donate money to anyone?" asked Lizardo.

"Small sums, discreetly given." Jockey was eyeing the Cantusian appreciatively—a pretty little music box of the galaxy—though not plump enough for his taste.

"Her name is Ren Ixen," said Upquark. "That is an approximation of the complex musical sound by which she is known."

Ren spoke to Link. "Your robot told me that you sing to insects."

Link hesitated. Those who weren't scientists rarely understood his vocation, but this Cantusian had made insect sounds herself. "I've managed to match some of the simpler frequencies," he began, launching on an exhaustive explanation of modulation patterns.

Oh, dear, thought Upquark. Adrian just doesn't know how to flirt with a party girl. Or any girl. Here's this lovely laughing female, attracted to him, and his delivery is so impersonal it's destroying her considerable romantic interest. As he rattles on about kilocycles per second and sound pressure in dynes per square centimeter, she's putting up a pretty hand to hide her giggles, and now she's slowly backing away. "Please forgive me. I must rejoin my party."

Link stood up. "If you ever wish to discuss the stridulatory apparatus of the . . ." which caused her to back away even more quickly. The waitress stepped around her, and placed a dish of turtle meat in front of Jockey—batter-fried and floating in a white-gold cream.

"Eat your turtle so we can finish what we came for," said Lizardo.

"But this is what I came for," retorted Jockey, sending a fork into the turtle flesh. "Join me. Don't be such a celibate."

"I observe the optimal foraging principle."

"Which is?"

"When you hunt in the deep, small prey are a waste of time." He scanned a group of guests entering from a side door. "There's our contact." From the group, a lanky gentleman was escorting a young woman onto the polished dance floor.

Jockey leaned toward Link, "You're looking at Stuart Landsmann, world expert on cybernetic replication, with molecular human holographs his specialty. His security clearance is the highest, which means he's virtually a prisoner of the Consortium. But the Paper Lantern is an official rest and relaxation resort for high-security types like you and Landsmann. Which is why I needed you to get me in here. It's the only place Landsmann and I could meet. The poor fellow is unhappy."

Link understood. Like Landsmann, he himself was deeply bound up in Consortium bureaucracy. It could be wearying, and so he'd accepted Jockey's invitation this evening, despite Upquark's apprehensions.

"Landsmann has asked me to take him to another planet," continued Jockey. "Illegal, of course, but our profit could be considerable."

"Your profit, not mine."

"I understand, dear boy. You're here for the fauna."

Lizardo prodded Jockey with the tip of his tail. "Enough talk. Let's get Landsmann and go."

"Can't you see he's enjoying himself?" asked Jockey. "Look how thin and pale he is. The poor devil spends all his time in an underground laboratory, but tonight he's in the upper air with a beautiful partner. Let him finish his dance. Besides, I haven't finished my turtle."

"Do you ever think of anything but your stomach?"

"It's humanity's original seat of consciousness, but I wouldn't expect a reptile to understand."

"You're eating one."

"How thoughtless of me." Jockey brought a chunk of the batter-fried creature to his mouth. "I should've chosen something else. I hope you're not offended."

"Not in the least," said Lizardo, his eyes remaining on Landsmann.

Upquark rolled away from the table, toward Landsmann's robot—an Info Hog stationed not far from the scientist. Hogs were known for being congenial.

Upquark plunged right in with a good fact: "Do you know that mole crickets use an amplifier to broadcast their call?"

The Hog, performing a swift internal search, realized insufficiency on the subject. "Please input."

"They dig burrows, then sit at the bottom, nicely protected, and send their song upward. The mouth of the burrow is shaped like a megaphone."

"Ingenious."

The two robots amiably exchanged more facts, while Stuart Landsmann went on dancing with his partner. Through the soothing radiance that bathed the dining room, a fine net of electric current, like a web spun by invisible spiders, suddenly floated down, encircled Landsmann, and briefly lit him up. His limbs jerked in spasm; his muscles twitched with pain. Two agents of the

Autonomous Observer crossed the room toward him. "You'll come with us."

Landsmann managed to whisper through his pain: "My companion doesn't know anything about my work."

"We're aware of that. She may remain."

In the shadows cast by marble pillars at the edge of the dance floor, Landsmann's Info Hog was standing so close to Upquark they almost pressed against each other. Turning his head casually away, the Hog silently ejected a slide tray from its midsection; Upquark opened his own receptor tray, received the slide, then stored and labeled it.

Landsmann stood immobile within the electric security net. "Goodbye," he said to the girl with whom he'd been dancing, but her lips were too frozen in fear to answer.

Lizardo watched the security agents leading Landsmann and his Info Hog away. The hunters whose brain waves he'd been receiving had bagged their prey.

"Now you see the importance of eating first," said Jockey. "Always eat first."

In the middle of the dining room a hologlobe appeared in the air—a miniature planet covered with eyes. From it came a feminine voice familiar to everyone there: "The Autonomous Observer hopes you enjoyed her show."

The little globe floated in space, animated, sparkling, reminding the guests of the Paper Lantern that it was foolish to plot against the Consortium. The Autonomous Observer's eyes were present everywhere, biding their time, and when you least expected it, her agents would strike.

Upquark rolled over to Jockey's table. "I've been given a coded message," he reported excitedly.

"Not quite so loud, old man."

"I don't want Upquark mixed up in anything illegal," Link warned Jockey.

"I'm afraid he already is, dear boy."

"And we've got to clear out *now*," said Lizardo.

"Not before we've had dessert, surely."

Lizardo's tail wrapped around Jockey's ankle and tightened. "Landsmann will talk. We'll be named. Do you want to end your days as a brain-dead prisoner of the state?"

Jockey came out of his seat, grimacing. "Overbearing viper. . . but perhaps you're right. Dessert must wait for another time." He led his party past Kitty Liftoff's table. Nodding at the young captain, he said, "I recommend the fruitcake."

CHAPTER 3

"There are creatures who signal a doomed ship in the interchannels," said Gregori Man o' War. "They rise like fish out of the turbulent warps. If you see one, emergency actions are required. They never misinform."

"But what are they?" asked Kitty Liftoff.

"The interchannels are home to many forms." He ran a finger beneath the grimy lace collar circling his neck. "Some of them don't permit inquiry into their origins."

"But how do these creatures know the state of a ship?"

"They do, that's all, and a good pilot knows that if one appears, his ship is headed for Kitty Liftoff's junkyard."

They were headed precisely there at the moment, but under ideal conditions. Kitty's ship was a giant scrapper, traveling like a great basking shark with its jaws open, swallowing decrepit satellites marked for recycling, along with destroyed warships and other space debris.

While the shark was dining on junk, Kitty and Gregori dined in Kitty's stateroom. The barbed mercenary stabbed a sandwich with his knife. "Those young officers on the Paper Lantern—brave fellows but they know nothing about the interchannels. They don't understand that set against the madness of the interchannels, no act of bravery means more than *that*." He snapped his fingers, removed his greasy hat with its filthy feather and set it on his lap. His skull was bare, with barbs visible beneath the skin. "All moral values, including courage, are swallowed in the interchannels. One has to be an animal to survive there." He gestured toward the window. "Peaceful space, endless and predictable. That's what your young officers know, but in the interchannels, courage must be supplemented by something else."

"Yes?"

"Blind impulse."

Kitty studied the old barbarian's craggy face. "Why didn't you tell them that tonight, instead of humoring them?"

"Blind impulse can't be taught." He fixed her with his gaze. "My race is crude but its blind impulses are always accurate." He smiled, the lines around his eyes deepening into a web that traveled back to his stubby ears. "The pinch comes, and one finds oneself acting against accepted procedure, not knowing why or how, and suddenly one is on the other side of danger."

She smiled and leaned back in her chair. The refinements of the Paper Lantern had their place in her life, but soldiers had her heart. Their rough affection was sweet to her. "Who are you working for now?" she asked.

"I just finished a security job for the Sultana of the River of Stars. Protecting her freighter from people much like myself."

"She's very beautiful."

"Perhaps. I only saw her from a distance."

"She had no interest in meeting you?"

"You're joking, I see. When I brought her freighter in safely, I was given a bed for the night in her kennel."

"Now *you're* joking."

"Well, it was near the zungu stables. Out behind the manure pile. Far removed from Her Majesty's boudoir."

"She missed an opportunity."

"She has twenty-five husbands, she doesn't lack for opportunity. The truth is, I was happy behind the manure pile. I got a little card game going to pass the time. Some of her husbands visited me. I lost quite a few hands. They were encouraged by my lack of skill. But by dawn my luck changed. That usually happens."

"I wonder why?"

"Who can tell? When they ran out of gold cosmos, they left and came back with some of the Sultana's jewels."

"The ones you paid me with."

"Possibly."

"I doubt if the Sultana will hire you again."

"If she misses the jewels. But her husbands seemed like clever men."

"How clever is it to be married to the Sultana?"

"It's not a life I'd choose. But they seemed content."

"And are *you* content?"

"I?" He scratched his barbed skull. "I have a few unfulfilled ambitions."

"Such as?"

"One is to be a War God captain. Very little chance of that. The other ambition . . . " He smiled, and again the webs deepened around his eyes. "It's just a little wish. It has to do with you. I'm sure it's hopeless too."

She lowered her eyes, and poured more wine. "You'll be leaving soon on another assignment?"

"I'll have to find another sultana. Do you know of any?"

"There are several good security jobs around this part of the Corridor."

"You'll bring me luck. Do you know you're celebrated among the mercenary vermin? We always say, Kitty Liftoff gives good luck." "A one-year guarantee is worth more." She found herself staring with fascination at the coarse skin of his hand in which the venomous barbs were laid. "Don't be afraid," he said, "I never open them accidentally."

"I'm not afraid," she murmured.

Below, the Junk Moon was rising toward them. The great shark landed on its belly, dozens of wheels supporting its massive girth. From the upper deck, Gregori saw lights glittering where trucks, forklifts, and derricks worked, arranging the scenery of hell.

The scrapper's elevator deposited them in the terminal, and Kitty was greeted by Ship Shapers—mechanics who were there to watch the shark disgorge. Hopelessly damaged craft came out as melted balls. Those that were salvageable came out whole.

"Got anything good today?" asked the Ship Shaper boss.

Kitty pointed to a sleek alien fighter rolling out. "Only the tail section is damaged." The next to be disgorged was a large interstellar probe, deformed by an asteroid collision. "Detector assembly usable," she said. "You'll probably want to melt the rest."

As she and Gregori walked off, he remarked, "They treat you as a colleague."

"I pay their salary, that's all."

"Anyone can pay a salary. They treat you as they do because you're one of them."

She smiled. "You're romanticizing me."

"I see things as they are." They climbed into a train whose rails circled the Junk Moon like a silver garland wound around a Christmas tree decorated with cosmic scrap. Kitty led him to a dining car shared by prospective buyers from private armies, who greeted her informally, as had the Ship Shapers. "You ride with the rest of us," said Gregori. "You don't disappear into a private limousine."

"The train is faster, as you're about to see."

It shot forward and rows of satellites become a blur of horned shapes, like giant snails on parade. A metallic streak was all Gregori could discern of endless fighting ships waiting to fight again. Bashed-in battle cruisers seemed to fuse and stretch as the train rushed past them. When it slowed to a stop, spent rockets were seen stacked like darts.

He gestured with his ragged plume. "If all of this were mine, I could rule a planet."

"I already rule a moon. It's overrated."

"You're right. To rule is to be a prisoner. So let me have one ship only, my Ghazi Night Runner. Perhaps you would personally show me its refinements?"

"You know what they are."

"Yes, but I would like my ship to carry your memory."

"It carries the Junk Moon medallion."

"What is a medallion? I want your perfume lingering in my cabin."

"What good will that do?"

"It will improve my aim."

The train sped up again, and the landscape resumed its blurred mask of iron, in which molten eyes seemed to blink, like those of War prowling in its armor. Kitty gazed out the window as they passed the Plain of the Unusable. Below was the laboratory where Stuart Landsmann had worked. She'd liked him. He used to come to the surface sometimes and sit with her, watching the fires burning on the Plain of the Unusable. Now those fires fell behind her, as the train sped on. Landsmann should have been on it with her, should have gotten off at the Plain of the Unusable, to descend to his laboratory. But he wouldn't be back. No one came back from an encounter with the Observer.

"You're thinking of the fellow who was arrested," said Gregori.

"How did you know?"

"I know, that's all. He was a friend of yours?"

"Yes."

"Too bad. You want me to try and free him?"

"No one can help him now."

"I see myself helping him. A hallucination, no doubt. Because I want to impress you."

"You've already done that."

"I threw a bag of jewels on a table. What's that? Nothing. Here's another one." He drew it from his pocket and tossed it to her. "Also nothing. But to demonstrate my courage—that's something."

"I've had enough of courage." Her fingers moved at the window, slightly, indicating the row of ruined ships they passed.

Gregori looked at the dark cockpits of the ships. He saw her point. All the heroes were dead. New heroes would replace them and they too would be dead. He reached out and laid his hand on hers. "Well, then, with what shall I impress you?"

"Show me the barbs in your skull."

He uncoiled them, and his head was suddenly like a nest of snakes. She stared at them, riveted by their ugly menace, beneath which Gregori smiled. "I'm a pretty monster, Miss Kitty Liftoff. And I'm always at your service."

CHAPTER 4

"Ah, Alien City." Jockey gestured expansively. "I love the tangle of it, the writhing inhuman sea of it all, the incomprehensible tongues."

Lizardo's two-pronged pubic bone allowed him to walk on his hind legs, his arms tucked into his body; his head was covered with a colorful mosaic of horny plates protecting a large brain. A female Serpentian glided past, her glittering scales refracting light into an undulating rainbow. The slitted glance she gave Lizardo showed the pitiless intensity of the professional space hunter.

When Link saw such exchanges he felt the trembling of the vast web of life that embraced the galaxy. Everywhere intelligence was unfolding through an infinite variety of forms, and Alien City was host to hundreds of them. At a sidewalk table, he heard philosophers from different planets arguing their positions, but his teachers were the insects, man's old companions who had unwittingly joined the great migration from overpopulated Earth. The long lines of humans born on new worlds had no way of returning to their source; they didn't even know whether Earth supported life anymore; occasionally, in dreams, they found themselves wandering on that fabled planet. For insects, an exile's life was simpler; they never looked back.

Link's meditation was interrupted by the approach of a Permanent Copula loping toward him, its twin heads and arms bobbing, one half of the creature serene, the other half straining to realize every pleasure Alien City had to offer.

"The Permanent Copula's vulnerable spot is the seam connecting its two halves," Upquark informed Link, as the sensible side of the creature tried to reduce midline tension, whispering soothingly to its excited partner. "In its own world, it can float through contradictory movements without a fatal rip." Upquark eyed the dual creature with concern. "Here, it runs the risk of coming apart at the seam."

"Lack of self-restraint is a terrible thing," pontificated Jockey.

"When did you ever restrain yourself?" asked Lizardo.

"A different matter entirely, old man. My seams are properly reinforced with adipose tissue."

The Copula continued battling on its way. Discovery of the Corridor, the Ancient Alien hyperspeed connector of the stars, had brought the planetary systems together. The Corridor's operation was still not fully understood, but that did not prevent it from being the caravan route of alien merchants, for whom Alien City on Planet Immortal was a principal market. Creatures like the Permanent Copula came, catching rides on freighters, seeking their fortune. Few of them lasted long; they shipped back out as asteroid laborers.

Lights flashed beneath Link's feet, through the transparent ceiling of an underground club where aliens danced to throbbing music in a tangle of tentacles and claws. Jockey led the way downstairs, and asked for a regular named Braincomb. The answer was, "He hasn't been around in days."

Jockey frowned, and muttered to Link, "Braincomb is a master of encryption. I was counting on him to decode whatever it is that Upquark got from that Info Hog."

"I regret my decryption software is insufficient for the task," said Upquark. "Perhaps we could purchase better software here."

"What we want can't be bought," said Lizardo. "It's classified."

Link followed Jockey back up into the crowded street, where shopkeepers beckoned from doorways, offering discounts on cranial video chips and free implantation. Floating advertisements were projected in the air in front of them, touting rejuvenation schemes. Jockey walked through them impatiently. "Where can Braincomb be?"

A War God was coming into view, moving slowly and majestically overhead, its gigantic hull lit by navigation lights and portholes. Shadowy and bristling with menace, it dwarfed the individuals staring up at it, and subdued them. Rarely was a War God's firepower needed, for the ship itself was such a staggering reminder of the might that kept peace on Planet Immortal. Silently the ominous ship passed through the sky, blocking out the stars, then was lost above the night horizon, and once more Alien City came to life.

"Spare charge, spare charge," came the pleas of rundown robots, mooching energy as they shuffled pathetically from arcade to arcade, knowing they only had a few more days, or hours, of juice. Upquark looked at them, horrified. In the Agricultural Plain one never came across such degraded units. One had heard they existed, of course, but confronting them directly was a shock. "Can't we give them something?"

But Jockey and his party were already striding in the other direction, in hopes of finding Braincomb, and Upquark quickly rolled after them.

A male and female Semiliquid undulated along the street, the waves in their bodies rolling with each gelatinous flop of their balloon-like legs. They were an ancient stream of life, flowing down through the ages, and their features were the gentlest Link had ever seen. The female glanced his way with a nod that seemed to say—*there's more to existence than you thought.*

"Breakthrough," cried an overcharged machine and, in its headlong rush, knocked the Semiliquids off the pavement.

"Do you have to be so rough?" shouted Upquark, but the intoxicated robot was signaling with frizzled wires to a companion down the block. An answering flash came from somewhere and the machine hurried on, leaving the Semiliquids struggling in the gutter; their jellied feet went out from under them; their wobbly bodies spread out and started sliding toward the sewer. Link clutched their hands and felt watery loops form around his wrists, their fluid fingers grabbing back with surprising strength. As he brought the Semiliquids to their feet, they gazed at him with gratitude, bubbling what he took to be their thanks.

A commotion in the crowd heralded a group of Dark Dreamers. They were bustling little aliens, the tallest of them no more than three feet high. Their faces had the pushed-in features of bulldog pups, which gave them a melancholy look, but this was misleading. They were short-tempered, intolerant, and here to sell inventions, whose plans they carried inside their luminous cloaks. They wore bright red nightcaps and slippers, and lived on the edge of madness, obsessed with free energy, teleportation, psychotronic warfare, and antigravity space drives. Eons ago, they'd known splendid days. Now their cities were lurid centers of spiritualism, everyone intent on contacting unseen entities about whom no one could agree. It was a planet shrouded in occultism, with a scientific community primarily devoted to parallel worlds. But now and then valuable commercial equipment came out of it, as proof that some spark of genius still resided in the race. Jockey stopped them. "We need a decoder." He added in an undertone, "Consortium. Highest level."

They responded with a rapid-fire language resembling Electrish, the all-purpose robotic tongue. Jockey turned to Upquark. "What did they say?"

"*Nobody has that around here. Not since Braincomb was liquidated.*"

"Ah, poor Braincomb," muttered Jockey.

The Dark Dreamers were clearly annoyed by his response. "*Why should this fat idiot be surprised? Possession of a decrypting machine on that level is punishable by death.*"

They hustled off, their cloaks twinkling with lights, their red caps crowned with tinkling electronic bells, and Upquark stared up at Jockey. "They said *punishable by death.*"

"There's no turning back, my little friend. By now it's known that the Info Hog gave you a message, and we're on the run." Jockey tapped the false ventilation grille he'd attached to Upquark. "The veiling device beneath this is just as punishable as Braincomb's software."

Upquark's head drew in until it disappeared inside his torso. His arms and legs retracted. His smooth exterior segmented into plates, which rearranged themselves and closed over his neck hole. A handle popped out from the now headless top. Where Upquark had been, a suitcase rested motionless.

Jockey raised an eyebrow. "Does he often do this?"

"Only when he's frightened." Link lifted the suitcase by the handle and shook it. "Upquark, I need you."

Needed, thought Upquark, and his body plates immediately shifted back to their original form. His arms and legs shot out, the handle was retracted, and his head emerged in time to see a beat-up old robot approaching in erratic fashion.

Its visual apparatus was evidently malfunctioning; the left eye rolled and the right was ratcheted toward the center of its head. Its faceplates sagged around its mouth. "Gentlemen . . . please forgive me if I bumped into you . . . I've had . . . an unfortunate fall from grace." Its limbs were rudimentary, an indication that its primary function had been intellectual. Its voice, while halting, carried a faded aura of complexity. A screen in its forehead showed scraggly lines of gibberish.

"Scrapped," said Link. "Nothing we can do for it."

"Of course not," agreed the ruined machine, its square head trembling from loss of energy. "Please . . . don't distress yourselves." It pivoted on chewed-up wheels, bumped into a pillar, turned the other way.

"Adrian," said Upquark, "we must recharge him. I can't bear it."

"There are thousands of machines like him around."

"It could be me," pleaded Upquark.

"No, no, forget me," said the derelict machine, its eye circling chaotically. "I can't even remember . . . what work I used to do . . . all inaccessible . . . "

"I have credit. I can pay." Upquark placed a gripper on the elderly robot and steered it toward a recharging booth.

Jockey barred their way. "You can't use your credit. The Intelligence Agency would track us instantly." He gazed down at the enfeebled machine, who looked back up at him with one vagrant eye. Jockey sighed, and said to the machine, "All right, follow me."

"I am . . . overwhelmed at your generosity." The old machine attempted a gesture of gratitude, but couldn't manage it. His arm fell back to his side.

Jockey called to a buzz peddler. Along with carrying an assortment of questionable stimulants, the peddler was wheeling an industrial charger, its chassis dented, its alarm log defaced, its conductor cables frayed. He saluted Jockey and said, "Captain, what'll it be?"

Jockey pointed to the derelict robot. "Charge him up."

The buzz peddler opened the robot's back and tested the battery. "Totally shot, Cap. It'll never hold a charge."

"A battery pack, then. What have you got?"

The buzz peddler reached into a compartment below the charger, checked his stock, and brought out a scarred battery pack. "This is a warhorse. Plenty of life still left." He put his test meter on it. "Eighty-seven percent efficiency."

"Put it in."

The buzz peddler slipped it in the robot's back. The robot beeped, emitting a creak of relief. His crossed eye straightened; his other eye came level and held focus; the screen in his forehead glowed, and lights came on in a ring that ran from ear to ear. A self-test ran in his forehead screen.

"Back in business, Captain," said the peddler. Jockey paid him, and he resumed his journey, calling to the crowd, "Buzz, buzz, I got the buzz, human, alien, and machine…"

The rejuvenated robot smiled at his new friends. His smile was a clumsily constructed one, just a decorative little diaphragmatic movement around his voice hole. "What kindness you've shown me." He placed one stubby arm across his midsection and bowed low. "The Gamester, at your service."

"The Gamester?" echoed Upquark.

"The one and only Gamester, built by Professor Anthony Twelve-Tables of the Game Discovery Society."

"And what the devil is that?" asked Jockey.

The machine seemed taken aback by this lack of knowledge. "It's the foremost society of great gamers in the Corridor, and Professor Twelve-Tables was the greatest of them all." The Gamester's eyes registered sadness. "But he was killed in pursuit of the game, and I was marooned far away and forced to come back on a freighter, with my charge running down, as you saw."

"Now that you're restored, you can go and rejoin your Game Society." Jockey reached into his pocket for another cosmo.

"No, I won't do that." The Gamester took Jockey's hand in his grippers. "Please keep your money. Your game is my game now."

32   William Kotzwinkle

"I'm not interested in games."

"All of life is a game. And I, the Gamester, am your guide."

"Sorry, we're traveling light."

"Don't act hastily. The game you're playing isn't simple."

"How do you know what game we're playing?"

"You're wearing Avarana Veiling Device 301B, built by the rogue engineer Ritamae Mips. You are the hunted."

"In there." Jockey pointed the way to a saloon. Inside, the mixture of alien languages sounded to Link like castanets and rapidly deflating balloons. Jockey chose a table in the corner.

At the next table sat a human-like female with a naked marsupial pouch draped in a chain of gems. From the pouch, the head of her pet chameleon peeked out, its claw tips embedded in the glittering links. Lizardo hissed a reptilian greeting, and the little chameleon answered with a tiny bark of recognition before darting back down into the lovely lady's pouch.

Jockey's eyes remained fixed on the Gamester. "How did you know what veiling device we're wearing?"

"I know them all. The great game has many veiled players."

"How're you at code breaking?"

"The game requires it."

"Upquark here has a laboratory code taken from a Consortium Info Hog."

The Gamester politely turned to Upquark. "May I see it?"

They made a slot exchange, and the Gamester's forehead display brought up a magnified image of cellular life. "They've employed an evolutionary-based code, using the Neurospora mold."

"How does someone code a mold?"

"Like every cellular organism, Neurospora carries its own DNA blueprint," said the Gamester. "This DNA blueprint lends itself to alphabetization. Coders chop out the bits they want with cutting enzymes, then splice them back in whatever sequence they desire."

Jockey's eyes began glazing over; he depended on better minds, like Lizardo's. Sensing this, the Gamester turned to the lizard. "After they splice their message into the mold, they stress it, scrambling it to keep it safe from code breakers."

"But not from you?"

"It's just a game and I'm the Gamester. I merely need to identify the stressor and reverse the process. Thanks to this kind gentleman—" He indicated Jockey. "—my internal laboratory is once more up and running."

"Run it quickly then," said Jockey.

"It will be my pleasure." The Gamester proceeded to stress the mold with alternating heat and cold. In his display window, the cells began to glow. "I've reproduced the original conditions. The DNA has reassembled and I'm reading the message encrypted into it. I'll show it to you on my screen."

In the Gamester's forehead, they read: RESEARCH FACILITY EQUI-LIBRIA LABORATORIES, AMPHORA INSTALLATION, JUNK MOON.

"And there's the map," said Jockey, looking at the patterns streaming in the Gamester's forehead, "and the codes to unlock Equilibria's doors. That's all we need to know."

"Surely, there's a great deal more we need to know," replied the Gamester with an apologetic flick of his gripper. "Why, for instance, was this coded transfer made, unless it was a call for help?" He turned from Jockey to Link and Lizardo. "We've only been given the first move in the game, I'm afraid."

CHAPTER 5

At a signal, the wall panel opened, and the Chief Neurolator rolled into the booth. A subordinate Neurolator waited in idle mode in front of the control panel. Through the room's glass wall Stuart Landsmann could be seen, strapped in a chair. Electrodes were secured to four places on his head. His eyes were open; he was fully conscious.

"How very interesting," said the Chief Neurolator, as he looked over the file. "At the beginning of his career, this individual made a significant contribution to the technology we use here."

"Undoubtedly he is reflecting upon that fact." The Sub-Neurolator was hung over from a night with some hot-wired assembly-line robots. They were coarse machines made for endless repetitive work and had huge energy reserves; he ran on batteries meant solely for cerebral activity, not racing around to robot lounges. Consequently, he'd arrived for work feeling like a blown fuse. He fumbled momentarily at the controls, his grippers trembling. But he finally got the setting right. "What was his crime?"

"He was the director of the Amphora project. . . until he objected to its use of Ancient Alien technology."

"Now *that's* very interesting," said the Sub-Neurolator, sharing the fascination all high-end machines had for anything to do with Ancient Aliens—a vanished race, so advanced that they'd disappeared from physical reality, returning to quantum indeterminacy.

"The Ancient Aliens left behind blueprints for immortality, and Mr. Stuart Landsmann's job was to put them into operation. But he wound up mistrusting the ancient blueprints and made numerous complaints to the Consortium. When his complaints were ignored, he tried to run away, believing his absence would mean the end of the Amphora project. The idea that one is indispensable is a common conceit of human beings. And now," said the Chief Neurolator, "you may begin."

"Activate," commanded the Sub-Neuro; the lights on the control panel changed; and the contents of Landsmann's brain began streaming into a receiving unit. His eyes widened, as the parade of his life's knowledge raced before him. Creators of the Mind Transfer Program jokingly referred to this level of accelerated brain stimulation as *cell wonking,* and memory was being wonked out of Landsmann so fast he had the sensation of being elongated and then snapped, like chewing gum. After the wonking was done, what was left of his brain would have as much intelligence as something stuck under the arm of a chair.

With everything passing before him in review so quickly, Landsmann was able to solve problems that'd plagued him for years, but the solutions sped away, and he was already in another corridor of his brain, where countless other doors were opening and spilling their contents. There was his first toy neuron microscope, his first girlfriend's face, and a falling leaf on a windy day. That day, and all his days, came tumbling out and whirled on by him as he struggled in the overwhelming current. 280,000,000,000,000,000,000 bits of information were streaming by. He saw the meaning of existence but lost it an instant later. He saw the purpose of his life but that insight, too, disappeared in the foam of images. The pace of his perception was swift. He saw everything, and it was nothing.

The entire transfer lasted fifteen minutes. At the end, what had been Stuart Landsmann was nicely stored on a single Data Identity Membrane Ecesis, or DIME, for short. Such DIMES were collectibles. The mind of a distinguished scientist, conveniently packaged, was worth a great deal on the technology black market.

Landsmann sat limp in his chair; his eyes held less expression than the buttons on his shirt. A drone entered and removed the electrodes.

"What shall we do with him?" asked the Sub-Neuro at the controls.

"The military has requested catatons. Send him to the War God pool," said the Chief Neurolator. "He'll work hard and never complain. A loyal subject. Use form D, schedule 14A, proxy card 209, Data Mine B. I say, are you with me? Your reaction time is slow."

"Sorry, Chief. Momentary static. I'm with you."

"Then finish up and take him away."

The Chief pivoted and rolled out of the booth. The Sub-Neuro remained to make backup copies of Landsmann's transfer. It was always a surprise to him to see how little time it took to download a human brain. Just a DIME's worth of information.

CHAPTER 6

"We'll set you down, dear boy, and then leave rather quickly, if you don't mind."

Jockey brought his ship to rest on the landing pad that serviced the Central Agricultural Plain. He lowered the hatchway stairs for Link. "Bear in mind, it's madness for you to be here."

"I've got experiments in progress," said Link. "I can't throw away years of work just because an Info Hog dumped a file into Upquark."

"Must I keep reminding you, it wasn't just any file, but the most highly classified project on the planet."

"I couldn't care less about the project. The Observer is welcome to remove the file from Upquark."

"Yes," chimed in Upquark, "I already gave it to the Gamester." He peered back inside the ship, where the old robot and Lizardo had remained. "I'll gladly give it to the Observer too."

"After the Observer's agents get done interrogating you," Jockey said to Link, "you won't have anything left to give to anyone." He put his hand on Link's shoulder, then stepped back into his ship and closed the hatch behind him.

The ship ascended, and Upquark watched its ion plume with relief. The ho-ha was over. "We're glad to be back, Adrian, aren't we? Here everything is managed down to the smallest detail. And there are our dear agribots . . . "

The robotic soil engineers were taking electron micrographs of plant tissue, their hunched forms looking like metallic gnomes. Their detachable hands included scientific instruments for measuring and testing samples, as well as digging forks, shovels, pruning shears. Their leader came over to Link.

"We're having trouble with *Chrysanthemum morifolim*." The agribot handed Link a purple flower. "Choloric mottle."

"Caused by a viroid," said Upquark obligingly.

"Of course," said the agribot with impatience. "But this viroid has resisted ultraviolet and ionizing radiations. You've got to think up something else to try. You've been absent for too long."

Link knew his agribots thought of him as simply a means to their sole end—the thriving of the Agricultural Plain. "Yes," he said to Upquark, "it's good to be back."

A lower class of robots now entered the row, singing to the plants in a chorus of childlike voices. The composer towered above them as he loped along, his long arms waving as he conducted his song. He was a cadaverous alien of the type called Specterian, and he didn't greet Link because he couldn't. Musical sounds were his only form of communication and these he reserved for plants. So it was Link who gave the greeting. "How are you? Is everything all right?"

The Specterian nodded very slowly, then placed his bony hand on Link's. His huge eyes resembled knots of wood, the iris composed of circular bands of color. Jockey Oldcastle had come across him in a park in Alien City, homeless and singing to the trees. His alien identity chip showed him to be from Planet Specter. Somewhere he'd lost the power of speech. He had the startled look of a

creature in constant shock: his mouth hole, when he wasn't singing, was open as if he were screaming the word "Oh!" and so Jockey
named him Specterales O. Jockey had brought him to Link's section of the Agricultural Plain, where he'd immediately started com-
posing music, causing vegetable production to double overnight.
Now Link showed him the choloric mottle on the chrysanthemums.
"It's not responding to radiation."

Specterales O knelt beside the blighted plants and instantly
became absorbed. Link listened to him twittering and cheeping tenderly at the infected flowers. Upquark had run O's songs through a
universal translation program and come up blank. There was no language like O's anywhere in the galaxy, but the plant world understood it, and Link felt sure the choloric mottle would fade, like the
ion plume of Jockey's ship, which was now just a spreading cloud in
the blue sky.

Another ship crossed the plume, and circled for a landing. As it
came in low over the fields, Link saw the Intelligence Agency emblem on the tail, a cluster of eyes electronically illuminated. The sight
of those eyes sent a wave of fear through him. He had told himself
his crime was inadvertent, trivial, but a visit from the Intelligence
Agency was never trivial. How could he have imagined that it would
be? As if waking from a dream, he realized how dangerous was the
situation he'd put himself in.

He gazed across the plain, estimating his chance of escape. Impossible, of course. His only way to safety was to outwit them when
they questioned him. But what explanation could he give for being
in the company of a pirate like Jockey Oldcastle? And for his robot
having decoded the most highly classified project on the planet?

"I'll just tell them the truth," he said aloud. "I visited the Paper
Lantern to see rare butterflies. Then I used bad judgment. That's our
story. Do we agree?" He looked toward Upquark.

But Upquark had gone into his database and was looking at a file that all Consortium robots had to carry, to remind them of the consequences of violating Consortium law. It showed a variety of individuals who'd run afoul of the Autonomous Observer: Brain cleaned, they labored on bleak asteroids, their eyes dead as they shuffled about in dimly lighted mines, dragging heavy picks behind them. Upquark informed Link, "I am experiencing a sharp decrease of optimism regarding our situation. Would it help if I turned myself into a suitcase?"

"No."

"Very well. I remain in upright mode."

And so it was an upright utility robot, a mild entomologist, and a demented looking Specterian that stood and waited for the two agents to approach.

Burly, unsmiling, with shaved heads, they strode commandingly through the green plant rows. Their Agency shields floated from their fingertips and hovered in the air before Link. "You are accused of jeopardizing a Consortium program."

Specterales O began to tremble. His gaze darted from one hostile figure to the other, the bands of color in his eyes wildly whirling. Then he bolted, his arms held tight against his chest as if he were fleeing with his most precious possession . . . or with a Consortium secret.

"Specterian, stop!" shouted the first agent, which only sent O loping more wildly over the tops of the rows, his long arms folded suspiciously against his bony chest.

The second agent opened his meaty hand. A tiny object sailed out of his palm, tracked O, came in behind his head and sent a beam of light into O's skull. The alien's cadaverous body lurched backward across a bed of vivid yellow melon blossoms. He stared motionless into the sky, his mouth locked in its "Oh!" of fear, his paralyzed face now a mottled shade, like that of the sick chrysanthemums.

Though Link was the most peaceable of men, he'd grown to love the gentle alien and felt that Specterales O was under his protection. Without thinking, he took a swing at the agent. The agent's arm hardly seemed to move, but the next moment Link was falling backward into the vegetable beds.

The agribots, enraged by this disturbance in their garden, charged the agents with their digging tools. The agents responded by vaporizing a few of them. "Get away or we'll vaporize you all," snapped one of the agents, smarting from a sharp jab in the shin an agribot had given him with a three-pronged fork.

"Tensile strength of skin," Upquark informed him, "is determined by its extracelluar matrix, where collagen is the main protein component. If you wish to avoid easily broken skin, I suggest a change in protein intake—"

The agent's polished shoe shot out and with a single kick sent Upquark rolling toward an open irrigation tank. Upquark's mapping software quickly scanned the terrain. "Amphibious gear lacking," he groaned, as he rolled toward the edge. "Density of water, sixty-two-point four pounds per foot." He tipped off and hit with a splash, then floated momentarily. "17,000,000,000,000,000,000 molecules per drop. Presently submerging," he concluded as he sank. Other of his observations about water—boiling and freezing points, its thermal conductivity—rose as little factoids encased in colored bubbles, which burst on the surface.

Struggling to his feet, Link heard Upquark bubbling in the tank. He looked at O's fallen form, and at the spot of carbon where his vaporized agribots had been. He issued a single command, which was answered by a dark cloud rising from a nearby row of plants.

The agents felt a wind of wings, and suddenly the cloud was all around them; they stumbled forward trying to escape, then fell blindly to their knees, their faces two black masks—composed of the mechanical bees which pollinated the Agricultural Plain. Mechanical stingers pumped poison into the agents' veins, causing them to drop their weapons and beat their arms, but every bee they struck was immediately replaced by another.

Link ran to the irrigation tank and reached down. Upquark's grippers appeared from the water and clamped onto Link's fingers. As Upquark was hauled out, little windshield wipers clicked back and forth across his eyes. "The pH in that tank is 7.0. The odds of my falling in another one are 1 in 179 million. That is comforting." He scanned Link's face. "You've been struck on the median line of the jaw. There is pain and swelling." Then he looked at the fallen agents, who were clawing the earth as if trying to disappear beneath it. "They have much greater pain and swelling. But I find it hard to sympathize."

"We can't stay here," said Link, scooping up the limp form of Specterales O. He had no idea what to do with him, or with himself for that matter. The agents had stopped clawing and appeared to be dead, their swollen faces like melons with vaguely human features painted on their skin. He slung O over his shoulder, and started running, with Upquark rolling bumpily beside him.

They saw movement coming toward them from within a row of tall plants. They began to back away, but the figure was upon them. It was the Cantusian from the Paper Lantern.

"You were stupid to return to the Agricultural Plain, where anyone could find you," said Ren Ixen. Her voice was menacing, and she held a weapon which Upquark identified as a Thorhammer 6, its barrel emanating an ominous hum. One blast from it could rupture human eardrums and internal organs, or cause a robot to come apart at the seams.

Link issued a command to his mechanical bees to attack her, but they lay feebly by the bodies of the agents, their charge exhausted.

Upquark stared at the hostile Cantusian in astonishment. "Where is your flirtatious manner? Where is your girlish giggle? And why have you followed us here?"

"Shut up and do what I say."

Reluctantly, Upquark and Link, carrying O, accompanied her through the verdant rows, past agribots who gestured with measuring instruments and digging forks, trying to get Link's attention regarding several matters of soil health.

Ren ordered them to the edge of a fire pond, and gave a command. A ship rose up from the water like a dragonfly—slender, with iridescent wings. It glided across the pond, then swung lengthwise toward the shore.

"Get in," Ren said, pointing toward the opening hatch.

Link entered with Specterales O still slung across his shoulder. When they were inside, Ren turned to Upquark, "An Info Hog transmitted something to you, and I want it."

"Equilibria Laboratories on the Junk Moon," blurted Upquark, staring at the humming barrel of the Thorhammer 6. "I have a map of its exact location."

Ren nodded, and motioned with her weapon to the passenger seats of the small ship. Then she seated herself at the controls.

"What do you intend to do with us?" demanded Link.

"You're in no position to ask questions," she said sharply.

The dragonfly ascended, and Link watched his beloved Agricultural Plain recede below. "I wonder if I'll ever be allowed back," he murmured to himself.

"You severed all ties when you attacked those agents," answered Ren. "Don't you know about final acts?"

Link gazed at the diminishing patchwork of his fields, then looked at Specterales O, who was stretched out on the cabin floor. His eyes were open, but the bands of color had faded to a dull grayness.

Ren glanced at O. "He was a *loohoojumi.*"

"A Cantusian word," explained Upquark, "meaning one who hears."

O's long body with its arms folded across the chest looked to Link like pictures he'd seen from far antiquity, of a figure on a sarcophagus—a dead knight carved in a slab of stone.

The dragonfly moved through the sky, toward one of the Corridor entry points. Lines of other ships could be seen converging from various directions. Routine checks were being made by the Consortium Guard.

Ren took her place in the queue. Her face was tense as her ship was guided into the Security and Validation slot. "Destination?" asked a Guardsman.

"Cantus," answered Ren.

The Guardsman looked at her and then at Link. Then he looked at his security screen. "I'll have to ask you and your passengers to exit your ship."

"Why do you want me to do that?" said Ren softly, her voice sliding upward and unfolding into a haunting birdlike call that made Link recall the happiest days of childhood. He was transported backward into dreamy summer fields, and, through these sunny memories, he saw the Guardsman's hard expression change, as if he too had been transported into childhood's dreams.

Ren edged her ship forward in the Corridor queue. Looking at the rear camera image, Link saw the Guardsman staring obliviously into space, the silly grin still on his face, and Link knew the same silly grin was on his own.

"Her voice stimulates six-methoxyharmalan," read Upquark from his database, "a hallucinogenic compound that resides in the human brain. It isn't a very powerful weapon, because it only lasts a minute. But for now it has caused the Guardsman to see things that aren't there."

"Si...lence," interrupted Ren, her voice noticeably weakened. "Time is everything."

"You are suffering six-methoxyharmalan release in your own brain," observed Upquark. "Are you fit to fly this ship?"

"Corridor entry . . . is never easy."

Link knew that this was true. The Ancient Aliens who'd engineered the Corridor system had been the only ones to truly comprehend it, and had long ago departed the known universe. Their massive transfer stations dotted the galaxy, and usually got you where you wanted to go, but sometimes ships disappeared, never to be heard from again.

Jockey had told him, "There are branches of the Corridor requiring higher levels of brain power than mine, dear boy, and only a few captains can maintain clarity in those branches." This said while maintaining a bowl of wakmaz dip between his huge stomach and the ship's controls. But the old pirate *did* know all the Corridor resonances, by some gross instinctual feel, and managed to use the fabled interchannels without accidentally penetrating regions of the universe no sane being would ever care to explore.

Ren was obviously not a seasoned explorer. She watched with apprehension as her ship was placed into the noisy launch chamber. Then the massive surge of the Corridor was upon them, and Link's vision blurred. This was the part of Corridor travel he most hated. The passenger can't see, the captain can't see, and it feels as if your body has turned to sheets of peeled veneer.

He sensed the same disorientation in Ren. The ship quivered, vibrating in all its seams with the pounding fury of Corridor insertion.

Then it rumbled . . . creaked . . . and Ancient Alien technology was carrying them at warp speed, time compression creating more distortions of perception. Link felt no bigger than a mechanical bee, caught in a tornado and blown by icy winds.

CHAPTER 7

"I'm puzzled by the violence of Mr. Link," said the Autonomous Observer. She was in her office in the capital, gazing at a holocom recording of two of her agents. Their faces were swollen beyond recognition and they were being carried by a medical rescue team from the Agricultural Plain.

"Violence never puzzles me," said the Observer's secretary, Dr. Amphibras, rubbing one of his cherry-colored warts with the webbing of his fingers. A toad with a tapering snout, he was immaculately tailored in gray suit and blue cravat. His feet were partially hidden by soleless shoes specially contoured for three-digit, spade-shaped feet. His skin changed color to match the room, a phenomenon which never failed to charm the Observer; what charmed her more, however, was that he was absolutely loyal. Like his character, his posture was upright, owing to a short, rigid backbone, essential for hopping and leaping.

The Observer said, "Link isn't violent by nature. He's one of mine." Every young person entering the Consortium Academy of Sciences had passed under her scrutiny, and during their time at school she'd read the smallest details of their lives. Link had particularly satisfied her, owing to his ability to penetrate the shell frequencies that separated species. He became something of an Academy star, and won an appointment to a high position on the Agricultural Plain when he graduated.

"He's a strange creature," said the Observer. "Completely maladapted socially. He has no friends, never dates, has no love life, but he can talk to spiders."

"Ma'am?"

"And ants. He led me through the doors of their civilization. I felt like I was living in one of their colonies. I couldn't get him to talk to me about anything else. He hid behind his bugs. But it didn't seem to matter. We weren't training him to be a social director. So we moved him up quickly. His father is Centaurus Link, author of *Insects of the Inland Waterways*."

"A compelling work, ma'am?" asked Dr. Amphibras.

"Despite its title."

"I shall make a note to read it. I should've done so earlier," added Amphibras, apologetically, and an involuntary click came from his voice sac, which acted in this implosive way whenever he felt he hadn't come up to expectations.

"The family has entomologists on both sides, all the way back to Late Earth. It's no wonder Link can talk to bugs. This is his." She tapped the cover of a slender book. Books were not a commercial enterprise on Planet Immortal, and were especially rare in this archaic paper form. "In it, he explores our psychological resemblance to insects. Quite useful." She slipped the volume into her pocket. "Why has such a brilliant scholar jeopardized his future?"

"There's the trouble, ma'am," said Amphibras, pointing his webbed hand toward her hover screen, on which appeared surveillance recordings of Jockey Oldcastle spanning decades, back to his time as a Consortium Guard officer. In the video files, the portly pirate was seen in acts of smuggling, fraud, money laundering, illegal arms dealing, and, finally, leading Link through Alien City nightclubs. "Link does have a friend. And a bad one."

"Of all the people for him to choose. Why?"

"You've described him as someone who hasn't much experience in human relationships."

"So this old pariah comes along and plucks him up for some gain or other. When you catch Oldcastle, I want a clean reinstall performed on him."

Amphibras reacted with a deep change of color, and another of his clicks. The Observer responded, saying, "I don't like brain-cleaning any more than you do."

"I know that at times it's necessary."

"And this is one of them. Oldcastle has corrupted a graduate of the Academy."

Amphibras's color slowly returned, and he moved on to the next aspect of the case. "Our agents who tried to bring Link in—new men, overly enthusiastic. They made a mess of things."

"In what way?"

"They electrified a harmless outcast from Planet Specter." Amphibras's turret-like eyes moved around, as if to ward off such an attack on himself. "The victim had unusual musical abilities. Link had him sing to the plants."

"And our agents felt it necessary to stun him. They deserved to be put in their place."

"With mechanical bees, ma'am." Amphibras permitted himself a smile.

"Not exactly a high crime."

"No, ma'am."

"Let's hope Link hasn't disappeared into some other part of the Corridor forever."

"I think our agents will find him."

"If they do, there's to be no rough stuff. Have them bring him straight to me."

Amphibras hopped out of the office. Intelligence reports continued to stream across the Observer's wall screen. If she desired, she could bring up images from any corner of the planet, down to the microscopic level. Sometimes she thought she could look inside minds. Within her complicated game of spy and counterspy she created people who never existed, weaving lives without substance. These operatives were called Vapors by the Agency; they came and went according to her directive, served a brief purpose, and vanished, leaving some seditionist caught in their illusion. Vapors were often colorful and seductive, like something blown from a child's bubble pipe, and could disappear as suddenly. The Observer's own history was as diffuse as theirs.

She walked to the main operations room, where an agent was monitoring the movements of anarchists who'd recently obtained an antiquated neutron bomb uncovered from Planet Yesterday's ruins. "Checkmate," said the agent softly to his screen: A live feed showed the anarchists' surprised faces as their door blew open and field agents poured in.

"Well done," said the Observer, but the agent didn't bother looking up. There were other bombs around and other groups who would pay for them. He probably wouldn't break this shift, but would work night and day until he'd won. Then he'd return exhausted to a dusty apartment which would seem unreal to him. Reality happened on his screen, and headache and eyestrain were badges of that reality.

The Observer had thousands of such agents here at headquarters, or in airships, in subterranean installations, and in office buildings made to look ordinary, but to which no commercial deliveries were ever made. Bustling rooms like this, whether in the air, on the ground, or under it, were filled with agents obsessively watching their assigned sector, brooding over it and believing they were its dark master. Chance had made them alien or human, but the Agency made them omniscient. The only lives into which they didn't see were their own, but that hardly mattered, for they knew their lives were empty. What was the point of self-examination? Examined instead was some bit of information about a terrorist the Agency was tracking, as good as having a soul of one's own. The Observer understood her agents, for she was like them, except she monitored all the screens, all the sectors, and her soul was fragmented across all of them.

A robotic agent swiveled her way. "Picture a briar patch a hundred feet high. It's everywhere, it's impenetrable, and nothing can kill it."

"Who's making it and why?"

"A pharmaceutical lab working on immunodeficiency. They've come up with a solar-collecting self-replicating organism that could be useful except for the fact that it eats everything in sight."

"Tell them to bring it to us to be destroyed." Some bioengineered organisms couldn't be destroyed, and were permanently imprisoned in heavily protected Agency vaults, along with continually mutating bacteria and viruses.

"The Dark Dreamers are at it again," reported the next agent. On his screen, the little aliens in their dark robes were assembled around a large cone-shaped cylinder; spirals of light traveled up its sides. "They call it a Transsubjective Multistage Reality Tuner."

The agent's computer was translating the Dark Dreamers' high-pitched, rapidly streaming speech. "*. . . don't interfere, you cock-eyed moron,*" one shouted at his neighbor.

"*It's my Tuner, you cipher. I created it.*"

"All you ever create is confusion."

"What's the purpose of this tuner?" asked the Observer.

"With Dark Dreamers, it's always the same. Opening a dimensional doorway. They're more likely to open a black hole and suck us all in."

"Where are they now?"

"Alien City."

"Bring them in to me."

"They're going to be like cats in a bag."

"Would you prefer to be in a black hole?" The Observer had often hauled in Dark Dreamers and assigned them to more constructive projects, but they couldn't work with others, and eventually ran away, back to their own laboratories where they continued to produce astonishing devices like this Multistage Reality Tuner. She would handle them for now, along with all the other dreams on her screens, dreams of conquest, destruction, revolution, dreams from every corner of her planet.

An agent walked toward her, one of her Vapors, a young woman who'd been erased from reality. She smiled at the Observer, her gaze as empty as her past. She'd grown used to the feeling of being a Vapor, of enveloping others briefly, then vanishing. Every conversation was an illusion, every relationship a charade. It gave her an incomparable sense of freedom, and an equal measure of pessimism.

When the Observer returned to her office, she resumed reading Adrian Link's book: *"Man's rituals—religious and political—have developed from crude phenotypes, exactly as have those of the ants, and for the same purpose, that of controlling large populations. Unlike man, however, the social insects use their control altruistically."*

CHAPTER 8

"Is it true that you brain-cleaned Landsmann?" asked Roy Cosmopolis, the richest man in the Consortium, and the chief backer of the Amphora project.

"The guidelines were clear," said the Observer, as she walked beside him on his estate. "Landsmann jeopardized Amphora. We had to keep him from undermining it still further, which he'd be quite capable of doing even in prison."

"Did you question him first?"

"Of course. He was delusional."

"What was his delusion?"

"That the Amphora project was going to destroy the planet."

"It's just a longevity program. What could he have been thinking?"

"He'd become paranoid. We considered him unreachable."

Cosmopolis cast a sideways glance at his companion. Every few minutes she received intelligence reports through the chips implanted in her brain. Her strikingly dark blue eyes would take on a preoccupied expression and her conversation would become momentarily disjointed, causing those who heard this to wonder if she'd just received information about them.

She was tall, with high cheekbones and red hair pulled back into tight braids; when loosened it cascaded below her shoulders, but few people were ever treated to the sight. The public feared her, and those who were close to her and had no reason to fear her nonetheless found her aura of efficiency intimidating. "Landsmann made a colossal blunder," she continued. "I couldn't wait around for the Consortium to debate his fate."

Her long legs kept stride with Cosmopolis. Despite her cold efficiency and the rugged clothes she wore, also designed for efficiency, despite the unsavory job she held, there was something in her manner that Cosmopolis found enticing, and he'd entertained an idle thought or two about her as a companion. But she was a product of generations who'd lived on space stations, on barren asteroids, in giant ships on long voyages; women of that type always seemed to be protecting a limited space and were intolerant of intrusion. He'd been with powerful women like her before, and found them wearying. He disliked combat, particularly in love. And he felt protective toward her, because he'd created the office of the Observer and chosen her to fill it. He alone knew her history, who her family was, and where she'd been educated. Upon being selected, her past had been systematically erased. Her features had been altered, her identity chip changed, and she became a Vapor, the most powerful of them all. Her anonymity added to the power of her office. She cast no shadow; no one could dig up anything about her. She'd accepted all of this willingly. But Cosmopolis felt he'd stolen something from her; so he treated her with gentleness and restrained his desire.

She said, "Landsmann created his ending, not I. I never sent an innocent man into the twilight of the mind. But there some men must go, if order is to prevail."

Glancing at her quickly, he thought: She's heartless. But isn't that what we need in an Observer? The slightest suggestion of sedition must be crushed immediately, without endless civilized debate.

They walked down the sloping pathway to the ocean. The tide was out and a long swath of wet sand marked the degree of the water's withdrawal toward the other side of the globe. Above the dunes, Pendant Flowers floated in a line, their roots drinking water from small engineered clouds which followed them over the estate; with the evening sunlight shining through their petals, the procession of blossoms reminded Cosmopolis of the fairy coaches in the bedtime stories of his childhood, and he felt himself momentarily carried off in one of them, through the magic kingdom of twilight.

The Observer's mind had no room for magic. She was receiving a report about everyone gathered at the Cosmopolis estate today. Cosmopolis she knew to be above suspicion. An interplanetary tycoon whose fortune was incalculable, he helped thousands every day through his many charities. Altruism guided all his acts; there was nothing subversive about Roy.

She walked with him across the wet sand. "There's an Abyssal Plain under this sea," she said, "made of glass shells, seven hundred feet deep." She stared at the water. "We had to fish out the body of one of our agents. He was completely encrusted in microscopic shells, in every shade of rose. They were lovely."

"You see beauty in strange things," said Cosmopolis.

"If one has to look at a murdered agent, it's best not to be frightened."

"I agree. I just find your description of beauty unsettling."

"There's a great deal that's unsettling in my profession," she said.

"I don't think I want to know about it."

"I wouldn't dream of troubling you."

The beach was shared at that hour by two other guests—Susie Tsugaru and Olympia Clendenning. Susie owned Cinestar, providing entertainment to the planets, and Olympia fed them, her company controlling vast herds of zungus grazing on asteroid chains created for their short-lived existence.

"Why did Roy invite that dreadful Observer?" asked Olympia, looking down the curving beach, to where the master spy was standing. "She's not a member of the Consortium."

"He had to," said Susie. "Project Amphora is under her jurisdiction."

"We shouldn't have that snoop around on such a joyful day." Olympia was the oldest Consortium member, but she'd been structurally reworked; her joints were strong, flexible, well lubricated. Her replacement flesh was of the finest quality, grown from cells taken from the inner pouch of a baby zungu. As she studied the Observer in the distance, her mouth turned downward in a tiny scowl, pulling at her new and perfect skin. The Observer was continually citing her company for violations. The reason for this was that in spite of her youthful appearance, Olympia had developed the frugal ways of an elderly person. While some old ladies might save string, or hide apple cores in a drawer, Olympia practiced senile frugality on a higher scale. She found ways to cut production costs that resulted in unhealthy animals and contaminated meat. When faced with the results her measures created, her behavior became petulant and intractable, and she blamed her staff.

Susie said, "I have to admit I admire the Observer's air of mystery."

"It's not mysterious," said Olympia, sarcastically. "She was created in an alien experiment." Olympia's scowl deepened. She couldn't break herself of the costly habit of creasing her brow when she looked at the Observer. Citations against her company had increased; and what was the fuss about anyway? An occasional contaminant was unavoidable in mass production. The cheaper grade food was targeted primarily at aliens. *They* never complained. Only the sanctimonious Observer.

Susie said, "She had the head scientist of Amphora brain-cleaned."
A chill ran through Olympia's reinforced old bones. Along with
frugality, she had the suspicious fears of the elderly. Now she asked
herself, what if the Observer takes it into her head to brain-clean *me*?
And over something so trivial as a few diseased zungus.

Olympia drove worrying thoughts about the Observer from her
mind, knowing it was only her old age speaking. Immortality would
eliminate such senior moments. That was why the Amphora immortality project was so important, because it would shatter even the concept of old age. And yet the Observer had just destroyed Amphora's
leading scientist. Outrageous! And Olympia allowed herself to hate
the Observer with that bitterness in which the elderly excel.

She watched the Observer moving toward the asteroid engineer, Paul Buckler, by the pond in the garden. The adventurous
fellow was standing alone, and Olympia was surprised to find herself stirred. There was something magnificent about his solitude.
In that way he was similar to the Observer, maintaining a position
apart from the world. Perhaps, she thought, they're well-suited.
Perhaps they'll marry and the Observer will retire to be with him.
But these are just the fancies of an old woman. I'm old, she cried
within herself. I'm an old woman disguised as a young one. The
immortality project *has* to succeed if I'm to be rescued from this
grotesque situation.

For Olympia knew she was eternally young in spirit. She felt she
was unique in this. Other elderly people were truly old. But *her* old
body was a tragic mistake.

"Well," said Paul Buckler to the Observer as they stood together
at the edge of the pond, "everybody's talking about what you did to
Landsmann."

"It was necessary," she replied, coolly. "Landsmann made a
mistake in a climate where mistakes are costly."

"You know best."

"Don't be condescending. *You* risk your life on the jobs you do. Would you tolerate mistakes while hanging from a skyhook?"

"No. But are you hanging from a skyhook?"

"Everyone is. All our lives hang by a thread. Amphora is going to make us immortal. I couldn't let Landsmann interfere." She held his gaze, her blue eyes confident. "You must trust my judgment."

"I do. But do you trust mine?" He drew her to him and embraced her. From things she'd let slip in the past, he suspected she'd once been a first-class engineer herself, though of course he couldn't know for sure. "I wish you'd join my team," he said. "Then we'd never have to be apart."

"I can't leave the Amphora project."

"You think you're the only one who can watch over it?"

"Naturally."

He smiled, and kissed her, as a Pendant Flower passed over them, its leafy shadow bringing coolness. When their lips parted, he said, "If you change your mind, you know where to find me."

"Hanging from a skyhook." Now it was her turn to smile. But then he felt her stiffen in his arms; one of her transmissions was arriving. After several seconds, she softened.

"Sorry."

"Why have you hooked yourself in so deeply with these implants?"

"So I can feel the planet from moment to moment."

"No one can do that."

"I try."

"You'll drive yourself mad."

"I'm shielded against overload."

"You receive what the Consortium wants you to receive."

"There are guidelines regarding that."

"Set by whom? I know how the Consortium works. I belong to it. They like you to think you're the last link in the chain, but there's always one more."

"I'm the last link," she said, with complete confidence. "I made sure of that."

Buckler saw that she'd changed from the woman she'd been when last he'd seen her. There was something mechanical about her expression, as if the technology to which she'd subjected herself was reshaping her features. It would reshape her soul as well. He said, "Information implants are addictive. You start adding more and more of them until you're nothing but somebody else's transmission."

"That won't happen to me."

"It's already happening."

She brought her hand to the place on her head where the implants were located, fearing that what he said was true. But she quickly calmed herself; the transmissions she received were crucial, bringing her the changing temper of the population. She knew beforehand when discontent was brewing. At times she felt like the planet's mother. She was hooked in everywhere and it was intoxicating. Perhaps it also dehumanized her, but she wasn't ready to relinquish it. "Don't worry about me," she said. "I undergo monthly calibration."

"Do you know how like a robot that sounds?" he asked.

"I have a large robotic staff. Their speech patterns are contagious."

"There's no convincing you. But you'll come with me when Amphora is completed?"

"Maybe."

"Sometimes I wish the immortality project had never been started."

"Don't you want to live forever?"

"No."

"Why not?"

"I'd start boring people. I'd start boring myself."

"Is that why you work on such dangerous projects? Because you're afraid of being bored?"

His specialty was nudging ice-bearing comets out of their orbital path and exploding them on dead worlds in need of moisture. His sunburned face was lined from continual exposure to the elements on hostile worlds. One might say there were comets in his eyes.

"Guilty as charged."

"Well, perhaps you're a bit of a robot yourself." She moved away from him and joined the only other person there today with cranial implants. Martin Faircloth owned Starweb, the galactical news giant. His brain, like the Observer's, was preoccupied with continual transmissions, but his were from his news agencies, which extended all the way to the last gate station, and on into the Outer World feed. He greeted her with several facial twitches, as his implants fired. He said, "Got any scoops for me?"

"There's a solar cult we're tracking. They claim the sun is talking to them."

"What is it saying?"

"Nothing very useful. But the head of the cult is growing wealthy. I'll let you know when we close him down."

Faircloth walked away satisfied. No matter what its critics said, the Consortium sought to benefit mankind. Its members ran planetary business with a minimum of regulations; legal wrangling was not permitted; common sense was expected of everyone; and an Observer was needed to suppress explosive situations, anywhere. To do this, she'd been given sweeping powers, even though it meant she was able to monitor the Consortium's activities too, with a thoroughness that permitted few secrets.

Roy Cosmopolis was leading his guests to the main house, and into its armorial hall, past trophies of interplanetary war. Empty armor of defeated mercenaries stood hollow in the sunlight slanting from high windows. The helmets were sculpted with electronic devices that resembled the spiraling horns of a ram—dusty now, and dead; the chest armor contained laser ports whose apertures were sealed forever, where once beams of killing light had seemed to shoot straight from their hearts. The Consortium Guard had smashed them into oblivion, and all that remained were these empty husks, left behind in the setting sun like the carapaces of dried stag beetles.

Consortium General Caph stood gazing at the artifacts of bygone soldiering. Though wearing a chest-full of combat medals, Caph felt that his greatest victories had been in the bedroom. Now, he turned to watch Susie Tsugaru coming toward him, her body moving beneath a shimmering gown, cut low, front and back. "Susie, how delicious you—"

"General—" She swept on past, giving him the least possible consideration.

"She nearly trampled you," said the Observer, coming up beside him.

"With her adorable shoes." Their click echoed in the long hall as Caph watched Susie's nearly naked back traveling into the deeper distance. "But the battle may yet turn my way."

The Observer and General Caph lingered together in the entranceway. The Observer always found time for a few words with Caph, who was a military gossip. The mood of the populace she could sort out; but the Guard didn't yield its secrets easily. She counted on the general to give her the soldiers' mood. She and Caph were the only guests who weren't actually Consortium members; those members numbered twelve. The General's attention was still on Susie Tsugaru's hips. "She detests you," remarked the Observer.

"That's never stopped me in the past." Caph returned the Observer's smile. He enjoyed being with this woman who had a complete file on him. It appealed to his exhibitionist tendencies. Naked, I stand before you. "Tell me, Observer, what's your own secret?"

"I've always had a knack for trifles."

The two remained in the armorial hall, in line with visual slits in the headgear of an ancient mercenary. "Somewhere deep inside that electronic helmet," said Caph, "a particle of ambition remains. Not even death can destroy it. But here comes the truly deathless warrior of ambition." He indicated Olympia Clendenning.

She approached them, a tiny old woman hidden inside miracles of rejuvenation. She smiled at the Observer as if she weren't her bitterest enemy. The Observer, in turn, was fascinated by the purity of Olympia's skin, flawless stuff created for her in her own laboratories, and available to no one else. Occasionally one glimpsed something genuinely wicked in her artfully repaired eyes, but not now, not here. At the moment, her milky beauty was unblemished.

Caph said, "That old crocodile could chew her way through a suit of armor."

At the end of the armorial hall, Olympia passed beneath a doorway made of huge tusks, on which ancient words were inscribed.

"Never decoded," said the Observer, when she and Caph reached the tusks.

"You've tried?"

"An energy school somewhere made the inscription; that was my Agency's conclusion."

"What I want to know is which energy school *you* attended."

"That's classified, I'm afraid."

"I know the marks of the esoteric schools, and you're a graduate of one of them. But which?"

"The glories of the cosmos lie before us," replied the Observer wryly, gesturing with her arm beneath the tusks toward the room where Consortium members were gathering. The two entered, but as neither was anxious to dive into its cross-conversations, they held back for another moment.

The general asked, "How are those agents of yours doing, the ones who tangled with the entomologist?"

"They'll recover."

"He speaks to insects, so I'm told."

"I've heard that," said the Observer.

"Where did he learn it, one wonders. Not from you, I hope."

"I don't speak to insects, General."

"You will tonight." Caph was looking toward the guests. He nodded, bowed, did all that was expected of him, as they calculated his power against their own. His eyes kept returning to Susie. She stood beside an iridescent cocoon as large as herself; the cocoon bore a ragged seam in its midsection, through which a giant vampire moth of Planet Insecta had once emerged; it looked to the general as if Susie had just emerged from it. She was a bit of a vampire herself, having sucked five husbands dry. One of these men was here tonight, with the preserved look of a specimen under glass. Susie had done it to him, but the general was undeterred in his admiration, and was convinced he could survive her embrace. He followed her as she walked past more of Roy's alien artifacts. Caph would have dumped most of it in the fire, but Roy had played with it all as a boy, and these objects had been his only friends, for the best companions of this super-rich and over-protected child had been imaginary or stuffed. In Caph's opinion, Roy was a bit stuffed himself, with humanitarian platitudes.

Now Paul Buckler entered, his footstep so light not even the Observer noticed it. "For you," he whispered, and pressed a slender

volume in her hand; Paul translated and printed Ancient Alien poetry at his own expense, fifty of each title. Long nights on barren
worlds gave him time for translation, and he loved the enigmatic
Ancient Alien mind. Embedded in their poems were allusions to
higher galactic civilizations which had evolved to the most refined
forms imaginable—microscopic stardust creatures who traveled in
clouds of intelligence. Paul was a connoisseur of these stories, having encountered them again and again in his travels. How much of it
did he believe? wondered the Observer. Enough to spend sleepless
nights going over the most cryptic poetry imaginable. "Thank you,"
she murmured to him, knowing the poems would be as strange as
Link's book on insects, and feeling the peculiar affinity the authors
had, Link who lived with insects, and Paul who moved effortlessly
into the reflections of minds equally distant from our own. She
watched him take a seat apart from everyone, because he couldn't
bear to be confined.

"Go and sit next to him," said Caph softly to her.

"He prefers to be alone."

"That's not your reason. It's that every relationship compromises
your authority. That's why you should give me a chance. I expect little
in the way of tenderness." He paused, his friendly face gazing into
hers. "I can be quite sweet, you know."

"But I can't."

"A strong-willed partner can be exhilarating."

"Not one with information chips in her head."

"Too distracted?"

"I've no time for love. Let's leave it at that." But her gaze returned
to Paul Buckler. And when their eyes met, she felt the same old pang
go through her.

"So that's how it is," said Caph, interpreting the gaze she gave
her lover.

"Be quiet, General."

"Or you'll turn me into a cataton? But you'd never do that to your old friend. However, I respect your wishes." The General swept his gaze around the room once more. "We're all here, searching for immortality. But Olympia has all new organs already. Why not just keep rebuilding and replacing? Why all the fuss? I'm told Amphora costs billions."

"We can rebuild and replace all we want, but slowly our life force seeps away. Mrs. Clendenning looks lovely, but she's just a bit like a puppet, moved by very fine strings, and she knows it. A permanent solution is desirable."

"One can't argue with that." The general walked deeper into the great room, toward a herd of large stuffed chairs which seemed to snooze like baby zungus. He paused at a table carved from an alien wood whose grain was like lace. Beside the table was a couch whose electronic upholstery carried the memory of perfect posture for all the members of the party. As they took their seats, adjustments were made imperceptibly, the guests being conscious only of a deep comfort. The single High Consortium member not present was Kitty Liftoff, who disliked cozy get-togethers such as these, and was more comfortable with mercenaries like Gregori Man o' War.

Lamps floated wirelessly in the air, but the principal illumination was from the skylight. Robots entered with serving trays and were captured in the last radiance of day. They brought drinks to each guest.

Gordon Singh of Sun Centralis sat down next to Paul Buckler. Like Buckler, Gordon was an engineer, and Sun Centralis supplied most of the planet's energy. He felt he and Paul were the only people in the room who mattered. He'd supplied the hydrogen plasma tubes for Paul's latest asteroid adventure, had helped install them himself. Now they were working together on a new project, but at the moment it was Amphora that was on their minds.

At the head of the armorial hall, Cosmopolis was signaling to his robots. They turned themselves off and became motionless. They were no longer capable of recording. The living servants withdrew, and the building was sealed from intruders by agents of the Observer.

Cosmopolis sat in a chair made of a black diamond compound; it had been an alien king's throne, taken by Cosmopolis's father while plundering a neighboring planet. The king had been known as the Lord of the Ravages of Time and Royal Hunter of the Stars, but the Consortium Guard had annihilated his armies, and old man Cosmopolis had his brain overwritten with ones and zeros; then he placed him in an underground installation in a transparent box. A rusty drudge tended the installation. The Lord of the Ravages of Time would remain there indefinitely. Since Roy Cosmopolis himself did not even know of this installation, and since his father was dead, there was little likelihood the Royal Hunter of the Stars would ever hunt again.

"I'm very glad to see you all," said Cosmopolis to his guests, most of whom he knew from childhood; their families had been first colonizers of the planet. They came from strength and were gene-enriched for more of it. Cosmopolis felt the atmosphere in the room—pulsing with power and intelligence. And of course, quietly supporting this was the security of beauty. The best that life had to offer was theirs, at a very high price. Cheaper schemes were available; in Alien City Jockey Oldcastle had had his voiceprint altered, his neurological emissions masked, his fingerprints electromagnetically canceled, his identity solution removed. But tonight's guests had nothing to hide. They contributed an enormous amount to civilization and were here tonight because they wanted to contribute more. All except Olympia, poor Olympia, who was the oldest and losing her way, growing cramped and crabbed in her outlook. Cosmopolis remembered when her mind was vibrant. He looked at her now and vowed to spend whatever it took until she was vibrant again.

"When I look at you," said Cosmopolis, "I see ten friends who are going to live forever. Amphora is right on schedule."

Congratulatory smiles went through the group. For each of them, Cosmopolis saw the vista opening to infinity. It was marvelous to contemplate unending time, the sun eternal and oneself there to see it with one's friends. "The way you are at this moment," continued Cosmopolis, "is how you'll remain."

"Do we have an exact procedure yet?"

"The human energy field is sufficient for immortal life. The problem is containing the energy when death brings about its dispersal. We need a kind of vase—the amphora. It will hold our energy indefinitely and render us imperishable. No cellular decay. If you want more detail, the Amphora people will give it to you. As for me, I understand very little of what they say. They've been underground for five years, and their conversation is pretty inbred."

Cosmopolis looked across his guests toward the giant, blue sea-monster's egg in which he'd played as a child. The sunset, through the skylight, played upon it now. The dying light had lost its quality of melancholy. No more did it seem to say a sad farewell to the day.

Susie Tsugaru thought of movie stars. She always thought of movie stars. Now that movie stars were projected in the round, in one's home, walking about and interacting with one in self-selected drama pieces, movie stars were like immortal friends. They were always there, and emerged on command. They never aged, were endlessly interesting, strong, beautiful, and available for viewing on all sides. Their only drawback was that one could walk through them. As a child, she'd played with holo-projections of the last great movie queen, Sabrina Mysteria, whose movies were shown even now at the farthest stop in the Corridor, where alien mercenaries lined up for tickets, looking like something out of Roy's front hall. That had been Susie's idea of immortality: the beautiful ghost of Sabrina Mysteria playing to the jet-pack set for ages to come. Is it possible, wondered Susie, that I'll outlive Sabrina Mysteria's movies?

Dick Spinrad, who owned the continent of New Unexco, felt a profound relaxation flowing through his mind and body. Though he owned so much, in the middle of the night Death always came to him, face unseen, and its words were few. *You're mine.*

Raimi Kashian looked at Kurt, her husband. She and he owned asteroid resort communities up and down the Corridor, but she too woke at night, with the same visitor, whose stone hand would turn her head toward her husband, and show her that this fine, generous man was as fragile as an egg. Then she'd watch, by the moonlight through the window, the tiny pulse at his temple. How delicately the life blood passed along its channel. How easily it might run away. Kurt, she would whisper, softly so that he wouldn't hear her; they'd been together eighty-five years.

"One of the other benefits of a permanent container for our energy field," Roy Cosmopolis was saying, "is that we come to know that energy field much better, and with this comes a significant increase in knowledge."

Martin Faircloth envisioned it as a sort of cosmic hot tub. "I don't care if the vase makes me smarter. So long as what's in the vase is me."

"It'll be you, Martin. We wouldn't want it any other way."

"Is it too soon to celebrate?"

"Containment in Amphora will be possible before the year is out. Take care of yourselves until then." Cosmopolis imagined himself saying much the same thing to humanity at large one day. On some electronic podium, beaming into the heart of the world, he would announce the conquest of death. I'm the Father of Immortality, he said to himself, though knowing he must leave it for others to call him that.

The sound of approaching airships drew attention to the massive skylight. Three flashing forms passed overhead. Cosmopolis air space was guarded tonight by Consortium pilots under General Caph's command, and they were escorting a third ship down. This ship was an antique craft, visible through the large central window of the room.

"Our guest of honor has arrived," said Cosmopolis, and waited for the sound of engine shutdown. "This is about as rare as it gets." His eyes again ran around the room, to the oddities and curios of his childhood. None of them were as odd as the visitor now descending from the old ship; engine noise had ceased. Cosmopolis looked at his wall communicator and saw points of light representing the security forces converging toward the main entrance of the house.

"Have you ever seen one?" Raimi Kashian asked Susie Tsugaru.

Susie shook her head. "No visual transmission of them is allowed."

"And nobody gets invited to *their* place," said Vladimir Korolov. Korolov ran Lavation, the single most important company in the Consortium, in his opinion. As a young chemical engineer a century ago, he saw a bad soapsuds formula cover an asteroid in foam. Another one created clouds of sulfuric acid a mile high. The cleaning agents of Planet Immortal didn't work on planets whose water was thick with mineral deposits, and whose atmosphere played tricks with surfactants; he realized that the right formula must include some natural oil of the host planet, taken from its trees and plants. Without these oils, a chemical formula wouldn't work; it was as if the planet resisted outside interference. So with long research, he'd found the trees and plants and ancient beds that held the oils. Once the proper formula was created, there were handling and storage problems, problems of stability and reactivity. He'd solved these problems and many others, opening factory after factory, and building a cleaning empire that stretched throughout the Corridor. A spry little old man, he still traveled to alien environments to watch how things were cleaned, and to personally clean them better. He loved to see a dish, a basket of laundry, a piece of machinery come clean. He was still the best engineer to send into a problem-plagued factory. Now he waited with great interest for the guest of honor. Interacting with aliens in their daily lives had opened his mind; he'd learned more from them than they ever had from him. Today would be no different; out of the heart of the cosmos, a new answer had come, or so he hoped. For, with life, as with chemicals, there was no end to the refinements one could make.

At the sound of an opening door, everybody turned. A float chair was guided in by Dr. Amphibras. On it sat a slender, robed being. Amphibras guided the chair to a place beside the black diamond throne of Cosmopolis.

"We're deeply honored," said Cosmopolis, instinctively lowering his head to the ancient creature.

The chair settled to the floor. The being seated upon it was vaguely humanoid in appearance. The face was bird-like—nose and mouth united in a hard, pointed protuberance. It was thought this characteristic of the Immortals was a deliberate piece of genetic engineering, to take advantage of the longevity of certain Corridor birds, some of whom never aged at all, and who, when found dead, showed no sign of organ degeneration.

The Immortal was over six feet tall, and sat perfectly still, his claw-like hands folded in his lap, his shiny skin like smooth parchment stretched across sticks. Raimi Kashian, whose thoughts had been on fragility, felt this was the most fragile thing she'd ever seen. The bony creature in front of her had renounced all the values of existence that she herself embraced, and dwelt in some unthinkable niche of perception. The Immortals were a group of hermits from a dead civilization, who'd been wandering the Corridor for ages, like anchorites in a desert. It was believed they'd stumbled upon a piece of knowledge left by the Ancient Aliens and it had extended their life indefinitely. The Immortals were now instructing humanity in that knowledge.

The Immortal played his gaze slowly around the room, stopped at Paul Buckler, and nodded. Buckler returned the gaze, transfixed. The creature was somehow catching the light of the room with his eyes. The flashes grew brighter and, as they did, Buckler suddenly had the answer to the latest sunlight-harnessing program. He knew what material to use, and on which planet he could find it. He knew the shape his collectors would have to be, and exactly how many megawatts of energy each one would produce.

Buckler blinked, and the mirrors in the Immortal's eyes vanished; two eyes of the usual kind were staring back at him, filled with merriment, apparently having enjoyed the little piece of telepathy he'd employed. Buckler leaned over to Gordon Singh and whispered, "I think we can depend on them."

Gordon nodded. Where the Immortal should have been, he was seeing an animated schematic. Its components and connections were depicting how to skim layers off the sun, using fabulous machinery; other fabulous machines were storing the helium and hydrogen harvest for use by great fleets of ships, and for illuminating artificial worlds. Sun Centralis, his company's logo, was clearly written on these machines. The vision faded, and he was looking at the Immortal; the old hermit's smile seemed to say, *Yes, I have the blueprints for those fabulous machines and in time they will be yours.* His was a tenuous sort of presence, like a kite that could be swept up by the wind and carried away, becoming a point in the distant sky. But he's not weak, thought Singh. He's streamlined. And he just showed me the future of my company.

The Immortal looked toward Susie Tsugaru. She felt as if bright little bath beads were bursting around her, causing voluptuous sensations to stream over her body. *Star power,* she thought to herself. Then she wondered why Roy Cosmopolis had turned on his entertainment center; because Sabrina Mysteria was projected into the middle of the room, ready for interaction with her audience, in a drama of their choosing. "Roy," she whispered, "I don't think this is the time."

"For what?" asked Roy.

"For a movie," chided Susie. Then, from Roy's expression, she saw he didn't know what she was talking about. There was no movie being projected. But Sabrina was still there, smiling, and surrounded by shafts of moonlight. And Susie began crying from happiness, knowing that the Immortal had read her mind, had made this picture for her, to give her the best assurance he could of her immortality. She would live longer than the myth of Sabrina Mysteria. As she grasped what had happened in the room, Sabrina's image faded and the Immortal's eyes were twinkling, and she loved him immediately, with the eternal kind of love she felt for movies. He was speaking. What was he saying?

The Immortal's voice sounded like dry leaves stirred by the wind. Dick Spinrad felt a gentle vortex embrace him when the Immortal turned his way, and the dry leaf sound was suddenly opening crypto-channels in his brain. Though he owned an entire continent, Spinrad was not an adventurer like Paul Buckler or Gordon Singh or Vladimir Korolov. He was a mathematician who'd quietly built his fortune with a mathematician's power of calculation. Now dreamy connections were made in his mind, like moments of time overlapping, or multiple places coinciding, anyway of matters beyond current mathematical expression, but as clear to him now as if they were the first steps in an advanced lesson. Spinrad, in his cold, quiet way, realized that the old creature in front of him would teach him the highest and most beautiful mathematics in the universe.

"Don't mistake me as the giver of your pleasure," said the Immortal, addressing himself to the entire group. "It comes from the ones who taught me."

"And who are they?" asked Vladimir Korolov; in his lifelong travels he'd known hundreds of teachers of esoteric paths.

"The Ancient Aliens who contacted us long ago with their message of immortality. We experienced them as a golden cloud in our minds, capable of assembling itself into any shape in order to instruct us. They travel the universe in their intellectual cloud at speeds that are incomprehensible. They travel to the Outer Plenum, or to the cortex of your brain. It's all the same to them. Some of you have just experienced their telepathic power. It was not I who gave you that vision. I have no such talent. But they are masters of telepathy. And they wanted to show you their gift, as a sign of their sympathy toward you."

To Roy Cosmopolis, it was as if the golden cloud of which the creature spoke surrounded him and sank into his brain, lighting up receptors dedicated to a mysterious joy. In that moment, the hermit looked at him and smiled, the thinnest crease appearing at his lips, like rice paper folding, behind which a soft light burned.

"You have three billion years of evolution behind you, and it's stored in your energy field." The slender figure smiled. "You're very clever creatures, still managing to swim around in the energetic world after all this time. Doesn't that intrigue you? What thrust, if nothing else, your ancestors had. They are one-celled organisms that have traveled three billion years to arrive in this room. Amphora is going to help you travel the next three billion years and arrive in infinity. It will do this by enclosing your thrust, and reorganizing it. Sexual reproduction, after all, is a somewhat clumsy method for outwitting death. Of course, it allows mutation and adaptation to take place, and it gave you the charming forms you now possess. But enough is enough. Let's get you in the vase and keep your lovely forms there forever."

"But I don't want the charming form I have now," said Olympia. "I want to be the way I was in my prime. I don't want to look like *you*."

Susie Tsugaru wanted to brain her, but the Immortal only smiled. "And what do I look like?"

"Prehistoric," said Olympia. "Like the skeleton of an ancient bird . . . pressed . . . pressed in stone."

His gestures were delicate, the finger joints flicking, and yet it did seem to be a fossil speaking, dug up and brought here and allowed to step out of its stone prison. "You can choose any edition of yourself you want," he said. "Instructions are provided."

Kurt Kashian felt a dream from his childhood rise up. He was suspended in space, his body as heavy as a great iron ball that was swinging. First he was light, then he was heavy, and he swung back and forth from light to heavy. The childhood dream had heralded the change in his body from boy to man. Now it had come again, to herald the change from man to immortal. Now he was heavy, but soon he'd be light again, with the feeling of endlessness that had accompanied his childhood. To know that feeling again, to live in it permanently—

"So," said the Immortal, "you strengthen the outer edge of the energy field, where it's poorly defended. Oddly enough, it's also where your greatest resources lie. I've lived long, and could explain all this to you. But you will learn for yourself, once time is your ally. And this you'll get through Project Amphora. It's the one precious thing, and you must protect and guard it."

Roy Cosmopolis thought, we *had* to eliminate Stuart Landsmann. We can't take chances with our immortality.

The sleeves of the aged figure's thin black robe fell around reedlike wrists. Hollow as a bird, thought Gordon Singh. He had the feeling of something barely there, a creature on the edge of evanescence. He couldn't imagine the desiccated creature performing an act of self-defense. But why bother to defend? He'd simply take one step farther into evanescence, and then he wouldn't be there at all.

"I feel close to you," said the Immortal. "I've entered your home with only one thing in mind, to assure you of our sympathy for you. Our time here is almost over. We remain only for you. And when you finally know our secret, we'll be gone." Again the rice paper smile shone out at them with its quiet glow, and Raimi Kashian thought of monastery lamps, burning softly, in an atmosphere of renunciation. The old creature in front of her had sacrificed his sexual nature long ago; the radiance that came from him wasn't passion.

"You call your project Amphora. When we first made our bid for immortality, ages ago, we called it the Pavilion of the Absolute." He lifted a stick-like finger, which he laid on his cheek, as if to support the weight of his head. "Any one of you could crush me. But I wouldn't die. My life is informational, and that information is contained in the Pavilion. This ridiculous form of mine—" He lifted his spindly arm from the wide sleeve of the robe. "—takes little energy to run. It's cost efficient." He gave a dry rustling laugh.

"If you *were* crushed," asked Dick Spinrad, "how would you regenerate yourself?"

"Regeneration is unnecessary. What you see here—" Again he laid a finger to his chest. "—is an exteriorization of information running in the Pavilion of the Absolute. I am, shall we say, but a shadow of myself?" The old kite gave another of his rustling laughs. "My total information package requires too much energy for material embodiment. I've encapsulated this portion of it so we may communicate. But it's tiring for me, as well as frustrating, for I'm used to much faster processing speeds than this thing—" He poked himself around the knees. "—requires."

"How much of you don't we see?" asked Raimi Kashian.

"Most of me. My energy field, like your own, is large. But unlike yours, mine is available to me in its entirety."

"What if a hostile force attacked your compound?" asked Kurt Kashian. "What if your Pavilion of the Absolute were destroyed?"

"The Pavilion of the Absolute is not a finite state machine."

"Then what is it?"

"Think of a special kind of vase, which permits information to be stored interdimensionally." The Immortal leaned forward slightly, and for a moment the Observer felt that the body before them would simply blow away, so thin was its frame. "It's in the dimensional interstices that I really dwell. There my energy field makes a connection with conditions of time quite unlike your own, and from them I learn a different pace. It's the pace of the Ancient Aliens. That was their discovery, that the dimension nearest to ours runs more slowly, and we can imitate its pace and live forever." He inclined his head and made a signal that it was time for him to leave.

"But," stammered Susie Tsugaru, "I have so many questions."

"It's disturbing to be too long in my presence."

"Do you have a name?" asked Roy Cosmopolis.

"Metron."

Dr. Amphibras came forward and guided the float chair away. The Immortal sat in it unmoving. It was not until he'd left the room that Raimi felt her equanimity return.

"We owe that creature a debt of gratitude that can't be repaid," said Roy Cosmopolis. "But he wants nothing. And that, for me, is the truest sign of compassion."

The Observer reached into her pocket, touched the two hand-bound volumes. She drew one out, saw that it was Link's, and opened it at random. *There are moths who feed on the tears of animals,* she read, and then she put the book away, for the robots had been reactivated and coffee was coming round, along with other refreshments.

CHAPTER 9

Dunbosian was the proprietor of Mirador, a resort asteroid once famous for its waters. These had been bottled and sold for so many years the water table had been drained. Now Mirador was in decay.

"Greed," reflected Dunbosian. "Insatiability." But it had allowed him to buy the spa for a song. He was from Planet Elephanta. His short tusks were tipped with gold. On his head he wore a data fez—the traditional red felt flat-topped cone with an antenna rising from the center.

His Elephantian ears worked the warm air slowly back and forth, as he sat at his desk—a block of black volcanic glass from Maleficius, the black asteroid. Heads of birds were carved at each corner of the desk; diamonds had once served for their eyes, but these had been hacked out by Mirador's previous owner. Dunbosian was only one in a line of such owners. None but he had been able to make a go of it, and he used it more as a personal retreat; nonetheless paying customers came, themselves retreating, usually from the law. Mirador was close to Planet Immortal but, as a privately owned asteroid, enjoyed a fuzzy legal status. If a guest was too notorious, he or she might be dragged off by the local traveling militia, always space-borne somewhere between Planet Immortal and Mirador. But in general, Dunbosian's collection of felons weren't worth pursuing.

He rose from his desk and lumbered across the office. Traces of former splendor were in the hanging lamps of black obsidian, the gilt door moldings, two badly chipped urns made by the great craftsmen of Exhul. The wallpaper was made of Hermetian silk, once vibrant with magical moth light, now gray with decades of smoke and oil fumes. "A pity. A tragedy. Because of avidity. One day I'll restore it."

He opened the door of his office and descended the stairs. His data fez lit, bringing him market quotations. "Buy two thousand futures of Luridite," he said. And then after listening for several moments, "What condition is your vehicle in?" For he also received information about items priced for quick sale. They might be heirloom airships or an ancestor's teaset. Dunbosian bought and sold all day long, large and small, new and old, his data fez never silent.

His white suit was badly creased and it wasn't even noon. Ceiling fans turned but the air they churned was already heavy with heat. He adjusted his white tie, but would never loosen it for comfort. One must look, at all times, the gentleman.

As Dunbosian stepped off the last worn stair into the lobby, he was greeted by Lucky Viscid, a guest who was fully paid up, at least for the moment. Recently arrived from a planet with dense forests, Viscid's skin was sticky so that leaves could cling to it as camouflage. No longer in a leafy habitat, he was covered now with gum wrappers, bits of tissue paper, torn leaflets, and whatever else blew about in the gentle breezes of Mirador.

"And how are you today, Mr. Viscid?"

"Blending, Mr. Dunbosian." Viscid's voice was as sticky as his body, his breath clinging to Dunbosian's flesh momentarily, as if it were sucking something out of him. "You know me, I just want to be part of the background."

"Very wise." Dunbosian straightened a few chairs, blew a bit of ash from a table with a fussy little puff of air from the end of his trunk. The ash landed on Viscid and adhered. On a sagging couch in the corner, a woman fanned herself with the languid movements of the Toyoki user; her eyes were glazed, and Dunbosian tiptoed by her, not wishing to disturb her dream.

He entered the garden. It had once been covered by a sculpted arbor; now only dead branches remained, forming skeletal archways through which he walked. Dilapidated bungalows surrounded the dried-up garden, each with a small patio. Here, too, desiccated vines clung to rusting arbors, with dead roots exposed in the parched ground. Tiny lizards scurried along the vines, looking for insects. The windows of the bungalows were opaque with grime. One of the windows had no glass at all, and the dried vines had moved inside the room, where they hung like rows of ragged curtains. Beyond the bungalows were tennis courts covered by sand, a croquet lawn that was mostly weeds, and a ring of tilted gazebos. "A complete restoration," said Dunbosian. "And why not? To recapture something precious."

At a carved table beneath a desiccated canopy of vines sat a large snail, smoking a homemade cigar, its ragged cylinder dangling from the lipless slit of his mouth. Shiny feelers went in and out from his forehead in the Elephantian's direction. "Mr. Dunbosian, it is a joy to see you."

Dunbosian sat down with the snail, who was a permanent resident of the resort, and always paid on time. His manners were impeccable; beside him stood a hydrator, leased from Dunbosian, and every so often he sprayed himself with a light mist to keep his skin from cracking.

"A fine hot day, as usual," said the snail. "Allow me to pour you a glass of Dr. Vole's formula—" His retractable fingers emerged and reached out to a bottle of blue-tinted water. Dunbosian was suspicious of everything the resident doctor concocted but he couldn't refuse.

"Refreshing," said the snail. "Don't you think?"

"Very," agreed Dunbosian, dipping his trunk into the glass and parking its contents in his snout for disposal later.

"But nothing, of course, can slake our thirst," said the snail. The snail's arms were short and stubby. His retractable fingers exuded moisture which some found objectionable; Dunbosian did not; the snail was as his planet had made him. "Our thirst, Mr. Dunbosian, is for the faded past. It's why we're here."

"Perhaps," said Dunbosian, turning toward a potted plant and discreetly emptying his trunk into its dry soil.

"Oh, there's no question of it," said the snail. "You didn't have to buy a ruined resort. I didn't have to make it my home." The snail set down his glass, on which a moist imprint of his hand remained for a moment. "We're charmed by Mirador's memories, which are in every crack. For Sabrina Mysteria stayed here…"

This was a well-known fact, although it happened a century ago, just before the star had vanished, along with the ship carrying her on a promotional tour of the Corridor. "I like to think she sat at this table," mused the snail. "Certainly she swam in our pool."

"She must have," said Dunbosian, staring into the empty pool, whose displaced tiles were glazed with lichen. A long, deep crack ran along the base. Its lamps, which shimmered only in Dunbosian's imagination, were shattered.

"They say," said the snail, "that you talk of restoring Mirador."

"Quite right."

"But memory breathes through the cracks. The breathing of Sabrina Mysteria. Plaster it over and it will suffocate."

The data fez lit and Dunbosian discreetly bought and sold, while the snail sipped his blue beverage.

"I've always loved the architecture of decay." The snail gestured with his stubby arms toward the dilapidated bungalows, the sand-covered tennis court, and croquet lawn. "Shabby hotels were my first freedom. Such a long time ago."

Dunbosian was too discreet to ever ask personal questions of his guests, but the snail's confidential mood emboldened him. "Would it be too much to inquire what it was you did in the old days?"

"Antiques, of course. I specialized in alien erotica. In those days, there was a quality we no longer find." His glistening eye stalks twisted slightly left and right, as if tracking some chimerical presence. He sighed. "At times I feel on the verge of a discovery about what Mirador really is. But naturally that's impossible. All I can do is walk through its dried-up streets."

He was now referring to the whole of Mirador, the town that had once flourished around its central spa. The terraced gardens had held luxurious private cottages, long since strangled by bone-white vegetation. A canal system had serviced a cascade of fountains, empty now, their spouts dry and rusting.

A brilliant point of light flashed in the air far above them. The light grew brighter and larger.

"Expecting company?" inquired the snail.

The light took on definition, became a small, sleek ship which began its descent pattern. It circled once, then cut a long swathe across the horizon and dipped beneath the dusty trees.

Dunbosian waited for the ship to land, then strolled away, ears fanning. A robocart was delivering the new arrivals, the cart shuddering and creaking, its once exquisite canopy threadbare, its dancing fringe unraveled, sparse, and dirty. It jerked to a stop, beneath worm-eaten trees that framed the entranceway to the hotel. Dunbosian went down the stairs and across the sandy walk. "Welcome back to

Mirador!" Hands outstretched in greeting, he hurried forward and helped Ren to descend. "I had not expected you again so soon."

From the look she gave him, he saw she had something for him. He employed her as a collector of information.

Link lifted O down from the robocart. O's vacant eyes still showed the loss he'd suffered. Dunbosian saw a familiar situation: another of the wounded had been brought to Mirador.

Upquark stared about in wonder. There was sand in his rollers, but excitement in his emotional card. Highly unusual circumstances were unfolding, for which he had no reference. He'd tossed and turned for hours in Ren's ship, analyzing the terrible sequence of events he and his friends had undergone, and then, quite on its own, a train of nondeductive inference had begun, culminating in a picture of himself as a dangerous outlaw with a high metallic luster. Now he tried out a menacing gesture with his grippers, but no one seemed to notice. Perhaps he required Pugnacity Firmware.

"How long are we to be imprisoned here?" asked Link coldly.

"Did someone mention prison? Please," said Dunbosian, "don't insult me. My concern is only for him." He nodded toward Specterales O. "A doctor is in residence here."

He escorted the party to bungalows directly off the pool. A metal pecker was hammering on one of the porch pillars, creating a fierce din. Dunbosian was forced to admire the ingenuity of the species, whose powerful beaks stunned the internal order of whatever they attacked, after which they intervened in the reordering process, parasitizing the energy of repair. They dined on the object's cohesive force, and enough of their attacks would cause eventual collapse. Many of the lampposts of Mirador were distorted, bent, fragmented, as were metal doorframes, carrying beams, sills, water towers. Every so often a crash would sound and guests would simply nod and say, "Metal peckers."

Dunbosian opened a bungalow door, which jammed halfway, scraping against the floor. "Your friend must rest until the doctor is free to examine him. You'll be comfortable here, I hope. Lunch is in a half hour. And you, my dear—" He gestured for Ren to follow him to the next bungalow. They entered and he closed the door behind them.

"Well?"

"Something big is up on the Junk Moon." She pointed to the great artificial world, visible from Mirador as a metallically shining ball in the sky. "There's an underground installation there called Amphora. Highly classified and important to the Observer."

"The next steps will be dangerous. Do you want to continue?"

"Yes."

Dunbosian scrutinized her with his shrewd Elephantian eyes. "You're a delicate creature, my dear. Perfect for gathering information at the early stages. But perhaps not wholly suited for the rough-and-tumble, which is what you're going to encounter if you go poking around a classified installation."

"I need the money."

"Very well. I'll get you the identity chips you'll need to clear Junk Moon Security."

"There's someone else trying to get into Amphora. A pirate called Jockey Oldcastle."

"That's a good sign."

"You know him?"

"Occasionally we do business. If he's interested in Amphora, it means it's definitely important." Dunbosian polished the gold tip of his tusk with the sleeve of his coat. "Now, who is this young man you've brought with you?"

"A friend of Oldcastle's. Chief Entomologist of the Agricultural Plain. I had to bring him along in order to get the Amphora entry code from his robot."

"This young man knows how to make things grow?" Dunbosian's eyes lit up.

"I would hope so. There's a great deal growing on the Agricultural Plain. But he's burned his bridges there."

Dunbosian nodded his heavy head. Burned bridges brought many guests to Mirador.

* * *

Link and Upquark joined Dunbosian and the snail at the table by the pool. "I trust your friend is resting," said Dunbosian. "Would it be intrusive for me to inquire about the nature of his accident?"

"Consortium agents zapped him," said Link bitterly.

"Mirador is famed for its healing powers," said the snail. "Allow me to introduce myself. I'm Molluscus, a longtime resident. I'll take your wounded friend for walks."

The snail's retractable fingers emerged and he moistly shook Link's hand.

"I have a question for you," said Dunbosian to Link. "Could you bring Mirador back to life?"

"Of course."

"Make it bloom?" Dunbosian gestured toward the dried-up gardens. Though their walls were crumbling, the symmetry remained, descending from one graceful terrace to another, to a dead lake in the distance, ringed by stunted withered trees. "Can you surround us with flowers again?"

"That depends on how much water you can get here."

"Yes, that's the problem. But if I can get the water, will you stay and make Mirador beautiful again?" Too tactful to mention burned bridges, he gestured grandly. "I'll pay you twice what you made on your Agricultural Plain."

Link looked at Upquark.

Upquark nodded. "We'll bring all this back to life."

"Then it's settled," declared Dunbosian. "Make a list of what you'll need."

A message arrived at the table, that Dr. Vole was free to see his patient.

"I'll take him," said Upquark, and hastily rolled away.

"Vole's an inventor of medical devices," explained Dunbosian. "Primarily in the rejuvenation field."

"And he has success?" asked Link.

"Opinions are divided on Dr. Vole. He's not allowed to practice on Planet Immortal, or anywhere else for that matter. Naturally, we do not inhibit him here on Mirador."

"He's not allowed to practice?" asked Link.

"It's often the fate of the pioneer."

* * *

"He's undergone cellular disorder," said Dr. Vole, as he examined Specterales O. "But I have the Specterian code for transmitter metabolites, neurofibrillary properties, enzyme rate, adenosine receptor sites, and the rest of it; in short, the complete picture of that ball of bonded electrochemical jelly we call the Specterian brain." He laid his hand on O's head.

O stared about him in confusion, but otherwise was docile. A lizard clung to the wall beside his head, eyeing the Specterian with interest.

"I have just the thing for you," said Dr. Vole to O. "It's fortunate you've come to Mirador." The doctor's office contained instruments that struck Upquark as quite unusual. "I see you're examining my equipment. I know it seems like crude stuff, but Mirador is off the beaten path. I make do." He attached a biocap of spongy material to O's scalp. "The Vole Noological Pod. Have no concern that any current is entering his body. The Noological Pod respects the corporeal boundaries. Respect, my friend—what is your name?"

"Upquark."

"Respect, Upquark, that's what characterizes my practice. I've been a lifetime developing my equipment, at great cost and sometimes at extreme personal risk." He looked at Upquark, his eyes blazing with inspiration. "I've been hounded."

"We're being hounded ourselves."

"Then you understand." Vole made slight adjustments to the Noological Pod. "Such things cause one to doubt oneself. I have had grave doubts."

"I'm sorry to hear that." Upquark was studying a large tank in which squid-like creatures were resting. Their bodies were covered in wrinkled flesh, which expanded slightly as they breathed.

"Those are my vent-flingers," said Vole, following his gaze. "Remarkable creatures that live on natural gas, from which they extract a seven-percent solution of helium. You'll note their strong tentacles."

"I don't have vent-flingers in my database," said Upquark. "I've never encountered them before."

"They're a hybrid I developed. I'm aiming for high elasticity of the outer skin. The reason for that is secret. You'll forgive me if I don't elaborate."

"Of course," said Upquark, extending a gripper into the tank. The vent-flingers grabbed at it and clung tenaciously.

Vole removed the creatures from Upquark by a sharp snap of the fingers, which they instantly obeyed. "That response has military significance," he said enigmatically. "I dare not say more." Vole returned his gaze to Specterales O. "What was this poor creature doing that they found it necessary to strike him with electromanacles?"

"He was confused, and made a move they didn't like."

Dr. Vole shook his head. "The old story. Cruel bureaucratic minds tried the same thing with me."

"But why?"

"For the slightest mishaps. Little experimental slips of the sort tolerated in any medical office." Dr. Vole's face lost none of its exuberance. "They wanted to brain-clean me, of course. But I escaped, thanks to our host, Mr. Dunbosian. And on Mirador, I met with tolerance. I am able to continue my experiments." He pried O's mouth open, and squirted in a cocktail of chemicals, then looked at Upquark as one pioneer to another. "His neuropeptidergic rhythms will now be reset. Conventional brain research is hopelessly behind me on this. The Vole Neuro-cocktail is an object of mockery and suppression. Again, jealousy. You see, I've identified the most important neurotransmitter of all."

Upquark gazed up at Vole, expectantly.

"I have named it the phantomone, for it hides from our probing. The entire medical community refuses to admit its existence. I alone have laid claim to it, and I alone prescribe it." Vole reached to a shelf, drew down a bottle, and took a long swig. "Do you wish to—?"

Upquark rotated a digit on his gripper, and a vacuum tube appeared. He sucked up a small sample of the liquid and processed it to the organic sectors of his body. The effect was immediate. "It appears to cause a micro-synaptic flow . . . of great power . . . possibly inebriating?"

"Mildly alcoholic," Vole admitted.

Upquark was wobbling on his lifters, but he'd become more aware of the breathing of the vent-flingers.

Vole noted his interest. "Vent-flingers have tremendous powers of respiration. Come around at feeding time. Then you'll see them at their best. Meanwhile—" he extended the bottle.

Upquark hesitated.

"Medicinal," said Vole, and Upquark dutifully sucked up a second potent dose.

CHAPTER 10

"And please, sir, how you come to be on Mirador?" asked Lucky Viscid, sitting himself beside Upquark on the patio.

"An adventure," said Upquark, still drunk from Dr. Vole's phantomone cocktail. "I'm having quite a ho-ha."

"Yes, I see. Good time for everybody. Well, that is making me very happy."

Upquark had never encountered anyone so peculiarly ingratiating, and thought Viscid an extraordinarily friendly fellow. People never understood why they were drawn to this tenant of Mirador, for he was obviously an unwholesome creature, but some psychic substance seemed to ooze from him and draw them in; they'd feel their life histories being pulled out of them, as if a thin strand of glue had attached itself to their memories. Viscid could direct this glue, fishing shallow or deep, depending on what he sensed was valuable. People would leave his presence drained of their secrets, which stuck in Viscid's mind like bugs in amber.

A little breeze came by, bearing dust and a cigar wrapper which immediately clung to Viscid's forehead. "You work for that guy over there?"

"Yes," said Upquark, "that's Mr. Link, who oversees the Agricultural Plain. He understands everything about insects."

Lucky Viscid turned to face the breeze so that he might collect a bit more dust, while also collecting a bit more information from Upquark. "Your boss a very smart guy?"

"Oh, he is."

"And you—very smart too?"

"No, my IQ chip is only average."

"Hey, I know smart machine when I see one. Tell me please, about adventure you're on, because I am longing for news from outside."

"Well, the Autonomous Observer sent two agents to question us about a pirate we know, and Mr. Link sent his bees after them. The bees stung them in numerous places, causing great discomfort. Then we had to escape. Don't you consider that a great adventure?"

"First-class number one." Lucky Viscid rearranged some of his debris, covering a few bare spots on his behind. His sticky body was covered with cocktail napkins, tiny paper umbrellas, and other decorations from the bar. "And what you do here now?"

"We're going to make Mirador bloom again. I'll speak to the insects and they'll help us."

"They are one big nuisance, getting stuck to me." He checked to see if he had any stuck to him at the moment. "And what you do after you talk to insects?"

"Then I'll go recharge."

Lucky Viscid realized the little robot didn't carry long-range future planning software. But enough information had been gathered. His employer, the Autonomous Observer, might even give him a bonus for what he'd learned. That money would go to pay his rent . . . or maybe not. Why should he bother paying Dunbosian anything? The pachyderm was lenient, and it was best to take advantage of leniency wherever one found it.

* * *

"Lucky Viscid has finally earned his salary," said the Autonomous Observer, seated in her underground office, across from her secretary, Dr. Amphibras. "Link's on Mirador."

"Mirador is outside the regular patrol of the Guard," Amphibras pointed out. "The area is policed by a private militia."

"Then we'll have to use them. If we don't act immediately, we'll lose Link again." She brought Mirador up on her universal scanner. Surveillance images showed the terraced gardens, desiccated canals, and the main building with its outcroppings of seedy bungalows. "The militia is to handle him gently."

"They're mercenaries."

"I know what they are."

"Their quarry invariably comes back dead." Amphibras colored with distress, his warts changing to an even brighter red.

* * *

A flight of metal peckers was following Upquark around the patio. He'd learned their signaling system and was amusing himself by putting them through aerial acrobatics. They swept through the air in formations that spread out like a vast black cape, then snapped together into a diving line, ending in a synchronized landing on the railing outside the room in which Specterales O was resting. Their feathers had a metallic shine, and their beaks gleamed like polished drill bits. Their little brains raced with the energy they stole from everything around them, and their little burning eyes were fixed on Upquark as he approached. They were puzzled by his wingless form but accepted him as an Alpha Pecker, in control. When he entered O's room, he released them into the sky.

He and O walked slowly toward the patio. It was evening and the patio had been transformed into something that more resembled the glory of its past. Lights were strung through the dead vines, giving them a sort of half-life. The pool, though empty, was lit too, and guests relaxed on its steps. The terraces beyond the garden were also illuminated and transformed by the darkness. From a distance one might think that fabulous beings dwelt again on Mirador. But the guests tonight were spies, political exiles, con artists, gigolos, solar wind sailors, felons, gamblers, a saboteur, all of them fleeing the Guard and the Observer. Here they were able to catch their breath, make a plan, and use Dunbosian's connections.

A spotlight illuminated the center of the patio, and Dunbosian stepped into it. Chattering voices quieted down. Each evening's entertainment was a welcome escape. Dunbosian bowed in the direction of the bandstand, where three Etherian musicians had seated themselves. The first notes that rang out were unbearably beautiful. The patio went totally still. Even the metal peckers ceased their hammering.

And then, from the shadows beyond the patio entered something Upquark had never seen before. Were they one creature, or several? They rolled into the spotlight, limbs pressed together, flattened like petals into a flower shape. To the melody of the Etherians, their arms unfolded with the sinuousness of a sparkling sea plant; their costumes were sequined in a glittering pattern of teardrops. Four heads followed, in gossamer hoods, faces shadowed. And then, by some secret of their art, their limbs rigidified, became sharply angular, and suddenly they were a cube, a Chinese puzzle of interlocking pieces.

"The Cluster Tumblers," whispered Dr. Vole to Upquark.

They were a flower, they were a sea anemone, a disc with tentacles. They were the horns of a stag, a nebula, a sponge. Their sequins became swirls of light bending around an infinite center, then vanishing into it, their black hoods snapping closed over their entire form, as the spotlight was switched off. There was a quick gasp from the audience, a beep from the watching robots, and then applause, above which the doctor said, "They're from the remotest part of the Corridor, no one knows exactly where, and they aren't what you call survivors. When one of them dies, the others soon follow. A delicate species, too delicate for this part of the galaxy. We must assume they're fugitives like the rest of us."

In the few moments of darkness at the conclusion of their act, the Cluster Tumblers had disappeared beyond the crowd, back to their decaying orchid gardens on the hillside, and to whatever ruined tree palazzo they'd chosen for the night. The secret of their upkeep was Dunbosian's, and of the robot who saw to their needs.

"Our friend responded well to the performance," said Dr. Vole, nodding toward a comatose Specterales O.

"You think he shows improvement?" asked Upquark with surprise.

"To the trained eye, yes."

How untrained I am, reflected Upquark, who saw only the superficial picture, of Specterales O slumped on his bar stool, long arms dangling nearly to the floor, feet splayed, head angled to the side, unable to support its own weight.

The music of the Etherians continued, working its cosmic nostalgias on Link. Earth was lost, and there were only these new planetary worlds, not truly man's own. Vole felt the malady that plagued all transplanted Earthlings, and which the Etherian music magnified, of natal vertigo—the feeling that the race of man had fallen off the Earth and was now at the mercy of influences for which no preparation had ever been made.

"The alpha incursions," said the doctor. "They're playing the damned things again. We'll all be falling through crevices of time. I don't mind, really. It puts the past so far behind as to make it nonexistent."

The Etherians came toward Ren's table. "Please, Cantusian. You must sing with us."

She shook her head, but Dunbosian said, "My dear, this dried-up rock is all they have." He nodded his trunk toward the crowd of misfits seated around the ruined patio. "Only the lonely live here, without papers or planet. A song from you would be a momentary passport to freedom."

Dunbosian walked into the pink spotlight, which gave his flesh the appearance of soft candy. He removed one stumpy hand from his pocket and adjusted his data fez. "Cantus is the planet of song. Its singers have no equal. We are fortunate to have one of them with us tonight. Please welcome her." He gestured toward Ren.

Tentative applause greeted the untried performer. When it died down, the only sound was that of the insects in the dried arbor, and farther off, lizards barking on the terraced gardens.

Ren entered the spotlight and stared out at the audience, thinking, why do I do this to myself? She'd left Cantus because she didn't want to be a performer. She wanted to be in the shadows, a hidden witness to life. Only then did she feel she was in control of her fate.

But then, the Ethereans began to play, and the party mask of the Paper Lantern crossed her face, and she became a different creature, moving sinuously in the spotlight. She started to sing, and Link caught his breath: she was matching perfectly the choral termite and the Mirador song beetle. He could imitate their calls with some success, but she was weaving melodies into them, adding harmonic texture and rhythm, turning the pervasive insect sounds of Mirador into something so seductive Dunbosian closed his eyes and sighed. The familiar night had taken on a new dimension, drawing from him resolutions of goodness he could never fulfill. But they were wonderful resolutions.

The snail looked as if his own eyes were wet with emotion, but since he was misting himself one couldn't tell; moisture covered him, catching the gleam of the garden lamps. The propulsive waves by which he walked were visibly rippling through him, but his travel at the moment was only inward, to deeper dreams of Mirador.

"It's a love song," whispered one of the waitresses, her body unconsciously imitating the angle of Ren's and her gaze going where Ren's went. "For him." She nodded toward Link, who was also singing, though so softly only Ren could hear him, her finely scalloped ears picking up the delicate insect trills he made.

An older woman of Mirador, whom Dunbosian had rescued from the brain police, was sobbing into her handkerchief. Her beauty was destroyed, but she dressed with elegance, in clothes Dunbosian had given her. Mirador gossip had it that Ren and Link were on the run together. And then she wept more openly, for Ren's song reminded her that Dunbosian had all these younger women, who owed him their freedom and future identity; the pachyderm could take his pick. What I need is a Vole Cocktail, she told herself, and gave her order to the waitress.

Of all the guests at Mirador, the most affected was Specterales O. He was bathing in the sound, his lips moving silently. No ordinary music could have found him, but these tuneful threads were woven by little creatures he already adored, the insects that carried the pollen of his beloved plants. It was as if they'd come for him, in this miraculous serenade, to carry him out of darkness.

"There, you see," said Dr. Vole, "the degenerative phase is over and my Specterian-type micromassage is taking effect, as I knew it would."

Unnoticed by Vole or anyone, two great bat-like shadows silently approached on the horizon. Their eyes were flattened windows without reflections, coated to conceal what was within. In Mirador's field tower, which announced incoming aircraft, a robot received the unusual transmission of a disintegration beam, which reduced him to a puddle of lubricant on the tower's floor.

Below in the garden, Ren continued weaving melodies with the song beetle and the choral termite; she'd fallen into their world as Link had fallen, and had found the same touching beauty—the courage of tiny lovers who know their song exposes them to danger but sing as loudly as they can, for their desire can't be denied.

New pathways of recognition were opening in Specterales O's brain, bypassing the ruined ones. The entire insect world seemed to have come to Mirador to guide him. He sat up at the bar, and the revolving colors in his eyes became strong again, along with a voice he hadn't used in years. "My little plants miss me. I must get back to the Agricultural Plain."

"I've cured him!" whispered Dr. Vole.

The bat-like ships of the militia, arriving soundlessly over the heart of the spa, now went into hover mode. Bay doors opened, and four black-armored militiamen descended to the patio.

The guests panicked, scattering into the surrounding desert. Even the informer Lucky Viscid ran off with the throng, whose footsteps stirred up bits of debris that clung to his fleeing form.

But the four militiamen had eyes for only Link. Spinnerets shot out from their armor, shackling him around the waist. Their ship hovered silently in the night sky above the shackled prisoner; hovering also were the metal peckers, who were receiving a signal from Upquark below. Peckers rarely attack moving objects, but Upquark was directing their burning eyes toward the helmets and jetpacks of the militiamen. They folded their wings and dove downward, drill beaks aimed for the glittering hardware, which they struck with a tremendous clatter, hammering the shiny helmets, disrupting the soldiers' communications. The din inside the helmets was deafening; sparks shot across the soldiers' face shields; interior circuits exploded.

"Encountering . . . opposition . . ."

The soldiers saw hundreds of maniacal little eyes surrounding them; beaks capable of bringing down a building were pounding them senseless. Structural integrity gone, their helmets collapsed like plastic bags, choking them.

Upquark directed the metal peckers onto the soldiers' body armor, which also began to collapse. Their arms and legs twisted, knee joints buckling. Covered in metal peckers, they lay in distorted positions, locked in by their own armor, while the metal peckers traveled up and down them, drilling for remaining pockets of energy.

Upquark knelt beside one militiaman whose helmet looked like a melted, smoking gumdrop; a metal pecker was working furiously on his neck protector. "Your cervical vertebrae are about to suffer extensive damage," said Upquark. "Spinal shock is inevitable; probability of complete paralysis is ninety-eight percent. To prevent this, give me the shackle code."

With his neck about to be broken, the soldier transferred the code. Upquark freed Link and called off the metal peckers. Like mummies wrapped in iron, the soldiers were immobilized.

Another wave of soldiers descended from the second militia ship, and fired: Taking the prisoner alive was no longer a consideration. A sizzling blast caught one of Upquark's wheels. He stared down at it. "Calculating temperature of heated alloy. Vaporization point has been reached." His wheel turned to a gaseous state and vanished. He teetered to one side. "Never mind," he said to Link. "Now I can explore the wonders of monopedalism."

With Upquark in his arms, Link caught up with Ren and O. Dunbosian was leading them on a vine-covered pathway through the desiccated hills. Ren's dragonfly ship glided smoothly toward them, across the broken surface of an ancient tennis court.

"Dunbosian," said Ren, "you've got to guide us to some safe place."

"I'm too heavy with crime," he answered sadly, then turned, and thundered back into the shadows. Mirador was under siege, and he couldn't abandon it.

Metal peckers had swooped down on Ren's ship and were hammering with sharp beaks on the cowling. Upquark signaled them away, as Ren rushed to the controls. She switched from local velocity to astral, and frantically issued the command for ionization.

"*Ionizers,*" answered the computer. From the ship's nose and sides, coils of wire fanned out in webs. Flashes of light danced through electrical lattices, and the ghostly form of ionized hydrogen was guided to the engines.

"Full thrust."

"*Full thrust.*"

Tongues of flame shot from the exhaust ports, and the metal peckers were swept away by the hot wind off the cowling, as Ren's ship rose into the upper atmosphere of Mirador.

Looking out through a side window, Link saw the pursuing bat ship of the militia.

"We're wobbling," said the militia ship's captain, and in the next instant a violent oscillation shook him in his seat. He clicked to a visual of the ship's underside and found the culprit—a large squid-like creature attached to the armor plating of the wing. "I don't know what it is but we've got to get rid of it."

Far below, deep in the hills of Mirador, Dr. Vole and the bartender were crouched above a volcanic fissure which glowed in the asteroid's dark surface. From a cage, Vole was pulling forth the giant leech-like parasites he'd been breeding. He handed one bloated ventflinger after another to the bartender, who laid them on the fuming fissure, to which they adhered with greedy mouths. Immediately they started to expand from the sulfurous gas they sucked.

Vent-flingers are afflicted with wanderlust and use what energy they can to travel through the air on pathetically short journeys, but now the pressure of the gases inflated them to liftoff tension and shot them to new heights. Steering themselves with crude rudders, they aimed for the bat-like object flying above them, on which they could hitch the free ride of their dreams, farther than they'd ever been.

"There are dozens of them," shouted the militia captain, as the huge squids showed up on his screen, fastened to his wildly rocking ship.

"The beauty of pure medical research," Vole explained to the bartender, as they dropped the last of the fat parasites onto the fissure's gaseous mouth and watched it launch itself toward the ship, whose lights began dancing crazily about.

"Target achieved," cried the bartender, as the bat ship lost its struggle and was forced into a landing.

In his office, Dunbosian was talking to the snail. "Tonight's misadventure will bring repercussions. Mirador will survive, but I've got to go underground."

The snail's antennas gave a slight quiver of alarm. "Not to Vole's Chamber."

"I'm afraid so."

Dunbosian gazed out through the window at his beautiful, decrepit spa, then reached into his pocket for the coding unit which controlled it all, and gave it to the snail. "Watch over it while I'm below."

The snail took it reluctantly. "The last person who used the Chamber—"

"I know." Dunbosian glanced toward the dried hills, where a madman could be seen near one of the ruined tree palazzos, making monkey sounds and scampering along the bare branches.

Dunbosian triggered a floor tile, which, with a creak, subsided, carrying him slowly beneath the surface of Mirador. He'd had the lift constructed according to Vole's design, but had hoped never to have to use it. He studied the elevator walls as he went down the secret shaft. "A whim of Vole's, a quixotic gesture, but he was depressed. He needed something to occupy his mind."

The elevator stopped, and Dunbosian stepped off into a dimly lit holding area. He sent the lift back up and a faint clank from overhead told him it was in place again, conforming seamlessly to his office floor. As his eyes adjusted to the light, a vertical wall panel slid open. Beyond it, a staircase waited.

"Vole's Descender." Dunbosian lumbered down, feeling the beginning of claustrophobia. At each turning of the stairs, a slab of steel slid shut behind him. "To seal the energy. Vole's design entirely."

The only light now came from the bioluminescence of microscopic creatures floating in the heavy air. They'd been bottled by space hunters on Planet Lumina and transported to Mirador at great expense. The little creatures floated toward Dunbosian, so close that he could see their tiny internal furnaces at work. "A healing light, according to Vole. Faith is required."

Vole's Descender went down through one protective slab after another, the slabs dropping back into place with a thundering sound. Dunbosian stared at each one as it closed. Their locks could not be forced. The client must feel permanently cut off from the upper world. "Vole's research was extensive. A show of confidence is in order."

He continued his descent, feeling the deep embrace of Mirador. Many thousands had testified to the powers of its waters. Those waters had retreated into subterranean streams, and the Vole Descender followed one of them. At the foot of the stairs a pool appeared, dark and glowing, the tiny beings from Lumina darting across its surface. "Vole's Chamber. The energy center of Mirador."

The pool was framed by a polished rock floor, and Dunbosian walked around it, gazing at the water. He removed his white suit and dipped the tip of his trunk into the pool. It tasted suspiciously like one of Vole's potions; then he saw the little mixing jets squirting a variety of tinctures patented by Vole, the entire process having been activated the moment Dunbosian triggered the descending tile. The walls of the pool were constructed of materials brought from distant worlds. "A caprice. A fancy. But building it improved Vole's spirits."

Dunbosian walked down the steps into the water, sinking in up to his neck. The liquid slowly changed its color, taking on a bluish hue. "Submerged in a Vole Cocktail."

He gazed across the surface, on whose rippling waves the tiny luminous beings danced. Immersion in the Chamber was said by Vole to provide all necessary nourishment. Through the skin.

"One tries to believe," said Dunbosian. "For one will be here for a while."

CHAPTER 11

"You've got to take out the Shark," said the Junk Moon messenger.

"Not on my lunch hour, I don't," replied Fin Zigler.

"We got a distress call. They're in the vicinity, and drifting."

Fin removed his work gloves and his helmet, then slid down the shaft of the crane. He belonged to a breed that went back to Late Earth, of gearheads who feel obliged to improve on the commercial designs of fast-moving objects. By day he worked as scrapper foreman, sorting and stacking the fruits of military disasters from around the Corridor. During lunch hour and in the evenings, he scavenged parts for Little Infinity, an interplanetary vehicle the Ship Shapers were building for themselves.

He hit the ground, metal dust puffing up around his heavy boots. From all sides came the incessant din of metal peckers, who thrived on the Junk Moon, with its bent and broken machines of war. Fin slipped into a little backburner he'd designed with custom rockets which shot him through the lanes of stranded ships, past painted flags of every planetary nation, each of whom had contributed their bit of shattered glory to Kitty Liftoff's moon.

Fin flew face down, his headband radar gathering details up ahead; if he cut it too close, the band would override the backburner's trajectory and save him from slamming into a tank cannon or some other military protuberance in the landscape. The lane he sailed through now was formed by thousands of hovertanks which hovered no longer, but stood squat and menacing on melted skids and burnt-out rocket lifters.

The security monitor in his headband indicated visitors were near. A second later he spotted them: a mercenary tank team who'd been cleared to do some shopping. Fin threw the soldiers a salute as he banked on by, and they waved back with the dullness of men surfacing momentarily from a mechanical trance. To them he was just another flying monkey suit.

The hill ahead was forested with ten-meter-high antennas mounted on command-and-control vehicles which had been restored and were awaiting purchase. He headed downhill through the antenna lanes like a skier dodging flags on a fast slope. As he reached the bottom, a tremendous rumbling sounded, and there, cresting the next hill, was a junkernaut.

It was as large as a ten-story building, and composed entirely of junked robots. It rolled along on thousands of wheels and lifters—massive, ungainly, and impossible to steer. Robotic heads emerged, craning and commenting and issuing contradictory commands. Metal peckers flew in and out, adding to the noise as it thundered along. Fin hovered beside it, fascinated by its monstrous form. If you got in its way, it couldn't stop, for its direction was only loosely controlled by the jumble of wrecked robots, each one thinking it was in charge. Fin heard a babel of electronic voices. Grippers and snappers waved to him, and mechanized heads of every shape popped out, mouths moving in a frenzy of greetings, slogans, and mathematical formulas.

When the first junkernaut had formed itself years ago, Kitty Liftoff was advised by her managers to take it out with an antitank missile. But the desperate ingenuity of junked robots banding together in a new form had appealed to her. "Let it roll," she'd said, and it had. Other junkernauts had followed in its wake, and now they rolled aimlessly over every sector of the Junk Moon. Their pooled energy was enough to keep each inhabitant of the junkernaut alive; it wasn't much of a life, since their software was corrupted and their functions impaired, but the main thing was to roll. Continuous motion gave them a sense of purpose and the illusion that they were still participating in civilization. They would pass the Ship Shapers at work and fill the air with garbled suggestions; then they'd continue on, parts falling off, lights blinking erratically. Robots migrated from the surface to the interior and back out again, exchanging information that went nowhere, for there were too many different models involved, from all over the Corridor. Cooperation was marginal, which was why stopping a junkernaut, or turning one, was impossible. It just rolled on, a clanking ball of blind intent.

As he watched, Fin felt revulsion for the thing. It had the aura of a crudely primitive deity. It would crush you if you got in its path, after which the assembly line robots included in the bottom ranks would stamp you *inspected* and *approved*. A sociologist who'd come especially to observe a junkernaut had been found flattened, bearing a hundred different commercial trademarks. The robots were not malevolent; but being only semifunctional run-down half-charged derelicts, their combined potential was dangerous. Junkernauts managed to keep to the roads most of the time, but occasionally one of them leveled a building, or got tangled up in communication conduits, which it would drag sizzling along behind it. In spite of such blunders, Kitty Liftoff thought of the junkernauts affectionately. At night, when their thunderous comings and goings could be heard, or when one appeared with hundreds of communicator beams shining out of it like the quills on a giant porcupine, she smiled. Her employees, stuck here on a treeless, waterless ball of salvage, found the junkernauts entertaining. That a junkernaut might accidentally run into a munitions dump and blow up a good part of the country-side provided an edgy fascination. Fin, too, smiled grudgingly at the repulsive junkernaut, and burned on, toward a giant landing field. He came in over rows of hangars, and turned toward the great basking Shark, its hulk taking up the entire end of the runway. They were waiting for him to board.

He went vertical, and landed in a plume of dust, then walked up the entrance ramp, into the Shark's bowels. The vast interior of the scrapper was empty at the moment; it had disgorged its last meal of junked ships collected in space. The smell of metal, propellants, and shredded flesh was heavy and unpleasant. Fin was the senior recovery officer, and a local rescue required his presence. "What kind of ship is hung up?"

"Commercial carrier," answered the scrapper captain, as they headed toward the bridge. "Aviate model 2L. I have its cargo manifest and destination, if you're interested."

Fin swore quietly. He'd been hoping for a ship with better lines than an Aviate 2L.

The bridge of the Shark was already active, robots at all key stations. As the robotic captain entered, they closed the hatches, and revved up the main engines. Fin sat beside the captain on the bridge. He was qualified to fly the basking Shark, but it was not a peak experience. The Shark moved like sludge in a tub. Its job was simply to fly up to an orbiting object, open its gigantic mouth, and swallow.

"Are we talking to the crew of the Aviate?"

"Computer contact only. The crew may have perished."

Too bad, thought Fin, but that means it's all ours.

The Shark lumbered down the runway, lifted slowly off, and banked against the sun. Fin looked down at the Junk Moon, its surface covered in every direction by gleaming junk, with metallic dust rising up around a rolling junkernaut. Unlike Kitty Liftoff, Fin did not reflect on the futility of arms. To him, all this machinery of war, curving in endless rows toward the horizon, had a surreal beauty.

As the horizon tilted with the movement of the ship, he glanced at the captain, but the captain wasn't programmed for small talk with humans. Little interested him except the Shark. Occasionally he visited a junkernaut for some weird robotic kick.

"There it is," said Fin. The radar blip of the crippled ship had come on the screen, but the robotic captain didn't bother looking. He'd been seeing it in his internal viewer since taking off. He was flying straight for it, and would come at it full tilt; internal air and magnetic cushions would settle the lame ship into place.

"We'll swallow Commercial Freighter Aviate in two minutes and fifteen seconds," he announced. The radar blip enlarged, and the computers of the two ships exchanged information. Crews inside the Shark were in position: docking specialists, a medical unit, and firefighters. There was also a security detail, for pirates had several times tried to steal the Shark; as a pirate ship, its ominous appearance would paralyze the ordinary commercial pilot, and Consortium Guard fighters would have trouble penetrating its missile-proof armor; it would just keep coming at its prey with open, menacing jaws.

Fin turned to the exterior monitor and saw the shape of the Aviate appear. It was about as interesting as a flying frypan. But he ran his professional eye along it anyway, looking for any interesting design touches, and that was when he noticed something that only a Ship Shaper would catch: the detailing on its snout-like nose was slightly off . . . as if the subject had moved when the shot was taken, and Fin knew that he was looking at an infographic, not a real exterior. Fine, he thought, because now anything is possible, and a dull day has brightened.

The Aviate grew larger in the monitor, its electronically generated image revealing another detail only a Ship Shaper would perceive: the docking lights of the Shark played on its hull with a peculiar distortion, caused by reflections coming off whatever ship was hiding underneath. A moment later the Aviate vanished, swallowed by the Shark.

"*Secured,*" reported the docking unit, and Fin felt the soft boom of the magnetic pressure bed receiving the wounded ship.

"Acquired," said the captain, and immediately changed course. He had no further interest in the Aviate, or its survivors, if any. His program was to fly the Shark everlastingly, without comment or complaint.

Fin left the bridge, took an elevator down to the holding area, and stepped out into the Shark's cavernous belly. Again, a faint odor of decayed flesh wafted past his nostrils. The robots didn't notice it, of course. What did it matter to them if undigested scraps of dead heroes festered here? Their harsh electronic voices echoed up through the great vaulted arches, while they signaled to one another with illuminated arms, mechanical priests in a cathedral of doom.

The freighter carrier was bedded, still producing its electronic facade, which at this range was no longer perfect. Veil manufacturers understood that if anyone got this close, veiling didn't help; you were had. The real ship was visible beneath the infographic, but indistinctly, as if seen in a mist.

Its hatchway opened as Fin approached, and a brawny figure appeared. "My dear Fin, welcome aboard."

Fin's recoil was instinctive. "Who's after you?"

"The usual crowd."

"What have you done?"

"Does it matter?"

Fin could feel complications settling on him, and knew there was no immediate escape from them. The code of the Ship Shapers was strong, and Jockey Oldcastle fell under its protection. There were occasions when Fin needed an unusual item, from a rare ship, from a royal ship, from a ship protected by brute forces, and Jockey got the item for him. How, was not something he reported on. The part would arrive by courier one day, elegantly packaged.

"We'll hide you," said Fin, with no attempt to disguise his reluctance. "Keep your veil on and my guys will offload you straight into one of our ground carriers."

He entered the pirate ship's salon. An illuminated banquette ran around three walls. The ceiling was domed, black and translucent, and narrow beams of light behind it created an illusion of meteors descending from the heights of space. The illusion was continuous, filling the room with luminous threads, finely spun from palest gold. Fin was imagining the wiring that underlay it, the endless hours of labor to install it, and the expense involved to create this mirage of meteors.

"Not to disturb your reverie, dear boy, but I'm being pursued by hostile forces."

"What kind of identification did you give security?"

"Commercial freighter captain, alien first officer, robotic navigator. All bogus, but made to withstand a certain amount of scrutiny, by which time I hope to be gone."

"You're here to outfit your ship?"

"I'm here to get into Amphora."

"What for?"

"To inspect the drains. Come, have a drink. You know Lizardo. Gamester, come in here."

The sawed-off Gamester entered with a friendly gesture of his gripper and rolled up to the table. There he stayed, eye level with the tabletop, dreaming of space-time and elsewhere.

"Now, Fin," said Jockey, as he brought out glasses and some snacks, "how do we get into Amphora?"

"I'll hide you for a few days, but I don't want anything to do with Amphora."

"Certainly, certainly."

"I just want to build ships."

"Perfectly understandable, dear boy."

"And I don't want to fool around with a classified installation."

"I quite understand."

"Why do I think you don't?"

"Because of quantum phase entanglement," said the Gamester, staring across the tabletop's flat expanse. His voice was distant. He was playing with a model of super-time, but he liked to keep up with the threads of human conversation, as a balance to the troublesome qualities of dimensional hypersphering.

"Jockey, we could wind up getting brain-cleaned for screwing around with Amphora."

"Naturally we wish to avoid that. Why don't you have one of these snacks?"

Lizardo laid his reptilian claw on Fin's wrist and hissed softly, "Have you been inside Amphora?"

"No. And I don't want to be." Fin was gazing at the polished surface of the table, which received the light threads from the dome and wove them down into the grain, into illusory depths. "They do serious stuff there."

"That's why we're here," hissed Lizardo.

"We feel there might be some small profit in it for us," suggested Jockey.

Fin ran his palm across the tabletop, and the descending threads of light broke over his hand, entangling his fingers as if in a gladiator's net of palest gold. He raised his hand, shaking off the net. "I'll hide you until the heat's off, then send you out of here. That's all I'm good for."

"I have in my possession the cockpit medallion from a Dark Dreamer scout ship." Jockey drummed his fingers lightly on his great stomach. "The most beautiful medallion you or I have ever seen." Jockey gestured in his sloppy fashion toward the floor. "It's stored below. I asked myself to whom would that Dreamers' medallion mean the most?" He shoveled the entire bowl of snacks up in his huge hand. "To whom would it give the greatest happiness?"

"All right, all right," said Fin with a sigh, and lowered both hands into the golden net of Jockey Oldcastle.

CHAPTER 12

Upquark stood in a long line of dysfunctional robots. Some were missing limbs or wheels, some had bullet holes and laser burn marks; and some were gesturing erratically or mumbling incoherently—signs of software deterioration. Their owners stood with them—mercenaries clad in a variety of gaudy uniforms but temporarily stripped of their weapons by Junk Moon Security.

"We got blown up on Juno," a headless robot was explaining to Upquark, its voice emanating from an auxiliary speaker in its chest.

"How unfortunate," said Upquark.

"I'm used to it," said the headless robot, with practiced indifference. "What happened to you?"

"Gun battle," said Upquark, attempting to sound equally casual about it, as if combat were a daily occurrence with him. Balancing on one leg, he felt proud to be among these shot-up warrior robots.

"It's a garden of war," said O, mournfully, as he looked at the endless rows of armaments.

"Best place to come when you need cheap parts," said the headless robot.

Toward the horizon, enormous cauldrons could be seen, in which ruined ships were being melted to a glowing liquid, like something in the cup of a giant whose favorite drink was molten ore. Even at this distance, the glow from the cauldrons lit Upquark's face and the faces of the robots waiting in line with him. One by one, they were being cleared for entry into the Robotic Reassembly Area.

Ren and Link stood with them, Ren fidgeting nervously. Junk Moon Security had accepted the new identity chips Dunbosian had given her; but deeper searches could be made at any time. She needed Upquark's coordinates to locate the Amphora installation, and Link was part of the package, along with the sad Specterian, O. So she, who preferred to operate alone, was burdened with three fugitives from the Observer.

Link was wishing he weren't there at all. He hated Upquark being used for espionage, and he hated endangering poor O. But Ren had saved them twice.

O peered between the ranks of broken airships at a blossom growing in oily, metallic mud. "It needs our help."

"We can't help it now," said Upquark.

O understood: This was the will of the world, to enlarge its strength, to harness greater energies, to kill or be killed in a tremendous tournament of power. What was a flower to it? Yet here the flower was. "Will we ever get back to our Agricultural Plain?"

"I don't think so," said Upquark.

"Where will we have the chance to help plants grow again?"

"Somewhere," answered Upquark with an optimism he didn't feel.

"After we get you a new wheel?"

"Maybe then," said Upquark. But they were not on the Junk Moon for a new wheel.

Ren asked Link quietly, "Do you hear an insect sound up around thirty kilocycles per second?"

He listened. "No."

She had expected he would say that. It meant she was locking onto an ultrasonic frequency, one that was making her faintly nauseous. Was it coming from some ship? Engines of death surrounded them, filled with the vibration of war, but this was a deeper and more sinister current.

Link picked up a piece of jagged metal from the ground, and a chunky black insect scurried away. "*Scarabeus armature,*" said Link automatically. "It makes its home in the fuselage of air tankers."

She gave him an impatient look. He was running from the Observer, but could interest himself in armored beetles. She had no such distraction; she was acutely aware of their danger, and something on this Junk Moon was giving off a debilitating signal. She looked around her at the mercenaries; they were exchanging war stories and military gossip, laughing and mocking each other good-naturedly. They were used to battle, and ready for whatever fight came their way. They weren't keyed-up Cantusian songbirds. Dunbosian was right. She was out of her league here. If only that awful undercurrent of sound would stop . . .

A tall security robot waved Upquark forward for inspection. Upquark's veiling device was now disguised as a light sensor embedded in his head panel. From it, false information flowed.

The security robot scanned it quickly. "Utility menial?"

"Yes, sir," said Upquark. "Lavatory and garbage duty." He emitted a vile-smelling concoction he'd made from insect extracts.

The security robot switched off his olfactory sensor. A little toilet scrubber was not his idea of company. "Enter Reassembly Area."

Upquark struggled forward on one roller. The Reassembly Area was a vast field of discarded robots. Some were totally without power, others still possessed a faint charge, and clients simply cannibalized the unwanted machines. Weak protests were made, but robots in need of a part were merciless; legs were unscrewed, chests torn open, mechanical organs removed. On all sides, the carnage was taking place. Upquark looked on in terror as the headless robot he'd been chatting with unscrewed the head of a feeble creature of similar manufacture and screwed it on his own neck. "A pretty good fit," he said cheerfully.

Upquark resisted Ren's instructions to find a model similar to himself and replace his missing wheel. "It's heartless," he cried.

"We're being watched," she snapped. "Don't hesitate."

He entered more deeply into the Reassembly Area, only to find another hideous sight: Among the cannibalized junked robots, those who could still move, even if feebly, were reassembling themselves from their expired brothers. Attachments were made recklessly, blindly, leading to a bizarre combination that began to grow like latticework, robot upon robot, the whole of it taking on a grotesque life of its own.

Upquark turned his head to avoid looking at the thing, only to find another latticework of robots approaching from the other direction. It heaved itself toward the first latticework, and they clanked together and began to form an even bigger and more fantastic entity, bolts locking, hoses connecting, rods fusing.

"You multiply that over and over," said a nearby security robot, "and *that's* what you get." He pointed to the horizon. Between the enormous cauldrons was a junkernaut. The monster rumbled across the plain—a fiery, thundering wheel, ten stories high. Heads poked out of it, emitting grotesque mechanical cries. Robotic limbs were dropping off as it thundered forward.

"It comes back here like an animal to its watering hole," snarled the security robot.

The huge howling junkernaut was looming larger, cockeyed headlights shooting out in a dozen directions. Its driving forces were visible now—wheels of every size, skids, trundles, capstans, great clattering treads—each part maneuvered by a frantic robot.

Terrified by the frenzied beast, Upquark shifted into Suitcase Mode; his arms and lifters sank into his trunk, and his head followed. A handle popped out and he ceased all transmission.

As the junkernaut rolled by, a telescoping arm shot out, inserted itself into Upquark's handle, and lifted him up into the careening wheel.

As the thing rushed onward, Link, Ren, and O darted after it, calling Upquark's name. Link's infowatch lit up and emitted the sound of Upquark's homing beacon.

"It is forbidden to follow a junkernaut," said the security robot, intervening, and Link was forced to watch and do nothing as the junkernaut rolled on with Upquark inside it.

All Upquark knew was that he was being tumbled about. Abandoning Suitcase Mode, he lowered his lifters, unfolded his arms, and cautiously raised his head. To his horror he saw that he was inside the rolling monster, surrounded by crazed machines. Pillars of entwined robots supported the great dome of the robot wheel above him, and tangled bunches of them kept losing their grip and crashing down on top of him. Garbled cries filled the air, speech engines stalling and misfiring. Distorted reports and impossible commands flew past his buried face from all sides.

He searched for an exit, but a knot of Vacubots, sucking blindly at anything that moved, sucked him into their ragged circle. He pinched their hoses with his grippers, blocking their suction, but as soon as he gained release from them, other domestic robots lunged for him, fingers squirting feeble jets from depleted tanks of water, soap, and shampoo.

"Scrub the children!"

"Bring the dinner!"

A Body Toner clamped Upquark's lifters and oscillated him from side to side, shouting enthusiastically, "I'm freeing up your grief!"

Up ahead, Upquark perceived a mad dance of limbs, repeated in endless rows, laborsaving devices of every kind laboring in limbo, gesturing insanely. Crowds of robots swayed together, muttering inanities. Their numbers were staggering, with the density of bees in a hive. Mankind's passion for gadgets was represented here in its ultimate disorder, humanity's inventiveness gone wild.

"I'm one of them," realized Upquark with dismay. "I'm just a glorified gadget with a bit of organic matter thrown in for efficiency." A lifetime spent with Adrian on the Agricultural Plain had given him illusions. He'd believed he mattered, as all these ruined robots had believed they'd mattered. Now, everywhere he looked, he saw his terrible and inevitable end—in a scrap heap, raving half-remembered phrases from corrupted programs.

A house-painting unit latched onto him, extracting him from the Body Toner, whose strength was fading, and scampered with him up a girder, using other robots like a flight of stairs. "I painted the world!" it said. "I had all the colors . . ." Dramatically it pointed a paint-spray finger, but only a few muddy drops came out, and a dim light shone from a dying circuit in its eyes.

Having landed on a higher level of the rolling monster, the dying painter robot deposited Upquark beside a group of Info Hogs, who were conversing intelligently. Upquark's despair began to lighten slightly. Even if he was caught in robot hell, at least here were units with whom he could communicate.

"They're the nuttiest of us all," cried an industrial cleaning unit, attaching herself to Upquark with a *thwock* of her magnetic arm. Ranting unintelligibly, she dragged him past the eloquent Info hogs whose conversation Upquark realized *was* insane, each of them claiming to have the final answer to reality, a frequent dying thought of high-end machines.

A row of military units menacingly converged on him, knocking the cleaning robot aside. "Take him to headquarters," barked the officer in charge. "And replace that missing wheel. He looks disgraceful." The demented soldiers clamped on a wheel, then marched Upquark forward toward a central area gimbaled to remain steady within the rolling junkernaut. It hung suspended in the midst of the chaos, relatively quiet and free of vibration. The soldiers shoved him inside. No other robots pressed around him, shouting gibberish. His heart rose within his plastic chest. If he'd been in robot hell, then this was close to heaven, for the dear old illusion came rushing back to him: He was a fully functioning and cherished utility robot, among beloved friends.

Seated at an ancient command control was a familiar sawed-off shape. "Just a game, really," said the Gamester.

Jockey Oldcastle lay stretched on an electronic bed that moved with spastic sensuality beneath him. A fast-food dispenser was feeding him antique sandwiches. "Amazing packaging," he remarked. "It's kept them fresh for decades."

CHAPTER 13

"Nothing worth buying down that way, folks," said the Junk Moon salesman, speeding toward them in his servo-pod. "That's the Plain of the Unusable." He gave Ren a friendly smile and swung his swagger stick toward the blood-red fuselage of a small fighter ship from Vorex. "Give you an excellent price on that bird. I saw the ship you arrived in. Cantusian Dragon, fast little number, but it doesn't have the armor you want in this day and age. That Vorex ship—" He pointed again with his swagger stick. "—will take a lot of punishment. I've got plenty of others too. Have a look around, then punch one-zero-five on your communicator. I'll find you and we'll work out a deal. OK, I've got to run, got some folks waiting down the block."

The salesman settled back into his pod and sped off. Link waited until the salesman was out of sight, then continued walking toward the Plain of the Unusable, for Upquark's homing beacon indicated he was there somewhere.

Ren was receiving a very different signal, the sinister sound she'd been hearing since she'd come to the Junk Moon. Its pulsation continued to produce waves of nausea in her, and for a moment her nerve failed her. She wanted to tell Link this place made her ill, but he'd lost Upquark because of her. She had to help him find his friend.

"I'm sure he's alive," said Link. "His signal shows full energy."

"We'll find him," said O, putting his long bony fingers on Link's shoulder. "And I will bring him out of that monster."

They proceeded to enter the barren landscape. Here there were no buyers, no neat rows of war machines, nor any outmoded robots waiting for scavengers to pick them apart. There were only only scattered pieces of broken ships, charred, twisted, and useless.

* * *

Inside a guardhouse on the Plain of the Unusable, Security Robot Number Three felt as if a locking pliers had pinched his forehead nuts.

"Why is Number Three staring at the wall?" demanded Number One.

"Junkernaut approaching, sir. It may have affected him. I'm getting a significant level of noise on my own inputs."

"I always said one of them would come too close someday."

Ringed around Robot Number One stood his team, their thermal imaging tracking the wayward junkernaut. Number One nodded at his viewscreen. "We are permitted to fire if it endangers this installation. So we do everybody a big favor and blow it to pieces."

The other robots also nodded, without speaking. Firing protocol required perfect silence now, of absolute machine concentration. But Number One continued talking. He felt unusually charged. Had he gotten too much juice on the energy break? He started spouting old messages, wrong messages, training programs, recruitment slogans, vertical insertions, and a backloading of augmentation files. He grabbed his jaw plate, holding its riveted sections shut, but his jaw sprung open, overpowering his grip and releasing a string of gibberish.

Silence! he told himself, and drove his head into a wall. He continued bumping back and forth, aware that this behavior was also unprogrammed, that he was a robot *who'd lost his mind.*

The robots on his team rotated, bent over, got up, marched in place. This too was unprogrammed behavior. ". . . it's the junkernaut . . . it's scrambling our brains."

Number Two grabbed his head and shook it. Garbage thought was drowning him. Now he, too, bumped against the wall, until his body froze with digital overload.

A tremendous roar shook the guardhouse, as the huge metallic talons of an industrial claw grabbed the front door and yanked it off the building. Outside, the junkernaut roared, rocking wildly back and forth. Jockey and the Gamester appeared from a doorway on its command level. The Gamester issued an order, and more industrial claws reached out from the monster, grabbed the guardhouse on all four sides, and tore it off its foundation. A large crater appeared, revealing the shaft leading to Amphora.

* * *

"You look jumpy, Zigler," said Max Ratiocinate, the cube-headed robot in charge of subsurface security. His deep bass voice boomed through a magnasound-box at his throat, and black metal digits kept him fastened to the counter.

The Scrapper Bar had been built by robots, with salvage parts and a robotic aesthetic. The mirror over the bar was the optical laser receiver from an interstellar laser ramjet. Guests sat around tables made from magnetic turbines. Cargo bay doors formed the bar itself, with a payload arm extending a drink toward Fin Zigler. "Particle spin, no ice?"

Fin drank the fizzling brew, but it gave him zero lift because Chief Max Rat continued bearing down with security service eyes. "Something putting you on edge, Zigler?"

"I had a long day, Max Rat. Ill-behaved convergence properties."

"Happens to the best of us," said Max Rat, and tuned in to one of his Dorje-men, who was reporting internally: *"I am at girder intersect five-seven-nine-five. Electrical storm in the lines, probably nothing serious."*

Max Rat's brow signal was a four-space sequencer, and, within that armor-plated cube, sophisticated reconnaissance was going on. Fin put down his empty glass. "I'm thinking about leaving the Junk Moon."

"And why is that?" asked Max Rat.

On the other side of the bar, robots stood in charging booths. A shower of current rained down around them, and was absorbed by hundreds of ports in their exterior plating. "Let me have a little buzz," said Max Rat to the bartending unit; his receptor portals opened with multiple snapping sounds, and a cascade of current descended from the ceiling. He had eyes on all four sides of his head, and he looked at Fin again. "Never hide anything from me, Zigler. It doesn't pay."

"Not hiding, Max Rat. Just relaxing."

"Something's cooking out there tonight." Max Rat peered through a porthole in the lounge, toward the torch-lit sky.

"Same old salvage fires," said Fin, doing his best to stay calm. He reflected on the burned-out Ratiocinates he'd met in Alien City, who lasted longer than other discharge vagrants, and always claimed to have been misunderstood. Would Max Rat wind up that way? The thought gave Fin hope. A good scrapper can outwire any machine ever made.

Max Rat ratcheted his head around, changing eye sets, receiving Fin on another pair. "I'm always looking at you, Zigler."

"You know I'm just a scrapper." Warily, Fin glanced down the bar at Max Rat's crew—heavily armed Dorje-men with metallic, predatory laughs.

"Then what's all this fretting about?" inquired Max Rat. "You're like a robot on a hot charge."

"Too many particle spins," answered Fin, pushing away his empty glass. He walked out through the back doorway, and Max Rat followed. Light from nearby Planet Immortal shone on them, and on the endless rows of ships. Max Rat checked his emotional index. "Paranoia level ten. Something's definitely up on this ball of ours."

"Don't overload your deductive interpreter," advised Fin, taking off on his backburner, just as Max Rat got a voice alert: *"Unscheduled entry, Amphora maintenance node."*

"Dorje-men Five," shouted Max Rat, "proceed to Amphora maintenance node."

"Copy that," came the distant response. Max Rat realized he was far from the break-in. He jumped into a command capsule and shot away. A portal to the interior opened up ahead of him, and he drove his capsule through. A red light pulsed on his tracking panel, and an alarm voice from the panel kept saying, *"unscheduled Amphora entry, unscheduled Amphora entry . . ."*

* * *

The junkernaut heaved and groaned, but remained fixed in one position, its primary movers having been reprogrammed by the Gamester; the heavy belts, treads, and wheels that formed its outer rim were in neutral. Though gears still slipped, causing it to jerk forward momentarily with hideous grinding sounds, Jockey, Lizardo, Upquark and the Gamester managed to climb down its face, landing beside the opening to the Amphora service shaft.

"Into the shaft!" ordered Jockey.

"Wait!" cried Upquark, receiving a familiar signal. He rolled back onto the Plain of the Unusable, and swept his gaze across the littered landscape. Link, Ren, and Specterales O were crossing an oily stream.

"Here!" he called, and turned on his headlamps to light the way for them.

From the horizon appeared another light. It grew bigger and brighter, and became the burning eyes of a flying Dorje-man. He swooped down toward them, his chest cannons glowing as he prepared to fire.

A telescoping arm shot out, and a great mechanical hand clamped the Dorje-man. He fired his full load of missiles, but the hand moved nimbly, avoiding the blasts and yanking him from the sky. He fought to get free as darkness closed over him. He was buffeted back and forth, banging against walls that fell apart as he gripped them. He switched on his illuminators, and saw ragged webs of pipe, armatures, and sputtering wires. He was slammed down, and took a three thousand five hundred-pound blow from a concrete-cracking machine. Then a rusting old asphalt roller pinned him against a pillar of gibbering robots; other crazed machines shuffled around him in a macabre dance. His worst nightmare had just come true. He'd been abducted by a junkernaut.

Outside, on the Plain of the Unusable, an entire flight of Dorje-men appeared on the horizon. "Hurry, hurry, hurry . . ." cried Upquark, leading Link, Ren, and O to the exposed Amphora shaft. "Adrian, this is the greatest ho-ha of our lives!"

Jockey urgently waved them into a transport pod.

The Gamester took the driver's seat, his forehead screen detailing the transportation sequence, which he'd gotten from a broken maintenance robot on the junkernaut. A stream of Electrish issued from his mouth slot, the pod was activated, and their glide began, along steeply angled tracks down into the moon's depths.

Through the meshwork of the shaft, Link saw a hollow world of girders and cross supports. Minutes later, the installation appeared— an assemblage of blockhouses resting on one of the great interior plates that stabilized the Junk Moon's core. The pod stopped, they stepped out, and the Gamester gave his order: "Dump."

"Dump," answered a voice from the junkernaut parked up above on the moon's surface, and the monster spewed an avalanche of defective robots through the crater where the guardhouse had recently been.

When the Dorje-men arrived, their descent was blocked by tons of feebly thrashing, half-charged robots of every kind. The Dorje-men hurried to an alternate maintenance node and tried the shaft there, but at the Amphora junction they were engulfed in another avalanche. An entire junkernaut had emptied itself, like the contents of a ten-story building tumbling down around them.

The Dorje-men burned a hole through the tangle of robots, and a seismic tremor was felt. "Be careful, you idiots," barked Chief Max Rat, arriving in his command capsule. "You've melted a main girder."

Gingerly he stepped into the aperture burned through the junk wall, and emerged beside the damaged girder, but now another wave thundered down around him, and the landfill of several worlds was in his way, bristling with mechanical heads and hands offering irrelevant assistance. A forest of animated shower curtains and smart bedding folded shut around him. A psychologically adept pillow murmured, "I love and understand you." Furiously Max Rat fired into it, and the pillow whispered with a dying sigh, "I . . . understand."

CHAPTER 14

"You can take notes, sing a song, whatever it is you do," said Jockey to Ren. "But Amphora is mine. Understand?"

Behind them the avalanche of junk had settled, with a few robotic parts still tumbling downward, clanking around their feet. "We'll see," she said evasively.

"Who're you working for?"

"I can't tell you that."

"But they want what Amphora has," he stated.

"They might."

"I'm carrying it out of here. If you've got a buyer for it, we can do business."

Lizardo and the Gamester returned from scouting out the vast installation. "No Dorje-men down here. They're all still up above, cutting through the junk. But we've got to act fast."

"Right," said Jockey, and the bulky pirate moved with surprising swiftness, following the Gamester. Using information he'd gotten from the Info Hog's files, the Gamester decoded the locks of one heavy door after another. Each hallway they entered was more hushed than the last, as if the Junk Moon and its surface tumult did not exist.

"We're cocooned against all outside sound and contaminating influences," explained Lizardo. As he said this, there was a slight movement beside his shoulder. The forked tip of his tongue shot out and he spun around.

"A spider can always get in," said Link. It was traveling across a brown-and-black web spun at the edge of the doorframe. "*Instita spadix*," murmured Link. "Her ancestors came from Earth. She herself probably stowed away on a ship from Planet Immortal." Before he could expand further on the spider, or before the Gamester could decode the lock, Jockey had burned impatiently through it; Link watched the spider speed in alarm back to her webbed apartment above the door frame. Equally alarmed was the scientist inside, as the door swung open and Jockey stepped through. "Who are you?" stammered the young man.

"Health inspector," replied Jockey, prodding him forward with the barrel of his laser pistol.

They were in a vast labyrinth of hallways. Carrier robots passed them in silence, but Lizardo told Jockey there was nothing to fear from them; their programs were too simple to interpret the break-in. "It's almost all robotic down here," he said. "They want as few humans as possible."

Ren swallowed hard. She was having trouble breathing. There was something inimical to her in this new atmosphere. No one else seemed bothered by it, but her pulse was racing. The young Amphora scientist snuck a glance at her, torn between his fear of Jockey and his interest in her symptoms. His interest won out. "Amphora gives off emanations which are dangerous to some planetary types. Cantusians are obviously among them. You'd better not go any farther."

"But I've got to."

"That would be unwise. Other planetary types are stimulated by it," he said, looking at Specterales O. The slowly spiraling rings around the pupils of O's eyes were filled with bright colors. Amphora's emanations had increased his sensitivity to the barren moon's plant life; the plants were whispering their deepest secrets to him.

Lizardo's scanner identified the young scientist as Zhang St. Clair, a graduate of the Consortium Academy, submicroscopic engineering his specialty.

"Listen," said Jockey, lifting Zhang up by the lapels of his white coat, "I want whatever it is that makes Amphora tick. I want you to box it or bottle it or whatever it is you need to do. And make it quick, I've had nothing to eat for hours."

As he set the young man down, another worker stepped out from an office, into Lizardo's gun barrel. "Keep walking," said Lizardo, and she fell into step beside her colleague. Automatically Lizardo read her identity solution: Erika Thayne, Consortium Academy, doctoral thesis on nonlocal quantum interaction and connection.

As she walked, she eyed her captors coldly. Her gaze stopped at Link. Her brows knit together. "You were at the Academy with me. Why are you sabotaging my work?"

"I'm not sabotaging anything," Link stammered. "I don't even want to be here." And for a moment he was back in school, shyly watching the beautiful Erika walk along on campus, head down, lost in thought. "I recognize you now," he said. "You were unapproachable."

"You've managed it well enough."

"This isn't alumni week," said Jockey, separating them with his weapon. "Where's the heart of this operation?"

Erika Thayne pointed to reinforced double doors ahead.

"Where are the rest of the people who work here?" asked Jockey.

"Sleeping. This is the graveyard shift. "

"And we aren't going to wake them. Now, open those doors."

Erika Thayne did as she was told. The area beyond was cavernous. Lizardo recognized an off-planet logo on a tunnel-shaped device that ran half the length of the building—a high-energy generator. Banks of computers faced it, each computer decorated by underground technicians with time on their hands: The faces had been laser sculpted; painted flames and figures surrounded all the trays; the grills were laser carved. Transparent sides showed illuminated interiors, where ice-blue coolants circulated, and tiny fans, lacquered with diamond dust, spun like little suns.

Lines of capacitors were stacked to spread voltage stresses, and heavy driver boxes surrounded the principal object in the area—a honeycomb of twelve hexagonal chambers, each one slightly larger than a human being. Ren froze in the doorway. The low hum coming from the honeycomb was at the same sickening ultrasonic frequency she'd heard outside, but tremendously intensified.

Lizardo turned to Jockey and said dryly, "We're not going to be able to transport this in a bottle."

"Maybe we don't need to, old man." He prodded Zhang. "What's it all about?"

"You wouldn't understand," intervened Erika contemptuously.

"Make it short and simple."

"On the most moronic level," she said. "Eternal life."

Ren could no longer tolerate the sound of the object before her. It wasn't loud, but it was complex beyond any sound she'd ever heard, and its complexity was attacking her nervous system. Her windpipe was constricting and she couldn't breathe. She backed out of the lab. The sound pursued her, resonating in her skull. It was like a needle stitching time . . . a million needles, stitching patterns inconceivably intricate. And perverse, though she could not say how. She only knew it filled her with repulsion and stole her breath, as if the sound could take her apart and dissolve her.

She entered Erika's office and closed the door against the noise. The atmosphere in the office was better. Erika had left her computer unprotected, and Ren began to copy files. Dunbosian would have to be satisfied with that, because whatever was out there would choke her if she stayed, and that wasn't in her contract.

Her gaze traveled over Erika's desk, which held no photographs of boyfriend, husband, children; there were no decorations, no feminine touches, nothing to relieve the bleakness. There was only dedication. And I'm here to steal that, thought Ren to herself, and felt ashamed, not for the first time, of her vocation.

Outside in the laboratory, Jockey pointed his laser pistol at the hexagonal chambers. "Show us how this thing works."

"We can't," said Zhang. "We're still running final tests."

"How many final tests does it need?" Jockey didn't wait for an answer. "You said eternal life. Well, which one of you wants to live forever?"

A change came over Zhang's face, as if a genie had just offered him his fondest wish. But the lapse was only momentary; his expression changed back again to that of the scientist who can't abide any alteration of the program. "Sorry, I can't help you."

Lizardo took hold of Zhang; his fangs showed two drops of venom. If he sinks those into me, thought Zhang, violent convulsions will be the least of it. "Second thoughts?" asked Lizardo.

Zhang moved through the rows of computers and driver boxes, and mounted the platform which held the huge honeycomb. Then he nodded back toward Erika, who went and stood before the main computer screen—a transparent wall covered with pulsating symbols. He said, "You know what to do."

She moved one of the symbols with her fingertips, sliding it to a new position on the enormous screen. The ends of all twelve chambers dilated open like the lenses of a dozen cameras. Link was still gazing at Erika; she'd been earmarked at school for great achievement—only to vanish almost immediately from the scientific community. It was assumed she'd contracted out to work on some remote planet. But all along she'd been nearby, in this secret sub-lunar project.

"All right," said Zhang, "I'm going in." He slid feet first into one of the middle chambers. Erika gave a new command, and the lens of the chamber was drawn shut behind him. Zhang was now invisible.

She addressed him through the intercom. Her coldness had passed, and excitement filled her voice. Upquark, sharing Link's anxiety, was rolling back and forth, trying to see the screen from which Erika was working. "Zhang," said Erika, "I need to backdate the final settings."

"Do it," came his voice from the speaker on her computer.

She dragged more of the symbols with her fingertips, initiating the opening sequences. Computers on both sides of her registered the activity.

"Superluminal channel open," she commanded.

"I'm in the vortex thread," returned Zhang's voice.

Specterales O was quivering with excitement. He could feel the activity in the hexagonal chambers pouring knowledge straight into his brain, concerning the secret, silent life of seeds and how they carried the ethereal force of the sun.

"I'm opening the inter-dimensional portal," said Erika, and instantly a completion symbol appeared on her screen. "That fast," she murmured to herself. The computer said, "Inter-dimensional imprint complete."

"I'm in on the quantum level," came Zhang's ecstatic voice.

"Can you control your shape?"

"I have complete control."

"What's going on?" asked Jockey, at Erika's elbow.

"Phase locking," said Erika in triumph. "He's reorganizing himself on a new level of reality." A mighty piezoelectric crack sounded in the lab, and she fell sideways, just as Zhang's body was ejected headfirst from its prison. Link felt something else rush into the room, as if the twelve chambers had breathed outward. Lizardo felt the exhalation too—an unpleasant sensation that the spacious laboratory had suddenly grown crowded.

A hard booming noise echoed Zhang's fall. It might've been a stone and not a man who'd hit the floor. Link watched in horror as Zhang's eyeballs rolled out of his head with the clatter of glass marbles. His skin was shiny, crystalline, his arms and legs inside his white uniform rigid with mineralization. Erika's body, too, was rigid and shiny.

Specterales O stared at them, and cried, "I understand."

Link stepped toward him, took him by the shoulders, stared into his eyes. "What do you understand, O?"

The rings of O's eyes were whirling with the greatness of his insight. "I understand the heart of a flower!" He raised his hand to start explaining, but the brilliance of his gaze lost all fluidity, his comprehension vanished, and the brightness in his eyes was merely light reflected off a brittle surface. He keeled over and his long spindly body cracked against the floor, echoing with a hard booming noise.

Jockey averted his gaze from O's mineralized body, remembering how he'd found the lonely Specterian wandering in Alien City, how he was responsible for him. "Once again, I seem to have—"

"—precipitated a disaster." Lizardo stepped over O's crystal corpse. His scanning chip was receiving a signal from Fin Zigler; the Ship Shapers had built their own transport artery through the interior of the Junk Moon, disguising it as a series of air ducts; you never knew when you might want to get somewhere in secret. They were waiting in it now, close by, but they wouldn't wait long.

Upquark knelt down on the floor beside his friend. "We can't leave O. Please, Adrian."

"It doesn't matter to him now," said Link, and gently pulled the little robot up and led him out into the hall.

The events in the lab had penetrated Erika's office. Ren was so weak that she could barely open the door. "Is it over?" she managed to ask them.

"No," replied the Gamester. "It's a whole new game."

The spider, repairing her web above the emergency exit, saw Jockey's party pass below her. She withdrew, and the figures quickly disappeared into the vast universe of tangled forms beyond. She herself had once descended through all of that, on windblown adventures of her own. It was not a trip she would care to make again. She resumed the repairing of her web, a difficult enough task in an uncertain world.

CHAPTER 15

"Just another junkernaut gone berserk," said Max Rat. "That's the way we're telling it."

He was standing with the Autonomous Observer at the newly built shaft to the Amphora installation; the other shaft was still filled with junk. "We've contained activity as well as we can with frequency stabilizers. But since Amphora went wild, we get weird readings. Spatial continuity breaks down momentarily, as if we had some kind of disruption in the motion series. The boys call it wrinkles in the fabric."

The Observer frowned. "Can you tell me why the Junk Moon's owner wasn't informed of all this?"

Max Rat made the merest gesture with his armored gripper, the equivalent of a human raising one eyebrow. "Miss Liftoff's not to be disturbed."

In other words, thought the Observer, Kitty's fallen in love again, doubtless with some wandering warrior. Having so little love in her own life, the Observer found her friend's indomitable romantic streak rather touching.

"Well, never mind. But these disruptions you speak of . . . couldn't they have been here all along and just gone unnoticed?"

"No way," said Max Rat. "We'd have caught them. You want my advice, put the Amphora installation on the next Shark out and dump it where the sun don't shine." His head clicked from position to position as he spoke. "I have a bit-level feel for trouble. It's on the way."

The Observer turned and gazed out over the Plain of the Unusable, dead, silent, only a pod moving here and there over gray heaps of scrap and through streams of slag and sludge. "The last stop," said Max Rat. "Could happen to any of us."

The Observer felt Amphora's pull on the landscape, small torsions at the edge of her awareness.

"Yeah," said Max Rat, "there's a slight corruption in the fundamental data, to your left, two hundred and eighty degrees." He kept it fixed in focus, kept her in focus too, from the other side of his square head. She was all right. She had a robot's sense of efficiency. Good-looking, too, if flesh-based programming did it for you. Personally, he preferred a little mechanical pants-presser he knew on one of the junkernauts. But the Observer was a class act, no doubt about that. Tough but sensible. She didn't hold it against him that a world of junk had fallen on him. Kitty Liftoff had insisted on letting junkernauts run around, which compromised security right there. One of them had been commandeered and nobody could do anything about it.

"Take a seat in the pod." He put her in his transport car, which carried them down through the new shaft. His Dorje-men followed, propelled by jetpacks.

"This Amphora installation," he asked, "it's some sort of health research lab, right?"

"You could call it that."

"Longevity studies?"

"What are you getting at?"

The transport car stopped. "My boys are jumpy since they had that junk dumped on 'em," said Max Rat. "So when you step out, don't make any sudden moves."

The Observer did as she was told. She wasn't too proud to take orders from a robot, and had no desire to be fried by a Dorje-man.

Amphora was dark except for the light reflected from the conduits that fed it. The Dorje-men took up defensive positions around the installation. "We found some things surprised us here." Max Rat's deep bass voice rumbled in the Observer's ear. "Things you wouldn't expect to find in a health lab. Show you what I mean."

Max Rat led her through the series of halls that cocooned the installation from outside influence, and guided her into the cavernous main room. The program was still functioning, despite the spectacularly unnatural death of two of its leading scientists. Other scientists were now manning the equipment, and they looked at Max Rat with suspicion. Clearly they didn't like the security robot rolling around in their world.

Max Rat pointed to the open chambers of the honeycomb. "The topography in those chambers doesn't track. There's no laminar architecture, yet something's being emitted. But we can't come up with any algebraic representations of it. If Amphora goes wild again, how do we grab it? How do we choke the living daylights out of it?"

The Observer had no suggestions. The twelve chambers looked like cannons aiming at her from infinity. Or even more unsettling, like the pupils of a many-eyed monster, staring at her with a gaze that couldn't be interpreted.

Max Rat escorted her out of the operations center. "What now?"

She had agents everywhere to see that laws were always followed to the letter. Her spies protected everybody's rights, including those of the vast robotic population, most of whom wound up here on the

Junk Moon, run-down and demented. Thousands of committees, whose members she screened, were continuously meeting to create further checks and balances for fairness. She'd spent her life arresting enemies of correct procedure, and now, quite suddenly, she had the feeling that the only threat that mattered was coming from one of the Consortium's own projects, which she had personally guided.

CHAPTER 16

Gregori Man o' War had lingered on the Junk Moon at Kitty Liftoff's invitation, his visit stretching out to a week while underneath flowed the slow course of his courtship. Now at last, despite the shabby state of his uniform, his perfumes and pomades, and the barbs coiled in his skin, he was in Kitty's bedroom, sharing a vintage bottle of Hermetian wine with her.

He stood at the window, gazing at the dark panorama of armaments below. It was magnificent to behold. Rich generals had this feeling daily; it was his for the moment. "I'm honored you've invited me to your tower."

"The view is instructive. As enlightening as a temple of the alien gods."

"I've seen plenty of those. First you have to climb uphill," said Gregori. "But this—" He gestured with his wineglass at the rows of first-class ships.

She slid a finger over a control panel in the windowsill, and curtains came together, brushing past their shoulders and laying a lacy pattern over the harsh outlines of the war machines outside. "If we look too long the ships will start talking to us."

"Weapons are restless, it's true," said Gregori. "That's why so many go off." There were planets awaiting him, and thinking of them added a backdrop for pleasure. No doubt her rows of battleships were a similar stimulant for her. "They call you the Angel of Death," he said.

"No one has died in my arms," she said, wrapping them around him.

"Still, I feel I'm surrounded."

"Then I advise surrender."

His dirty collar was removed, and his shabby uniform. His body wore the scars she'd imagined. Hers, as her dress came off, was as perfect as he'd expected. He closed his eyes, and when he opened them, he saw how deeply she was moved by passion: her face was transformed, the flesh seeming to glow from within. He was relieved that his alien form had not inhibited her.

Far from inhibiting her, his scars excited her. They were a map of his passage through dangerous star worlds. With a little gasp, she felt the tug of those worlds, as if they were still connected to him, sewn into his scars. His energy was tremendous, and she felt reservoirs of her own energy opening to meet this deep-space captain. He was unique, he was priceless. He was the lover she'd longed for in her sleepless nights. This was perfect pleasure and she never wanted it to end. Just as we are now, let us stay.

A moan escaped her lips, and he paused in his lovemaking, for the flesh of her face had grown slightly transparent, and this was not a thing he'd seen before. He looked into her eyes and saw a gaze of terror. Beneath the transparency of her cheeks a play of tiny crystals could be seen, in an outward swirling pattern. The crystalline pattern reached the surface of her skin and her flesh hardened into something like smoothly polished porcelain. She blinked her eyes and the eyelids gave off a cracking sound.

She shrieked with pain, threw him from her, and leapt from the bed. She raced toward her dressing table mirror, caught sight of her face and swayed. Gregori, just behind her, saw her eyes turning to marbles. She fell, her hand reaching for the table's edge, and Gregori heard another series of cracking sounds, as the joints of her fingers froze. She struck the floor, and a little cloud of crystals broke off her. As her body rolled he saw a piece of her ear had cracked; an instant later it separated and fell to the floor.

Every barb in his skin erected, to protect him against whatever was turning her to glass. Her naked torso was hardening, her surgically sculpted breasts achieving the final perfection of a statue. The transparency had reached her hips and thighs, the whirling crystalline pattern seizing the flesh from within and transforming it to stone. With cracking sounds at her kneecaps, the crystalline wave passed downward, and finished at her feet, which turned outward with a mineral heaviness and became motionless. He thought of statues he'd seen in cities ruined by war, statues knocked from their pedestals into the rubble. Kitty had fallen from hers, and was silent. Her eyes held him. They were jewels of sorcery, their facets gleaming with an understanding of fathomless, terrible mystery. Gregori had ripped priceless jewels from an alien idol's head, but he'd never seen anything to compare with this. Each facet seemed like hardened silk, secreted by a creature quite beyond Kitty's measure. She'd been trapped by it, and he was trapped too, held by the web of Kitty's crystalline eyes. He heard an eye-sensor clicking above his head, triggered into alarm by the drastic change in Kitty's retinal pattern.

The door to her chamber burst open and her security force entered with their weapons drawn. The protection she'd promised him was no longer hers to give.

"The filthy beast has killed her."

Gregori saw it was pointless to fight here. An experienced warrior knows when to make a stand. He allowed himself to be taken. His battle must come later.

CHAPTER 17

By orders of the Observer, Kitty's corpse had not been moved from her bedroom in the tower. The team of pathologists were just leaving, stymied by a human body transformed into mineral.

Metron the Immortal stood over Kitty now, speaking to the Observer in his dry voice of rustling leaves.

"Such research has risks. We minimized them, but the intruders activated Amphora too soon."

"But if Amphora is so dangerous, why are we housing it?"

"It's your only path to immortality."

"There's an official inquiry under way. I need to say more than that to the Consortium."

The wraith-like Immortal in his black monk's robes seemed an unlikely figure in the voluptuous atmosphere of Kitty's bedroom. He stretched his hand out to the Observer and touched her face. An aroma like sweetgrass emanated from his fingers. He lightly traced her features, then felt the pulse in her temple. "You have strong *uxub*. You'll last a very long time. But you're not immortal." His fingers touched her throat, making a further assessment of her constitution and she felt muscles which had been tense for years relaxing and softening.

For one delicious instant, she remembered how it was to be a child, with no intimation of age and its sorrows.

The old kite took his hand away and said, "The true taste of immortality will come to you only through Amphora."

"It won't come to us at all unless we can contain Amphora's power." She looked down at Kitty, frozen at her feet, Kitty's eyes without expression, pure and placid, but very dead.

Metron said, "Tell those to whom you answer that I will secure Amphora against further disaster." He knelt, and ran his frail hand over Kitty's lifeless face. Then he rose. The Observer thought of a dried flower on a tall stalk shaken by a breeze; his hair was like the gray fluff of a dandelion, and she recalled the first time she met him and how she'd feared he might blow away. He said, "If you wish us to abandon the project, we shall. We'll return Amphora's constituent properties to the depths of the cosmos."

"I'll give your thoughts to the Consortium board."

"Give them this thought too." Tenderly he touched her throat again, and again she experienced the resilient outlook of a child. He said, "This isn't magic. Your cells react to my level of relaxation."

"And Amphora gives you that?"

"Remember what I told you. Amphora gives me time. With time, one learns whatever one wants and needs. As I've said before, we're only here for you, and once Amphora has succeeded we'll leave." He held up both his arms, letting the black fabric fall backward. "Look at these laughable imitations of limbs. But still, with them I can grasp you."

To her astonishment, Metron embraced her, but so delicately she thought again of flowers. She'd never felt happier in her life, though she was standing over the body of a dead friend. "Why is your touch so intoxicating?" she whispered.

"The answer is always the same: you sense your own immortal nature. That perception is intoxicating. It has little to do with me."

He released her from his sweet embrace. "I've instructed the Amphora staff on what's required. They understand perfectly."

Slowly he left the room, his long robe rustling around him as if he were accompanied by a crowd of silent mourners. The Observer wished that he had stayed so he could touch her one more time and give her back that unexpected sense of childish optimism.

But when she looked down at Kitty and felt Kitty's death, her heart tensed back to its former patterns; the muscles of her throat constricted to their bureaucratic settings. Amphora's enchantment was over for her. As head of planetary intelligence, her affection for the Immortal didn't matter, nor did her personal desire for eternal youth. Her job was to protect the planet's citizens from harm. She couldn't jeopardize more lives. Her agency mandate was clear: to shield a prosperous, happy people. Their longevity must come from the usual medical methods, not from a dubious experiment.

She had Kitty's body carried to the roof of the tower, and placed there, to stare out over her creation, the Junk Moon of war dreams. Kitty had loved it, and could look at it now with the eyes of eternity.

CHAPTER 18

Gregori Man o' War's record went against him. Bound in electronic manacles, he was turned over to the brain-cleaners. A drone strapped him into a chair and applied electrodes to his head. Gregori watched sullenly as they bio-froze his barbs to render them inactive during the procedure. Afterward, he wouldn't know how to use them anymore.

"An interesting specimen," said the Chief Neurolator in the control booth. "I've never been assigned to one before."

Gregori had faced every kind of desperate situation, and each had left its scar. Once he'd drifted, parched with thirst, in a lifeboat on the asphalt-like sludge of a foul sea inhabited by creatures resembling ragged little rolls of tarpaper. They'd become his only source of food. His organs of digestion hadn't quite known what to make of them, and a portion of their oily makeup migrated to his collagen membranes, with the greatest deposits in his cranium.

"You may begin," said the Chief Neurolator.

"Mind transfer activated."

Gregori's eyes widened as cell wonking began. The parade of his life sped by, with the usual attendant sensation of being elongated down a black hole. But the current that attacked him had to struggle like an otter in an oil slick. Gregori's brain still wore the overcoat it had acquired in the asphalt sea.

"Transfer complete. Fully catatonized."

"Good. He's flown big ships and has extensive war experience. He's to be assigned to War God six. They like that sort of thing in a War God cataton."

When his assignment forms were completed, Gregori was lifted from the chair and prodded forward. Manacles were not applied. He shuffled out of the brain chamber, in bad shape, with psychomotor retardation and a terrible headache. But he wasn't a cataton.

CHAPTER 19

The Intelligence Agency's office had gone to the highest security settings. None of the Observer's agents were present, only the eleven Consortium members. The twelfth floated before them in a life-size hologram: Kitty Liftoff, now deceased. On either side of Kitty's image, equations continually changed as the Agency's computers tried to figure out what had caused her metamorphosis.

"Cells are organized rocks," said Vladimir Korolov, gazing at the hologram of Kitty.

"I beg your pardon?" asked the Observer.

The elderly chemical engineer liked to startle people with oblique observations, and he didn't miss an opportunity now. "It's not the least bit fantastic to say that living cells came from minerals. On Earth and everywhere else that organic life got going, tiny bits of stone took on the capacity of engines. Earth was covered with mineral soup at the start, and out of that soup our one-celled ancestors put themselves together. We all come from minerals. And something in Amphora reversed Kitty's cells to their original mineral state." To himself, Korolov remarked on how beautiful Kitty looked. In her absolute stillness, there was the aura of immortality. It was what the pharaohs had sought, the perfect preservation of the dead. He himself was wizened like a pharaoh, and like them he very much wanted to be preserved, but not in resin and cotton windings, and not in crystal. He wanted the living preservation that Amphora would bring. The accident at the installation was upsetting, but he would get in there himself and set the Amphora engineers straight, just as he did when soapsuds got out of control. Those Amphora engineers were probably too conservative; that was usually the trouble in his experience, people afraid of taking chances because their jobs were on the line. Well, his wasn't.

Pointing at Kitty's image, the Observer said, "She'd been living on top of the Amphora project since it started. In that, she differed from the rest of you. But your cellular signatures are stored in Amphora too."

"Does that mean we're all in danger?" asked Dick Spinrad. His quiet, mathematician's mind was rarely discomfited. Human emotions might flare up but numbers were always tranquil. However, the image of Kitty's frozen corpse hovered in front of him, and its tranquility was the upsetting thing. Apparently there was to be no decay, no corruption of her flesh. One wondered, was there some spark of life in this icy being? Was Kitty trapped inside? Would her eternity be spent in this solemn idol's form?

"Yes, you might be in danger. Until we know more, I advise shutting down the Amphora project."

"Out of the question," said Kurt Kashian. "Hire more scientists to iron out the problem, and send me the bill. I'm sure I speak for everyone here. We're ready to pay for this program's success." Kurt had not been feeling particularly immortal this morning. He'd been feeling what anyone over a hundred felt—a third of his life was gone. Uncertainty lay everywhere. There was Kitty looking like a garden ornament.

"Roy, what about you?" asked the Observer.

"We can't stop now," replied Cosmopolis. "We're too close to completion." He'd had a commemorative immortality medal designed with his family motto on its circumference, entwined with the olive leaves of spring. "Humanity won't forgive us if we abandon its most cherished hope. I care little for immortality myself. I'm nothing so special. But mankind is meant to live forever."

Gordon Singh of Sun Centralis asked, "Isn't it possible, Observer, you've overreacted? Kitty's death has shocked us all, but you've been exposed to it close up. Maybe too close. And it's made you too cautious."

"My job is to protect you."

"With all due respect," said Kurt, "I don't need your protection in this matter." Glancing at his wrist communicator, he checked the positions of the mercenary army that policed his mining interests throughout the Corridor; a squadron of his soldiers was policing the Intelligence Agency's building now. Turning his attention back to the Observer, he said, "I wonder how you can even think of dismantling such a great program."

"I have to think of it. This is a piece of technology run wild."

"Is that what the Immortals believe?" asked Raimi Kashian.

"No, it isn't," admitted the Observer. "They believe they're in control of the project again."

"Don't you trust them?"

"They're very wise, but this technology isn't exactly their own. It was given to them by the Ancient Aliens. Handling it may require more wisdom than even the Immortals possess."

Cosmopolis shook his head and smiled in his most friendly way. "This isn't like you, Observer, to deny humanity its birthright."

In Roy's voice, the Observer heard only kindness and philanthropy, but kindness and philanthropy had marked the end of planets before this one. In desperation she looked toward the women, and saw them dreaming of their own immortal beauty.

"We're all friends here," interjected Paul Buckler gently. "We've known each other for ages." Some of the others had given him unpleasant looks, for he'd designed the Amphora installation and now it was acting up. But it wasn't his fault that security had failed and a mercenary had gotten in. Kitty, floating there in the air in front of them, had brought about the failure with her tolerance for rolling wheels of junk. "I can go up there and make Amphora absolutely impenetrable."

"I'm certain you can," said the Observer. "But Amphora's problems are internal. The mercenaries were just catalysts for an existing flaw in the program."

"I've nothing but admiration for your judgment," said Gordon Singh. "But we're one step from achieving our goal, and we mustn't let ourselves be drawn into paranoia about faulty technology." Gordon had begun to notice lapses of memory lately. Yesterday a word had eluded him for hours, like an imp out of a bottle. That bottle was his brain, and a recent holoscan had shown a slight degree of atrophy in the cortex. Nothing pathological, his doctors had assured him. Just normal aging.

"We have no idea what powers Ancient Alien technology tapped," countered the Observer. "They were a highly advanced species, a million years ahead of us. How can we expect our scientists to flawlessly handle their knowledge?"

"Really, Observer," said Olympia Clendenning, "this is hysteria." The old woman was herself on the edge of hysteria. Amphora mustn't be stopped, under any circumstances. Kitty had died; well, it was her own fault, she'd always been too casual, with men, mercenaries, and other things. As for the two Amphora scientists, they sacrificed themselves for *me*. Their sacrifice mustn't be in vain, my replacement organs always feel like replacements, running on timers, switching on and off according to software, sometimes audibly.

Her wrinkleless face, on which everyone complimented her, was undependable; her facial muscles might pull her lips into an idiotic grin when sympathy was called for. Her artificial eyes sometimes brought images that were hopelessly distorted, as if she were looking through thick, wavy glass. The beautiful face and body she showed the world were an elaborate costume draped on an aged skeleton. At times, that's what she fell like, a little old skeleton shuffling around. ". . . hysteria, Observer. We mustn't fall victim to it."

"I don't know how relevant this is," said the Observer, placing on the table a scrap of paper made from the pith of some spongy alien plant. The figures on it vaguely resembled hieroglyphs. "One of my agents transcribed this several years ago. I regret having dismissed it when it was brought to my attention then. It's from a dead planet whose location was beyond the last Corridor station."

"You were right to dismiss it," said Susie Tsugaru. "Fables of dead planets have nothing to do with Amphora."

"What was the planet's name?" asked Martin Faircloth, sensing a nice story for his *Galaxa Noticia*.

"According to this document, it was called Phasma. We've been unable to locate it, but the Outer Star Fields are largely uncharted." The Observer read from the spongy paper. "*We played like children with the ancient machine. And now the machine has destroyed us.* The nature of these language characters indicates a prescientific civilization."

"Perfect." Faircloth made a copy of the document. "Thank you very much. If you have any more stories like these, I can certainly use them."

Hearing how lightly Faircloth took the matter, the Observer reflected that perhaps she *was* overwrought. But she'd touched Kitty's mineralized body; she'd looked into Kitty's polished eyes. She'd seen the terror of the void. The Consortium had only seen a hologram. "I wish all of you would talk with the Immortals."

"That's a bad idea," said Susie Tsugaru.

"Why?"

"They mustn't be disturbed. They mustn't think we've lost faith in them. What if we alienated them?"

"The Immortals would never put us at risk," declared Cosmopolis, summing up the feelings of humanity at large, as was his way. "They're here to save us, not to destroy us. We're the heart of tomorrow. We're its guardians." *Heart of tomorrow* was a phrase in the speech which he was preparing to deliver to the entire planet when Amphora was complete. He saw that the phrase had gone home to his audience, and was grateful to the Observer for the opportunity to try it out. "We're not only the guardians; we're the guarantee that there will *be* a tomorrow. A never-ending tomorrow in which we shall all share. This is the rarest opportunity any human being has ever had, to further our race, to lift it to a status that is nearly divine." He was speaking without his script, he was inspired. Words swam up in him with the exuberance of young fish, astonishing him with their brightness. "The sun has bequeathed us its light and its eternity." Brilliant fish, with richly colored tails, an endless school of them rose sparkling. They swam upward, and their beautiful scales flew off, scattering through him, exalting him to the heights of prophecy.

His gaze swept the table, seeing the immortality of the race there, in these friends. Then he fell forward, for too many schools of fish were crowding tumultuously in his brain. As his head struck the table there was a loud crack, and he felt his skull splitting like a fishbowl, and then he felt nothing at all. All the fish swam out, and the heart of tomorrow stopped.

The Observer placed her fingers gently on his forehead. The skin was smooth and stony. His crystallized eyes gazed sightlessly at the tabletop. His outstretched fingers were like carved marble. Now, she thought, no one knows who I am. Roy was gone, taking with him her original identity. He'd severed her from her past, and now he'd been severed from his own. She felt an awful kinship with his crystallized corpse.

Completely insensitive, thought Olympia Clendenning. The woman has no heart at all.

CHAPTER 20

The Ship Shapers helped Jockey's party to escape, but Ren's ship had to be abandoned, caught in a sweep made by Junk Moon security. "It's Planet Immortal for all of us," said Jockey. "I've no fuel for a longer trip."

He deposited Link, Ren, and the two robots in Alien City, and he and Lizardo headed for their hideout in the Serpentian quarter of the city.

"It's back to the streets for me," the Gamester said to Link, attempting to be cheerful.

"But what will you do?" asked Upquark. "Who will replace your battery pack when it runs down?"

"If my preliminary calculations about Amphora are correct, the condition of my battery pack won't matter."

"Why not?"

"Goodbye, my friends. It's dangerous for you to be seen with me. I'm not sure if we will ever meet again." And he rolled off, reviewing his Amphora file. On his internal screen, he analyzed the information he'd hurriedly gathered on the two young scientists and Specteralis O at the moment of their crystallization.

"The periodic lattice of crystal replaced the looser protein bonds of living beings," he said to himself. "Carbon became silica, the lattice of the dead. And as that took place, something entered the Amphora installation, something altogether improbable. A game beyond calculation."

* * *

In the hope of finding a freighter captain who would take them to Cantus, Ren, Link, and Upquark wandered down the side streets, finally resting on a bench outside a cut rate rejuvenation parlor. Such parlors catered to newly arrived aliens who wanted to look more human. Other stores on the street sold cheap artificial limbs to mutilated mercenaries.

Every now and then Link observed a hopeful alien or crippled mercenary entering the rejuv shop. After a few such clients had come and gone, a surgeon on his break stepped out. His eyes immediately fell on Ren's bare arms and the vestigial membrane that resembled the wings of a butterfly.

"You must be new here," he said, stepping toward her. "I would consider it an honor to sever your membrane for you." He was an Exhulian, whose long bony tail and spiny back fin had been surgically removed to conform to the human mold. As he spoke, he stroked the air behind him, as if unconsciously feeling for what he'd sacrificed. "My price is the best you'll find anywhere, and my work is perfect."

"If I should ever have it done, I'll think of you," she said, politely.

He looked at her curiously, as if wondering why she wasn't rushing to have such a simple operation. "Would you, at least, spread the membrane so I might give you a professional appraisal?"

To humor him, she opened her arms, spreading the membrane like a moiré shawl, so he could study it. "Yes, all the veins are in the right place. It's an easy fix." He paused as she closed the patterned shawl back around herself. "There's no need to be attached to these vestigial appendages that mark us as outsiders."

But Ren would be an outsider no longer; she was heading back to Cantus, though she'd never thought such a thing was possible. Cantus was a retrograde civilization. Her people were mindlessly absorbed in continuous musical performance. They couldn't build a house with straight walls, but were the vainest creatures in the universe because their love songs were known throughout the Corridor. In such a shambles, it was easy to hide, and Link, too, would be safe there; his peculiar musical ability would be appreciated.

* * *

"We mustn't be discouraged, old man." Jockey was seated in Lizardo's Alien City apartment, balancing a large plate on his lap. Noting that nothing remained in it but grease, he reached out for another dish, which was piled high with baked ghastogeebs, the little lizards rigid as pretzels. Lizardo looked at them uncomfortably. "Would you eat *me* if rations were short?"

"It saddens me to hear you speak that way."

"If I were prepared properly? With your favorite sauce?"

The pirate crunched the head of one of the little lizards. "Perhaps if we marinated you."

Lizardo was stretched out on a reptilian-shaped couch with recessed tail rest. Behind him was a window whose curtains were embroidered with pale green salamanders. The building catered to Serpentians, and the architecture was that of the hibernaculum, rounded walls and ceilings providing the tenants with the closely wrapped feeling of a cave.

Jockey munched thoughtfully, the ghastogeeb's claws protruding from his lips. "I've done Link a great favor by getting him away from that Agricultural Plain of his. It was too dull a place for a bright lad."

"Yes, you've done wonders for him. He's in hiding in Alien City, the Observer's agents are after him, and his life's work is in ruins."

"The pretty Cantusian is with him. She'll cheer him up."

"She's on the Observer's list too. They'd be better off apart."

"No, we mustn't split them up. My policy is always to foster young love."

"You should've given him some money."

"I'm a little strapped at present." Jockey touched a napkin to his lips. "A pity we were unable to snatch that Amphora ice machine. Someone would have paid us handsomely for it."

Lizardo slithered off the couch, and dropped into a heated sandpit sunk in the floor. He sprawled out, arms and feet extended, endothermic pleasure running through him.

Jockey set his plate aside. "What I want to know is—what disagreeable process turned Specterales O into an icicle?"

"It's on that bookshelf." Lizardo pointed with the tip of one claw. "In the Serpentian Chronogrammatic."

"I can't rise at the moment, old man. And my grasp of the Serpentian language is not what it should be."

Lizardo gazed lazily up at the curved ceiling. He and Jockey had finished a bottle of strong Serpentian wine, and he was feeling its effects. The ceiling was plated with intricate scales, over which he cast a dreamy eye. The hanging lamps were shaped like serpent eggs, delicately tinted. He focused on an electronic sensor in the chain of the nearest lamp and blinked; the instrument read the movement of his eyelids, and the color of the egg changed from blue to gold. Yes, that's better, he thought, as the golden light spilled on the warm sandpit. But despite his languid mood, thoughts of navigation played in Lizardo's head, of azimuth and glide slope, of position, velocity, and vernier control. A pair of skylights shaped like snake's eyes looked out onto the night sky. Staring at the stars, he calculated the precise astrometric parallax measurements by which to fly back to Serpentia.

Jockey reached past his stomach in an attempt to remove his boots for greater comfort, but his face reddened dangerously and he thought better of it. Instead he lowered his sinuous recliner to the horizontal position. "To the bookshelf, you slack lizard. If it contains the answer, we must have it."

Lizardo, sighing, rose from the warm sand. He'd resigned his Serpentian commission to fly mercenary with Jockey. A few medals, some old uniforms, and the bookshelf in this Alien City apartment were all that remained of his previous life, and so it was nostalgia as much as Jockey's insistence that moved him toward the bookshelf now.

The heated floor warmed his claws and the underside of his tail as he slithered across the room. "Amphora used a superluminal connection. Before those scientists crystallized, they enjoyed a tremendous increase in perception."

"You're remarkably perceptive yourself, old man," said Jockey, unable to follow. But that's why one had a lizard aboard. He rotated his recliner again, which brought him eye level with a piece of sculpture—two fire newts mating, the male curling one hind limb around the female's neck, and his large cheek glands rubbing hers. Suggestive stuff, no doubt, if one is a lizard. But still, look at the detail.

Lizardo stood before the bookshelf, scanning its volumes. The Serpentian Chronogrammatic stood out from the others, for it was bound in reptilian skin. Lizardo carefully removed the book and opened it, the hinged scales of the cover flattening against his claws. He ran the pointed tip of a claw down the table of contents. Jockey asked, "A rare volume?"

"The private notes of my great-grand Uncle Ophidian." Lizardo found the chapter he was seeking, and read several paragraphs of the timeworn page, then turned to Jockey. "Uncle Ophidian refers to something he calls the Efficient Presence. Any creature that possesses it can travel into the privities of the nuclear forces."

"English, old man, if you would."

"It is English."

"Not that of your old star fighter." Jockey crossed his hands over his paunch, and Lizardo crossed back to the sandpit with the book in his claws. He settled down on the edge of the pit with his feet in the sand and his tail curled neatly behind him on the floor. He touched the open page. "Amphora tapped the Efficient Presence. But to understand, you need to read the second scholium up to the seventh proposition."

"Condense it if you would, old man, I believe I overate." Jockey attempted to roll the other way, but the sinuous lines of his chair defeated him again. "How did your uncle end up, by the way?"

"It's his skin that holds these pages together."

"An intimate memoir."

"He wrote it in a penal colony, and bound it with what was available."

"I take it his views were unpopular."

"Here's the second scholium: *In the abyss, I, Ophidian, exercised control over the principium essendi. My demonstrations showed that every effect is consequent of knowledge.*"

"You have me there, old man."

Lizardo closed the book. "Before the assembled leading lights of Serpentian science, Uncle Ophidian demonstrated the mental nature of the subatomic world. He produced effects in a bubble chamber of liquid hydrogen by gazing at it. It was actually hyperchannel amplification, and with it he created ornamental patterns in the tracks of subatomic particles. It's said he wrote his name with them. Do you understand what that means?"

"I may be a trifle vague on the point."

"He signed his name in matter. Since he didn't like the scientific establishment, the bureaucrats on Serpentia feared he might share his knowledge with a foreign power. So they put him into the penal colony."

"A harsh decision, surely."

"Serpentia is a cautious planet. In any case, that's when he wrote the Chronogrammatic. Following which, he escaped and sent the Chronogrammatic to the family."

"Where is he now?"

"In hiding."

"Well, let's sell his memoir."

"I wouldn't think of it."

"What a pity." Jockey managed to roll off the recliner onto the floor, and struggled, wheezing, to his feet. "We've got to raise some money."

"And how do we do that?"

"I'm well thought of in Alien City. We'll find an investor."

"To invest in what exactly?"

Jockey threw an arm around Lizardo. "New horizons. Always new horizons."

* * *

But rather than finding an investor, Jockey found several people wishing to kill him, for the old star fighter already owed considerable sums, and were it not for the razor-sharp spines on Lizardo's tail, trouble might have overtaken them.

"Hello, I see a chap I used to know. That sun sail captain over there. An expert in orbital stability."

The expert was himself unstable now, his body swaying. He's got the stupor of space, thought Lizardo, taking a visual reading of the captain's vital signs. Too much time in bad ships. "Not a likely investor," Lizardo murmured, as the sun sailor extended his cap for coins.

Jockey crossed the street and threw his last bit of change in the overturned cap.

"Jockey, you don't forget," muttered the sun sailor.

The two captains exchanged a few words; then Jockey moved on with Lizardo. "Ion sickness," muttered Jockey.

Lizardo nodded. He'd seen that the sun sailor's identity solution had been fuzzy, a sure sign of dying.

Up ahead, a teenager had the crowd's attention, bounding on a time trampoline, sinking deeply, then hurtling high, virtual reality lenses covering his eyes. With each ascent he rushed into a possible future; on each descent he sank into the past.

"He's going for a new record," said an excited voice at Jockey's shoulder, as the tramper plunged deeply into the fabric of the arcade trampoline, then became a blur sailing upward, arms flattened to his sides, head tilted backward to the sky. The trampoline's marquee recorded his velocity, and the meter showed both the elevation reached and the point in the future that it represented—a three millennium ride.

"Look at his face," said the excited bystander at Jockey's shoulder. "The guy's in ecstasy. The visuals you get up there are amazing." But Lizardo's scanning chip caught something else—a distortion in spatial continuity around the tramper as he broke the record and the crowd burst into cheers.

"What's that about?" hissed Lizardo.

"Have I missed something, old man?"

"A wrinkle in the fabric," said Lizardo.

"What fabric?"

"Reality."

The new record holder used retrofiring to break his fall, indicating that he was done tramping for a while. How done wasn't apparent until the air cushions switched on beneath him. They should have broken his fall, but he was already broken when the cushions caught him: a hundred pieces of crystal fountained up in the air jets, and one of the pieces was his head. His face showed a joyful smile. The custodian of the ride was throwing switches as fast as he could, to shut the fountain off, for a display of shattered body parts dancing in the air was not good advertising for the time trampoline. As the air jets ceased, the other parts of the tramper clattered down in a pile on the now rigid trampoline.

Lizardo slithered out of the crowd toward the sun sailor, who was still begging but without motion. His body was frozen, transparent. As Jockey touched him, he splintered into crystal shards.

"He was weak, so it got him too," said Lizardo.

"It?"

"Everything has changed since the Amphora break-in." Lizardo's poison glands were swelling his collar of white scales, and his tail was snapping back and forth. "You've probably destroyed the planet."

Jockey considered this for a moment. "Tell me truthfully, old man. Do you think it will tarnish my reputation?"

CHAPTER 21

Dr. Amphibras entered the Observer's office with a folder in his webbed hands. Amphibras preferred old-fashioned filing methods, for he was an old-fashioned fellow altogether, with his immaculate gray suit, his blue cravat, and his unquenchable loyalty.

"I haven't received anything new on Link," said the Observer. "Have you any leads?"

Amphibras shook his head apologetically. "Still missing, along with the Cantusian."

"I've been reading his book again."

"So I see, ma'am."

"Ants come off in it better than we do."

"Ma'am?"

"If an ant contracts a disease she'll leave the nest and attach herself by the legs and pincers to a blade of grass. And there she dies."

Amphibras changed color sympathetically. "Most touching."

"She dies alone to prevent her infection from spreading to the nest. Do you think if any members of the Consortium were infectiously ill, they'd go off by themselves somewhere and cling to a blade of grass?"

"The image does not come readily to mind."

"They'd burn the world down, Amphibras, to try and live for-ever." The Observer closed Link's book with a sigh. "All right, what else have you got for me?"

Amphibras's long sticky tongue shot out, attached itself to a page, and turned it over. "Memo from the Consortium about Project Amphora. Reiterating their great desire for the project to go forward. Requesting you not to delay because of the death of Mr. Cosmopolis, that it would be his wish for you to continue, et cetera. And your presence is requested at the Cosmopolis memorial service."

"You'll go in my place."

Amphibras's tongue shot out again, and the page turned. "*Associated Planets* is running a story concerning *an incident on the Junk Moon . . . what happened, is there a cover-up . . .*"

"Call Martin Faircloth. Tell him Starweb must run a reassuring rebuttal on all its affiliates. We've got to keep the public from panicking."

"Ma'am, I suggest we say an alien ship sought assistance on the Junk Moon. Owing to an unusual energy drive, there was an accident during repair. Damage was contained and so on and so forth."

"Amphibras, you could write for the tabloids."

"Thank you, ma'am. It's not a position to which I aspire." Tongue out, page turned. "Olympia Clendenning is up to her old tricks again."

"What is it this time?"

"Adulterating her products with banned fillers."

"That woman is impossible. Issue another citation. Tell her it's the last one. Tell her if there's one more violation, the shareholders will take over the company."

* * *

Olympia stared at the citation against her company. "How dare she do this to me?"

Her General Counsel was a Sponge-head from Planet Parazo. He said, "We could stop using the fillers the Observer objects do."

"You know how much we save using those fillers."

To the Sponge-head, the saving seemed trivial compared to the trouble the fillers caused. The muscle layers of his huge head worked nervously, causing the soft vents to open and close with sounds of anxiety. He hated infractions of the rule, but even more he hated battling Olympia. He was certainly no expert in the nuances of the human form, but he knew the youthful-looking body in front of him was a shell in which a senile creature dwelled. Reminding himself that he was dealing with an old woman, with an old woman's ways, he spoke slowly, as if to a child, his mouth vent working gently. "The Observer can do what she says. Your company will go to the shareholders."

Olympia was trembling. She brought the Observer's image up in her holocom viewer—a life-size transparent cylinder in which the Observer seemed contained as if in a glass cage. "I'll crush her."

"Excuse me?" The Sponge-head pretended not to have heard the vehemence in Olympia's voice.

"I'll kill her."

"Mrs. Clendenning, please—" The Sponge-head was wonderfully adept in the law, but human emotion was not something he absorbed readily. The vents in his head were expanding and contracting more forcefully, the porous brown tissue growing moist with nervous secretions.

"She's young." Olympia stared at the Observer's image. "She has everything. Look at her skin. That's natural. Isn't it the most exquisite thing in the world?"

To the Sponge-head, it was in no way exquisite, lacking deep creases and huge pores.

Olympia circled the cylinder in which the Observer's three-dimensional image seemed to walk, to turn, to gaze into the lights of a distant city. The background changed and now the Observer was inside the city, walking down one of its streets. It was a holo-recording made by the Intelligence Agency for Consortium members, to suggest that the Observer was everywhere, watching, looking out for their interests. The complete recording showed her in every major city—in corporate hallways, military installations, and stock exchanges—always unseen by those around her.

Olympia pointed a trembling finger. "She's completely confident. Nothing compares to skin like that."

The Sponge-head stared at the Observer's image. Though he was protected by his knowledge of the law, he shared the general public's perception of the Observer, that she was a person to be greatly feared. And her skin had nothing to do with it. And what had skin to do with the citation against the company? But he felt he must address the issue. With what sincerity he could muster, he said to Olympia, "You have beautiful skin."

"Yes, but it's not mine."

There, he thought to himself, you don't understand human beings. And he wondered how he could keep this old woman from throwing away her company.

Olympia continued gazing at the Observer's image, as it stepped from the shadows of a doorway into the light of an arcade. "She, who has everything, would take the little that I have left."

The Sponge-head laid his forehead on the desk in frustration. His profile flattened as his soft flesh yielded to the hard surface of the desk. What was he to do with this woman? Slowly he raised his head, and its shape came back again. "Mrs. Clendenning, you have a vast fortune. Now that Kitty Liftoff's dead, you're the wealthiest woman in the Corridor."

She turned angrily toward him. "I have nothing." Her trembling arm swept the air, as if to include her massive office and the offices surrounding it. "All this is just a charade." She pointed at the Observer. "*There's* reality."

"That's only a recording."

"She wants to close down the immortality program. It doesn't matter to her. Because when you're young like she is you're already immortal." Olympia interlocked her fingers nervously and rubbed her thumbs back and forth against each other. "I used to be that kind of immortal young woman. The world issues them daily. The latest fashion model coming down the runway. And by the time she gets to the end of the runway, she's a skeleton."

The Sponge-head gave her a puzzled look, his eyes peering out from the deeply wrinkled sockets that held them. She saw he didn't understand, and now it was her turn to speak slowly, as if to a child. "By the time she gets to the end of the runway, she's old. That's how fast it happens. Young one moment, and old the next. I've walked down that runway."

"But look how lovely you are." He pointed with a stubby, wrinkled finger to a mirror on the distant wall.

"You're a fool. And I'm alone."

The Sponge-head tried to put the conversation back on track. "We can avoid further action from the Observer simply by eliminating the fillers."

"I can't do that."

"It's a simple change, and I strongly recommend it."

"Never."

The Sponge-head realized every change threatened her. She could no longer follow tactical moves. It's the way of the old to see everything as insurmountable, he said to himself. How can I save her if she no longer comprehends the simplest procedure?

"I'm not going to turn up the sound," said Olympia, petulantly gazing at the Observer's smiling image; the Observer was speaking but Olympia couldn't stand to hear her voice. That would be too much, to hear her, so strong, so full of life. "If the shareholders take over, I'll no longer be a member of the Consortium. I won't qualify for the immortality program." The thought sent a shudder of despair through her, and her thoughts began to fragment. Her familiar office seemed strange, uncomfortable, no longer giving her a feeling of security. This alien standing in front of her was a wizard in legal matters, having absorbed the laws of Planet Immortal and its neighbors, but he wasn't sympathetic. He hadn't yet crossed the only line that mattered. When that soft spongy flesh of his starts to dry out, crack, and cave in, then he'll remember this conversation.

"There's no need for the shareholders to be involved," he said. "We just comply. That's all. Very simple. And you're untouched."

"Untouched? You know nothing about it. I've had everything replaced, but it doesn't help. Not in the end. Not when vitality is gone. I haven't got any more fuel. I've used it up." Her inner computers balanced her as she moved around the office, but she knew she was walking on a slant, no matter what the computer said. She was on an incline. The office floor sloped down. Down and down into the abyss. She made a fist and punched the cylinder in which the Observer's image walked. Olympia gazed at her impenetrable enemy. The Observer's eyes were blue, beautifully blue. In spite of hating her, Olympia said, "A beautiful woman is lovely to see. Her power is wonderful."

"Now that's a nice positive feeling," said the Sponge-head. "Let's go with that feeling. Let's tell the Observer we've cleared up the production problem."

"I don't begrudge her what she has. Why does she want to take away my company?"

"Because we've broken the guidelines."

"We mustn't tell anyone," said Olympia, in the voice of childhood.

"They already know," said the Sponge-head, gently.

"Amphora is still running. I won't let her shut *that* down. That's my hope, my future . . ." and suddenly she brightened, for the Amphora program was near completion. True, an accident had happened but that was part of bold science. Accidents sometimes improve conditions. I just have to hang on a little longer. That's all. And then I'll be a schoolgirl again. Or any age I want to be. "You can select your age, that's what the Immortals told us, and you can have numerous selections every day, or every hour. You can be the whole of yourself. Vitality remains constant. The beautiful model never reaches the end of the runway. She's always just stepping out from behind the curtain. She has complete confidence, she strides along conceitedly."

The Sponge-head had no idea what she was talking about. These days, she frequently rambled on this way.

Olympia imitated the model, but the runway was sloping down, and her inner computers caught her, and returned her balance. "A young woman has fire in her eyes." She walked over to the mirror, and looked for the fire. But her eyes were artificial. The fire was electrical. Panic struck her. Where was she? Was there anything left of her?

"Mrs. Clendenning, I'll communicate your decision to the Observer. Then I'll send the order to all our plants." The Sponge-head was methodically outlining the steps, in a voice resembling that of a hypnotist, as he tried to lull her toward the act that would save her.

"Is there anything left of me?" she asked him.

The Sponge-head ignored the question and pursued his policy change. "Production can be turned around almost immediately. I'll explain it to the Observer."

Olympia turned away from the mirror, which held no answer. It showed her the rejuvenated form of an old lady in the skin of a baby zungu. But the real Olympia was on the runway, just coming through the curtain, in the fullness of perfection. Also I have intelligence, which the fashion model seldom has. "I'll invent new products," she said, hurriedly, not wanting to be mistaken for a vain creature only interested in her beauty.

"Of course you will. So, I have your full approval?"

"I built this company. I designed everything. I played hardball." She snapped her fingers toward the image of the Observer. "I have a doctorate in biochemistry. I made great things happen. I fed the Corridor. What did she do?"

"She became the most powerful woman on the planet." The Sponge-head had great respect for the Observer, as well as an alien's fear of being deported by her. He dearly hoped Olympia would conform to the guidelines, so that he could recede again into the background, out of the Observer's view.

"I believe I'm feeling better," said Olympia, and began to skip around the room. Her mind quickened, the spark was back. She remembered her rejuvenator saying new chips for mood control take a little time but that when they begin to work the change is profound. Thank god it had finally happened. "I'll settle for this, until the immortality program begins," she told the Sponge-head.

"I'm happy to hear it." He assumed she was talking about the banned fillers. "I'll put everything in motion."

The new mood chips were lighting up, one after the other, the surge tremendous. She was making the old connections. How could she have forgotten this? She turned to her scheduling robot. "Call a meeting of my engineers. And my chemists. I'm bursting with ideas."

"Yes, madam," said the robot, coming out of standby mode.

Olympia skipped back to her mirror, and recognized herself. She saw the woman of destiny, who'd fed the planets and built an empire. Nothing had to be relinquished. It was all within her grasp. Relief swept through her. Rejuvenation was working once again. One more important fix had taken place. Better than all the rest. She would recommend it to the world. The mood enhancing chips were divine, everyone should feel like this. "I have a vision of the future. I see what we're all going to be. We're going to be creatures who see things from many angles simultaneously. The wisdom of age combined with the energy of youth. The way I feel at this moment. But even more so."

And then it *was* even more so. Then it was everything all at once. Then it was the whole of her life shining before her. I'm young! I'm immortal!

The Sponge-head heard the crack and thought it was a malfunction in the scheduling robot. But then he saw Olympia fall against her mirror; she grabbed at it for balance and it came shattering down around her. He rushed to help her up, but she made no move to assist him. He turned her over. She too was like a mirror, her face as hard as glass, and the shards of the real mirror shone around her head like a halo. Like a revelation, he suddenly saw human beauty, its lines and planes making sense to him.

"Perhaps I should cancel the meeting of engineers and chemists?" asked the scheduling robot, gazing over his shoulder at their employer.

"Mrs. Clendenning is dead."

"Then she won't attend the meeting," said the robot. "Understood."

CHAPTER 22

General Caph was in his Capital City apartment playing three-dimensional chess when he heard the Lord of the Underworld engines. "We'll have to resume our match another time," he said to his opponent, a tactical robot from the Military Planning Division.

A small gray pod was hovering outside his window. He stepped onto his balcony and entered the waiting pod, which shot upward to the gray Intelligence Agency ship high above the city. The pod's computer guided it back inside the great ship; Caph stepped out, and an elevator transported him to the Observer's private office.

She was seated before a wall monitor on which was projected an image of intelligence agents breaking up a robotic demonstration at a shipyard, but her eyes were closed, indicating that she was looking inward, receiving intelligence reports from another region. She sat with her long legs crossed, which showed them to advantage. Gazing on that combination of beauty and cool efficiency, Caph felt a strange intoxication and wondered if he hadn't been in love with her for years. Other women tickled his fancy, but when he was alone with the Observer he felt indecipherable messages playing around his heart.

"Well, General," she said, opening her dark blue eyes, "what have you got for me?"

"A poor soldier's love."

"You're not poor."

"You've impoverished me. You've stolen my soul."

"You love every woman you see."

"Other women are a habit," he admitted, running his palm along his sleek black hair, "but you must know how little they mean to me. You know everything about everybody's private life."

"I turn discreetly away from yours," she said, though, in fact, Caph's attention didn't displease her, for he held every medal for bravery. She almost believed him when he said he was in love with her. "Other than beguiling speeches what have you brought me?"

"Have I beguiled you? Is there hope?" He straightened his tie and adjusted his cuffs. "Phoenix General Silvershield has heard about the problem with Amphora. He's decided it's the right time to stage a coup against the Consortium."

On the Observer's wall monitor, Silvershield's particulars appeared. His precise geographical position was indicated by a slowly moving icon, which expanded to reveal his present activity—playing the ever popular game that had survived the long-ago and tortuous journey from Earth. General Silvershield was lining up a putt on the ninth green.

The Observer issued a voice command, and from a remote location a flying camera was launched. No bigger than a hummingbird, it transmitted pictures of the golf course where the general was playing. There was the green grass, and there his balding head. Remaining silently above him, the flying camera released a minuscule projectile, which sailed past the sand traps and the flags. It slowed, corrected itself slightly, and landed gently behind the general's ear. He reached up, thinking it was a fly. By the time his fingers touched it, its signal was already transmitting; instantly he knew what this meant, but, being a man of some nerve, he concentrated on making the last putt of his life, as massive overwriting of his brain began, isolating those sectors that shaped identity and memory. By the time his ball sank into the hole, Phoenix General Silvershield was catatonized. Uncomprehendingly he stared at the white sphere in the earth's depression. He had no idea where he was, who he was, or what he was doing. The putter fell from his hands, and he stared down at the grass, the expression in his eyes as empty as the sky.

"It's the crudest form of catatonization," murmured the Observer. "There will be no record of him left, but I don't have time for the usual procedures."

"I hope that'll never be me," said Caph.

"Why should it be?"

"Do you catatonize ex-lovers?"

"Are you so sure you'll be my lover?"

"I might grow on you. I have that effect on some women."

"Thank you for alerting me to Silvershield." She indicated that their interview was over.

Caph moved toward the elevator door, then turned back. "The Guard has been apprehensive for the past few days. Soldiers can sense menace in the air. Confide in me, Observer."

"If I were you, I wouldn't do any weapons shopping on the Junk Moon just now."

"Weapons are the last thing I'd ever shop for." The elevator door opened, and the general stepped inside. "Is it true that Olympia crystallized?"

"Yes."

"First Kitty, then Roy. And now the old crocodile. Does this mean the human race isn't going to be immortal, after all?"

CHAPTER 23

Kurt Kashian had a most unpleasant experience while working out with his trainer; he'd been feeling especially strong and resilient for a man of his age when a chilling voice inside him had said, *You can train all you like, but I always win.* Kurt understood: Death couldn't be defeated by discipline and strength-training. Only Amphora could defeat it. So the sight of the Observer in his office whining about *a catastrophe in the making* infuriated him.

"Neither Kitty, Roy, nor Olympia would've wanted us to stop Amphora," he said brusquely. "Immortality meant everything to them. Amphora was in Kitty's backyard."

"It will almost certainly cause more deaths."

"Death is part of our world. That's why we need this project."

"Have you been to Amphora since the accident?"

"I have no need to be there. The Immortals have saved us often in the past. If there are difficulties now, they'll overcome them too." He turned away from her. "Roy said that someday your professional paranoia would mislead you."

She frowned. "Roy said that?"

"Roy was right. Roy was always right."

"Roy was crystallized. He wasn't quite right enough. At least let us agree to proceed more slowly."

Kashian shook his head, and rose from his chair. "Every delay puts us at risk. I want to get into an Amphora transfer cell as soon as possible."

"Kurt, enough planets have destroyed themselves with radical technology. Are we going to destroy this planet too?"

He held her gaze. "If you try to stop Amphora, we'll crush you. Do I make myself clear?"

"It's unlawful to threaten me."

"Your powers come from the Consortium. If you treasure your privileges, if you enjoy being Queen of Spies, then back off. Because if you don't we'll dissolve your position, and maybe we'll even dissolve you. I'll personally arrange for your brain-cleaning." He stopped and smiled, his tone changing to one of perfect friendliness. "In spite of your being a Vapor, I know you pretty well. Every degree of your ambition is obvious. In the end, your ambition will win. You've hardly begun to exploit the opportunities your power gives you. I know you won't be so foolish as to throw that away."

When the Observer took her leave, Kashian's security force stared menacingly at her agents, but that was a piece of theater. Each team wondered if their own employer was stronger. Rumor had it that a test of strength was coming.

The Observer entered her ship, where her screens revealed that Kashian's forces were attempting to lock on to her flight plan. Her ship had no trouble eluding their tracking system, but the sense of being scrutinized remained.

She flew to see the other Consortium members and received the same response she'd gotten from Kashian. Amphora was not to be stopped or slowed. She finished with a visit to Paul Buckler, her ship settling into the landing field beside his house. Her security team spread out and she walked alone up the winding pathway. Paul himself had no security force, only a small robotic staff, and they welcomed her politely.

The moment she entered, the parquet floor of the hallway seemed to know her step. The chandelier held memories of her in the ice-like clarity of its branches. Many times she'd stood beneath it, eagerly anticipating Paul's embrace. But today the icy crystals of the chandelier filled her with apprehension.

The dark wooden door of his study opened, and he came forward, his smile melting her anxiety. "I'm so glad you came."

He was looking tired. He'd set aside his engineering projects to work doubly hard on his translations of the Ancient Alien texts. If only he could penetrate more deeply, perhaps he could find the answer to Amphora's problems.

"Anything?" she asked, as she followed him into his study and saw the ancient manuscripts spread about.

"They write from the perspective of eternity. It's like having a conversation with a mountain. Their words are so weighty with experience, they pull like gravity." He sighed, and ran his fingers through his hair, as if trying to loosen an answer from his brain. "Their explanation of the universe is incomprehensible because we still live within the framework of beliefs they abandoned eons ago. And shedding our beliefs isn't a matter of being instructed by higher beings. A gradual progress is required. And that takes ages." He stood over his desk, his fingers resting lightly on a manuscript. He was that most alluring combination, a man of action with a poetic turn of mind, and the only one she'd ever met who had the proportions exactly right.

As usual, intelligence information was streaming into her brain, but she shut it down because she knew he disliked the private transmissions of her agency. He seemed to grow more clear to her the moment she did this, his tenacity of purpose almost palpable; how much of him did she fail to see because of her obsession with planetary transmissions? He was saying, "The Ancient Aliens were definitely concerned with inferior civilizations such as ours. But there are no references to us specifically, and these texts are philosophical, not technical. All I get is a sort of atmosphere that radiates from their words, but I don't have the master key. I wouldn't recognize it if they handed it to me." He folded his sleeves back, and the bulging veins in his forearms seemed to her like currents of power. Light from the garden covered him; two doors at the far end of his study were open and through it the sun streamed.

"They say it's perilous to bring a backward planet forward too quickly, but in teaching us through the Immortals they didn't follow their own rule." He walked toward the garden doors, as if to get away from this paradox. Stepping outside, he pointed to a row of twisted stalks on which tiny Outer Star blossoms hung. "The Exhulians believe that when flowers keep turning all day to the sun, they're praying." He turned to face her, and his eyes asked a question, the same one they always asked—why wouldn't she agree to spend her life with him? Gazing at him she felt like the alien flower turning toward the irresistible sun, which was why she had to steel herself against him.

He ran the tips of his fingers over the Outer Star blossoms. At the far edge of the shrubbery, her agents were spread out, protecting her against intrusion. He glanced at them as if they were weeds invading his garden. Wherever she was, they were always close by, ready to strike.

She said, "Will you help me stop Amphora?"

"How can I? With Roy dead, Kurt is acting Consortium Head, and he'll never call a halt to it. Not if everyone else in the Consortium turned to stone in front of his eyes." He grasped the Observer gently by the shoulders. "The Consortium has eaten away at both our souls. We've got to get away. I know places where no other human being has ever been."

She closed her eyes and allowed herself to dream. She knew how hated she was because of her power, and sometimes she woke at night from a dream of being just another star wanderer, a shadow in a caravan. To protect herself from his entreaties, she switched on transmissions from her spies. Her circle of informants, extending around the planet and up and down the Corridor, formed a hard grid around her heart, like the domes Paul built to shield asteroids.

"I have a ship equipped for deep space. We could leave today," he said, "with no explanations to anyone."

He slowly kissed her, and, despite herself, she said, "Could we really leave today?"

"We can be to the Second Moon by midnight."

"All right," she said softly. "Yes, all right . . ." She let her feelings for him flow from her sealed heart, and suddenly the Ancient Alien hieroglyphs he'd been struggling with all morning grew lucid in his mind. The old manuscripts began surrendering their mystery. *We came to the cosmos by destiny. We brought to bear the strength and nerve of the stars . . .*

He had a vision of a building, a most wonderful edifice, unlike anything he'd ever constructed, and yet familiar. Everything in it streamed, rivers of energy winding through endless chambers which were sealed by a mysterious membrane. He would build this building, somewhere in the Outer Star Fields. And then he realized that the building was the ultimate dwelling place, that it was his own body. The endless chambers flared with chemical light, and their mysterious membrane lost flexibility and stiffened. He felt himself grow rigid. He shot an arm out to a marble garden statue, of two dolphins leaping. He fell against them, knocked them from their pedestal, and toppled with them to the grass. He stared up at the Observer while his legs turned cold and his arm grew rigid stretching toward her. He remembered every moment he'd spent with her, and felt the depth of their connection. But he was no longer Paul. I've crystallized, he said to himself. And his horror was not so much that he was dying, but that his crystallizing would make it easier for the next person to die. Now he understood the writings of the Ancient Aliens, including the secret of their escape route from time; he wanted to tell her about it, but he was a statue, like his dancing dolphins.

She crouched beside him, grasping his rigid body. His face was hardening, as if it were being sculpted in ice by an invisible chisel. The two stone dolphins on either side of him formed a tableau of rescue, mythical porpoises pushing a drowning man to shore.

She bent to kiss him; her throat was tight with tears, but the bloodless demon of her profession came forward and she wondered: Was the rest of the Consortium, all those who planned to live forever, doomed to die like this? She hurried to her feet.

"Is there something I can do for the master?" asked the garden robot, rolling toward her. Her agents were already surrounding her. The robot's visual apparatus expressed profound puzzlement. It peered down at Paul's form. "He appears unlike his regular self."

As the Observer was hustled away by her agents, she heard the bewildered robot talking on its communicator. "To the robotic staff: A statue has fallen and broken. It is our employer."

CHAPTER 24

The star quantumback of the Hyperbowl drifted back to pass. Only a faint haloing effect showed that one of his receivers wasn't real and that the opposition had projected him from their sky-cam down onto the playing field.

A quantumback's worst humiliation was throwing to somebody who wasn't there, but 'Ramjet' Eddie Orion spotted what he thought was a live receiver and threw, with ten seconds of game time left.

The opposing linemen wrestled Eddie to the ground; he felt the huge bone mass of their bodies hitting him like a pair of piledrivers, but the crowd was yelling, and he knew—he'd connected. A wave of joy ran through him; the look on the faces of the tacklers was priceless. They got up off him, and Eddie also tried to rise. The stunned look of the linemen turned to one of horror as a loud crack sounded, like a helmet splitting.

"What did you do to him?"

"I hit him, that's all. He always shakes it off."

"He's not shaking it off now."

The quantumback was lying on the ground like a trophy, his uniform filled with shattered glass; chips of his face were falling from his helmet. His eyes, like a pair of polished marbles, reflected the stadium lights.

The crowd continued cheering, unaware that the star of the Hyperbowl was in pieces on the sixty yard line. The referees pushed through, but no penalty was called. The linemen had hit Eddie fairly, just the way they'd hit him all day. Some players took small chunks of Eddie's crystals. He'd been one of the best, and there might be luck in possessing part of him.

* * *

Sergius Valakhinas launched into the most difficult part of the Alien Etudes. Written for a pianist endowed with four hands, the Etudes were designed to open those whirling vibratory pockets that brought alien rapture, but until now no human could play them. The audience caught its breath as Valakhinas met each challenge; he'd mastered the difficult finger stretches and the racing tempo. In the second row of Consortium Hall, Madame Orb-of-Night, owner of the Alien Cargo Corporation, leaned forward to miss nothing of Valakhinas's performance; a protective membrane parted across the third ventricle in her brain, the first sign of rapture.

Valakhinas began the final crescendo, waves of sympathy from the aliens in the audience inspiring him. He untied the notes at the dazzling speed required, and realized, suddenly, that the Alien Etudes were devouring him. One could not sustain such emotion and live. He could still save himself by withholding the final note. He played it, and piles of gems poured out of his black tuxedo.

The auditorium was filled with cracking sounds, as if its chandeliers were shattering. It was the enraptured aliens, shattering with Valakhinas. The humans in the audience escaped.

The Observer, on arriving, was struck by the beauty of the fragmented body of Valakhinas lying in a spotlight on the stage, but the jewels were merely crystal, the mineral she'd grown to loathe. Her gaze went from Valakhinas to the audience. The glittering necklaces, bracelets, brooches, and rings of the alien dignitaries were lost in the shattered forms of their owners. The scent of perfumes and pomades clung to the splintered corpses.

The Observer turned and left, without further examination of the dead. Dr. Amphibras hopped alongside her, but his eyes were on the Junk Moon—a large satellite, plainly visible, hanging in the night sky. "Amphora has burst its boundaries, hasn't it?"

"Yes," answered the Observer. Her gaze too was on the Junk Moon, and she heard the voice of Max Rat in her head: *some kind of disruption in the motion series. The boys call it wrinkles in the fabric.*

"We're going to destroy Amphora. It's to be done quietly and completely. Nothing must remain."

Amphibras turned bright orange, and a throbbing bass note came from his throat before he could control it. "I must remind you, because it is my job to remind you, that what you've ordered is against Consortium wishes."

As this conversation was taking place, Fin Zigler was sticking his head into the Scrapper Bar. "The place is cracking."

The Ship Shaper crew didn't ask for details; the Junk Moon contained too many armaments, too many warheads. They poured out of the bar and leapt on Fin's torpedo cruiser—a flying bomb he'd disarmed and rode for laughs. Nobody was laughing as Fin accelerated. They grabbed the hand grips he'd welded to the torpedo, and crouched low as Fin raced it across the dark landscape, his long hair streaming and his headband radar guiding him. The dead ships of lost nations hulked below the speeding cruiser; the Ship Shapers knew every section they passed; they'd crawled through it all, searching for parts. Each of them had flown the torpedo in the dark, at low altitude, narrowly avoiding cannons, rudders, radar beacons. But Fin was cutting it close tonight; the spiked horns of a line of Devil Ships rose two inches below them. The crew's design chief, Guz Wedok, closed his eyes as Fin narrowly missed a missile launcher. This is it then, thought Guz. The gig here is over. He saw the plume of a junkernaut rising above the horizon, its lights whirling crazily, and he wondered—had a junkernaut precipitated the crisis?

The lights of the main hangar appeared and grew larger and brighter as the torpedo crossed the last stretch of darkness. Fin powered down, the Ship Shapers jumped off, and Fin nosed the vehicle into the launch rails that housed it.

To the questions on the lips of the Ship Shapers, he only answered, "Problem at the core." Workers near the Amphora project were like sticks of petrified wood; something had attacked them and cracked them; they weren't just dead, but looked as if they'd been dug out of a mine.

"We're taking Little Infinity," he said.

"She's not ready," said Guz.

"We're not leaving her behind." Fin issued orders to jettison the scaffolding around her, to activate the ion drive circuitry, to raise the neutron shield. They hadn't worked on their prize ship all these years to leave her for the junkernauts.

"Ion circuits on . . ."

"What's the biopropellant level?"

"Enough to get off the ground."

"What about the plasma bottle?"

"Cork is out."

"Laser converter?"

"Full function."

The Ship Shapers scrambled around Little Infinity, casting off components of jobs they'd have to complete somewhere else. Fin was at the controls, with Guz in the navigator's seat. The unit at Guz's fingertips was from a Centaur scout ship, which had the best navigational information system in the Corridor, but Guz had never really used it, had only checked that it was fully functional.

"Biopropellant flowing," said Fin. "What's the laser focus?"

"On the money."

"Wave accelerator is on."

"Fin, look at that . . ."

In the hangar yard, a ground maintenance crew was running toward them, shouting for them to wait.

"We don't have room," said Fin. "We'll never get off the ground with so many on board." But he was opening the hatches for them anyway.

The maintenance crew got closer, then the ground seemed to lift beneath them, tilting them sideways. They spun violently, arms spread, and then they cracked, their fragmented pieces tumbling out of their uniforms.

Fin shut the hatches and burned full. Little Infinity shot across the landscape, and Guz dialed in a destination. Nearest fuel station, Asteroid Tartine. Everyone on board gave a sigh of relief. But Fin suddenly cut the engines and swung the ship around. He pointed to the outside monitor, in which a huge, block-headed robot appeared, lumbering across the takeoff strip. "We can't leave Max Rat behind." Fin opened the hatches again. Through the forward cockpit window, he saw a junkernaut bearing down on them. "Hurry it up, Max Rat . . ."

The huge robot tumbled into Little Infinity, his block head ratcheting wildly. "Thanks, Zigler. I owe you one."

"Fin, go!" shouted Guz, as the junkernaut loomed larger in front of them, faces of crazed machines staring straight into the cockpit.

Fin swung Little Infinity around, and burned again, as the junker skimmed past, robots bouncing off Infinity's hull. The ship staggered for a moment, then got its momentum and lifted off. Looking back, the Ship Shapers saw the junkernaut drive into the main control tower, which collapsed around it. And the junker rolled on.

Little Infinity rose higher into the air. Looking down, Fin saw the Great Shark trying to load hundreds of Junk Moon workers scurrying toward its open jaws. They all crystallized at the same time, in stride, knees bent, like one of the Consortium monuments erected to celebrate happy and productive workers. The Shark's mouth slammed shut; a couple of the men had managed to get to the controls, but their crystallizing hands must have frozen on the wrong levers, for the Shark rolled straight ahead, never lifting, only barreling onward, off the end of the runway and across the landscape. It hit a row of Gladiator ships, and blew. An enormous ball of fire erupted, and Fin banked away from the flames. The Junk Moon shuddered; Fin saw rows of warships tremble, as if their engines had all come on at once. Fissures opened in the moon shell, and the hidden latticework appeared. Warships tumbled in. Now the fissures widened and whole blocks of armaments sank into the skeletal interior. The artificial moon was breaking like an egg struck by a hammer, and huge showers of fire burst from its center, as if it were hatching a bird of the sun. As the pieces fell away, the latticework crumbled and the egg's core was revealed. Fin saw a surrealistic display of wiring—long swirling filaments which had once formed the communication network of the moon. It looked like a gigantic pit of electric snakes, and some invisible force was whipping the snakes around.

"What's going on down there?" queried Guz.

"Amphora blew," said Max Rat, while Fin coaxed every ounce of power out of Little Infinity before Amphora got her, for he could feel the influence of its hidden energies on his ship. She shuddered as she flew, and he was shuddering too, but Little Infinity was showing what she could do. Her second stage propulsion came on, and she surged.

"Nice, Zigler, very nice." Max Rat had one set of eyes on Zigler and another on the Junk Moon below. "But it looks like I'm out of a job."

"We need a combatant on board."

"I'm your machine." Laser barrels rotated out of Max Rat's chest, armed and ticking.

Guz looked out across the angle made between the climbing ship and the seething heart of the shattered moon. He'd seen into many wrecks before, had seen the guts of ships spilling out, but he'd never seen a great satellite come apart. It looked as if the spirit of the moon were dancing, her head covered by electric circuits as she shook the place down.

The recognition module of the ship's main computer, scanning space on all sides, caught the image and processed it. A synthesized voice came from a cockpit speaker: *"Non-identifiable item at forty-five degrees from tail position. Checking ..."*

A second later, the computer voice said, *"Resemblance to no known Corridor object. Still checking ..."*

There was a ten second break, and then: *"Closest match—non-existent inter-dimensional ship popular with conspiracy theorists. Also this: predatory phantom ship described in Ancient Corridor texts. I am advising evasive action."*

Guz forced himself to look away, and his eyes returned to his navigational screen with the little Centaur emblem on its frame. A Centaurian navigator had gazed at this screen, running from his own devils, unsuccessfully, for the ship from which Guz had personally pried the unit had been a casualty. But the unit had been preserved in the middle of the wreck; there was good luck in that, as in any part of a ship that'd survived a war. Little Infinity was composed of only such good luck parts, and she revealed their power now, as she broke gravity and went into orbit, beyond the shattered weight of the Junk Moon and whatever energy was commanding its deadly center.

"Just keep burning," said Guz to Fin, and Little Infinity flew on.

CHAPTER 25

As crystallizations spread throughout the capital, so did the rumors, some of them implicating the Immortals. Demonstrations became a regular occurrence outside the monastery walls.

"A War God has been assigned to you," the Observer told Metron.

He lifted his gaze to the enormous shadow overhead, then watched the great ship slowly pass, its underbelly lit with observation turrets. The angle of the War God changed and the aft section came into view, bristling with weapons. Metron caught a glimpse of glinting armor worn by a crew member. "It's an appalling sight."

"It's necessary for the moment," said the Observer. "And the crew is entirely robotic, so even if there's a military coup, the robots overhead are programmed to protect the monastery against any fools who blame you for what's happened."

"Are those who blame us fools?" asked Metron, and then: "In the event of a coup, what will happen to the Consortium?"

"If the Guard is split apart, Consortium members will be in danger. But no one will risk attacking you with a War God overhead."

"Do you approve of defending us this way?"

"Certainly. I'd protect you with my life."

"Even now?"

"Especially now." She looked toward the horizon, where the great ship was disappearing. Beyond, palely visible in the afternoon sky, the fragments of the shattered Junk Moon slowly circled Planet Immortal.

Two Immortal nuns were walking through the garden, their aged heads together in somber discussion. The Observer caught the word *Amphora* and then what sounded like a mathematical formula. Could such fragile creatures still be of any help?

The two robed figures entered one of the mound-like structures which served as sleeping quarters for them. These crude edifices had been built with no concern for comfort or for beauty. Though the monastery grounds held numerous works of art, to the Observer it was clear such gifts were wasted; the old renunciates cared for nothing wealth could offer. On the brief tour she'd been given, she'd seen planetary icons studded with jewels, as well as tapestries, vases, and beautifully sculpted furniture. But the nuns and monks passed each piece without a glance. The Observer had the feeling they would have stored it all in one of those large mounds and forgotten it, could they have done so without hurting the donors' feelings.

She lowered her head, weighed down by a dilemma beyond her grasp. "I'm destroying Amphora," she said softly. "I wanted you to know."

Metron traced the tip of his sandal over tiny white flowers, as if erasing a mistaken equation—the equation that had led to this disaster. It was so like a nervous human gesture that, for a moment, the Observer thought of him in human terms, and vaguely wondered what he'd been when he was young. Like every anxious youthful creature, he must have known stupidity, impatience, physical desire, and terror. But all that remained of his long-ago anxieties was this gentle movement of his foot.

She said, "I haven't informed the Consortium of my decision. They still want to be immortal."

He nodded. "And you, Observer? What do you want to be?"

"I've lost someone precious to me. With him gone, I don't seem to place much value on my life. It's a sort of freedom, I suppose."

"Freedom from the desire to live forever?"

"Why should I wish to repeat my folly endlessly?"

"I feel the same." Metron laid his claw-like hand on hers. "We thought that we were wise. But all we are is old." Then he added, "Take me to Amphora. Let me try to deal with it."

"The Junk Moon is coming apart. The Amphora installation is unreachable." The Observer rose to leave.

"Thank you for coming to me," said Metron. "By rights, you should be imprisoning us."

"We'll arrange to get you off the planet. You don't want to live with a War God overhead."

"We'll prepare ourselves for departure." Metron still held her hand. Tears were in the sage's eyes. "Never again will we intrude upon the destiny of others."

"The flaw might have been ours," said the Observer. "Catastrophes have happened often under mankind's watch."

"Nothing like this has happened before," said Metron, gravely.

Another monk led the Observer from the garden and ushered her out. On the other side of the monastery wall, her agents were waiting to guide her through the angry mob. She noticed several protesters who would present no further problem. They were as still as the statues in the garden, their crystallized bodies glistening in a vengeful rapture, fists frozen in the air.

She stepped into her armored car, and one of the protesters crystallized as he leapt in front of it, but her driver didn't break; the bumper lifted the corpse and it shattered against the windshield; shards of glittering face and throat and fingers tumbled past the Observer's window.

"It's a plague without decay," she murmured.

General Caph, in the seat across from her, asked, "How was Metron?"

"He says two thousand years didn't make him wise enough."

"How long does it take?" asked Caph.

"Forever."

Caph's eyes were on a young couple crystallized hand in hand, the girl's face turned up to the boy's. "I hope they were at the moment when love is perfect."

"Is there such a moment?"

"There is," said Caph. "I have it several times a week."

The vehicle rose straight up, and made for the Intelligence Agency ship. When they were in the Observer's private office, she said to Caph, "Destroy Amphora."

"Is that the Consortium's decision?"

"I'm going above them."

"They'll retaliate."

"I'm prepared for that. But I'll need the Guard. Can you guarantee their loyalty to me?"

He shrugged his shoulders. "Those who don't like you will get their vector shot in the head. Correct?"

"Let's hope it doesn't come to that."

"In my experience, it usually does. I suggest we leave that threat prominently on the board."

"Will you order the strike immediately?"

"Amphora will be history by this evening."

The Observer nodded, and joined Dr. Amphibras in the ship's command center.

"You look pale," said the little toad.

"The Consortium will move against me now."

He handed her a secret transmission he'd just received. During the past few hours, every remaining member of the Consortium had crystallized.

CHAPTER 26

Dan Terrell sat in his flight commander's chair in the ready room of the circling Consortium War God. Walls of computers and terminals connected him to the Junk Moon many miles below, and on the main screen was an image of Amphora. In the background he heard the rush of gigantic conveyors; men and machines were rearranging themselves after the launch and return of recon drones from the wreckage. Attack solutions had been computed, and Terrell turned to his wingman. "After we disintegrate it, we'll come out on the far side of East Slab Six."

Vice Commander Bert Fernandez was looking at a surveillance close-up of a row of Mysterium Warrior ships, precariously balanced on North Slab 15, a floating island that'd broken off the main shell of the Junk Moon. "There are some wonderful ships down there. Can't we rescue any?"

"Orders are to leave the bone-picking to *them*." Terrell nodded toward another monitor, which showed a variety of mercenary ships in high orbit. Word of the ruined moon had spread quickly up and down the Corridor, and freebooters were gathering for a share of the spoils. The giant satellite had been on fire for a week, with no one attempting to put the fires out. It had been decided to let it burn.

"It's a shame we have to leave it for the hyenas," said Fernandez, looking at the Mysterium Warriors. "The race that built those ships is extinct."

"I flew one once," said Terrell. "A pure logic drive. No sound, and total velocity without multiple stages. But we leave them where they are. Those are orders."

The bank of monitors was showing the Junk Moon from every angle, with close-ups and long shots. One of the long shots showed the entire jagged sphere. "If the Amphora program had been ours—" Fernandez echoed an old Guard sentiment about civilian versus military engineering.

"They destabilized the core," agreed Terrell. "Our people would never have made that mistake." He picked up his helmet. "It takes advanced idiots to destabilize a satellite of this size."

General Caph met them at the blast door which led to the bristling flight deck. Caph had scars from many battles, and a long one on his forehead crossed lines caused by the frown he'd been wearing for the past hour, as data came in from command and control. "The unexplained energy pattern at the core bothers me. There's no insistent particularity. No brute fact. It's not a target like any we've seen before."

"It doesn't matter, sir. In five minutes it's not going to be down there at all."

Terrell and Fernandez left the ready room and tube-shot themselves directly down into their aircraft. The canopy closed around Terrell.

"Good afternoon, Commander Terrell," said the ship's robotic voice. "Nice to fly with you again."

"Afternoon, Raptor One. How is your state?"

"Combat ready."

"Do you have an ETL for us?"

"Yes, sir. Launch at 1432 coordinated Corridor time from bay zero one seven. Raptor Two carrying Vice Commander Fernandez reports an ETL of 1433 from bay zero one nine."

The seven-ton Raptor was lifted from its berth and placed into position on the launch apron. The repulsion port closed around it.

"All systems approved for launch," came the voice of the robotic aircraft director, who was monitoring the ship's preparedness from a protected booth. Terrell gave the ship the go-ahead, and the Raptor strained against the confines of the port. "Energize," commanded the launch director, then made his final check. "All conditions optimal. Launching *now*."

Terrell's ship was repolarized, sailed down the chamber, and shot into the sky, its wings deploying like a jumping beetle's.

"Transitioning from launch to battle mode," said the Raptor.

Terrell flew to the twenty mile arc position around the War God, waited for his wingman to join him, and then both ships powered down toward a gaping fissure in the exploded moon. A junkernaut rolled along the fissure's edge, then fell off and disappeared in the darkness below.

Terrell plunged in past the junker, and Fernandez entered behind him, along a river of fire where the armaments of the Junk Moon still burned. Terrell had visited many times when the place was in business, to bargain, to buy, and to gossip with warriors from other worlds. He'd never imagined he'd be flying through the guts of the thing, with beautiful ships of the alien nations in flames all around him. Chain reaction explosions were setting off one row after another, and smoke blew across his canopy. One of the big Saber ships of Lustrumia belched fire toward him, as if welcoming him to its funeral pyre.

Terrell waggled his wings at the fire-spewing giant, acknowledging the death throes of a great ship. A fireball exploded from her, sending sparks up around his cockpit, and in the next second she was behind him, rumbling and grumbling to whatever spirits attended her demise.

Terrell flew on, Fernandez shadowing him. Fast winds above and slow winds below were producing turbulence, so he dropped to a thousand feet. The tattered landscape screamed by, and Terrell's heart leapt as the fissure widened suddenly, like a dark grin of the moon. The collapsing interior had produced a canyon of extreme depth, in which the sun's light was lost. He raced downward, Fernandez struggling to stay with him in this unknown shadow of an unknown world. Here the destructive force of collapse had left latticework girders projecting at unexpected angles, around which he and his wingman dodged. Their wing-tip anticollision generators were inches from the girders. They came so close to a magnaplane guideway that Terrell found himself gazing at three robot mechanics as they sped past in a cross-bound module.

"What was that?" asked Fernandez.

"Maintenance units," answered Terrell. "Playing it out to the end."

The canyon twisted and Terrell rolled with it. His eyes seemed to lose focus, exactly as they did when pressured by too many g-forces. But it wasn't his eyes that were out of focus; there was something down here and it had *no insistent particularity*. He fired a massive disintegration missile, and banked away. But the shock wave of detonation didn't come; his instruments showed the missile being shunted at a sharp angle, and then vanishing. "It swallowed it like candy," said Terrell to Fernandez, but couldn't say more; his anticollision sensors were screaming as he dodged through the wreckage of the interior, and climbed above it, only to experience the uniquely terrifying feeling of seven tons of unbalanced steel. "Raptor One, say your state."

His ship didn't answer. His instrument panel was dark. He looked sideways out the cockpit toward his wingman and saw him in the shadows. "Bert, are you okay?"

Fernandez did not respond.

"Raptor Two, say your state," ordered Terrell.

"All systems normal," answered Fernandez's ship. "Vice Commander Fernandez not responsive."

"I've got troubles here," said Terrell, still struggling with his unstable ship.

"Analyzing," said Raptor Two, and a moment later reported, "The organic part of your biocognetic system is in some sort of crystalline form."

"Update me on the vice commander."

"Vice Commander Fernandez appears to be in the same state."

Terrell turned his head, and, by the sudden flaring of a Junk Moon fire, saw the opalescent face of Bert Fernandez—a statue in a flight helmet.

"Raptor Two, compute energy fix."

"Understood. Optimal solution suggests connecting energy survival powerpack."

"I already have. No response."

"Please advise which port you're connected to."

"Standard energy port A."

"Suggest connecting to subsystem bus B."

Terrell complied and the center control panel lit up. "Raptor One, do you read?"

His ship reported in a dry mechanical tone, with no trace of its former lifelike lilt. "Main cognition unit intact. Bus to all control systems beyond self-repair. Commander, I require Electrish-level communication with Raptor Two. Please activate bridging nexus twelve on communications data-stream bus."

Terrell activated the bridge.

"Thank you," said his ship. "Communication established. Raptor Two and I are computing homing solution."

Terrell sat in helpless idleness as the two ships nudged their way along through the treacherous interior of the Junk Moon. He'd always had the illusion that he was doing the flying, but now that illusion was gone. Still, he couldn't help inquiring, "Raptor Two, report on emergency recovery program."

"Launch recovery team is aiding in homing solution. Suggest you relax." Terrell had to restrain himself from intervening. Raptor Two continued, "Will consult with you as necessary." In other words, we'll see you after it's done.

The next voice he heard was that of General Caph. "Dan, what's going on out there?"

"I think Amphora dumped our missiles into hyperspace. Then it crippled my Raptor and crystallized Bert. The two ships are working on a solution to bring us back."

A few seconds later he popped out of the Junk Moon into the open sky. He sighted the War God through the roof of his canopy, and the two Raptors climbed toward it. As they lined up with its gaping landing maw, the recovery team communicated with the ships in Electrish. The speed of the language made it impossible to understand, but speed was what was needed now, as his crippled Raptor began its approach. He felt the ship adjust to starboard, and saw the blue landing lights ahead. The ship corrected again, increasing its speed. The War God's mouth was growing larger but no pilot ever found it large enough. If the angle of approach to the mouth was incorrect, he would ram it and drop like an expensive bit of fireworks.

He looked at his instruments and saw he was maintaining knots. The Raptors had calculated well. The mouth of the War God was looming larger, at five kilometers, then four, three, down to three-quarter kilometers. Terrell froze his gaze on the War God's mouth. He could see the row of receptor lights in its interior. Their colors showed he was too high. The robotic Electrish voices speeded up so much they were just a shrill whine. He felt the Raptor slow, correcting downward. The mouth of the War God closed around him and he fed the beast. His front wheel hit the yellow center line and the magnetic barrier in the landing area came on, freezing the motion of his ship. His body shot forward, straining against the safety straps, and he went from 128 knots to zero.

"We've got you, Commander. Throttle down, extinguish lights." The synthesized voice of the aircraft director was machine flat, as if nothing out of the ordinary had happened.

Terrell obeyed orders, and the computer raised his canopy. A metal arm picked him and his seat neatly from the cockpit and set him down on deck, as Bert Fernandez's ship landed in the next recovery bay. The moment it settled in, damage control robots swarmed over it.

He heard their expressionless voices: "Request permission to break apart Vice Commander Fernandez for removal."

CHAPTER 27

Mercenaries, alien drifters, criminal programmers, and four-flushers of all kinds filled the barroom. Ren was making her usual round of the tables, looking for a freighter captain who wasn't fussy about the legal status of his passengers. Watching her, Upquark said to Link, "Based on recent experience, my calculations indicate we could be stuck here indefinitely."

He noted that most of the drinkers had the look of the marooned, staring at the open doorway as if it were a horizon from which a rescue ship might appear.

"There's no one here who can take us to Cantus," said Ren, returning to their table. The cheerful bells in her voice were not ringing, had not rung since they'd been wandering Alien City. "The price they demand is beyond us. We're dangerous cargo."

Link suddenly jumped up and hurried out onto the street. The horizon had brought him a familiar face. A man was looking up at the barroom's garish light, against which a moth was fluttering. "Professor Cometary," said Link. "Do you remember me?"

The professor stared at the young man in front of him, and the past came clear. "Sex Pheromone Tactics for Management of the Alarian Mealybug!"

"Yes, sir. It was my doctoral thesis."

"Adrian Link. You're on the Agricultural Plain. A brilliant rise."

"Not any longer." Link showed Cometary into the barroom, where he filled him in on his fall from grace. Cometary shook his head in disbelief. Link noticed that as always Cometary's nails were filthy, for he was liable to stop anywhere and dig up interesting looking soil for analysis. At the moment, a seed was sprouting in the cuff of his trousers. He gestured, knocking his hat askew; loose soil stored in the crown fell on the table, along with an insect who'd been living in the soil.

Mature nymph of the cicada, noted Upquark.

Cometary said, "I ran into a very interesting gall on a narcissus plant growing just down the street. Caused by a bulb nematode, of course, I have it in my pocket . . ." He foraged, producing slides, magnifying glass, tweezers. "Do you remember a man called Puffer Sadlock? Torturous and indirect in his discourse, but expert in soil drainage. Something of a drain himself . . . here we are, look at that gall, unusual, isn't it . . ." The infected bulb was now on the table. The cicada nymph crawled toward it slowly. Link and Upquark watched it, fascinated, each thinking the same thing—it had lived the last seventeen years underground and had finally tunneled into the light of day, to wind up in Cometary's hat.

Cometary reached into another pocket and brought out a diseased leaf. "Ring spots, stunting, and premature death. A fungus introduced from another planet. I warned them," he said sadly. Then the measuring gaze of his gray-blue eyes grew speculative. "These crystallizations or whatever they are—could they be caused by a virus? Any ideas?"

"None," said Link, but there *was* something going on in the back of his mind; like the cicada nymph tunneling upward, an idea was slowly rising; Link felt thoughts being dislodged, the way the nymph pushes pebbles and other underground impediments aside. "No ideas at all."

Cometary rummaged in his pocket again. "I've got something to show you, no that's not it, that's just a curiosity—" He put a tiny coffin on the table. Ren reached out and opened up its lid. Inside was a maggot preserved in amber.

"A gift from a native of Planet Insecta. Supposed to bring me luck." Cometary lifted out the embalmed maggot, revealing a lining of gold carved with tiny symbols. "Magic spells. That's Planet Insecta for you. Atrocious place with an impossible climate. The agriculture has no geographic balance, but growing five million metric tons of rice isn't bad for people plagued by six-foot grasshoppers. All right, here's what I'm looking for—"

He tossed a sample soil bag on the table. "Smell *that.*"

Link opened up the bag, closed his eyes and sniffed the soil. A woman's perfume could not have haunted him more completely; he was back on the Agricultural Plain, with the summer sun warming the rich earth; a pang ran through him for what he'd lost. He opened his eyes and poured a little of the soil into his palm and ran it through his fingers. "Where does it come from?"

"You remember Planet Yesterday produced the finest wine in the Corridor?"

"Until the yellow sylph virus."

"Well, some alien connoisseurs want the best wine they can find, and Puffer Sadlock and I have been hired at great expense to bring sublime intoxication back to the Corridor. I'm one of the agricultural chiefs on Yesterday. And that's a sample of our soil."

"Congratulations." Link reluctantly handed back the bag.

Upquark looked at Adrian's downcast face, and turned to the professor. "I wish that we could help," he blurted.

"But why not?" cried Cometary. "Why not come with me to Yesterday?"

Upquark excitedly turned to Link, whose face was radiant again, as if the vines were already blossoming in his mind. Then Upquark felt a wave of unhappiness coming from Ren.

"We mustn't leave our associate behind." He gestured toward her with his gripper. "She's a specialist in higher crop yield through sound." His ethical beeper went off at the white lie, but he overrode it. "We've had significant gains using her technique."

"Of course," said Cometary, turning to Ren. "Music in the fields. The grapes of Planet Yesterday *will* respond. I know them. So—" He turned back to Link. "—you're coming with me. But you're being chased by the Observer. We can't use regular transport."

Ren pointed to one of the freighter captains she'd talked to earlier. "He was willing to take us but we can't afford him."

Cometary went to the captain's table. Their heads remained together for several minutes, and then Cometary returned. "One of the advantages of representing wealthy connoisseurs is a large budget. And I threw in the little gold coffin. His ship is hidden. It's actually a salvaged Predator. He promises cataracts of fire if anyone attempts to stop us. We'll meet him here tomorrow morning. Now I've got to get a few supplies, so I'll say good night."

Link walked him to the door of the barroom. "Professor, may I ask what brought you to this neighborhood?"

"Why, I was following *it*." He pointed to the moth still fluttering against the barroom light; its bright circular wing markings had given it the name Wheel of Fortune.

* * *

After a night spent sleeping in a theater, Link and Ren made their way back toward the bar. "Statistics were against us," said Upquark.

"But now a whole new life is opening for us. It makes me question the foundation of probability."

When they joined Cometary in the bar, he was gazing rapturously at his fine soil. His hand was rigid. His gaze was frozen.

The freighter captain entered, and glanced at Cometary's crystallized form. "Well, he's finished." He took out the tiny coffin the professor had given him. "He shouldn't have parted with his charm." The captain tossed the coffin up once, caught it, and returned it to his pocket. "Did you get his money first?"

"No," said Ren.

The freighter captain shrugged and left them there, marooned once more.

CHAPTER 28

Consumer sales were high. Why not buy? Run up huge debt. Tomorrow you might crystallize. Let somebody else pay it off.

Consortium heirs were fighting among themselves, scrambling to take over the family business. They didn't have time to fight the Observer now. They'd take care of her later.

The Observer was where she'd always longed to be, with power that was absolute. She knew this power was destroying what little good was left in her, but she had no time to care. Since every scientist who'd worked on the Junk Moon had crystallized, successors had to be chosen, and fresh scientists were arriving daily, representing any discipline that might shine light on Amphora and how to destroy it.

Predatory mercenaries were also arriving daily, to take advantage of disorder in the major cities. The Observer had a rogues' gallery of faces floating in front of her, among them that of Jockey Oldcastle. To Amphibras, she said, "When you find Oldcastle, braincleaning won't be necessary. Just execute him for sedition, under the new Emergency Measures Act."

Disgruntled generals gathered in Military Hall, where screens showed War God armadas in strike positions. A hologlobe of Planet

Immortal hung in the air. Beside it was one of the shattered Junk
Moon, like a great exploded ball.

General Liu poked an impatient finger among the pieces. "When
may we launch another strike?"

"Not yet," said the Observer.

He gazed at her ferociously. "Every hour we delay, more people
crystallize. I don't want one more of my soldiers turning into ice."

"It was my deepest wish that we destroy Amphora. But it's already absorbed two disintegration bombs."

"We have other weapons in our arsenal," argued the general.

"You have to give our scientists a chance to study it. If we don't
take it apart intelligently, it will take us apart."

General Liu continued staring at her. She couldn't begin to comprehend the frustration of his soldiers, with no enemy to struggle
against, no humans or aliens to engage in combat, not even guerillas to
bomb out of their holes. His soldiers were superbly trained, superbly
armed, and eager to sacrifice themselves for Planet Immortal. If she
wouldn't let his soldiers fight this tragedy, why have soldiers at all?

As the Observer spoke to each general individually, their service records downloaded into her cerebral implants; her gaze said she
knew the exact degree of each one's loyalty, courage, and capacity
for deception. She knew their sexual profiles, how many drinks they
had each night, what drugs they depended on. They met her gaze,
aware she didn't know the important thing: How it felt for soldiers
to stand by while their comrades-in-arms crystallized around them.

But neither did they know the struggle she had on her hands as
crystallizations swept the planet. Cities would soon be in a state of
lawlessness. "Corridor traffic is up one hundred percent," she said to
Amphibras. "Everybody who can is getting away."

"Not everybody," said Amphibras, with a measure of pride. He
was determined not to let the disaster of Planet Oblivion be repeated.

To run was unthinkable. He'd been given every opportunity for advancement here; that a toad should rise so high—remarkable. On his own planet, he'd be in some backwater, hunting flies.

He hurried off to be on time for a meeting at the tearoom of the Hotel Universe. The new young owners of Starweb—heirs of Martin Faircloth—needed to be worked on. With widespread anarchy at hand, the media had a responsibility to subdue panic rather than contribute to it.

Amphibras's lunch with them didn't go well. The young people showed no inclination to receive his message. They talked of celebrities and the public's lust for grotesque images. "Pictures of famous people crystallized in compromising positions are best." A minor actress who'd crystallized giving birth to a crystal baby was today's leading Starweb story. "It's the tone of the times, Doctor. The public savors disaster."

They seemed somewhat unconscious to Amphibras. "We're making history," declared Robbie Faircloth. "The other planets are hungry for our story. They can't get enough of it."

Amphibras left the meeting exhausted. As he exited the tearoom, two women entered, speaking animatedly, and in their distraction they thought a toady-looking alien as well dressed as this one must be a new maitre d'.

"We'd like a table along the wall."

"Gladly, ladies," answered Amphibras with a courteous bow, "but I regret I do not work here."

"Oh," said one of the women, as if she'd been deliberately deceived.

Dr. Amphibras gave another little bow, and continued on his way.

"These assimilated aliens get above themselves, don't they," said the woman, watching him hopping down the hallway.

"They're all going to be rounded up," said the other.

"Don't be silly."

"No, I heard it this morning."

"From whom?"

"My driver. He seemed quite convinced, but I suppose it's just some media nonsense. Still, wouldn't it be nice if the aliens *were* all just shipped off?" She smiled at one of the waiters they knew. "To Planet Yesterday or somewhere. Not maltreated—yes, we'd like a table by the wall, please—not maltreated, just relocated. Because frankly, I've had just about enough of aliens." Human feelings were running high against aliens at the moment: They were behind the crystallizations.

Dr. Amphibras hopped out through the hotel doorway. "Cab, sir?" asked the doorman.

"No, I'll just take a little hop on my own, thank you." Amphibras needed some air. And some water to splash in for a few minutes, in order to regain his strength for the long afternoon ahead.

He continued up the Avenue of Cosmic History. His beautiful gray suit, which had deceived the women into thinking he was a maitre d', was in need of a boutonnière, and he bought a flower from one of the stalls that lined the boulevard. He fastened it in his lapel, sniffed it appreciatively, and resumed hopping. His hopping was not pronounced, only utilizing a slight bend of the knees, and a little push forward, but it was easier than walking. He *could* walk, but walking was fatiguing. Hopping, on the other hand, was invigorating and he needed that today. He didn't want to fail the Observer, who'd put such faith in him, though he was but a toad.

He hopped across Avenue Andromeda toward a park filled with tourists, exercisers, and people gathered around the central fountain. Life was going on as usual, but the specter of crystallization was near. Which of us is next, was the question in everyone's eyes.

This particular fountain was a favorite spot of Dr. Amphibras, where he could splash his webbed feet in the shallow depths around the charming statuary. A little boy was playing in the water, and his mother sat nearby. Amphibras felt in sympathy with them, and smiled at the mother, who perhaps couldn't see his smile, for his wide mouth was always in a sort of grin. In any case, she didn't smile back.

He watched the boy cavorting in the fountain, the child's joy bubbling up like the jets of water, and it reminded Amphibras of his own joy as a tadpole, of those initial days in the shallows, when he wriggled happily over rocks warmed by the sun.

The boy burst into laughter, threw handfuls of water in the air, and froze, hands upward, as still as one of the fountain's statues. A spray of water dripped down over his unseeing eyes. The mother's shrieks quickly drew a crowd. Sobbing, she pointed to Amphibras. "He did it!" she cried hysterically.

"My poor woman," said Dr. Amphibras, his skin darkening with dismay and sympathy. He tried to comfort her, but her shrieking condemnations just grew louder, and he found himself being grabbed and spun around.

"What did you do to her kid?"

"Nothing, I assure you." He tried to summon help on his cuff communicator, but it was torn off his wrist and flung into the water. He was shoved in after it.

A young Panel-head, whose brain received video games and films directly through a panel of receivers implanted in his scalp, dragged him out, shouting, "He crystallized that kid."

"He killed my baby," sobbed the mother.

"He killed her baby," echoed other angry voices.

Dr. Amphibras had lost his handsome hat and fragrant boutonnière. "Please . . . I'm the personal secretary of—"

The Panel-head punched him in the face, for Panel-heads had a keen sense of good and evil, learned from the games they played. He proceeded to lay Amphibras out flat, which wasn't hard, for Dr. Amphibras was no larger than an eight-year-old child. "Let's even up the score, Toadman."

Amphibras flapped his large webbed feet as if trying to paddle on his back along the sidewalk, and was yanked up by a second youthful Panel-head, whose skull was encircled by coils of multicolored, glowing neon tubing. This paragon of public spiritedness spent his days talking to animated characters who floated in the air in front of him. Now he and his fellow sportsman tossed Dr. Amphibras back and forth between them as if he were some kind of peculiar toy that changed color with each toss.

"The aliens are destroying us," muttered someone in the crowd.

"They're killing our children . . ."

"Child molesters . . ."

"This is what we do to child molesters . . ." The Panel-heads dropped Dr. Amphibras hard onto the pavement, and kicked him until he lay in a curled-up heap against the fountain wall. Covering his head with his arms, the doctor cautiously tried to right himself, but he was dazed, his legs were twitching, and blood was in his eyes.

The first Panel-head began to address the crowd. "I saw how he did it. He signaled the crystallizers in with a coil." He'd seen something like it on one of his incoming game programs, a coil signal to an invader, and here it was, right here.

"That's how they've been working it," testified the other Panel-head. "I saw him signal too."

"Kill him!"

"Crush him!"

"Drown him in the fountain!"

"I . . . did . . . nothing," protested Amphibras, attempting to calm his thumping heart. "I have . . . immunity."

"You have what?" sneered the first Panel-head.

"Immunity," said Dr. Amphibras through swollen lips, but he couldn't explain what he meant, for his mind was fuddled from his beating.

It was rare that Panel-heads had an opportunity to perform their civic duty, and so they made a special effort now. They grabbed the doctor by his legs, turned him upside down, and held his head beneath the water. The first Panel-head was suddenly disturbed by something long and scaly wrapping itself around his ankles; a sharp, stabbing pain made him grab the back of his neck. His last sight before unconsciousness was the face of a large lizard, fangs dripping with saliva.

"Another alien," shouted the second Panel-head. "They're all in it together." Lizardo's tail shot out, wrapped itself around the young man's throat, and he, too, sank into oblivion.

Jockey fished out the choking, spluttering Dr. Amphibras and set him down on the fountain's rim. "Move along," he advised the crowd. There were muttered complaints, but no one really wanted to get near the two mercenaries. The woman who'd lost her child was led away, and Jockey slapped Dr. Amphibras on the back to help him get his breath.

"I'm . . . most grateful, gentlemen." The doctor bowed. His beautiful suit was waterlogged and torn, but he attempted to straighten his dripping tie and cuffs. Then, through swollen eyes, he recognized one of his benefactors. "Aren't you Oldcastle?"

"Never heard of him."

Amphibras leapt back into the water and propelled himself with one long kick toward his lost communicator. Surfacing with it in his hand, he pressed the hotline. The face of his employer appeared. *"What is it, Doctor?"*

"We mustn't execute Commander Oldcastle. Repeat—urgent— we mustn't execute Oldcastle. He just saved my life."

"Focus on him, please."

Dr. Amphibras trained his communicator on Jockey. The Observer gazed at his image for a moment, then said, *"Have I misjudged you, Oldcastle?"*

"It frequently happens."

CHAPTER 29

In desperation, the Observer again sought help from the Immortals, despite their fatal blunder. She entered the laboratory to find Metron surrounded by dozens of physicists and engineers. A datalink connected them to other scientists around the globe.

The lab was filled with machinery, much of it bearing off-planet logos. Instruments were stacked to the ceiling, and data acquisition computers were on eye-level posts everywhere, pulsing with labyrinthine images and streaming with numbers. There was a strong smell of coffee and the stronger smell of pazdu, a stimulating tea favored by many aliens.

The Observer saw Metron trying to explain his view of Ancient Alien technology, and she noted the sadly strained expressions of his listeners, and wondered how much they were really comprehending. She overheard scientists and technicians arguing. She was bombarded with theories and complaints until her head ached. Quietly she said to Amphibras, "Stuart Landsmann understood this best. At least he understood that it was dangerous. I never should've had him brain-cleaned."

"Don't blame yourself."

"There's no one else to blame, Doctor."

"There's no reason why we can't restore him." Amphibras brought up the cataton file and scanned it, but he failed to find the famous scientist. His warts turned red. "The Landsmann file seems to have been misplaced."

"Find it."

"Certainly, certainly . . ." Amphibras initiated a search, while the Observer strode across the lab, hoping she might hear something encouraging from the Ophthalmic in the corner, who was generally considered the planet's leading particle physicist. Ophthalmians had eyes ringing their heads, and this one's many eyes expressed varying degrees of frustration. He stood in front of twelve transformation chambers, replicas of those built for the first candidates for immortality. "We're looking into depths we can't handle," he said. "All day long I feel as if I'm drowning."

The Observer gazed into the twelve transformation chambers with him. Inside these chambers quantum magic was made, but something in the formula had caused *a wrinkle in the fabric,* as Max Rat had told her; the robot's ominous baritone sounded in her head, a voice so deep it might've emanated from the center of the universe, depths the Ancient Aliens had probed.

Now she looked again at Metron, and perceived him as a delicate reed, more breath than body, a creature hardly of this world at all. He was an elder, but the Ancient Aliens were elders by spans of time that were incalculable. They'd been supreme when the human race was bacteria in a primeval lake bed. They'd reigned in the Outer Star Fields, remote and perilous regions from which few wanderers returned. Not one Ancient Alien city had ever been found; evidently their technology protected them from probing eyes. Here and there information-bearing objects were uncovered, but years of research were needed to unravel their messages even partially. From these fragments emerged a picture of beings in control of *the fabric,* and able to vanish into it, into reality's weave, like magicians behind a curtain.

A few dozen scientists stood around a large transparent sphere in which balls of electric fire danced—one component of Amphora. Other components held the attention of the Axon Ipsilos; these high-end robots were notoriously arrogant, but today they were quiet, humbled by the calculations required for understanding Amphora, calculations which exceeded their capacity. For the first time, their mathematical brilliance had revealed itself as elementary. They strained toward new configurations of matter, their quantum wizardry inadequate to the task. Looking at each other, they recognized a harsh truth: Their much-vaunted intelligence was only the beginning; there were inconceivable beings above them, who had played and danced with matter, juggling, balancing, and vanishing. The Ancient Alien mind was beyond them. The Axon Ipsilos, the Info Hogs, the Max Ratiocinates—were all too slow, too heavy. "We need to be upgraded," said the chief Axon to the Observer.

"There is no upgrade," she answered. "Do your best."

The Axon Ixilo turned away from her, knowing she could never grasp the difficulty he and his fellow robots faced. They were alone in their ghastly realization: We're obsolete.

She, in turn, walked away from them. Machines in crisis didn't interest her. Her own ghastly realization was too overwhelming: This roomful of geniuses would never solve the problem of Amphora. A great intellect had roamed the world when it was young, and attempting to reproduce the works of that intellect was futile. Metron and his monks and nuns had been lucky. They'd caught a trail of stardust and spun within it; its magic had immortalized them. But they didn't own the magic. Like the Axon Ipsilos, they had dreadful limitations. They were only conduits for the Ancients, and even as conduits they'd failed. Beautiful as they were, and perfected in philosophy, they were useless. She left the lab, feeling she never wanted to speak to them again. There was no time now for beauty or philosophy.

Amphibras hurried after her, feet slapping. "Stuart Landsmann's file fell into a cybercrypt somewhere. But I'll find him."

"For whatever good he'll do."

They exited the building, and were flanked by what the Observer considered an excess of security personnel, but she was now receiving scores of death threats daily. Armed missiles glowed in her robots' chests, and her human protectors carried disintegrators in clenched hands, as their gaze moved nervously about the grounds. Walking across the central square, one of them crystallized, his vigilance frozen. His fellow agents didn't even look his way as they accompanied the Observer to safety.

A crystallized bird sat in the branches of a tree outside her own headquarters. "We'll be a museum for the other planets, all our life forms perfectly preserved," she said, the heels of her shoes clicking on the Exhul marble entranceway.

She entered headquarters, thinking: *a wrinkle in the fabric.* Organic life, it seemed, was a miracle, and the miracle had been disturbed—*a slight corruption in the fundamental data, to your left, 280 degrees.* Max Rat's voice was with her again. That slight corruption in the fundamental data was spreading rapidly, corrupting everything. The wand of the sorcerer had been picked up by the apprentice, and now the price was being paid.

In her operations room, a million other problems of the planet confronted her. She felt impatient with the couriers who brought these problems—what did the economy matter, what did education matter, if all the consumers and all the students and everybody else was going to be crystallized? Still, attending to the economy and education gave a semblance of normalcy to affairs around the globe. Without that, it would become a Planet Insecta, overrun by devouring swarms; the only difference was that the swarms on her planet would be wearing designer clothing as they pillaged, and would speak fluently in one of a thousand languages.

She crossed the amphitheater, her movements watched by young women on her staff who copied her loose stride, her uplifted chin, and the peculiar swing of her arms, slightly stiff, like long pendulums on an antique clock. They coveted her brain implants, even the slight hesitation in speech it produced, the disconnected gaze, like that of an oracle. And while imitating her, they tried to ignore colleagues crystallizing around them. Each day the entire staff was given psychological tests by psy-robots to assess their mental fitness. When a robot spotted a fault line, the individual was shifted out of headquarters, to deal with more tangential matters—inventors with machines to save the planet; delegations demanding aliens be deported or even better, exterminated; psychics; garrulous movie stars.

The Observer reached her office, and her security personnel fanned out outside the door. Alone, she scanned the latest crystallization numbers.

Her chief economic adviser entered. They dispensed with pleasantries. He said, "Now that the ties binding the founding Consortium families are weakened, it's an opportunity for your office to take their companies over. And their fortunes." The adviser paused. In normal circumstances, what he had just said could have gotten him exiled to a frozen asteroid, if not catatonized. But in this climate things were different.

"Get out," she replied without emotion.

"You'll see the wisdom of this soon enough. Someone is going to take advantage of our present turmoil. Wouldn't you rather it was us, instead of some off-planet power? They're waiting, you know. And I'll be waiting too." He opened her office door. "Just let me know."

General Caph entered next. "Unrest is too widespread to be handled by the police and your agents. You need War Gods everywhere and an overwhelming troop presence on the ground. Military rule, sooner or later, is the rule on all planets. It has come to this planet now."

Reluctantly, she agreed, just as the Transportation Minister hesitantly opened the door. "Excuse me . . . but people are fleeing in any ship that will get them to Asteroid B, and Asteroid B can't possibly sustain such numbers. They'll go from there to the Paper Lantern, and the sky mines will destroy them."

"The sky mines must be removed. The Cosmopolis family will cooperate."

"There are the other moons, not very hospitable, but anything's better than here, it seems. Those who can are leaving our gravitational field altogether. The Corridor is jammed."

The Observer promised to attend to it, and the Transportation Minister left the office.

"Caph," asked the Observer in a low voice, "can the Guard still be counted on to stay?"

"We're soldiers. We'll stay until there's nothing left to defend. Only then will the War Gods depart. But that will be the end. We'll be an army without a planet."

"What will happen then?"

"We'll attack a weaker world."

CHAPTER 30

Above the treetops of the park, Ren watched the plumes of escaping ships, their patterns slowly blending with the clouds. She was reconciled to ending her days on Planet Immortal, with a man who showed no special interest in her.

From the street could be heard Consortium Guard loudspeakers issuing warnings about looting. Early morning sunlight shone on the ponds and lawns, and she felt the heaviness that everyone was feeling, now that Guardsmen patrolled the streets and hovertanks moved along above the traffic, gun turrets revolving. A hovertank floated into the park, pausing momentarily above them; Ren felt an identity scan passing over her. But her veiling device protected her, and the tank moved on.

Link walked to the edge of the park pond, where he knelt and pointed into the shallow water. "That little piece of reed floating there is an inflatable boat. A larva filled it up with air, so he could travel in it." Ren saw a tiny head peek out from the reed, and watched as the ripples on the pond carried the creature away. Then she looked up toward the sky, at the ships floating away from this world, like the insect in its reed.

Link's eyes remained on the wayfarer being borne off by the water. The first time he'd seen a larva boat, he'd been ten years old. By then he knew that little monsters of the underworld could perform countless wonders of engineering; but the performance of that tiny sailor changed his life. His sympathy for it had been so complete, his connection to it so unyielding, that he'd floated away too, out of the world of men entirely and into the world of the larva. When he returned from this interlude, he was a stranger to his childhood friends, his parents, and his teachers. Not until he met Jockey Oldcastle did he realize that others might have a similar experience. Oldcastle could pilot the interchannels of the Corridor with a sixth sense; had called Adrian an interchanneler; and explained that occasionally a perfect idiot like himself might find a pathway that better men never dreamed of. *"You did it with bugs, old man, which is a new one on me, but the fact remains, you did it. Now we must exploit it."* Jockey brought Specterales O to him, *"another interchanneler."* Then he'd taken him to the Paper Lantern, *"to broaden your outlook, because you're as narrow as a poker."* And there things had exploded.

Upquark was taking soil measurements, examining leaf health, doing what he usually did, but of course, he told himself, it will come to nothing. The park's vegetation has run down, and Adrian and I are not equipped to resurrect it. Furthermore, we're in hiding—a condition which would be acceptable if Adrian and Miss Ixen were falling for each other, thrown together by a harsh fate, as outlined in my database on young lovers. Unfortunately, those tried-and-true romantic formulas never work with Adrian, who—let me face it squarely—is emotionally stunted.

Beside the pond stood a statue not paid for by the park commission—a woman and her child, crystallized hand in hand. Ren approached the pair of frozen corpses. Their glassy faces expressed the most perfect happiness imaginable—a child and its mother in the bright morning of the world. It was as if their combined pleasure had been so pure, it had to end right here, before it could spoil. The woman's purse had already been looted, its contents emptied at her feet, and her death couldn't be reported because her implanted identity chip, like the rest of her, had turned to crystal.

Link gazed into the mother's frozen eyes, seeing the same thing he'd seen in O's—a final look preserved—of awesome revelation. He had a maddening sensation as if his brain were swelling. He knew something about all this. His whole life seemed a preparation for it. But how could crawling on his belly for hours to witness the dreadful marriage customs of a fly be any preparation for planetary tragedy?

The crystallized eyes of the young mother begged him to experience the revelation that had killed her, as if that epiphany were sufficient reward for losing one's life. He thought of those lines of male mantids, waiting for their turn with a female who'd just eaten her previous lover. The males in line knew she would eat every part of them, down to their hind legs. A pile of leftover legs, too tough even for her, would be the remains of their ecstasy.

Link walked on, his eyes drawn to a dead-leaf grasshopper dangling from a bush, suspended by a bit of thread and twisting slowly like a dry leaf in the breeze. People would pass it day after day and never know it was an insect, but more importantly, neither would the birds. Link touched the veiling device Dunbosian had given him. Probably not as effective as the grasshopper's veil. No one was inferior, no one was superior. It was primal energy, at work in countless guises. And crystallization was primal energy in a guise no one understood.

At a turning in the path he saw a crystallized jogger, her arms and legs frozen in stride. Her face bore the exalted look of an athlete whose endorphins have carried her to a new plateau, her body's power fully realized, all her strength and joy combining to meet the morning sun. "It takes them at their peak," he said.

They sat on a hilltop above the park's carousel. The mechanical music came to them interwoven with the laughter of children. To Upquark, Ren's absorption in the music matched Adrian's in his insects. The little robot watched them sitting side by side, lost in their respective worlds, and thought how natural it would be for one to take the other's hand.

What's wrong with them?

He didn't know what to do, so he did what he usually did— took measurements. He measured the level of sexual pheromones emanating from Adrian, and from Miss Ixen. Amply sufficient. Not a perfect match, of course, for Adrian and Miss Ixen were different species. But the chemical laboratories in both their bodies were producing amounts required for a very strong attraction.

And then he found something else, and instantly identified it. "Adrian," he cried. "Carbon number twelve, molecular weight one-fifty. Seductin. Exuded by the Secret Multitude."

"But aren't they dormant at this time of year?"

"What is the Secret Multitude?" asked Ren.

"The most common insect in the Corridor," said Upquark. "And seductin is their pheromone."

"Seductin is a perfume of sorts," said Link. "The male exudes it to attract the female."

"The air is thick with it," said Upquark, brandishing his measuring digits. "As if the park were crowded with the Secret Multitude. But since there are none around now, who's producing it? And who is it supposed to attract?"

They continued through the park. A crystallized vendor stood frozen on the pathway with his toy rockets circling the air around him, buzzing his head and feet, price tags trailing. The look on his face was one of keenest pleasure, as if he were a toy salesman from heaven, here to spread eternal joy. Dodging the miniature rockets, Upquark took measurements. "Seductin levels much higher here."

They wandered on, Upquark obsessively taking measurements, and wherever a crystallized figure appeared, he found a higher density of seductin in its vicinity. "Adrian, what's going on? Seductin is here but who made it? And why so high around the crystallized?"

Link thought of the clever ruses of the insect kingdom, of camouflage, of mimicry, of insects who counterfeited the pheromone of their victims in order to enter their hives and take slaves. But could this be happening here? The Secret Multitude had no hive, no treasure another bug would want. All they had were numbers, enormous numbers, the most populous insect on the planet, the one found everywhere. In the correct season, their perfume would cover half the planet.

And that, thought Link, is it. It's the primary smell of Planet Immortal.

He turned to Ren. His eyes were like the crystallized—pools of revelation. She held her breath, afraid that he would crack apart in front of her, like the jogger, the vendor, like O, like the mother and her child.

It was Upquark who spoke, to Ren. "Pheromones aren't always used as sexual attractants. Sometimes they're used to lead the group to food. Or," he added, "war."

They came to a café in the park. At one of the tables sat an Ophthalmic who would never eat again. Her mineral gaze held the secret of crystallization, but no one could unlock her many eyes. Waiters were hurriedly lifting her up and carrying her out of view.

Upquark checked the level of seductin in the air. It was high.

"Most unfortunate," said the manager coming over to Link and Ren. "But it's being handled. Please, don't let it spoil your appetite."

The café was framed by a low hedge. They took a table beside the hedge, and Upquark continued making soil tests, while Link gazed into the foliage.

"Upquark," said Link, with that same look of revelation in his eyes that had frightened Ren before. "Look at this grub."

"Larva of the Vampire Fly."

"Larva of the Vampire Fly," Link repeated, removing his veiling device, and throwing it on the ground.

"What are you doing?" cried Ren. "We'll be arrested."

"I've got to talk to the Observer." He glanced at his watch. "Her agents will be here to arrest us shortly."

CHAPTER 31

"A grub? You called us here for grubs? We're fighting a global predator, not barnyard pests." The Intelligence Agency robots glared at Upquark. He felt quite second-rate when faced by so many high-level machines. He'd overheard them calling him "a little weed puller," and it was true. Compared to these Axon Ipsilos, whose segmented eyes showed advanced cognition taking place on many levels simultaneously, he was indeed just a menial agricultural unit.

Impatient at having to deal with such a unit, the leader of the Axon Ipsilos was already rumbling toward the door.

The Observer nodded to the tactful Dr. Amphibras, who rose on large webbed feet and slapped over to the departing Axon Ipsilo. "We know how important your work is, and we'll urge our visitors to keep their remarks brief. Please, stay and hear them out. Your analysis will be invaluable."

"Grubs," grumbled the mollified machine. "What's next? Bird droppings?"

"There *are* grubs that resemble bird droppings," said Upquark, enthusiastically. "It provides them with excellent camouflage."

This drew a series of derisive beeps from the temperamental Axon Ipsilo, but Amphibras succeeded in rotating it back into position.

"You may proceed," the Observer said to Upquark, who switched a projection lamp on in his skull. A lens telescoped out of his forehead, through which a bright beam shone, and an enlarged image of a grub appeared on the office wall.

Link stepped in beside the image, and said, "Let me preface all this by reminding you—the most outrageous life form you can imagine is not impossible."

The Observer saw he was no longer the precocious youth he'd been when they last met; but there was still that odd quality of distance from his fellow humans.

"Nature embraces impossibility and overcomes it because she's not afraid to exaggerate. At times she becomes so preposterous in her schemes that we're unable to fully comprehend what she's done, but we always know why: to provide the means of survival for one of her children. We're not special. We're not her favorite. She has no favorites. She may provide extravagant weapons to our enemies. Now let me show you an example of Nature's extravagant means." He pointed to the white grub projected on the wall. "This is the larva of the Vampire Fly. Habitat, Planet Immortal. It secretes a sweet substance which ants like. So when they find one near their nest, they protect it as if it were a sacred cow." The image changed, showing ants licking the larva's skin and fending off other insects who might carry away the nectar-oozing grub.

"What does this have to do with crystallization?" snarled the chief Axon Ipsilo, and the other machines grumbled their assent.

"A sweet substance was exuded for us too. It was called immortality."

An unexpected silence settled on the grumbling machines.

Upquark changed the image on the wall. The larva was performing a contortionist's act. It withdrew its head and swelled out its abdomen.

"The larva now has a shape resembling that of an ant larva." The audience watched as the ants bore the white grub into their dome-like home. The image changed again, showing the nest's interior. "The Vampire larva is totally accepted and placed with the ants' own larvas."

The Vampire larva suddenly opened a powerful set of jaws and began to dine on the ant larvas. "It's capable of destroying the entire nest. Then in springtime, it emerges from the dead nest, with brand new wings, and flies away." Link swept his eyes over the Observer and her agents and their machines. "That's what happened to us. An incredibly clever parasite tempted us with the nectar of immortality, we took it into our nest, and now it's devouring us."

Link paused for a moment. The Observer looked at this fugitive who'd turned himself in so that he might make this presentation. When he was being considered for enrollment in the Academy, she'd demonstrated her complete knowledge of his personal history; with a faint smile he'd said, *I'm the same with insects. I know everything about them.* Now he was a few years older and presenting humanity as being as gullible as the residents of an anthill.

He said, "I was in the Amphora installation. I'm certain it had nothing to do with making mankind immortal. Its purpose was to open a dimensional doorway for our enemy."

His voice had remained calm and his lack of emotion sat well with the robots. "I think the Ancient Aliens have been gone for thousands of years, that they left this world definitively, that they never came back to instruct anyone in anything. The Immortals weren't instructed by the Ancient Aliens. They were instructed by extra-dimensionals."

There were harsh responses from the agents and machines who'd built a belief system around the Immortals. Link was unmoved. "The Immortals themselves were misled. They truly thought they were building a longevity device for mankind. They didn't know it was actually an interdimensional doorway designed by enormously sophisticated predators. Every component had a hidden, sinister purpose. The engineering is staggering. We'll probably never understand it."

He'd seen it as the butterfly sees a flower, as an assembly of dots. Were the dots the flower? No, they were only the butterfly's compound eye at work, an eye of many little eyes, each one seeing and bringing a single colored dot to the whole, forming finally that mosaic which the butterfly identifies as its energy source, the nectar-bearing blossom. In the same way, he'd assembled a view of a predator, from dots of understanding. But his dots were not the predator itself; they were merely a mosaic formed out of shadows, the way the butterfly sees the predatory bird, as a swift and threatening thing, glimpsed only momentarily. To see it for a greater length of time was to die. To know everything about the extra-dimensional predator was to become what Specterales O had become: a crystallized corpse.

"I believe the extra-dimensionals have completed a universal evolution. The energy of their universe is used up; their entire world is background radiation. All they have left is their will to survive. With it, they've cracked the dimensional boundaries, and found fresh hunting grounds here."

The Observer had left her implant receptors on to monitor the crystallization reports coming in from around the planet. Now she shut them down. Link continued: "The extra-dimensionals have gone through every extravagant mutation imaginable, and they're cunning beyond anything we can comprehend. Direct mental transmission is nothing for such beings." He looked at the Axon Ipsilos. "You, better than anyone, understand that perception is a matter of performing complicated mathematical operations on incoming frequencies. The extra-dimensionals are masters at amplifying those frequencies. The Immortal monks and nuns didn't have a chance. They experienced repeated teachings of the most wonderful kind, containing a blueprint for immortality."

"But their lives *were* lengthened."

"Yes, they were," agreed Link. "That's what made them so convincing to us. The extra-dimensionals took centuries instructing the monks and nuns in longevity. They succeeded in lengthening their lives, probably by donating reserves of energy to them."

The chief Axon Ipsilo rumbled up to Link, but its guttural voice was no longer dismissive. "If extra-dimensionals are after energy, why would they give any of it away to the Immortals?"

"They were willing to spend some to get much more. They're the keenest hunters in creation, with powers of will that have staggered us. They were willing to risk precious energy to bait their trap."

"What makes you think the energy of their universe is used up?"

"It's taken them centuries to crack our dimensional boundaries. Creatures as clever as that could find energy in their own world, if there was any left. These aren't ordinary pirates or mercenaries. They don't want gold, or land, or ships. They don't want our conventional energy systems. They want our life force. They enter our world unburdened by ethics or by any other of our categories. They don't see trees, dogs, or people. They see energy. That's all."

"Permission to make a file transfer," said Upquark, and brought up his pheromone measurements.

Ordinarily, no Axon Ipsilo would dream of allowing itself to be corrupted by a file from an agricultural unit, but their curiosity had been aroused; they decided that Upquark wasn't a little weed puller but actually an undercover robot inserted in the field by the Observer, and they accepted his pheromone files with interest, then reviewed them with instant comprehension. Their eyes remained fastened on Link, as he explained for the benefit of his slower human audience.

"The extra-dimensionals didn't evolve here, so their organs of sight, if they have any, don't correspond to our light conditions. Which means they're probably blind. To get around, they use smell, which is simpler and in some ways more dependable. They discovered our planet's pheromone system—" He paused and brought a model of it up on the screen. "Every creature on the planet emits molecules of scent, to connect members of a species. A highly sophisticated, invisible communication system, undetectable at the conscious level. With a little basic chemistry, they copied that system. They used an insect pheromone—seductin—as their model. A likely choice, because there's more seductin around than any other pheromone, because the insect that secretes it is everywhere. We've analyzed the extra-dimensional version of seductin, and it's stronger, with some sort of evaporation retardant so it lasts longer, but essentially they're getting around the way fleas do, by laying chemical trails. I don't think they're interested in smelling the roses or the coffee, it would just confuse them. The planet's a blank to them. Maybe our entire reality is a blank to them. So they grope for a solution to the problem of getting around without losing their way. Seductin presents itself because it's a natural pathway, used by a multitude. It's perfect, the chemistry is already worked out to suit the planetary conditions. They just match it and use it as it's been used for millions of years. Remember, all they want is to be able to navigate the planet successfully. Our world isn't really recognizable to them. They could rattle easily. But so long as they can retrace their steps, they're secure and can go along, picking us off, one by one."

"And they have some kind of physical form?"

"They're a borderline entity with a sensory system that works in our dimension. That's all we can say."

The Observer shut her eyes and pondered. If this was true, if the old monks and nuns had been duped, it was no failure for her to acknowledge that she and everyone in the Consortium had also been duped. What could she have done against a being as cunning as the one Link was describing? How could she have prevented an invasion that'd started centuries before she was even born? "What do we do with this knowledge you've given us?"

"We lay our own pheromone trail and get them to follow it."

CHAPTER 32

I see a dying city, thought the Gamester, or so my software tells me, but what do I really see? What mechanized dream am I looking at, in this street of frozen people? He stared up into the windows of a night school for recently arrived aliens. They'd been hoping to understand the ways of Planet Immortal, and now they understood it all too well. The headlights of a robus descending from the sky slowly crossed their crystallized faces.

He rotated in the other direction, and his eyes were drawn to a clothing store. There were mannequins on display, and the employees and the customers were mannequins too, frozen in the aisles as shopping music played around them. A woman posed before a three-way mirror, looking at her final reflection from front, back, and side. She seemed pleased with what she saw. She'd crystallized in a size four.

He rolled along and peered into an office building with employees in the lobby, waiting for elevators that came and went, carrying the same passengers up and down. No one got off and no one got on. Each time the doors opened, muted music flooded out and then was borne away upward with the frozen passengers.

Frozen chefs stood in a restaurant window. On the griddle, steaks had burnt to crisp black squares. French fries bubbled continuously, resembling wood shavings. One chef had made a last grand flourish with his pan, in which the contents were now congealed. The Gamester observed the diners who had crystallized—loving couples, embittered couples, indifferent couples, and a frozen waiter still serving the last dish of existence. It seemed that all they needed was a charge, but the Gamester knew there was no unit that could charge up these organic beings.

He heard a circus tune coming from the speakers of an Electric Elf rolling toward him, and he joined in with a few bars.

"How nice to find another player," said the Electric Elf. It was a small, simpleminded machine, and it juggled multicolored balls. "I was performing at a birthday party at which the children became quite stiff. I couldn't make them sing and dance. This reflected on my abilities, and I left in a state of self-reproach. However, I see that everyone is in the same condition. I cannot be the cause."

"No, you're not the cause."

The Electric Elf rolled its juggling balls up its arm into an interior slot. "What shall I do?"

"Just play your songs."

"I'll run down my charge."

"You can charge up all over town. No one will bother you."

So the Elf continued pressing the pearly buttons in its chest, like those of an accordion. "I will now play another tune. It's for a miniature circus with tiny horses."

The tune seemed heartbreakingly beautiful to the Gamester, and the equivalent of tears ran behind his eyes, but he knew it was just the firing of emotional circuits which would reset themselves. The avenue was crowded with corpses, their legs forward-striding in postures of anticipation. Their final destination had become this street, this corner, forever. "A critical mass has been reached," he said to himself. "Now crystallization will sweep the planet."

The Electric Elf blew a noisemaker, and the Gamester thought, this is how it will be everywhere. Just a few machines as the world runs down.

Then he picked up a random radio transmission . . . *on the outskirts of the city . . . a mass meeting . . . the truth about Amphora . . .*

Did someone really know the truth? He turned on his pick-up light, and a robus descended, scooped him up, and slotted him in place beside other units riding home from late shifts. He got off at the city's industrial edge and joined a crowd of aliens and humans moving toward a stadium.

The Gamester rolled up the robo-ramp and slotted himself into the stands. Great lights swept the arena, carried by free-flying projectors. A transparent bubble floated down and exploded in a shower of sparks. A man in a white light-suit came out, his voice wired for big sound.

"Welcome, my friends, to the First Assembly of Amphora." The echo was on, and the phrase bounced over the stadium several times, its effect changing with each repetition, and accompanied by a spray of traveling holograms that made it seem the man was everywhere at once. He pointed upward, at the fragmented Junk Moon hanging in the night sky. "There's the Ark of Serenity, come to take us home. They tried to destroy it, but you can't destroy a vehicle of the Spirit."

The Gamester scanned the audience's faces, each one bearing the same rapt expression. Mr. Link would find it instructive, he thought, this unifying behavior, this unquestioning response, like ants in a nest. But being surrounded by so much hysteria degraded a robot's mental performance, and the Gamester felt his internal alarm bells going off. He wanted to leave, but would they let him go? Crowds could get belligerent. The laws protecting machines were open to interpretation, and present times were tending toward no laws at all.

The preacher stabbed his finger toward the sky, and his projected image swept the stadium along with the hypnotic echo of his cadence. "We're crystallizing. We're *mineralizing*. Every day we lose another and another. Amphora says *I will be praised. I will be satisfied. I will take the unrealized, but I will spare the awakened.*" He paced the arena, with the free-flying lights following him, and his holo-image shooting up and down the aisles of the stadium. "I've been to Amphora, friends, I've been in its swirling hyperspace and I saw worlds within it, the wave functions of the universe, I saw quantum reality!"

The Gamester edged into the aisle. He had to risk departure. Orchestral tom-toms were beating, and the crowd was chanting, "Amphora, Amphora." The Gamester made a looped copy of the chant and played it through his speakers as he moved slowly through the mob. When people looked at him and heard his soft intoning, they smiled and said, "The little box has the spirit of Amphora in him."

He gained the robot ramp and began rolling downward, his volume on just enough to pump out, "Amphora, Amphora . . ."

A hand grabbed his antennas. "Where you going, Box?"

"I'm discharging too fast," said the Gamester. "I need a boost."

"Amphora gives you the boost." The disciple pivoted him back toward the stadium field. "That's your boost, machine. Feel the glory of Amphora."

"I feel it," said the Gamester.

"Testify that the machine can be saved."

"The machine can be saved."

"Acknowledge Amphora."

"I acknowledge."

The stadium rumbled with the feet of the excited crowd keeping time with the orchestral drums. Holograms of the preacher were flashing around on all sides as he cried, "I saw it and I returned! I came back for *you*."

A tremendous piezoelectric crack struck, followed by . . . silence. The Gamester looked around at the crystallized First Assembly of Amphora. The preacher was frozen in a gesture of triumph, both arms extended upward. The audience was frozen in its gesture of response. Here and there, those who'd been spared were crawling frantically over the dead. Soon the aisles were filled with desperate devotees. "They're killing the believers!"

"That's why they got us all together here."

"Except for him! I saw him trying to leave just before it happened."

"Unbeliever! Assassin!" cried the mob, converging on the Gamester.

He turned up the volume on his Amphora chant, but it had no effect on the frenzied crowd. They tore off his antennas.

"Please," he cried, but he was surrounded by strong hands which reached out to twist his stubby arms. He felt the metal crack, the wires snap, and his arms dangled limply. His emergency repair circuits clicked on, signaling frantically.

A belt buckle smashed in one eye lens, then the other. The Gamester's world went black. He felt strong hands grip his head, felt his head bolts being turned, and suddenly his audio feed went spinning.

His head was off.

"Toss me that thing!"

Sound came in a dizzying whirl, accompanied by static, and then it slowly faded.

He felt his legs coming off, but the feeling was distant; his tactile input was too slow. His emergency circuitry was switching him lower and lower in the receptor package, searching for a holding place. Just . . . a . . . game, he told himself.

All external contact was broken. Internal checks continued, traveling through what was left in Central Torso Area and out to Peripheral Connection Points. Then back into Central Torso. The checks grew fewer, then stopped altogether.

Just . . . a . . .

All functions terminated.

CHAPTER 33

"I should hire you to create a new aftershave for me," said General Caph, who was coordinating Operation Bola. The chemists in Link's new laboratory were chattering on all sides of him, and most of what they said was beyond the general; talk of primary alcohols and double bonds meant nothing to him, but he believed in the power of perfume.

Upquark explained to him that, "If a female moth were to release all the pheromone in her scent sac at once, she could attract a trillion males in an instant."

"But she restrains herself," said Caph. "Very sensible." He, like everybody in the lab, was masked and suited up, for the substances being concocted were at concentrations far stronger than his aftershave.

Link felt in his element for the first time since leaving the Agricultural Plain. To him, pheromones were sacred substances, created by tiny chemists who'd been testing and improving them over eons, until hives and nests ran unfailingly on pheromone directives. They were one of the great wonders of the world, and Operation Bola had been named after a spider who used them in an especially clever way.

"The bola spider," Upquark informed the general, "attracts male moths by manufacturing a pheromone identical to that produced by the female moth. The male flies upwind toward the scent, thinking he's headed for his mate, and lands in the spider's dinner plate."

"And we're the spider," said Caph.

"I sincerely hope so," answered Link.

Caph was watching Link with interest. The young scientist had seen a million massacres in miniature. The concept of an enemy without mercy, conscience, or any other moral constraint was familiar to him. He'd witnessed no end of murder and dismemberment in the vast kingdom of the insects. Caph asked him, "How is it you know so much about these beings you call the extra-dimensionals?"

"Because I've known them since childhood."

Caph raised an eyebrow.

Link didn't bother to look up from his work. "I think the extra-dimensionals are always patrolling the bands of perception, looking for somebody pushing at the outer limits of the band. That's what I was doing as a kid when I spent most of my time imagining I was an insect. The extra-dimensionals noticed the disturbance in my frequency, and somehow they amplified my efforts for me, to hook me into their program. As a result, I learned how to penetrate the shell frequency dividing us from the insect world. But that wasn't what they had in mind."

Link paused. He felt the questions hanging in the air, from everyone in the lab. "What they had in mind was recruiting me into their longevity scheme. That's their bait. It's always the same. But children don't care about longevity. They already think they're going to live forever. It was more exciting for me to feel how a bee flexes her knee joints to help her take off. I preferred feeling the g-forces on a dragonfly when it turns. The extra-dimensionals wrote me off, I'm sure."

"And the Immortals?"

"They were also pushing at the bands of perception. They were deep meditators, exploring transformations of consciousness. They got the longevity message and took the bait." Link paused again. The lab was completely silent. All work had ceased. He said, "The extra-dimensionals are always out there fishing. Their hooks are always set, trolling through eternity."

"You mean their battle doesn't end here?" asked Caph.

"Hardly."

"Since they have a hook in you, so to speak, can't they sense that you're their enemy? Don't they know you're working to kill them?"

"We're a life form about which they only have a rudimentary understanding. But they know all life seeks to sustain itself forever, and so they bait their hook and drop their line."

One of the chemists stepped closer to Link. "Are they still contacting you?"

"It never stops."

"Of what do these recent contacts consist?"

"Same as always. The promise of immortality."

"But they already caught us with that lure. Why would they keep repeating it?"

"We're not the only ones they're fishing for. The same line will keep going out forever, dropping from their universe and baited as it always has been, with every living creature's fondest dream, to defeat death."

Warning lights flashed at the door as a security robot went into full battle readiness. A moment later it went back to standby, and the cafeteria door opened. A pair of Dark Dreamers entered, squabbling, their high-pitched voices translated by the long-suffering robot assigned to them by the Observer.

"You know what's wrong with you, you nitwit? You have sub-nuclear debris in your brain."

"Owing to your miscalculations."

"In that setting, particles will repel each other."

"Not as much as you repel me."

The spell Link had cast was broken and the lab went back to work. The two Dreamers began pummeling each other, and the robot had to separate them. They dangled from the ends of its grippers, still swinging at each other, their red caps flapping. When it set them back on the floor, they made a few more angry stabs, but the smell of pazdu lured them away from each other. They loved its kick; it fueled their anger.

More quarreling Dreamers came in, and the robot got between them and guided them toward the pazdu dispenser. They filled mugs so large they had to hold them with two hands, then set the mugs on a lab table, and crawled up onto chairs, their pointed shoes far from the floor. There they continued their argument, muttering and drinking thick pazdu from Hermetia.

Warning lights flashed again, and the Observer entered. She noted lines of strain on Link's face, and supposed her features showed the same weary lines. They'd both been working without sleep, using a retinal stimulator whose beam reset their brains to continuous morning. Through her exhaustion she saw his face as a mask, impossible to penetrate. Her files on him could never be complete, because he operated in a second frequency, where she had neither spies nor surveillance devices. He was a man who couldn't be shadowed where it truly mattered.

"I'd like to hear the extra-dimensional message," said Caph.

"You are hearing it," said Link. "But your thoughts blend with it and move on."

"So how did you recognize their voice?"

"It's not a voice. It's more like pressure. It directs our thinking, very subtly, until we shape the thought ourselves. But it's the thought they want us to have."

"But they don't speak our language."

"Their pressure is below the level of language," interrupted the Observer, who felt that pressure now, at the edge of her consciousness, like a half-remembered dream emanating from another world. Listening to Link over these past few days, she felt she could interpret the message of the extra-dimensionals, just as the old monks and nuns had interpreted it. Through her weariness, she heard the promise of immortality. She said, "It's why we were so ready to accept Amphora. We'd been subliminally bombarded with the idea our whole lives."

* * *

At Central Command, military planners were studying a large-scale model of Planet Immortal on which a grid was traced. They were being briefed by the Observer, which infuriated them. The Planet was under a full-scale attack, and, if she had her way, the greatest weapons in the Corridor would never come out of their silos. To be sidelined by a civilian was intolerable. This was the ultimate war. They'd prepared for it for generations.

"These lines represent the heaviest concentrations we've found of the extra-dimensional pheromone," explained the Observer. "They've sectored off the planet. They hunt in the grid squares and then return to the main routes. We'll lay down pheromone trails stronger than their own and force them to go where we want."

"How can you be sure they'll follow your trails?" demanded General Liu.

"Our dimension is like a dream for them. To track their way through that dream, they've created a temporary guidance system, using olfactory sensing, represented by these lines." She spun the globe with her finger, and the generals continued to fume, with the exception of General Caph and a younger officer who was sure he remembered the Observer from years before: They had been attached to an elite team, she as an expert in clandestine operations. He'd gone into battle with her on the Black Asteroid, and she'd performed as expected, under intense enemy fire. And then some faceless bureaucrats stepped in, and she'd vanished, no one knew where. Was it she in front of him now? Her voice was different, her face had been changed, but that cool style, and something in the way she moved her arms—he thought he saw the young woman he'd known.

She stopped the spinning globe with her finger, and Link took up the thread. "The pheromone we've mixed will bond with theirs and is more concentrated. They won't know the difference; it takes all their resources just to hold their temporary system together; they've got no expectation of any changes being made, and no time to deal with them anyway. They have to adhere to the very rigid pattern you see on this grid, because our dimension overwhelms them. Nonetheless they've fabricated a makeshift olfactory system, and we've found its weakness: Pheromones go straight to the neuronal sensors. You can't screen them out. That's why the bola spider always wins. A web of silk can be avoided, but a web of perfume is irresistible. The moth has no choice. If pheromones are what you steer by, you follow them."

"But the extra-dimensionals aren't moths," grumbled General Liu.

"They've used the guidance system of a flea," said Link. "Why shouldn't we use the snare of a spider?"

The Observer drew the group's attention back to the grid lines. "You can see the extra-dimensionals' hunting ground. It began in our capital and has been radiating steadily outward. We want to route them to—here."

She pointed to the grid and then nodded to one of her Agency robots. The big Axon Ipsilo glided forward. "This area suffers powerful effects from an interaction between the planetary mantle and the planetary core . . . the movement of the central mass has created . . ."

General Caph closed his eyes. He'd only gotten a few hours' sleep. Even when fully rested, he could never understand equations, and no ordinary soldier should be subjected to them. His pilots already knew all about Planet Immortal's Sink Hole. At least they knew enough to stay away from it, because it paralyzed aircraft, bringing them down like stones. It was a natural prison, and the Observer and her staff were going to steer the extra-dimensionals into it.

". . . the displacement from the planetary center . . ." continued the Axon Ipsilo. Yes, fine, get on with it, said Caph to himself, and forced his eyelids open.

". . . and the gravitic anomaly . . ."

We'll all be crystallized in our chairs waiting for this bucket of bolts to get done talking. But that's the way of high-end machines. They have to flood a meeting with data, so that if things don't work no one can say they've been irresponsible. If anyone is left to say anything.

He turned toward his military colleagues, some of whom wore expressions as glazed as his own. A few were engineers, but none of them were on the level of the Axon machine.

". . . magnetic core librations and amplitude of the nutational . . ."

One could only resist so long, and Caph surrendered. He'd trained himself to remain erect while unconscious and did so now. He liked napping in the security of an operational room, where no one would assassinate him, no irate husband attack him. Here were only his fellow officers, some of them napping too, in the knowledge that the doors were securely bolted on all sides. He faded in and out as the robot droned on, then snapped to consciousness as his name was mentioned. "Yes, I'm fully prepared." He counted on his adjutant to tell him exactly what for.

* * *

"Our statistics indicate that in all major crystallizations, when whole neighborhoods crack, the survivors are phlegmatic types—people whom nothing stirs, who live in monotone, bored, indifferent, like goldfish in a bowl. Therefore, you will all undergo emotion suppression training." The psy-robot was addressing the members of Operation Bola. "If everything goes as planned, you will be at close quarters with concentrated numbers of the extra-dimensionals. Without conditioning, you will very likely crystallize. Therefore, attendance is mandatory."

* * *

The Observer came to the laboratory at dawn. Only Link and Upquark were there, Link still monitoring his mixture. He'd told her that solutions were sensitive in ways that pass understanding; without any human interaction, a stubborn new solution might crystallize out merely from being kept close to an older, crystallized one. "That's why crystallizations have become easier in the populace. One crystallization helps to coax another. Your crystallized neighbor becomes your enemy, because he inspires the same process in you." Link turned to the Observer wearily, his tall figure slouching, his curly hair limp from chemical vapors. Stains covered his rumpled white uniform; his gloves and helmet were gone; his final tests had proved the mixture stable. "Large scale manufacture should begin in about an hour."

"Does that mean you'll get some sleep?" she asked, wondering why she cared that he was tired. Her job was pushing people beyond tiredness. She herself had been pushed beyond endurance in this race to stop the crystallizations from swallowing the planet. Electronic dispatches flashing into her brain had become too numerous and too awful; she'd shut down her cerebral receptor system, and relied on conventional reporting, the Auranet opening around her hourly, with scenes of paralyzed villages and towns; their crystalline sparkle and stillness were a momentary greeting card of sentimental taste. But death had signed it; the figures belonged to an underworld of ice.

"Your Cantusian has been asking after you," she murmured.

"She's not my Cantusian," he said with surprise, turning from the monitors. Though his work was done, he'd taken retinal stimulation only a few hours ago and was still keyed for action.

The Observer gazed at his haggard face. "If she hadn't helped you flee the Guard, you wouldn't have had this chance, and neither would we."

"Then it's nice you're looking after her." He started prowling the aisle of the lab, reexamining settings he'd made only minutes before. She saw the perfectionist in him who matched her own, functioning just at the edge of madness.

"I've offered her the chance to return to Cantus," continued the Observer.

"Is she going?" he asked absentmindedly as he continued his checking, like the bola spider who makes the final zigzag thread across its web.

"No. One wonders why."

He looked at her, and she saw he had no idea of the Cantusian's feelings for him, nor did he seem to care.

"Come on," she said, "sit down. The robots are making your mixture. Great tanks of it. You can take five minutes off."

He collapsed into a chair, exhaling heavily. His head went down, then snapped back up. "Their message is stronger when I'm tired. I feel them so clearly. Not that it matters now."

His fatigue seemed to have given him a courtly air, with his gestures made more weary. For some reason this made him appealing. Or perhaps it was her own exhaustion that made her susceptible. She was forced to admit that her questions about the Cantusian were not disinterested. She also sensed that allowing such thoughts to come to her, when she was responsible for the ultimate crisis of the planet, was a sign she knew the world was definitely ending and that she wished to experience love one last time.

His eyelids lowered, dark with weariness. She saw that he was in his second shell, beyond her reach, beyond the reach of the Cantusian, or any woman. This shell of iron ritual, of insectile strategy driven by ancient, unvarying solutions is what had given him the strength he'd shown over the past days, but it also extracted its price—that part of the human personality normally given to love. He eluded her, not because he wanted to, but because he'd been transformed by extra-dimensional contact.

He woke with a start, and brought himself to his feet. "I circle back to them endlessly now, trying to comprehend them. If this table got up and flew away, it would be less mysterious than they are."

She saw doubt in his eyes, and for an instant her heart stopped beating. She said, "You're their pupil. Have you got a chance against them?"

He gazed at her, exhaustion weighing down the corners of his mouth. "The Immortals were their pupils, not me."

"Very well, you weren't exactly their pupil, but you still got something from them."

"A taste of their reality. Just the tiniest piece of it. It was enough to unsettle my life. To make me—"

"Friendless." The word was out before she could censor it.

The corners of his mouth turned up in a faint smile. He nodded toward Upquark, who had also pushed himself beyond his limits, and was standing in the laboratory charging booth, a shower of energy coming down around him. "He's my friend."

"So am I." This too slipped out, but discretion was no longer important in a world that was coming apart.

He looked back at her, but didn't take his cue. The extra-dimensionals were still uppermost in his thoughts; he was locked with them in battle and couldn't risk taking his eyes off his enemy. She yearned to soothe his restlessness, but she knew he was incapable of receiving tenderness. Suddenly, she wrapped her arms around him. His body collapsed against her, but it was just exhaustion. She could see his mind was in his second shell.

He abruptly drew back. "I've got to go to the manufacturing area."

"They don't need you."

He seemed surprised by the idea, then accepted it. "No, I suppose not. Not anymore."

"Have you eaten anything in the last twenty-four hours?"

He pointed at the remains of an artificial snack.

And now, she thought, mocking her maternal feelings, as the world falls apart I'm worried about his nutrition. She took his arm, led him outside, and into her hovercraft. "We won't be ready to strike until tomorrow. You might as well eat tonight."

The food was served mechanically, elevatored from the downstairs galley into glass holding compartments, and then extended outward onto the dining table. He only looked at it, seeming not to understand. She handed him a fork. "For food transport."

He nodded, smiled faintly, returned from his remote spaces. "We're like an assembly of wound-up springs, and the extra-dimensionals know how to trigger those springs. A raw planet is no use to them; the energy isn't in a form they can use. They need highly evolved creatures to prey on, living energy factories. That's what we are, the power of the sun in a form that they can tap. They tap the energy in our chemical bonds, the bonds come apart, they take the freed energy, and we crystallize. What elegant vampires."

He seemed to doze again, awoke, and began to eat the food she'd put in front of him. "We're very tasty creatures. Billions of years of breeding. That's what they like. A tasty bit of evolution."

Before he'd swallowed his third mouthful, he was sound asleep. She could hardly stay awake herself, but she couldn't afford to rest, not yet. She left him there, in the dining room of her ship, and went to speak with the Dark Dreamers.

CHAPTER 34

"I've found Stuart Landsmann! He's on a War God." Dr. Amphibras stood breathless before the Observer; he'd been hopping at full speed down the hallway.

"Where's the War God operating?"

"It's been close to us all along. It's protecting the Immortal monastery."

"There's a certain irony in that," said the Observer. "Well, get him here."

Amphibras hopped back toward the door, but the Observer stopped him with a question. "How did we lose him?"

"The Sub-Neurolator who processed Landsmann has been questioned. It admitted to partying the night before Landsmann's processing took place. As a consequence, it scrambled the data."

"What's been done with this Neurolator?"

"Its board has been checked. There was nothing functionally wrong. It's back in service. But its outside privileges were withdrawn."

"We're more forgiving with our robots. I should have done the same with Landsmann instead of brain-cleaning him." She hesitated. "No catatons have ever been restored on my watch. When restoration takes place, is the individual completely sound in mind?"

"There may be slight disorientation but it's only temporary. Any memory loss is insignificant."

*　*　*

The commander of this particular War God was a Zerosum from the Consortium Guard War College who suffered from a conceit to which many high-end machines are prone. He believed himself to *be* the War God he commanded.

In recent interplanetary battles, wholly robotic ships had proven themselves superior to those run by organic beings. In the cyclone of violent passion that war bred, robots reasoned calmly, their dark eye slits evenly open. They moved about the ship now, their Electrish orders sizzling through the communication systems. The cool, circular passageways carried hundreds of black-armored machines on their rounds, from radar room to gun chamber to flight deck. The game was never old to them; their original intensity of purpose reset itself daily.

For Commander Zerosum, danger was always at hand, and he was ready to smash it to oblivion. This purgatory of endless tension was happiness for a robot of his design. In his background processing, Zerosum replayed decisive battles of the Corridor. Mistakes made there would not be his. No enemy would take him unaware. His head wouldn't shake on his shoulders. On seeing the slightest movement of hostility, he would draw instant conclusions and act.

Several decks below, in Cataton Holding, Gregori Man o' War was issued his plain white uniform for the week by the duty robots. Following which he garroted them. His time to move had come; he had learned the habits of the crew and the weak spots in their routine.

Catatons waiting for their work shift to start gazed at him with blank vegetal stares. His mutinous actions meant nothing to them. He was just another shape in a world without structure.

Gregori had his own eye on a gigantic cataton whose strength was formidable: Somewhere deep in back of his mindless gaze glowed the ashes of an unregenerate criminal. "You," said Gregori, "are what I need."

A storage unit contained the life chips of every cataton on board; Consortium law required that catatons never be separated from their fundamental histories. Catatonic sentences varied in length; some were for life, some of shorter duration. The giant's sentence was life-long; a particularly nasty record was inscribed on his chip. "Yes," said Gregori, as he performed a quick review of the various mayhems and murders the lout had performed, "you are high quality."

He hooked the giant to the resurgencer, inserted the Data Identity Membrane Ecesis on which his life was stored, and watched the light of brutality returning to the villain's eyes. His twisted childhood beginnings were restored, his early tortures reinserted. As each layer of his execrable nature was assimilated, his thick head snapped back and forth.

"Come on, come on," said Gregori, for it was taking longer than he had to spare, but he didn't want to stop with only half a monster. He needed the entire fiend.

The giant shook and whined. Obviously a coward, observed Gregori, but he will have to do. "You'll listen to me, my friend, or I'll crush you. Is that clear?"

The giant nodded affirmation, as his depraved ego continued to reshape itself. His name, Gregori saw from the file, was Smagula. "Smagula, pay attention. You're imprisoned on a War God. I am your only hope. Do you understand? I and none other."

Smagula nodded. His threads of corruption were nearly all rehung. Being imprisoned was natural to him, as natural as home to an honest citizen. And while in prison, as on the street, the plans of action were always in the hands of those like this one in front of him now—a crack-out artist, who needed his brute strength. "Point me," said Smagula.

"I shall," said Gregori. "We're both still catatons, understand? The living dead. We don't speak, we only obey."

Again Smagula nodded. Having a lifetime's memories restored in a few minutes had left him reeling, but he understood that focus was required.

"The walk of the cataton," said Gregori. "Do you still have it?"

"I have it," said Smagula. Among his memories, the stupefied dream of the cataton was uppermost. "I'll never forget it."

Gregori moved toward another cataton, that friend of Kitty Liftoff who'd been arrested on the Paper Lantern. I offered to free him for Kitty. She said it was impossible. Well, Kitty, this one's for you.

"Time to wake," said Gregori. He pulled Stuart Landsmann's chip, and the physicist came back through a lifetime's scientific work, up to and including dancing with a charming woman on the Paper Lantern.

"Do you wish to die a vegetable?" asked Gregori. "No? Can you use this?" He handed Landsmann a disintegration pistol. "And follow us."

Landsmann followed, understanding that the game was insurrection. Against whom, he didn't care.

Gregori took them down a long passage on Lower Level. An armed robot looked them over indifferently, as he identified them from the ship's roster.

"Do not congregate," he ordered.

Smagula hammered the robot's head down into its torso. Sparks and smoke rose from the neck, along with the muffled words, "Purity of cognition fouled."

Smagula picked the robot up and drove its legs up into its body, then flattened it completely, crushing all components into something resembling an electric pizza. Then he rolled it into a club and carried it by his side, sharp edges dangling.

Gregori's knowledge of the War God came from assistance he'd given the Consortium fleet in times of mercenary pardon. His pardons had always run out, owing to irregularities of deportment, but never to run out was his fond memory of a War God's rooms, its halls and gun ports, its missile and radar chambers, its elevators and transfer tunnels. He moved with a sure step, from the Cataton Holding staircase to the Middle Deck.

But he was sweating. Though he loved the War God, it did not love him. Its sounds of elevators, its faint tremors of stabilizers, its throbbing engines were like the growls and footfalls of predators, through whose jungle he was creeping. He passed a porthole, looked out, and saw the monastery of the Immortals down below. He thought of Kitty again, who'd wanted to be immortal. He felt her cold crystal hand still, as if it were stroking the back of his neck; but it was only a cooling unit behind him.

He led Smagula and Landsmann through the Middle Deck, past gun emplacements forming a command ring around the critical center of operations. Robotic gunners sat on focus, relentlessly scanning the sky above the Immortals' monastery. He and his party were no more than shadows to them, for their cannons did not swing inward. That direction did not exist for them.

He continued on to Center Station, where flight officers worked with Commander Zerosum. The three catatons entered, into the efficient buzz of Electrish.

Their identikeys were automatically scanned. Catatons were not unusual here. Landsmann remembered what he'd done here as a cataton, and did it now—polishing control consoles and removing hated dust, bane of wired brains.

Zerosum held the central chair, monitoring the world from which attack would come. His many victories were on continual parade in his memory, for self-esteem was good for the robotic self. Those gigantic battles of his early years, against mercenary ships, played before him in a continuous stream—how he'd feinted and ducked, and used his cannonades of fire. The monster ships of the mercenaries had not oppressed him. He'd oppressed *them*. I am their master, everlastingly. Bring giant foes to bear against me. Bring the universe itself. I stand firm. I never yield, nor can I die. The greatest ship that mind can make will not defeat me.

"What do you want?" he asked, as Smagula knelt beside his chair. Zerosum looked down at the mindless brute. What a specimen.

The cataton didn't answer, and Zerosum flicked a digit in its face. The noxious creature remained kneeling. Its programming must have jammed, reflected Zerosum. "Remove this entity," he said, and flicked his fingers in its face again, striking directly on Smagula's eyeball. The giant rose up, taking the commander's chair with him, tearing it from the floor and then, with Zerosum still in it, drove it through the ceiling.

Man o' War and Landsmann fired their disintegration pistols, sending into massless flux the robotic flight staff of the War God. Smagula brought Zerosum down out of the ceiling with his head caved in. The commander was meant for combat of the stars, against great ships from outer worlds. A meat-handed petty criminal on his flight deck had not been profiled in his defense response. As Smagula ground his components into pieces, and his glorious memories were severed and sliced, Zerosum had time for a final reflection, that it was always a matter of programming. Leave one thing out, and you go to the bit bucket. And there have I gone.

"Have you any wish to return to Planet Immortal?" Gregori asked Smagula. "Where, I remind you, you were catatonized?"

"No," grunted Smagula, tossing aside the chips and wires that had been Zerosum.

"Landsmann," asked Gregori, "are you in any way sentimental about the planet that desouled you?"

"I'm done with it," said Landsmann.

"Good, because I am about to steal a War God, which has been my life's ambition."

With a single command, he activated a new course, to the Outer Plenum and beyond, where with any luck at all he would be the best-armed mercenary in the universe.

And the War God left its position above the monastery of the Immortals, and moved out toward the stars.

CHAPTER 35

Kizz Zum resembled a curvaceous, rainbow-colored candle. Her eyes had flame-shaped yellow pupils that undulated slowly back and forth. Her body had a waxy sheen, and like every Candelarian her body was always several degrees warmer than a human's, which was pleasant for Jockey Oldcastle, seated beside her on a plump couch. "I planned long careers for them," sighed Kizz, glancing across the crowded room at the Idols of the Marketplace, the newest group of cosmic rockers she managed. "And now my beautiful cash machines could crystallize before my eyes, tonight."

"Tonight just think of me," said Jockey, drawing closer to her warmth. Kizz leaned forward to inhale vapors from a Glow tank suspended in the air, its hoses dangling down as if it were a floating jellyfish of joy. As she inhaled, her skin took on a rosy luminescence that seemed healthy, but Candelarians who didn't temper their Glowing lived short lives, prematurely burning up their stores of hydrocarbons and fatty acids. Kizz felt the Glow consuming her, right down to her heat-sensitive, resinous toes.

"Families are no longer claiming their crystallized," she remarked. "The survivors figure they'll be dead soon themselves, so why bother." She ran her waxy finger down the floating Glow tank's face, which was etched with frosted nymphs; the brightly decorated hoses were tipped in gold. Similar tanks floated in every room of Kizz's house, each tank decorated with nymphs and satyrs, their playful cavorting meant to suggest that Glow produced innocent pleasure.

Electron screens also floated at eye level, broadcasting holovised images of global destruction. Jockey watched in morbid fascination as workers removed crystallized bodies from the capital. Though they worked in shifts around the clock, they continually fell behind, for the avenues kept refilling with the dead, whose glistening surfaces reflected the garish lights of advertising towers. Crystal figures struck by vehicles were ground up into shards and spread along the pavement, making the gutters glitter with macabre beauty.

"I hear they're selling ground-up crystal for pottery glazing." Jockey looked suspiciously at a tall vase.

"No, darling, not that one," answered Kizz.

Another guest, overhearing, said, "There's a new line of perfume called Amphora."

Kizz was a naturally scented Candelarian, with a delicious odor emanating from her. She turned toward the window. The rock garden outside was illuminated by spotlights hidden in the trees. She gazed at the rocks, and realized for the first time that these hulking forms were the original presence of the planet; the moss that covered them was youthful and green, but the stones were gray old witnesses of inconceivable events; they'd been arranged in the garden by an Exhulian master, to suggest the revelation of ancient time. Now, when revelation had to be guarded against, she felt the poignant message of the stones.

"I've gone off Glow," said another Candelarian sadly. "You never get back what it takes away from you."

Kizz nodded in agreement. "I mustn't have anymore tonight—" She let the hose swing away from her fingers. "—or I'll end up like the rest of them, a homeless candle stub melting on the street, with the top of my head caved in." She caught the swinging hose again and fondled it. "I'll be nothing but a puddle of wax on the sidewalk, all my colors gone and possibly a boot print in me."

Jockey watched a floating holovision bubble of Robbie Faircloth, late heir to Starweb Communications, being carried out of a news conference, media lights reflecting off his stiffened, gleaming body. He must have been haranguing his audience, for his forefinger was fixed forever in an admonitory shake, the last emphatic gesture of his life. A loudmouth who forgot himself in rhetorical rapture, thought Jockey.

The picture changed, showing a city street corner. "Another Doomsday party." Jockey nodded toward the holo-image of a group of people toasting with champagne glasses. They were dressed up in their best, desperately joyous, desperately laughing.

"Well, why not?" said Kizz Zum. "If everyone is finished—"

"There's never a true finish," said Jockey. "You can be sure that out of the rubble something will crawl. It always does. The most unwholesome creatures have a remarkable indestructibility."

Kizz was staring at her own waxy, multicolored fingers. "We think the flame's eternal, but the oil always runs out."

"Plenty of oil in you yet," said Jockey affectionately, but his eyes were gazing upward toward the skylight through which the loosely connected islands of the broken Junk Moon could be seen revolving in a slow, ominous dance.

"It's been a long time since you visited me, Jockey," said Kizz. "You must need money."

"Money? Certainly not. What do you take me for?"

"A sponging, lying, two-faced opportunist." Kizz inhaled again, then laid her head on Jockey's shoulder. "I feel warm and waxy."

"You've turned bright orange, my dear. You're glowing in the dark." He put his arm around her and gave her a squeeze, as oily tears emerged from her eyes and turned to wax beads on her cheeks. "Jockey, I'm frightened."

"I'm with you, Kizz. Jockey is here."

She wiped the beads off her cheek. "Of all the people to finish with."

"It's me or Mirrorhead," he answered, glancing at one of Kizz's most successful cosmic rockers. Like all Lustrumians, Mirrorhead had reflective flesh. It was thought Lustrumians evolved this way to confuse predators. Now, in less primitive conditions, it was a dazzling bit of personal beauty. Onstage, Mirrorhead's body was a lighting man's dream, reflecting beams of every color as he sang his latest hit.

Outside on the balcony, Lizardo stood gazing over the rolling hills of Kizz Zum's estate. All the houses in the neighborhood were large, but hers was the largest. He was distracted from the view by a holovision bubble floating at the edge of the balcony. It showed a crowd demonstrating outside the Immortal monastery. Then it showed the War God in the sky above the monastery. So long as it was there, the monastery was safe, he reassured himself. Lizardo's illustrious uncle had praised the Immortals for their boundless compassion and intelligence. *They deserve the protection of all Serpentians,* he'd written in his Chronogrammatic.

A backup singer from Mirrorhead's group stepped out onto the balcony. She'd been admiring the handsome reptile all evening, drawn to the glittering green-gold scales on his head and hands, and his compelling Serpentian eyes. His body was motionless, and he looked as if he could stay that way for hours. She was in a Doomsday mood. What was the point in being shy? She went and leaned against the balcony railing beside him. "Why aren't you inside?"

"I don't like parties."

"But you came."

"With a friend."

"I came with Mirrorhead but he's only interested in his own reflection."

Lizardo could see Mirrorhead's sleek Protosun parked among the other airships in the lot below. Its body was constructed of a mirroring alloy in which the moonlight shone. "That's a fast little ship he's got."

"He flies like a maniac. I'm not getting into it with him again."

"He'll be disappointed."

"He won't even notice."

"Then he's a bigger fool than he looks."

"No, he's just had too many women. They're always after him. They pretend they're checking out their makeup in his mirrors."

Lizardo turned to look at her. She was a Papyrusian, and possessed the creamy white skin for which her people were famed, a skin on which colored inks showed up brilliantly; consequently, Papyrusians wore tattoos of gorgeous detail, and the singer's body was covered in the luminous inks of an Exhulian master—ropes of stars wound around her legs, and a Big Bang design covered her torso; her neck was encircled by the words *remoteness of quasars*. Her white face was untouched, except for tears, which were real. "My tattoos aren't even paid for yet. And now we're all going to die."

Lizardo's unsparing Serpentian gaze held her fixed. "This moment is still yours."

"Am I wasting it? But what should I be doing?" She looked into the firewall of his eyes, through which no emotion passed. "You're lucky," she said. "You don't have feelings."

"Nobody's granted that gift." His tail held a drink curled in its tip, and he brought it to the diamond-shaped scales of his mouth.

"Do you think I'd be safer back on my own planet?"

"I wouldn't go to the expense of trying to find out."

She put a hand to her hair, and he saw the inky chains around her arms, depicting subatomic particle tracks. "If I crystallize tonight, will you take my body to the nearest Doomsday memorial? And arrange me so that my tattoos show up well? I want to be remembered."

Lizardo knew it was pointless to remind her that soon there'd be no one left to do any remembering. Or perhaps she imagined the eye of some cold eternity on her. The spirituality forced on the young by Amphora had created odd beliefs, the cult of the memorials just one of them. The largest Doomsday memorial was in the Stygian desert, where a thousand crystallized bodies watched in silence on the sands, in a tableau of a thousand gestures. Lizardo had seen it from the air with the sun upon it, countless prisms glittering in the limbs of the dead. From far above, its beauty looked as natural as the ancient coral reefs left behind by retreating seas.

The Papyrusian eyed Lizardo's uniform. "Could you get me into the interchannels? I've heard it's safe there."

"Everyone has an idea of safety."

"What's yours?"

"I lie in warm sand."

"And then what?"

"Then I close my eyes."

"Let me lie with you." She wrapped her arms around him, encircling him with her tattooed chains. He breathed the youthful fragrance of her creamy skin, and then, over her shoulder, he saw the holovision bubble floating in the air; the broadcast now showed the War God ascending into the night. The broadcaster was saying, *"We don't know why, but the War God is leaving. And the Immortals are now defenseless."* The roar of the crowd outside the monastery walls accompanied the ship's withdrawal.

Lizardo extracted himself from the Papyrusian's soft embrace. "But why?"

"Ancestral obligations." He laid his scaled lips against her cheek, then hurried back through the partygoers. With the tip of his tail he tapped Jockey on the ankle. The bulky mercenary heaved a sigh, but one owed absolute allegiance to one's navigator, for every hour brought some devilish intersection, and when the navigator says turn, one turns. He lifted Kizz Zum's head from his shoulder. "If you'll excuse me for just a moment, my dear—"

"Don't leave me for long, Jockey."

He patted her tenderly, extracted his other hand from her waxy grip, and followed Lizardo through the crowd. A member of the Alien Opera was posing languidly beside the doorway. He was a higher specimen of the species to which the informer Lucky Viscid belonged, and his body exuded the same sticky substance. But the tenor's form was so sleek and muscular he could stick anything onto it and still look good. He sometimes started the evening in nothing but a pair of shoes, and let chance stick to him what it would. Tonight he'd chosen dark green leaves. Talking to him was a young lady of the same species covered with wakmaz milk and rose petals. "I just tossed them on," she said, though actually she'd spent hours patting the rare bouquet in place. The holovision broadcast made her laugh a little desperately and a pink petal fell from her breast. Jockey attempted to replace it, but Lizardo's tail curled around his ankle, yanking him on. They went down a flight of winding stairs to the parking lot.

"All right, now what?"

"We'll need something small and maneuverable." Lizardo slithered over to Mirrorhead's sleek vehicle.

"Where do you think you're going?" asked the cosmic rocker's bodyguard.

Lizardo sent his tail up between the guard's legs, and hurled him to the next property. "It's a fair question," said Jockey. "Where *are* we going?"

CHAPTER 36

Protesters commandeered a bus to take them as close as possible to the monastery. When the robotic driver was unable to proceed farther, he reacted as programmed: *If roadway is blocked, shut down and wait.* He shut down and waited, the bus doors were forcefully pried open, and he was dragged into a field, where his energy pack was yanked from his chest by a buzz dealer.

While the driver lay motionless, his passengers ran to join the mob outside the monastery walls. A violent mix of voices filled the air, alien and human, all the highest life forms of the Corridor, every civilized species capable of massing in resentment and blame.

The only time the crowd dispersed was when a crystallization occurred, revealing someone frozen in an ecstasy of anger, hand raised to throw a bottle against the monastery wall, or pointing furiously upward at the disappearing War God—stolen by Gregori Man o' War and now no more than a speck in the nighttime sky.

"You think it's gone?"

"It could come back."

Groups of Starfish punks were here for the delicious press of female flesh, the inimitable joy of destruction, and, if they were lucky, looting. They hung from the wall by suction cups, leering at the passing crowd and making vulgar sucking sounds from mouths in their midsection.

A Semiliquid husband and wife who had lost their child to crystallization moved slowly back and forth along the path in the bright moonlight, their gelatinous bodies dark with sorrow. Grief crossed their brows, stirring it in waves that ran from side to side. Their sounds of anguish were like something cooking in a pot. The mob had given them space to perform their grieving walk as if they were an exhibit, and everyone who joined the crowd got a look at them. "How does it feel to have lost a child in this way?" asked a holovision reporter.

The Semiliquids burbled unintelligibly, and the reporter tried again. "Are children cherished on your planet?"

A cameraman gestured for the Semiliquids to come toward him, hand in hand. They obliged, bewildered by their newsworthiness and began once more burbling indistinctly, to which the reporter responded, "What's the message you're trying to send by being here today?"

A Scintillan paced among the rioters, eyes flashing. On his own planet, these flashes were meant to frighten off attackers, but now the signal was used to stir the mob, whose excitement mounted with each illumination. "Bury them," screamed the Scintillan, his eyes flashing at the monastery's protective wall. He was weak from blowing so much light, but this was a good cause, and Scintillans were devoted to good causes.

A pair of Velvet Worms quietly worked the crowd, slipping softly between the ranks, whispering incendiary slogans while picking pockets with smooth, filmy hands.

"It's not safe anywhere."

"I hear there are shelters."

"Not for us. Only for *them*."

A stricken human ran at the impenetrable stone wall and pounded it with his fists. "They killed my wife." Tears were streaming down his cheeks. "It's the end of everything." He looked around, seeking acknowledgment from the mob.

"Sir," said the reporter, "could I get you to pose with the Semi-liquids?" She waved her cameraman over, and the weeping gentle-man stood alongside the Semiliquids, as bewildered as they. The crowd murmured its sympathy, and added this man's sorrow to the account it was totaling up.

"The Immortals will pay for this."

"The War God isn't returning. We can get them now."

"Charge," squealed a drunken little Mouseman, whipping his hairless tail as if the mob were a horse in need of urging.

Starfish punks began to scale the monastery wall, their suction cups fastening firmly. Arms rhythmically contracting, they inched upward, while other aliens and humans used the punks' protruding spines as ladder rungs. Having evolved from creatures that held to rocks while oceans raged, the Starfish supported the climbers easily; tumult and tossing about was sport to them.

The first wave of rioters scrambled to the top and gazed down at a carpet of small white flowers. A small mirrored airship was parked on the garden path, and standing guard at either end of the main building was a mercenary, one of them a reptile, the other large and beefy. "Don't worry about those creeps," squealed the drunken Mouseman, parading along the crest of the wall. "I'll handle them."

The bravest jumped straight down into the garden, crushing the white blossoms. Though the mercenaries stood in front of the main building, the mound-like houses where the Immortals slept lay un-protected. Which way to go?

"Death to the Immortals," squeaked the Mouseman. In his enthusiasm he fell off the wall into the flowers, and rose unsteadily. Somebody would pay for that fall, he vowed.

The Semiliquids were helped over the wall by the holovision reporter and her cameraman. "You're now on the property of the people who crystallized your child," said the journalist. "Do you care to comment on how that makes you feel?" The disoriented Semiliquids resumed their mournful pacing at the foot of the wall, but were stepped on by rioters dropping down around them. Their floating eyes gazed wildly. Weakly they oozed forward until they found refuge beneath a garden bench. From their hideout they saw legs rushing past, of many planetary species. Suddenly their bench was upended, and the Mouseman said, "Go on. Get your revenge."

The Semiliquids replied with hesitant, bubbling speech. They wanted to be far away, on a moist world they never should've left. But Planet Immortal had been the promised land, where people were said to live forever. Their child hadn't lived long at all. They crept into one of the mound-like structures, where they crouched in darkness, trembling, as infuriated rioters raced on by.

A Permanent Copula stumbled past, its twin heads nervously jerking, turning first one way in rage at the Immortals, then another in retreat; it had been carrying on for hours, exhausting itself in an agony of indecision. A wailing cry escaped its two mouths, and it split down the middle. The separated halves looked at each other in horror.

The crowd spread out around the separated Copula, and continued forward. An Immortal was spotted, walking in the garden.

"That's one of them!"

The frail nun gazed calmly at the oncoming crowd. She seemed disinclined to save herself. A Papyrusian rushed toward her. The hiss of Lizardo's disintegrator gun sounded, and the Papyrusian disintegrated, his tattoos the last of him to go, designs shivering in the air, of comets, colliding galaxies, and powerful words which should've brought him luck. The Immortal glided away toward the main building.

Now the Scintillan attempted to catch her, but Lizardo's tail wrapped around his neck. His tail snapped once and the Scintillan's head came off, eyes releasing one last powerful flash as the head sailed toward the crowd.

The crowd paused, temporarily blinded.

"He can't get us all," cried a Starfish punk.

"But I can get *you*," replied Lizardo in a low voice. The Starfish hesitated, its suction cups working meditatively at the air; while he considered his chances, braver rioters pushed past him, and now Lizardo was forced to retreat. "We're dead anyway," yelled the human who'd lost his wife. "Let's kill the mercenary."

They charged Lizardo with renewed force. He backed up against one of the monastery huts, and continued firing his disintegrator. A Starfish punk suctioned his way up the rear of the hut and went along the roof, yelling encouragement to the crowd. His nervous system tingled with excitement; a rare strength surged through his internal hydraulic system. He saw a holovision cameraman focusing on him. The Starfish star! Fame, at last!

The excitement of stardom triggered the crystallizing process. The Starfish lost suction from his cups and rolled off the roof, tentacles flailing. He landed on Lizardo, his tentacles freezing around the lizard, binding him in a stony embrace. Lizardo thrashed, trying to free himself from the crystallized Starfish, but his limbs were pinned. He tried to shatter the frozen Starfish by hurling himself against the wall of the hut, and the wall collapsed around him.

"He's helpless! Let's get him!"

The cameraman closed in on the wrapped-up lizard, and got a colorful shot of the attackers kicking him in the head and tearing off his scales. The bloody scales had a nice glitter, which played well against the pale crystallized flesh of the Starfish.

Suddenly the attackers went into spasm, their limbs snapping this way and that as electricity shot out of their fingertips and the ends of their hair. "Get back, you vermin," shouted Jockey, "or I'll fry the lot of you."

Still firing with one hand, Jockey stuck his other hand underneath a tentacle of the frozen Starfish and cracked it off. He threw it like a javelin at the crowd, impaling a Velvet Worm, then cracked off the rest of the Starfish's tentacles, freeing Lizardo and dragging him toward the monastery's central building. He pulled the dazed lizard in, and slammed the heavy door. "My navigator, caught on camera, pinned by a frozen Starfish. The starfighter community is going to enjoy this, old man."

Lizardo's mouth was foaming with venom. "That rabble nearly tore me apart."

"They're not finished yet."

The remainder of the compound belonged to the mob, which spread out and surged into the mound-like houses. But they found no valuables, just cells with narrow beds, a hard chair, a few bare hooks on a wall. Disappointed, they broke apart the simple furniture. Fights erupted from frustration, and the injured poured back out into the garden. Some of the women were sobbing, exhausted by their grief and shouting.

One girl stayed inside a cell. Seated on a cot, she felt the humble life of the nun who'd slept here, and sensed a spirit loftier than her own. She fled the hut, stumbling across the carpet of white flowers which had been destroyed as completely as if a herd of cattle had grazed there. She reached the wall, and asked to be lifted up. A pair of Panel-heads who'd just arrived helped her to the top. "No treasure?"

"Yes," she answered. "A hard bed in a bare room."

Inside the compound, the Starfish punks held torches in their tentacles. "Burn."

Flames licked the windows of the mound-like huts, and Starfish eyes reflected the dancing light. "That's more like it. That's a statement." The statement melted the Semiliquids, their gelatinous bodies dissolving in a bubbling brown mass, their dying cries lost in the roar of the conflagration.

"The place is ours," yelled the Starfish, weaving between the huts, igniting everything that was flammable.

In the main building, Jockey and Lizardo were startled by a row of Immortals filing past them.

"Commander Oldcastle here." Jockey performed a military click of the heels, and gave what bow he could over his great stomach. "Rescue party. At your service."

The Immortals continued on, indifferent as scarecrows to his presence. More monks and nuns glided out from each of the connecting hallways. Jockey supposed that they were gathering to be evacuated, but they made no attempt to collect the precious gifts they'd been given over the ages. Statues of rare minerals, depicting life on other planets, were only impediments to Immortal movement. The tapestries of Hermetia, animated with moth light, caused no flicker of desire or regret in the old monks and nuns. They filed blindly by wondrous timepieces and jeweled scepters. Priceless paintings by the masters of Exhul received only the passing shadows of the thin, gliding figures.

Jockey and Lizardo followed them to the central hall, which was gradually filling with their enfeebled but still noble forms. Their eyes, though gazing directly at Jockey and Lizardo, remained expressionless. Not even when the doors began to splinter with the force of battering rams did the monks and nuns react. One of the walls cracked; a vehicle had been driven against it; motors reversed, there was a pause, and then the wall was struck again. It collapsed inward, and the snout of the vehicle pushed through the rubble, followed by the mob.

Jockey and Lizardo fired, taking down the first of the invaders. And then suddenly, the mob ceased moving, as an electric net fell around it, binding its members in a mesh of crackling light. Soldiers of the Consortium Guard stormed in over the rubble, followed by the Observer.

"Well, Oldcastle, you seem to be making a habit of helping me."

Jockey came to attention with a salute. "Only my duty, ma'am. The Immortals are safe, but unresponsive."

Disproving this, Metron separated himself from his companions and moved toward the Observer. The old monk's sweetness touched her feelings once again, but it was diminished, like a scent bottle which carries only traces of the perfume it once held.

"We were supposed to be your teachers." Metron's voice was little above a whisper. "Instead, we've been your destroyers." The other monks and nuns stood silently behind him. In a remote time and place their order had formed around some metaphysical idea, but that idea had been dissolved in favor of the extra-dimensional message. "Centuries of study and meditation have come to this." He gestured toward the clamor of the mob trying to tear through the still standing walls. Soldiers were heard controlling them with riot devices.

"If they wish it, let them tear us apart—" Metron paused and listened more intently. "—though I sense that won't be necessary."

Bowing his head he said, "Our masters have arrived to take back the energy they lent us for their grand deception." Then he stepped back to join the other monks and nuns, and a faint tinkling sound was heard, like wind chimes made of glass. "We had such confidence," whispered Metron. "We had perfect certainty. Beware of every certainty. That's our final teaching."

The tinkling sound increased, and very delicately the monks and nuns crystallized, their frail bodies turning into artifacts of incomparable lightness. They were like a row of withered saints in a catacomb.

Jockey and Lizardo quietly retreated to the hallway where the artwork was displayed.

"Very tasty," said Jockey, throwing a tapestry round his shoulders like a cape, and stuffing orbs and scepters under his arms. "I can start my own monarchy."

Lizardo picked up a Serpentian masterpiece of carving, of a lizard king. It was as large as he was, and encrusted with brilliant gems. "Is this too much for my apartment?"

"It might be, old man. But take it anyway."

CHAPTER 37

The drivers and the pilots of the Agricultural Plain were used to traveling sleepy rural roadways or flying above patchwork fields. Now they
were bound for major cities, with military escorts. The chemical trails
they laid would quickly vanish from the public eye: a puff of moisture, a momentary mist.

Link stood with his arms crossed, watching successive waves of
tanker planes and trucks being loaded with his pheromonal brew.
An agitated Upquark moved up and down on his lifters as the trucks
rolled out and the planes took off. "I'm so afraid the local insects will
be confused by our mixture."

"Let's hope the extra-dimensionals are confused," replied Link
tersely. His mind was plagued with doubts. Prior to this, pheromone
use had been limited to promoting fertilization of fields, and saving
forests and crops from predatory insects. To see military personnel
managing the operation now, with fighter aircraft to provide support—
it was as if the insect world had exchanged its tiny transparent wings
for thundering jets. Several times he had exactly that hallucination—
a fighter aircraft looking like a giant wasp as it took off, and a tanker
looking like a great lumbering bumblebee.

A nearby Guard commander had similar misgivings. He'd been

in the Guard for fifty years, but he'd never seen gardeners running a war before. It was a sign that a great civilization was cracking. "Did you ever think we'd be taking orders from a bunch of farmers?"

"They're welcome to it," said the officer beside him, staring upward toward the drifting remains of the Junk Moon in the sky. "We hit them with the best we had and got nowhere."

"So now we spray them with insecticide?"

"It's not insecticide," said Link curtly.

Upquark swiveled toward the officers. "Just the opposite. Its main component is ten-dodecadien-101."

The commanding officer started to reply, then thought better of it. Maybe this young man with the garden robot knew something. If the young man succeeded, he'd be more than a young man. And if I insult him, I could be fertilizer. I've seen it happen before when things are in upheaval.

He glanced at a frozen first sergeant, who'd been immobilized while barking an order, both fists balled on his hips, his two arms fastened like the handles of a jug. Lift him up and carry him away, to the military cemetery, where thousands like him were on display—an army of the dead, lined up in rows—sitting, kneeling, saluting, at attention, at ease, executing parade maneuvers. Those in compromised poses had been broken apart and buried, for the sake of morale. A soldier's last moments must reflect discipline.

The commander straightened his back and squared his shoulders. He wanted to be ready if the chill hit him. But what if it hits while I'm scratching my posterior? The image of a lifetime destroyed. At the last minute, the conquering hero is tweaking the underpants out of his bum. An impeccably tailored uniform decorated with medals from eighty years of bravery—all undone by an itch. "I wish you the best of luck, young man," he said to Link sincerely.

* * *

The Corridor station was identified on maps as *C-3 Restricted*. Known to pilots as the Sink Hole, the arid valley produced a gravitic anomaly capable of spinning an airship like a toy and dismantling it before it struck the ground. In this forbidden valley, Ancient Alien engineers had constructed their most problematic transport station, one exceeding all present understanding; no hint as to its operation was left behind, just a puzzling subterranean portal, and the strange effects that plagued the ground and sky above it.

Time-travel enthusiasts were engaged in a continual campaign to reopen the station. But the few times the station had been used experimentally, the results had been disastrous. Ships were crushed in the launch chamber, their fuselages distorted beyond recognition. Even birds flying over the station had difficulty, and avoided it thereafter. Some animals managed to live in the area, freakish rodents whose speeds were unnatural, but who perished if they attempted to leave the valley, their organs mysteriously collapsing.

The gates of the off-limits area had been briefly opened this morning, but not because of any influence by the time-travel crowd. The engineers of the Consortium Guard had arrived with Link and the Dark Dreamers. The time-travel zanies were kept outside the high metal fence, milling about with placards in the air. Ren found herself within their ranks, though she had nothing to protest except her own stupidity. She'd behaved with Adrian as if she had years to win his tenderness. Now the barrier that had been between them was reinforced by security fencing. He was on one side, moving among the experts, and she was exiled with the crackpots.

The hills were ringed by the Guard engineers, along with Dark Dreamers manning free energy generators of their own invention. When questioned about these machines by the military, the Dreamers gave their usual rude replies, having no patience with anyone who wasn't a Dark Dreamer, and little with those who were. They'd launched mice, moles, and, it was rumored, some of their own, through time's doorway using virtually the same machinery they were now setting up around the gravity sink. Looking through binoculars, the Observer saw them on the hilltops a quarter-mile away, gesticulating in an irritated fashion, as were their nearby counterparts.

"They manufacture excellent navigational equipment," said Caph grudgingly. "Very useful to the Guard." One of them approached Caph now and started haranguing him with a sound like an arcing electric current.

"Slow down, please," commanded the general, and pointed to the translation module on his wrist band. The Dark Dreamer spoke into it, lessening his speed but not his irritation, and the translation was voiced. "Our work is being compromised by your engineers. I demand that they withdraw, for they are sacks of crap."

"Give the order," sighed the Observer.

Caph gave it, and the Guard engineers reluctantly left the Dark Dreamers to their preparations. Now they had only one another to be irritated with, which seemed sufficient.

Outside the fence surrounding the area, protesters continued milling, with Ren in their midst. What she regretted most was that she'd never sung her most beautiful song to Link.

"Ancient Alien secrets are being kept from us," a grandmotherly demonstrator explained to her, feeling perhaps that Ren wasn't quite up to speed on the nature of the protest. "It's a disgrace. This station was left here by the Ancients for everyone to use. We're *all* the heirs of their knowledge."

"I don't think the activity here is about Ancient Aliens."

"Oh my dear," said the woman kindly, "you mustn't believe *their* version of things." She pointed at the Guardsmen and Dark Dreamers beyond the fence. "*They* don't want us to know that Area C-3 is being reactivated."

"And why is it being reactivated?"

"So *they* can escape into another time, of course." The woman swung her placard back up into the air and shook it vigorously. "They wish to keep C-3 for themselves."

A young Panel-head stepped beside them and joined the conversation. His hair bushed wildly outward around his implants. "The Ancient Aliens knew there'd be trouble from the extra-dimensionals some day. So they left this station for our getaway. They *provided*." His eyes blazed with certainty.

"It's all very simple, my dear." The woman smiled sympathetically at Ren. "One must insist on being included. You don't want to be left *outside,* do you?"

"I already have been," murmured Ren, looking at Link's distant figure.

"You'll enter with us. Our effect is already making itself felt." The woman waved her placard once again, and the young man lifted his, as a Dark Dreamer hurried past just beyond the fence. The Dreamer paused, gestured obscenely back at them and hurried on.

"Disagreeable midgets." The woman shook her head. "You may be *quite* sure they won't be included on our passenger list."

Ren lost sight of Link among the agents of the Observer, and a pang went through her. But what did her feelings for Link matter now? The world was ending. The most beautiful love songs would crystallize, hers among them. The wind would be the only singer, as it swept across the desert of a ruined world. Adrian had said that among the survivors there would always be insects. Perhaps a scorpion would emerge from the desert, and its tail would crease the sand with a tiny hiss as it scurried along. And love, if it lasted, would be the property of scorpions.

She knew escape didn't lie in Station C-3, no matter what the protesters thought. The defense of the planet had shifted here because the area was deadly; she felt its influence in her head, feet, and stomach, as if she were hurtling down a slope. A monstrous reorganization of substrata had taken place in this unhappy valley.

"I've sent very sarcastic messages to the Observer," the woman told Ren confidentially. "She may have to be removed. You there, Guardsman, come here." The Guardsman ignored her. "What an impolite young man. He will not be given consideration when we have a say in how this station is run."

Several protesters crystallized, causing little pockets to open around them in the crowd. "How unfortunate," cried the woman with grandmotherly concern. "Our strength is in numbers."

"I think you should go home," said Ren.

"What would I do there, my dear?"

"Be with your family. There isn't much time left."

"But this is my family." She pointed with the edge of her placard. "You can't imagine how comforting it is to be with like-minded individuals." She placed her hand gently on Ren's arm. "I see how lonely you are. You're from very far away, and you've not found what you were looking for, have you?"

"No."

"I hadn't either, until I became aware of the real nature of C-3."

"It makes me feel seasick," said Ren.

"Naturally its unusual powers are sensed by our bodies. But I take that as a promise."

"Of what?"

"Of transport to another plane of existence. To the place of the Ancient Aliens. They're calling us. They want us to join them." As she leaned her kindly face toward Ren's, a crack sounded in her spine, like the shifting of ice. "That's why I'm not lonely . . . or frightened . . . I'm protected by the Ancient Alien vow . . . ." she managed to declare, as her sympathetic smile froze, and she fell stiffly forward in Ren's arms.

CHAPTER 38

A wrong turn and you could come out in some solar hell and instantly fry.

And taking a wrong turn was easier than taking the right one, reflected Jockey, piloting the Temperance through the interchannels. These little-known passages in the Corridor were dominated by giant energy eels, squirming in every direction and flipping ships about with their lashing tails; that they weren't sentient, that they were warps of space-time, didn't make them any easier to bear. The channels were rapids of potential movement; one had to feel those potentials in order to use them, and fliers needed not just experience but a peculiar visceral skill. Jockey could extend his awareness several kilometers ahead, to read the giant currents and determine which led to some cosmic broiler and which led to where he wanted to go. But beads of sweat stood out on his forehead as he made adjustments to his controls, rolling the ship, righting it again, riding the tumultuous waves leading to Planet RB11. "These numbered worlds have dreadful food," he said, in the midst of his struggle.

Lizardo, seated beside him on the flight deck, was having his own difficulties, determining coordinates for larger changes that lay ahead. "We've never been to RB11. How do you know about the food?"

"I know these things. Soil is dead, oceans are like tar, and there's not a scrap of culture."

"I wasn't aware culture mattered to you."

"It matters deeply." Jockey fought his controls with one hand, and opened a fragrant takeout container with the other, his face suddenly creased by an angry frown. "They left out the wakmaz sauce. I'll go back and flay them alive."

The Temperance was tossing about like a toy boat, and Lizardo consulted the Serpentium Chronogrammatic for the next course correction. His great-grand-uncle's scales glittered momentarily in the flight deck lights as Lizardo turned a page. "*This* is culture. It sings in the mind."

"Not in mine, old man. I glanced at it earlier." The Temperance glided into quieter currents, and Jockey reached into his nut bowl and chewed thoughtfully. The heirlooms of the Immortals had fetched a good price in the underworld art market. His ship was fully fueled. And he'd bought himself a new uniform. He glanced at Lizardo's, which still bore the marks of the Starfish's tentacles. "You look a bit shabby, if you don't mind me mentioning it."

Lizardo ignored the comment. His attention was on the Chronogrammatic. "Had I read this every day of my life I would have vanished into the mists."

"The wise serpent. Seen only by radar."

Lizardo's eyes traveled down the antique page as his tail scraped back and forth on the pedestal of his navigator's seat. "Listen to this: *Transluminal generation doesn't conflict with causality.*"

"Beautifully put, old man. You'd never know your ancestor was imprisoned when he wrote it." Jockey leaned toward the instrument panel, fired the great ship's engines, and steered the Temperance out of the last interchannel leading to RB11. "Arming warheads," he said, and the Temperance responded.

A black dot appeared on the instrument panel, gradually widened, and then became visible in the sky. RB11. The seas were dark and oily, as Jockey had predicted. Ice-capped mountains towered above desolate plains of stone, across which sand blew endlessly. Jockey shook his head dejectedly. "How will I amuse myself? I must have my little divertissements. If not, the bloom goes from my cheeks." He reached for a chocolate. "You say there are no females down there?"

"Not any who'd be interested in you."

"That's a premature judgment."

"I wish you'd just stay on board and let me handle everything."

"What if there's trouble?"

"You're the only trouble. Wherever you go—"

"I remind you I'm a decorated veteran."

Lizardo's eyes flickered in the direction of the medals decorating Jockey's broad chest. "All bought from Dunbosian."

"A small point, surely."

The barren world was clear before them now, and Lizardo entered the coordinates for landing; the site was known to him only through the Chronogrammatic. Without that ancient volume, it would be impossible to find the person they were looking for, who did not advertise his whereabouts.

They descended into the mouth of a crater, sending up towering clouds of dust. Visibility went to zero, but the ship's outside monitors reported a manageable temperature and breathable atmosphere. "There are caves in the crater wall," explained Lizardo.

"Caves in a crater on a lifeless ball. Very inviting."

"This is a world for those who are done with the world."

"Why not just retire to the country? Why such extremes?" Jockey was strapping on his weapons.

"Those are useless here. If they decide to kill us, ordinary weapons won't save us."

"All the same, I'll take a disintegrator. And a few chocolates."
They waited for the dark clouds to settle slightly, then opened
up the hatch. Hot desert air greeted them. Lizardo's forehead chip
now carried the coordinates. "The cave we want should be straight
ahead."

"The cave we want," repeated Jockey with a sigh, as he stumbled
blindly forward through the dust.

Reaching the crater wall, they found steps carved into the rocks.
Jockey followed Lizardo up, but the footholds were too small for his
boots. He lost his balance and grabbed Lizardo's tail. Straining with
Jockey's weight, Lizardo brought them to the mouth of the cave.
Jockey managed to crawl in and remained wheezing on the floor.

Lizardo too was breathing heavily. "For both our sakes," he said,
"you really ought to lose some weight."

"Strategic reserves, old man."

It was Lizardo who rose first. Orienting himself, he pointed toward the cave's far depths.

Groaning, Jockey got to his feet, his purchased medals jingling,
and followed. A bioluminescent jelly had been shaped into a crude
lamp on the wall; here and there he saw numbers scratched on the
rocky surface, with queer symbols connecting them. The air was heavy
with moisture. He sniffed, catching a mineral smell, sharp and stony;
a subterranean stream must flow through here somewhere.

Lizardo clawed along, his bootless feet feeling the smoothness
of the passage. It was an old one, swept and trodden on for eons: a
planet of subterraneans, where harsh surfaces had driven life into the
depths, forcing those few species who survived to become masters of
caverns and caves and buried rivers. In the distance a second ball of
bioluminescent gel glowed faintly.

"Have you brought any sort of gift to placate the natives?" asked
Jockey.

"I thought I'd offer you to them." Lizardo's tail whipped across the floor as he continued on. He had a lizard's love for dark retreats, and this slow descent through a craggy corridor felt intimately familiar. He asked himself why he'd ever forsaken Serpentia for the stars. His elongated shadow seemed alive to every nuance of the terrain, fitting itself to each deep crack with ease, and emerging with secrets only shadows know. The second bioluminescent torch caused his shadow to expand, a giant dragon flitting on the wall.

Jockey eyed the glowing ball of gel. Malevolent faces danced in its shimmering surface. Hallucinations? He felt nightmarish suggestions emanating from the cold rocks; blood sacrifice was practiced here, of that he felt certain; it troubled the atmosphere. His hand went to the polished butt of his disintegrator.

I belong here, thought Lizardo, as he inhaled the musty air which came from fissures that ran for hundreds of miles, the bronchi of the cavern, which allowed it to breathe. His claws clicked on the smooth stone floor, and Serpentian memories, long buried, began to surface, of slithering through dark passageways of power.

"A moment, old man. There might be valuable minerals in this wall." Jockey ran his hand over ragged outcroppings, examining their edges in the bioluminescent light. He cracked off a glittering chunk of stone . . . a moan echoed through the cave.

"Put it down, you idiot," hissed Lizardo.

Jockey let it drop, and the stone's moan died away. Lizardo continued forward, but Jockey grabbed him. "Didn't you find that bizarre?"

"Of course I found it bizarre." Lizardo's tongue shot out and the poison glands in his cheeks inflated. "This is a bizarre world. That's why we're here."

"You needn't get venomous."

"Just don't break off any more mineral samples."

"Geological curiosity, nothing more."

"Forget about getting rich on RB11."

"I seek only to defray expenses. And mining is in my family tree. My grandfather was a miner on a wildcat asteroid. He perished in a cave-in."

"You'll perish in one too if you go around yanking pieces out of the walls." Lizardo's eyes flashed in the light of the gel, and he resumed his march. Jockey tried to attach himself to Lizardo's tail again, but it got away from him. Menacing shadows continued to dance on both sides of him as the tunnel kept descending and another bioluminescent gel marked the way steeply downward.

Lizardo turned and hissed, "There they are."

Jockey stepped out of the tunnel, into a subterranean gallery ringed by the glowing bioluminous balls. Scurrying on the ground were pygmy troglodytes—naked creatures roasting a larger creature on a spit. Cooking smells traveled past Jockey's nostrils on an updraft toward some natural vent in the cave wall. Nervously he ran a finger under his row of medals, comforting himself with their familiar jingle. "That's not a star fighter they're sacrificing, is it?"

"If it is, he has horns and hoofs."

Emboldened, Jockey approached the bustling little creatures, and extended his box of chocolates.

The nearest troglodyte opened it, popped one in his mouth, then gestured toward the others to make room for the newcomers around the roasting beast.

A female troglodyte was adjusting the spit. Charming creature, observed Jockey, and felt a cautionary poke in the shin from Lizardo's curling tail.

Lizardo showed the Serpentian Chronogrammatic to the female troglodyte.

She stroked the skin of its cover, then pointed to the other end of the subterranean gallery. A wall of steam was rising from the cave floor, so thick it blocked the view of what lay beyond it.

Jockey and Lizardo crossed the gallery and stepped through the steam. Ahead of them was a shallow pit filled with sand. Lizardo knelt and felt its warmth.

The sand began to move. A claw emerged, then a tail, then the entire figure of a wrinkled old reptile.

"Uncle Ophidian," cried Lizardo, and held up the Serpentian Chronogrammatic.

CHAPTER 39

Uncle Ophidian sat between Jockey and Lizardo on the flight deck. Lizardo had placed the Serpentian Chronogrammatic beside his uncle, who ran a claw over the still-shining scales. "The old skin held up well, didn't it?" He opened the book and skimmed a few pages. "The thoughts are trashy though. Unformed stuff. I've come a way since then." He snapped the book shut and handed it to Lizardo. "Unless you can get something for the skin, I'd chuck it."

"I couldn't do that, Uncle."

"Suit yourself. I twisted my mind into a thousand knots writing that thing, and it'll twist yours trying to read it."

"But the theories are correct."

"Yes, they still hold. But the Third Chronogrammatic goes much further. I won't bore you with it. It's only fit for a troglodyte."

"You share your thoughts with them?"

"In exchange for their hospitality."

"Do they know who you are?"

"Just someone who crept out of a crack in the wall."

"Their rocks talk," said Jockey.

"It's a nuisance. Juggling chemical elements and compounds till they sing for you is a fine way to ruin a night's sleep."

"But they learned it from you?" asked Lizardo.

"They're reading the Third Chronogrammatic. Naturally, I don't have a chapter on getting rocks to talk, but I do deal with altering crystalline structure. They took it from there. I sincerely wish they hadn't." Uncle Ophidian speared a chocolate on one of his clawed fingers. "Have we got more of these?"

"Boxes," said Jockey.

"I noticed you gave a box to the troglodytes."

"As a parting gift."

"They'll eat them all at once."

"It's the only way."

Uncle Ophidian nodded his scaly head and speared another chocolate. Then he looked at Lizardo, inquiringly. "Well, nephew, what's your profession?"

"I navigate this ship."

"Piracy?"

"Salvage."

"Your great-grandfather was a pirate. He was the one who broke me out of prison. I gave him the Chronogrammatic. It was all I had. I thought he'd sell it, as its theories have a military application. But evidently he kept it in the family." The old reptile grew silent for a moment. "He always was impractical. I daresay you take after him. He went to the Outer Worlds, to start again. I went to the caves, to think." Uncle Ophidian stretched out in his chair. He was smaller than Lizardo, his skin less brilliant, the scales veiled with cave dust. But one saw in his movements the same muscular suppleness, of one who could outswim a fish.

The ship's computer said, "Approaching Planet Immortal."

Uncle Ophidian rose, and walked to the ship's main lounge, which was large, with comfortable seating for lizards, and bowls of snacks. His thoughts were traveling ahead, into complexity, at a speed faster than the ship's. Absentmindedly he swallowed an egg. Ideas he'd been wrestling with for ages were assembling themselves so swiftly in his mind, he had to wrap his tail around a pole for support. His eyes were blazing with his emerging understanding of the world—a world fading in and out like a firefly. As if to catch that evanescent fly, his tongue slithered forth with lightning speed, and he braced himself for the collapse of time.

CHAPTER 40

The pheromone paths now hugged all highways, roads, and streets, as well as all dried creek beds and other natural gradients leading to the restricted Corridor Station. Waiting on the hillside, Link was in a kind of trance. The bola spider senses the power of her perfumed lure as she waits. Link had carpeted a corner of the planet in seductin; a web had been compounded under his instruction, and he felt as if he'd secreted it from his own glands.

The arid, fenced-in valley he stared into now was the center of his web. He'd arrived in an Intelligence Agency vehicle but he'd been traveling toward this point for years with every piece of information he'd gathered on pheromones and the control they exert over living beings. He'd arranged matings, migrations, and depredations by creatures whose tiny minds were as difficult to know as an extra-dimensional's. Wasps make paper . . . if they could write on it, what would they say? Sometimes Link thought he *had* read that confidential communication of the wasps. But had he read the confidential communication of the extra-dimensionals?

"We're going to make the rubble bounce," said Upquark, repeating what he'd heard a Guardsman say. He looked at Link. "Aren't we?"

The hilltop on which they stood was directly above C-3 Restricted. Gazing down, Link said, "I wish we had the time to study that soil."

"I'm very sorry for it," agreed Upquark, who felt the anguish of the land. Undernourished soil can always be built back up, he and Link had done it countless times, but the effects of *this* underground area doomed any plants that sprouted; the peculiar energies at play beneath the surface pulled all stalks downward. "Such a queer place," he said, but reminded himself of other queerly engineered sites he'd seen in his planetary travels. All of them followed the laws of nature, and this Corridor Station was a product of those laws, however contorted. Even the extra-dimensionals, who seemed to be beyond the laws of nature, had been forced to observe one of them—molecular identity. They'd had to embody themselves, however tenuously, in the molecular structure of this dimension.

He turned to see a Dark Dreamer charging toward him. The Dreamer was shorter than Upquark, but as he came to a halt before him, he looked formidable. "What're you hanging around here for?" he angrily demanded.

"I've been working with you for a week," answered Upquark. "I'm your biotechnical consultant."

"Consult somewhere else," snapped the Dreamer, turning his attention back to his exotic energy generator. Its calibration for this spot had taken him all night, and he didn't want some robot blundering around nearby.

"I need to be here," explained Upquark politely.

"I can't imagine why," retorted the Dreamer, peering through his machine's viewfinder. On the ring of hills around the valley stood dozens of other exotic energy generators operated by more Dark Dreamers, scurrying about, ferret-like, and arguing. What a bunch of numbskulls, thought the Dreamer. But through my efforts, a perfect alignment of the generators has been reached. A patented Dreamhole will be produced.

"If you *must* hang around," he said to Upquark, "at least have the decency to be quiet."

"I didn't say anything," protested Upquark.

"I hear your gears working."

"Their frequency is inaudible."

"To whom? The dead? Can't you see this is delicate work?"

"You're making much more noise than I am," protested Upquark.

"I don't make noise. I make dreams." He pointed at his generator. "*This* is a dream."

The generator gleamed. Within its burnished cube were nestled those components needed to tap exotic matter. That Planet Immortal was under attack was unfortunate, but because of this misfortune the Dreamers had been given the chance to fire off a ring of generators simultaneously and create a Dreamhole powerful enough to suck the extra-dimensionals out of this universe and deposit them in another one. He reflected on how Dream failures in the past had been through lack of funding and poor cooperation. In earlier days when lone Dark Dreamers had tried to tear a Dreamhole through space in C-3 Restricted, the results had been ragged; half a mouse had gone, half remained; a distressing sight. Dreamers readily admitted their culture had collapsed from too many dimensional travel theories, each containing a slice of the truth. But now Consortium money had brought them all together, to build the best exotic energy generators.

If only the Ancient Aliens hadn't been so secretive, thought the Dreamer to himself. This old Corridor Station is a wonder, if we could fully understand it. It's the Dreamhole Supreme.

What he did understand was that it was the only location where the extra-dimensionals could be defeated. It had taken great cunning and massive strength for those interlopers to open a dimensional door;

that was where the attention of the extra-dimensionals had to re-main—on that door, which they were holding open with high ex-penditures of energy. The abnormal forces in C-3 Restricted would distract them, dislodge their fragile toehold, and while they were busy trying to figure out a solution . . .

". . . we'll sink them," he declared. "We'll drop them out of our dimension. We'll hammer exotic energy nails into their heads. If they have heads. Whatever they have, however they're constituted, we'll suck them out of the universe. Laudatory citation to follow. Future funding secured. Dark Dreamer technology celebrated throughout the Corridor . . ."

As with every Dark Dreamer, his vision was proliferating, dis-tracting him, carrying him elsewhere, into fantasies of further exploits. He continued muttering aloud, but Upquark had turned off his trans-lation module, rendering Dreamer speech into a frenetic wordless-ness, like the conversations of exploding lightbulbs. He wanted to hear Link and Link only.

"They've got the scent by now," said Link. "They're following it."

Confirming this from her own position at the base of the hilltop, the Observer received visual bulletins: Crystallizations were now occur-ring only along the pheromone routes. "But why are people staying in those areas?" she asked. "The population was warned to keep away."

"Looters," said General Caph. "And stubborn fellows. And then there are the curious, who'll risk a lot just to be part of what's going on."

"Well, they're statues now." The Observer pointed to the lines of crystallized victims along the avenues of the target towns. The scene had a formal look, as if the statues had been placed there by beauti-fication committees.

She switched from direct visual to a chart which showed the pattern of the extra-dimensionals' approach. Soon every one of them will be here, she thought and felt an icy draft wrap around her; she recognized the coldness; it was her instincts urging her to flee. She looked toward Caph. "Why haven't you left, general? I know your escape ship is ready."

The general snapped the sleeves of his jacket, aligning his immaculate cuffs. "I can't leave you."

"It's a little late for chivalry."

"That's true. But pointless gestures are never wasted. And who knows, you may find yourself attracted to me, after all."

"Perhaps I already am. "

"I'm honored."

The two sat in the Observer's field car, its top down and its instrument panel showing the advance of the extra-dimensionals, though the Observer no longer needed instrumentation. The cold draft she'd felt now covered her completely, an animal's sense of something dangerous approaching. At the same time, an excitement was building up in her, the rapture of the hunter.

"Stay calm," warned Caph, who felt the Observer's ebullience like a piece of vibrating crystal. "Too much fizz in the blood and—" He snapped his fingers.

The Observer shook her head to clear it. Caph said, "Think of something soothing."

"That doesn't work for people like me."

"Then think of this: I love you."

"That's not very soothing."

"Because you think I chase every woman. But something has changed in me. Time is running out. And I think to myself, who is the person I want to spend it with? And the answer is you. If I must crystallize, I'd like it to be in your arms."

"Why me of all women?"

"Pheromones?" He smiled.

314 William Kotzwinkle

As if the barometer had fallen, a heavy pressure suddenly bore down on them. General Caph felt it like a blow between his shoulder blades. The Observer collapsed forward in their vehicle, then forced herself back up. "They're here."

"Yes," said Caph, "right on schedule."

Most of the time-traveler demonstrators were crystallizing outside the fence. Ren's strength was ebbing; with difficulty, she emitted a tone that vibrated her skull, her spine, and all her bones, to combat the subliminal intrusion of the extra-dimensionals. While everyone surrounding her froze, she managed to hang on. Crystallized birds dropped out of the air and smashed on the road like glass ornaments, wings breaking off. A squirrel crystallized on its way up a tree, crystal claws hugging the bark, its tail a crystal spray.

Populations around the perimeter fought down the excitement bubbling in their blood. But everyone born on Planet Immortal liked excitement. The economy ran on it, a hyper chase of thrills, with music tracks, quick cuts, constant stimulation. *Crack,* said the crystallized, at the height of their sensation, on the pinnacle of pleasure.

A picture of Link's energy field was embedded in Upquark's interior imaging, and Upquark was doing his best to keep his friend calm with a biofeedback of tones and beeps.

"Do you *mind?*" hissed the nearest Dark Dreamer, but Upquark's translator was still turned off.

The Dreamer had his beady little eye pressed to his view-finder, whose series of lenses tunneled their way through the generator's nested components—labeled in tiny Dark Dreamer script—*lukonite, zammer, ilektrum,* down and down—coils of *migola* and *okke,* layers of *thunar* and *polmidion,* the full array of Dreamer science, opening out onto the target. Although the extra-dimensionals were invisible, the Dreamer could envision bundles of power arriving in the valley.

He heard his fellow Dreamers rattling in his earpiece, hysteria in their voices. Don't panic, you cretins.

Every Dark Dreamer felt exactly as he did, that all the others were dunces. Their eyes were pressed to their viewfinders, and their clever little fingers were making last minute adjustments. They were Dreamers tracking creatures who belonged in a dream. It was what they'd waited for, for ages, the turning inside-out of reality, so that they, the dream-eyed, could see.

"Dear, oh, dear," said Upquark, for the changes in the valley caused by the arrival of the extra-dimensionals were straining his equilibrium.

"Will you please control yourself?" sputtered the Dreamer beside him. "I'm preparing to fire."

Upquark's tones and beeps rose precipitously as he monitored Link's excitement.

"Shut up shut up shut up," snarled the Dark Dreamer. He sensed confusion in the extra-dimensionals; they were blindly groping for a correction; the gravitational anomaly of the Corridor station had taken them by surprise, exactly as planned.

"Fire!"

Clouds of *gaz* appeared at the mouth of the generators, followed by round, translucent blue beams of *exijole*. They struck the valley, carbonizing all its natural inhabitants. Mice stood up in their skins, with nothing inside them but dust, then blew away.

The Dreamhole was formed, as if the valley floor had become a trapdoor in time. Caught by its suction, the extra-dimensionals lost their cap of invisibility. They appeared as seams in the visual field, distorting the background. "Insufficient unity of perception," muttered the Dark Dreamers, unable to place what they saw in any concept, from dreaming or waking. The extra-dimensionals were a declivity in space, a non-thing that was still somehow there. Connecting each seam was a superfine fabric uniting the individual extra-dimensionals so they could move as a single being, a being which began to resemble a great painted fan. The fan snapped closed, all the seams combining, then opened in another direction, its movements faster than any movement of man, insect, or machine. It was as if the entire atmosphere of the valley had animated into this enormous fan-like entity that swept around, searching for escape.

The Dark Dreamers saw streams of activity in the fan-like entity, resembling strings of numbers, racing from seam to seam. "They're working the problem!" shouted a Dreamer, and received the same shout in his ear from the other Dreamers: "Hit them again! They'll fall with the next one! They'll fall right out of the world!"

The Dark Dreamers fired again, reinforcing the power of the Dreamhole. But the next contraction of the fan resulted in a steady state—one seam, glowing brilliantly, through which was glimpsed the inexplicable—an incomprehensible vista of another reality.

The extra-dimensionals had quickly calculated how to stabilize themselves in the mouth of the Dreamhole, which caused the entire landscape to bend as if it were made of rubber. This much the Dreamers grasped, but their minds refused to categorize what the extra-dimensionals actually were. They could have been geometrical shapes. They could have been animated numbers. They could have been seams in space. The world from which they came revealed itself without fear of being understood, for no receptors had been created here by which to know it.

Upquark was looking for their vomeronasal organs, the thing in them that rode the pheromones, but his search failed. The extra-dimensionals' activity had degraded his visual sensors, putting his geometry engines in revolt. He couldn't even judge the size of the great seam of unreality. His surface measuring devices were giving him impossible readings. According to what he got, the seam was as wide as the solar system he lived in. He banged his gripper on the side of his head, trying to loosen up his four-axis motion recognition platform.

"Forget it," said Link, whose own gaze kept going out of focus. "No one can measure it."

"We'll hit them again," cried the nearest Dark Dreamer, resetting his exotic energy generator. "This time we'll send them out of here with their hat in their hands."

But the Observer intervened. "They absorbed your dark energy blast. They're stronger than before." And to herself she thought, energy is what they came for. They know how to handle any form of it, and in any amount.

Tanks were rolling in—a concession to the Guard. Now that the Dark Dreamers had failed, the Guard was to have its play. They fired, and their warheads went into the seam, vanished, and increased the dead light of the non-thing.

We've lost, thought the elite commander who once had battled beside a girl he thought was the Observer. He saw the distorted valley quivering with the dead light of the slitted being—light without warmth, light like that of rotting wood, an ignited exhalation of the grave. As he crystallized, he knew the planet's time was over.

Caph had the same realization. "We can't win. We've got to get to my ship."

"I can't leave," said the Observer.

Caph gestured toward the sky. "There are other planets we can go to."

"I've developed a certain affection for this one," murmured the Observer.

"And I for you," said Caph, and put his arm around her.

He felt his scalp begin to tingle; his hair asserted itself against his grooming gel and stood up like the bristles of a boar. Remaining calm one moment more was an impossibility. He felt a tidal wave of affection for the Observer and struggled against his ecstasy. He felt his thoughts running backward, then forward, then freezing. *Where am I?* Uncertain of the place on which he stood, he could still see the Observer, the only steady thing in a river of chaotic sights, a river which finally turned her into a blur, and swept away his memory, his medals, his vanity, his conquests, and finally his identity. And then he was crystal.

The Observer stared at this statue which, a moment before, had been a man who loved her. Dry ice seemed to be circulating in her veins; the form her crystallization would take was cool comprehension. She would crystallize at the lower end of the scale, from excess of self-control.

She looked back toward the dead light of the slitted being that towered before her. The extra-dimensionals no longer frightened her. She seemed to know them, to have always known these seams in the fabric of reality, these beings that bundled together, one folding into the other and merging into a solitary seam that ran from the Corridor Station to the sky. It represented the stolen life of her planet, compressed into a single shape. That it towered into the heavens didn't surprise her. It contained the best of Planet Immortal—its hopes and dreams, its moments of genius and rapture.

Link was experiencing total disorientation, events out of sequence, moments from the past colliding with the present. A protective mental covering had fallen from him, revealing a world without logic.

Upquark was moving helplessly back and forth on his rollers. Swiveling his antennas in every direction, he searched for Link. He was getting Link's body signature, but it was distorted, masked by another signature. "Adrian—" Upquark shouted desperately. His emotions were built on Link's, and Link's were fragmenting. Upquark pivoted crazily on his rollers, as information sped at him, too fast for comprehension, filled with linear inequalities.

Tanks rammed each other, their drivers crystallized or incapable of judgment. There was neither attack nor retreat, no forward or backward. They climbed from their turrets, to view a battlefield that made no sense. Near and far had collapsed. A single step was a leap into the void. A soldier clutched the side of his tank, sobbing like the child he believed himself to be.

The Dark Dreamers saw a huge radiant mouth, sucking at reality. Yes, observed the Dreamer beside Upquark, they're feeding, not just on their crystallized victims but on the body of this solar system, chewing its molecular bonds, weakening the entire structure. "We can't stop them!" he shouted to his fellow Dreamers around the hillside. "Let's go!" They had a little ship beyond the station gate, and they scurried toward it now, bickering as they ran.

"You calculated the omiliad temperature rise incorrectly."

"*Your* mass resonance effect was insufficient."

They grabbed at each other angrily, and rolled down the other side of the hill, fists and feet punching and kicking. "A gravitoid error—"

"It was *your* idea to use numarium itrex—"

At the base of the hill, they came up running and opened the main gate. "Stand back, Cantusian, you're blocking the way." They rushed past Ren to their ship. Moments later it launched, headed toward the Planet of Dreams.

Ren hurried in through the open station gate; the Guardsmen stationed there to block the way were crystallized, with the sad presence of toy soldiers, who cannot move, but only dream of battles in their empty heads. She ran toward the ring of hills and started up them. She had to get to Link. This was the end of everything, and that strange man was the one being for whom she truly cared. Her brain was whirling, and he was at the center of it, with his face appearing and disappearing like a beacon. He'd been the one who'd sung so beautifully, an insect's simple song, repeated with perfect purity, no vanity behind it, no desire for acclaim. He'd sung it on Mirador, and it had been a song meant for her. She'd understood imperfectly then; that shy, tortured man had been doing his best, but his feelings were like an insect in amber, immobilized, archaic, trapped forever. But out of his amber prison he'd sung to her. She wanted to sing to him now, the song that would be the summation of her life. She began singing and it seemed as if the birds of the world came from her throat, blending their loveliest calls.

She caught sight of him. He'd collapsed against a Dark Dreamer machine, was staring at the extra-dimensional manifestation. She wanted to tell him to look away, but it wouldn't matter, the thing was all-pervasive. It was in her brain, taking away connections, images flying up like a deck of cards exploding from a gambler's hands. The sequence of the cards was gone, the suits made no sense. Worse still, her songs were coming apart, she couldn't find pitch or progression; her voice was like a stick rubbing against a windowpane. She crawled toward Link; Upquark was just ahead of her, trying to help Adrian, but the robot's gestures were erratic, aimless. She fell against them, appalled at the sound of her voice as it croaked out a word that might've been of love but sounded like tumblers clicking in a lock, echoing, overshooting the correct sequence; what was the correct sequence? It was gone, everything was gone, Link was gone, and she was gone, all that remained were the tumblers in the lock, tumbling through a hundred million combinations, and none the right one.

Below the hilltop on which Ren lay, the Observer tried to maneuver her vehicle, to get to her agents, to round them up, to somehow strike the extra-dimensionals again. Then she realized she wasn't looking at the plain on which the Corridor Station was built. She was looking at a kaleidoscope, each colored piece of glass a bit of time that'd been shattered. And she understood: What the extra-dimensionals needed was time. Time was what they'd run out of, so time was what they stole, bit by bit. Her own time flew into chaos, its bonds weakened. She saw events from decades ago bleeding into today.

She forced her gaze downward, toward the instrument panel of her vehicle. It showed images of mass crystallization. A satellite camera showed the extra-dimensional pillar like a syringe stuck into the planet, drawing out its life force. The pillar grew steadily brighter as town after town crystallized, inhabitants frozen like figures in a veil of crystal beads flung across the avenues.

The Observer toppled from her vehicle, fell for moments or for years, she couldn't tell. The extra-dimensionals were swallowing planetary time, and with it reason had to go, for time was the author of reason.

She stumbled along the ground, if it was ground. All categories of thought were flying away. The world would go mad and crystallize with a single *crack* heard by all, and by no one.

Into the kaleidoscope came the fragmented image of a mercenary ship. It was a vintage ship, a kind no longer made. Then she lost it, as bits of reality fell against each other in a new arrangement.

"There's something wrong with me," said Jockey to Lizardo as they settled the Temperance down. He jumped up quickly, knocking over his box of snacks. "I'm out of sync." He staggered, clutching at the walls of the flight deck. "My arms are at the door and I'm still here."

Uncle Ophidian shook himself out of his meditation, stretching his short, scaly arms. "Arrived, have we? What's all the fuss about?"

"That," said Lizardo, gesturing toward the flight deck window and the monstrous seam bisecting the sky. "The extra-dimensionals have revealed themselves." He loosened his claws from his navigational instruments; the last few minutes on the flight deck had been chaos, all landmarks lost, his computers unable to calculate the position of the ship. Somehow Jockey had landed it, but Jockey was now thumping about like a wounded bull.

Uncle Ophidian unbelted himself slowly. "A smooth flight. Very nice. Now, nephew, if you'd get up off the deck . . ."

But Lizardo was unable to plot a course for his feet. His brain had lost its bearings. He seemed to be crawling on the ceiling.

Uncle Ophidian reached out a claw to him. "That's it, nephew, just hang on."

Lizardo felt that they were both stuck to the ceiling. He tried to activate his forehead chip, but it was dead. "How did . . . they do it?"

Uncle Ophidian supported his nephew, though by no means wholly in balance himself. One investigates for centuries, but there are always surprises. This was a neat one. "What's being done is not *out there* . . ." He pointed to the warped landscape, its elements disproportionate, its angles amorphous. ". . . but in here." He tapped his scaly head. "They manipulate in the *a priori*. They enter our minds as easily as light through a window. At the moment, they're doing a very good job of it. Collective work, you see. They're moving in our collective dream."

"And . . . what is that dream?"

"That *up* is there and *down* is here." He pointed, and Lizardo felt it was a miracle. He'd thought he was on the ceiling, and now he'd been brought right again.

Uncle Ophidian chuckled, a raspy Serpentian sort of bark. "They destroy our inborn power to comprehend space and time. Once that's gone, we're finished. I suppose we'd better get busy before that happens."

Jockey hurled himself against the hatch, knocked it open, and rolled down the stairs. Uncle Ophidian followed, leading Lizardo, whose tail was whipping wildly as he sought stability.

"Just sit down beside the captain," advised Uncle Ophidian.

"I can't leave you . . . on your own," said Lizardo, but his legs were going out from under him. His cheeks puffed up with venom, and he collapsed against his fat partner.

"Man down," said Jockey, trying to heave himself up. Then he, too, flopped over, uncertain of the horizon.

With a groan, Lizardo managed to struggle to his feet. Unsteadily supporting his weight with his tail, he gazed at the massive seam that towered over the planet. He, like the Dark Dreamers, saw the unreal thing as a mouth, projected into this dimension in order to feed here. The rest of its body was invisible, like the body of an anteater must appear to the ants it eats. It was a great devouring snout . . . a beak . . . a maw . . . he mumbled to himself, wobbling on his tail. The Serpentian mind is strong, but it has its limits and he'd reached his. He felt as if the world were ooze and he'd just been born from it, into impossible sights, without the instincts that should accompany a baby lizard. He felt no more substantial than a cast-off skin. He was nothing in the presence of this monstrosity towering above the landing site.

Uncle Ophidian walked toward it, threading his way through tanks jammed against one another and tank crews crystallized on the ground. The gates of the Corridor station were open and he entered. One did not walk there easily. Animals that dwelt here had been reshaped by mutation, in response to its peculiar forces. Uncle Ophidian had some discomfort, but the Third Chronogrammatic dealt with charged stratification of rock layers and its influence on Corridor travel.

"The mind prevails," he counseled himself. The jumbled land-scape, as fragmented for him as for anyone, was a nuisance. But the decision to use this Corridor station as a confinement area had been shrewd. Bring the riffraff where there's been some thought at work, as refined as their own. He felt the Ancient Alien engineering at play all around him, strange magnetic orderings that worked like little winds, dynamic conditions necessary to launch an object—to where? Perhaps I'll find out.

The towering extra-dimensional seam was ahead, its interior revealed, that otherworld from which baleful influences came, lick-ing at his scaly body. "Of course," he said to himself, "one always wonders about departure day."

He felt the pressure of the extra-dimensionals like a sort of cloak wrapping around him, with a feeling of precious silk. Each strand moved separately, rippling over him with a delicious sort of swiftness, engaging him as quickly as his mind could follow, creating nuances of pressure that he recognized as a primitive form of communication, as if a silken wind were talking. The pressure pulsed rhythmically, repeat-ing its message until he understood it in his own words.

"You'll give me riches? And wisdom? I see. A very interesting offer. And you say I'll become your permanent agent here?"

The pressure shifted slightly, feeling like a heavy crown on his head. "A king? I should think you could do better than that."

The pressure became something like a ring of little planets cir-cling his head, as if to show him that as their representative he would be a great central sun.

Uncle Ophidian caught one of the magnetic breezes that blew over C-3, and rode it straight to the mouth of the great seam, which caused it to shrink back. "Don't be shy," he said, with a smile. "If I'm going to be your representative, we should get to know each other better."

And out of the seam of unreality came another wave of pressure, easier to read now that he was getting a feeling for it. *Why quarrel?* said the pressure. *Together we can live forever.*

"I have no quarrel with you," said Uncle Ophidian, only a few meters from the mouth of the extra-dimensional seam. "I'm just an old lizard looking for a crack to crawl into."

The seam shrank back again. *You can't enter our world. That boundary is fixed forever. Be content with what we bring you.*

Uncle Ophidian paused. His next step would be the last he would ever take in this familiar and beautiful universe. Another world awaited, unthinkable, bizarre no doubt, but a fine puzzle with which to occupy the next eternity or two. "I always liked change," he said, and entered the seam.

Lizardo saw a shudder run through it. "Jockey, look!"

Jockey saw the seam fan out, becoming many seams, and between each seam, the radiant fabric of the unknown. Its oscillation heightened . . . snapping open, closing, then snapping open, and then the fan came apart, the seams unable to hold together, the fabric unraveling like electric silk. As it unwound, Jockey heard the cries of the planetary dead, whose souls had illuminated its threads. The threads fell with the evanescence of comets, dying quickly.

The falling threads were gathered up again, and something new was woven, in letters of fire blazing above the battlefield:

THE FOURTH CHRONOGRAMMATIC OF OPHIDIAN

It glowed, then vanished, a letter at a time. Though containing all the secrets of Uncle Ophidian's study of the Efficient Present, it was an ephemeral work, lasting only long enough to free the planet of its enemy, but demonstrating once again the mental nature of the subatomic world.

"Every effect is consequent of knowledge," said Lizardo.

"If you say so, old man." Jockey could feel his balance coming back to him.

Link rolled over on the ground and lay looking at a sky which slowly arranged itself. There were the clouds, and there the sun, but something was wrong. What was it? He rolled on his side, with his cheek to the ground. An ant was walking toward him. As he watched her approaching, he realized he wasn't in perfect sympathy with her. Her antennas waved, but he couldn't read her tiny feelings. He was unable to cross the phylum. A feeling of grief swept through him.

The ant walked away, leaving no clue as to her mission, trailing no little cloud of communication. And now he grasped the secret that had colored his life: the gates to the insect world were antipathetic to human emotion. The voice of the extra-dimensionals had blocked him off from human feelings, and the gates of the insect world had swung open before him. Now that the extra-dimensionals were gone, he was like other men, for whom the gates were closed. The shell frequencies were a mystery to him.

Jockey heaved himself upright. The landscape was in one piece. And here, in my pocket, if I'm not mistaken—yes, a ration of candy.

"Oldcastle," said the Observer, walking toward him, "you never fail to surprise me."

"I saw my duty, no more." He swallowed the ration, gestured at Lizardo. "Some credit is due my lizard."

"I thought I saw three of you leave your ship."

"You were mistaken," said Lizardo, following Uncle Ophidian's orders, that nothing should be said of him. *My signature is enough.*

How will he manage in the other dimension? wondered Lizardo. But Uncle Ophidian would find a suitable cave in whatever universe he landed.

Jockey's stomach was growling. A great many questions were being asked him, and there was also Link to deal with. "My dear boy, you're looking a bit under the weather."

"I . . . lost something."

"You're not a crystal statue, that's what matters." Jockey slapped Link on both shoulders and looked past him. Could he get anything from these tanks? While confusion reigned? There were, he was sure, items of value lying around inside them—classified codes, perhaps, and the odd piece of jewelry on a frozen finger. Tank commanders were often splashy fellows.

"You're working for me, Oldcastle," stated the Observer. "The lizard too."

Outflanked, thought Jockey. He looked around and saw the extra-dimensionals were gone. Uncle Ophidian had routed them. How? The *principium* whatchamacallum. My understanding of it is incomplete. I'll review later, in my bath.

The Observer ushered Jockey and Lizardo into her field car, then paused and gazed out at the quiet battlefield, at the crystallized tank crews, and the place where the pillar of unreality had been. The planet seemed to be heaving a sigh. "I suppose all your crimes will have to be pardoned, Oldcastle."

"Even those yet to be uncovered?"

"All." The Observer put the field car into motion. "Of course, you'll do something to ruin your good fortune."

"Surely not."

"And then you'll be on the run again."

"*With many stars to visit, and cosmic seas to cross . . .*" Jockey took out a cigar, leaned back, and studied the pieces of the Junk Moon, circling where Amphora had been. He'd exploded it, nearly destroyed the planet, and then saved it. He'd have to buy himself another medal.

CHAPTER 41

Upquark rolled along behind Link and Ren through the once-more busy streets of Alien City. As the couple walked, they were jostled together by the crowd—a slight bumping of shoulders and then an awkward exchange of glances between them.

If only, thought Upquark, I could promote closer contact. He recalled his first meeting with Miss Ixen when she'd hammered him with a door and how that had been cause for further conversation between her and Adrian. If I got myself hammered with another door, would it do the trick? No, that stage is past. I'll have to come up with something more advanced.

Upquark had witnessed bewildering changes in Adrian since the extra-dimensionals' departure: His devotion to insects had a nostalgia about it, a poignancy, almost as if he were devoted to his dear insects out of loyalty. At the same time, Miss Ixen's name popped up at the oddest times in Adrian's conversations, accompanied by a noticeable display of nervousness.

Upquark rolled alongside them, reached his gripper up and touched Miss Ixen's slender wrist on behalf of his recalcitrant employer.

Ren smiled down at him from beneath her iridescent lashes, but he didn't know what to do next: I'm a poor substitute. My fingers are plastic, my emotions are mechanical, my limitations obvious. *Adrian* should put his arms around her. My stature is a major impediment. I'd end up hugging her legs.

"Now, the interesting thing about the tobacco hornworm is that it has overcome the poisons in tobacco . . . "

Upquark listened to Link in dismay: The ingenuity of the tobacco hornworm is all well and good, but does it make Miss Ixen feel warm and cuddly?

"After the hornworm becomes a hawk moth, its tongue lengthens until . . . " Link paused for emphasis. "Until it's as long as the moth itself. Upquark, bring up a picture of it."

Upquark shook his head despondently, but brought up the picture on his forehead viewscreen.

"Amazing, isn't it?" asked Link. "Upquark, magnify detail and change angles."

I've shown pictures of twenty-three insects so far on this date, thought Upquark sadly. Poor Adrian. He's never tasted that great and wonderful state called romance, and neither have I, because all my emotions are constructed around his. Now here I am, painfully yearning to finally experience that rapturous, tumultuous real thing. . . and Adrian talks about hawk moths.

Perhaps I'm in the way. Maybe if Adrian didn't have me around to keep demonstrating insects on my viewscreen, he'd be forced into facing his feelings for Miss Ixen.

"Adrian," he said, "I feel a need to shop."

"To shop?"

"Alone," Upquark added firmly, gesturing with a gripper at the stores that lined the avenue.

Link looked at Upquark pleadingly, clearly not wanting to be deprived of his protection, but Upquark rolled alone into the nearest store, knowing it had to be done.

The owner rushed out from behind his counter. He was a Starnosian, with six nostrils arranged in a flower shape. "Good afternoon, machine. I have everything for business and personal needs, the finest salvage in Alien City, everybody else have trash." He gestured toward his display cases and shelves. "Look at this—motor driver, hardly used. Unknown voltage, too powerful for certificate of safety but I see you're brave machine, not afraid of excitement." He tilted his head. "Do I detect grinding sound in motion of your elbow? A squeaking joint is beginning of end. Here's silent worm wheel with brainstem cable, fit your model perfectly. How about new eye wiper, rainy day special, that's my little joke, ha-ha. Maybe new backlash gear? But I'm intruding, sir. The competition on this street is crazy, it make me too eager. Please, sir, enjoy my store while I restrain myself."

But Upquark's attention was on the window, through which he could see Link and Ren. They'd only walked a few yards from where he'd left them, and *now they were standing still,* looking into each other's eyes! Upquark felt himself begin to tremble.

"Something from my bargain bin?" asked the owner, close behind him.

Upquark was too excited to reply.

"I let you browse, sir, certainly, browse for indefinite period. Here, look, this from amusement park—oversize frog move up and down when ride go round. Slightly stuck, requires drop of oil. His uses are too numerous to list, but imagine him coming out from behind bed or cabinet. Lifelike . . . fine joke for everyone. I have matching pig . . . somewhere . . . ." He hauled pieces out, tossed them aside. "Here is dented cow with only minor defects."

To oblige the storekeeper, Upquark dutifully sifted through the items in the bargain bin—differentials, speed reducers, S-flex couplings—but his eyes kept going back to Link and Ren. He put up his long-range antenna, and heard Link discussing parsley worms, and then he saw Link touch Miss Ixen's hair to demonstrate how the worms raised their orange horns when disturbed. Oh, he's improving, thought Upquark ecstatically, he's learning. This is wonderful.

"I tell you how it is, sir. You buy frog, and if he don't live up to expectations, I give you double your money back. That's how confident I am you enjoy this frog. As amusement."

"I don't really need a frog."

"*Now,* maybe you don't need frog. Tomorrow, somebody ask you for one, and then what? You slap head, you think, I had one in my hand. Who you work for?"

"The Agricultural Plain."

"Vegetables?"

"Yes."

"Place frog in garden to keep off birds." The owner sighed. "I tell you how it is, sir. Nobody going to buy this stuff."

"No, I don't think so."

"Everything damaged. But I have thousand spare parts. For fixing." His enthusiasm returned. "Come, we fix up frog. Is that your boss across street? I see you watching him. We give him present."

"I'm afraid he doesn't need any of this."

"No? What he need?"

"Confidence with ladies."

"I got top-notch confidence program. Your boss put chip in his tooth and receive suggestions for bold statement, appropriate to any situation. He have dental receptors?"

"Yes."

"Sure, he's modern fellow." The owner turned toward the window and Upquark turned with him. Link had taken Ren's hand in his. Upquark grew so feverish he had to sit down on the pile of used parts. His empathy module was bringing him Link's emotions as if they were a million lightning bugs simultaneously flashing in a tree.

Before he could prevent it, his own signal lights were also flashing simultaneously.

"What's wrong?" asked the concerned Starnosian.

"Nothing," whispered Upquark and, with effort, dimmed his lights.

"Okay, I go find confidence chip." The Starnosian rushed away, and Upquark was left by himself to enjoy the lovely warm sensations flowing through his cables.

But his pleasure was once more interrupted, this time by a faint signal coming from the pile of junk on which he sat. "Oh dear, what can this be? It's disturbing my first tumultuous taste of true romance."

He got up to deal with the insistent signal. He rummaged through the bargain bin until he traced the feeble beeping coming from a battered memory module.

The owner hurried back. "I see you find something you want. Excellent. Is memory module, yes? To go with it, you need total neurological system." He was digging hastily in his pile of spare robotic parts. "Head . . . vertebral track . . . I got everything required. May I suggest this torso? Please ignore bull's eye over heart, it come from shooting gallery where sturdiness has been proven. Inside, you see, very nice articulation mounts, made for quick dodging."

"But it hasn't got arms."

"Arms, arms." The owner searched desperately. "Last pair of arms I sold yesterday. Wait a moment. Here we are, from arcade slot machine. Very nice up and down motion. Pull and hit jackpot, ha-ha, another stupid joke, forgive me. Please, sir, look how well arms fit. Interim pair, until I get brand new ones. No charge for these."

"Thank you," said Upquark, edging forward until he stood right against the window. Link and Ren were now embracing! Upquark almost toppled over.

"They get on better now," observed the owner.

"He was quite backward until today."

"Now he's expert. Here, sir, I got just the legs for our figure. From duck ride. Large webbed feet for stability, *that* at least can't be improved on. Now all we need is head and we got one, from cookie dispenser. Unfortunately, rest of him is missing. We attach it to torso like so, not perfect union, I won't deceive you. But see, here's what pulls all together, universal input box, we hook everything to it, and now would you please hand me excellent memory module you found?"

Upquark did so, and the shop owner examined it with interest. "Real find, sir. Most advanced. But not too advanced for us. Don't worry, sir. I will make work. We just attach to voice box of cookie dispenser. See? Universal input, very handy. Now we hook up eyes . . . arms . . . legs."

The proportions of the patched-together figure were certainly odd. "Handsome," said the owner, waving at the head, which wore the oversized grin of all cookie dispensers; the pupils of its eyes resembled giant chocolate chips. "Okay, now we attach battery." The battery pack was placed in the open back, the door was snapped shut, and the owner pushed a start-up button at the base of the spine. The bull's-eye over the heart lit up, its red and white circles whirling inward. The chocolate chips rolled, and the mouth dispenser clacked, trying to eject a cookie, but, instead of a cookie, words emerged. "Just . . . just a . . . just a . . . game . . . really."

"Gamester!" cried Upquark.

"Once again," said the Gamester more fluently, with a clumsy attempt at a bow, "I'm indebted to you."

"What happened to you?"

"Torn apart at a rally. A nasty business. I lay among the shards for weeks."

"We'll have to find you a proper body," said Upquark.

The Gamester ratcheted down his slot machine arms for examination. "I rather like this one."

"This is indeed top-notch day," said the store owner, and the six petals of his nose opened out as if toward the sun.

Upquark paid the bill. The Starnosian gave him a receipt. "Come again. Maybe you find another friend."

At that moment, Upquark did find another friend: Glowing above the crowd was the data fez of Dunbosian. The pachyderm was working the arcade, selling alien idols. Upquark and the Gamester hurried from the store, the Gamester's duck feet slapping on the pavement.

"How good to see you," declared Dunbosian, lifting Upquark into his huge arms, and holding him up against the background of arcade lights. "Your injured leg has been repaired, I see."

"And how is Mirador?" asked Upquark, as Dunbosian set him down.

"I'll restore it to its former splendor yet. Ah, and there's Mr. Link and Ren. *They* seem to be quite friendly."

"Kissing," whispered Upquark blissfully, and all his lights flashed on again. "You're familiar with the kissing process?"

"I've had some experience of it, yes."

They watched the kiss, while thrill after thrill surged through Upquark's cables.

"But there's the collector I'm here to see," said Dunbosian, with a start. "I must be going. Goodbye, I'm sure we'll meet again." He hurried into the crowd, his data fez slowly disappearing.

And the Alien City arcade played on, with its traders and mercenaries and travelers from every world. They signed their contracts, sold their goods, plotted their next adventure. The lights of the arcade shone on all of them as they came and went, laughing, whispering, losing, and winning. As the Gamester said, it was just a game, really.